FIC 8985
YOU

Young, Al
　Ask Me Now

Discarded

ASK ME NOW

BY THE SAME AUTHOR

Novels

Sitting Pretty

Who Is Angelina?

Snakes

Poetry

Geography of the Near Past

The Song Turning Back into Itself

Dancing

Co-Editor

Yardbird Lives!

Calafía: The California Poetry

Al Young
ASK ME NOW

McGRAW-HILL BOOK COMPANY
New York   St. Louis   San Francisco   Düsseldorf   Mexico   Toronto

Copyright © 1980 by Al Young. All rights reserved. Printed in the United States of America. No part of this publication may be reproduced, stored in a retrieval system, or transmitted, in any form or by any means, electronic, mechanical, photocopying, recording, or otherwise, without the prior written permission of the publisher.

123456789BPBP876543210

Library of Congress Cataloging in Publication Data

Young, Al, 1939-
Ask me now.
I. Title.
PZ4.Y67As   [PS3575.068]   813'.54   80-421
ISBN 0-07-072360-5

Book design by Anita Walker Scott.

For permission to reprint copyrighted material the author is grateful to the following copyright proprietors:

   Dave Etter for the poem "Ask Me Now": copyright © 1975 Dave Etter.

   Frank Music Corp. for lines from "If I Were a Bell" by Frank Loesser: copyright © 1950 Frank Music Corp; © renewed 1978 Frank Music Corp. International copyright secured. All rights reserved. Used by permission.

   The Living History Centre for the Dickens Christmas Fair poster: copyright © 1978 The Living History Centre. All rights reserved. Used by permission.

Published in association with
SAN FRANCISCO BOOK COMPANY.

To the memory of
PAUL EMERSON
(1930–1979)
Journalist, sportsman, and lover of literature and the performing arts

I poked squirming leaves in my ears,
sucked dry the nectar of sweet blossoms,
curled up in the big bosoms of trees.

I wanted spring to make me gasp for breath,
to make me ache in root and branch,
to cut me up with long knives of sun.

But it was her diamond ring that did it:
that shattered my eyes, broke my nose.
And her laughter left me weak and dying.

> DAVE ETTER
> (*a poem inspired by and named after
> Thelonious Monk's* ASK ME NOW)

Ask me how do I feel,
Ask me now that we're cozy and clinging.

> FRANK LOESSER
> (*from the Broadway musical* GUYS AND DOLLS)

So I play the ball, not the man. I wait until
the shot's in the air; then I knock it down.

> WILT CHAMBERLAIN

1

By Christmas he knew he'd be ready for an oxygen tent. This hadn't always been the case. As a child, he'd loved the holiday season with its promise of good times, good talk, good feelings, good things to eat, the Yuletide bonanza of goodies galore. But now, as a grown man who had to do the providing, he had grown to loathe the spirit of cash flow that permeated this time of year.

Even as he stepped out of the shopping center meat and poultry market, lugging two bags filled with turkey, ham, eggnog, liquor, and what not, something told him that this year wasn't going to be much different from last, when things had hit an all-time low. He stood for a moment in the late-morning drizzle, trying to remember where he'd parked the car. Scanning the enormous lot, he thought he could make out a lemon-colored Ford station wagon facing him a dozen rows ahead. Quickly calculating the distance and time it would take, he decided to make a dash for it, hoping his packages wouldn't get too drenched.

Halfway there, he could see that this particular wagon had a luggage rack mounted on top. His didn't. By then everything was wet, including the dumb tennis shoes he was wearing. He had taken the Channel 6 weatherman at his word when he'd announced that the Bay Area could look forward to warm, sunny days through the weekend with highs in the low sixties and lows in the upper forties. He should've followed his daughter's advice and expected just the opposite.

Well, this was something! Now he would have to do some more wandering around to look for his machine, which he was afraid to drive because it had been shorting out on him lately. Some bug in the electrical system. He had no choice but to push his luck until Thanksgiving was over. Then he could take the car in for repair while it was still on warranty.

This drizzle was quickly turning into a mild downpour. Damn! If he caught cold again, there went all the family plans. Come on, Durwood, pay attention! Where'd you park that sucker?

Then it hit him. He'd entered the mall from the other side, way around by Woolworth's. Good thinking. What he had to do now was cut back through the main arcade. At least he'd be dry for a few minutes.

Mobs of ugly people were crowding the central arcade, where some kind of drawing was taking place. Because of his height, most people automatically moved out of his way. He never had to do much pushing. This time he slowed down to read the sign that he'd only glanced at previously:

WIN A FREE TRIP TO RENO

2 DAYS FOR 2

DRAWING TODAY AT 11 A.M.

Standing under the Woolworth awning, he spotted a Chinook, a small Datsun camper, with a watchful German shepherd in the front seat and instantly recalled pulling into the space adjacent to it. Well, downpour or no downpour, he was practically home free now. One last sprint and he'd be warm and snug inside his own vehicle, even if it did unnerve him to drive it.

Once he got there, having trudged all the way, he found the space unoccupied. He clutched his bags desperately to keep them from slipping. The Ford was gone. How could this be? His car wasn't there. With a lump in his throat, he took one last frantic look around him. Even though the lot was packed, there wasn't another yellow car in sight. To add to his aggravation, the German shepherd had his snout poked through the rolled-down portion of the camper window and was growling at him savagely. What in the hell was going on?

He took his time walking back to the arcade to find a pay phone to call Dixie. What was he going to tell her? Rain was coming down mercilessly now, drenching him and soaking the bags. His toes were squishing inside his watery canvas shoes and socks, but he no longer seemed to mind. He simply couldn't understand why the car wasn't there where he'd parked it an hour and a half ago.

"What do you mean you can't find it? I never heard of such a thing."

"Well, you're hearing it now. It's nowhere in sight."

"How can you say that? Have you looked everywhere? Did you even bother searching the lot?"

"Dixie, I looked all over. It just isn't there. I know where I parked it."

"The *whole* lot, Durwood, did you search the whole lot? I'm your wife, remember? We've been through this and *been* through this. It's boring. You thought you knew where you'd parked it that time in L.A., too, and turned out it was in a different parking garage on another block."

"Can you come pick me up in the Vega?"

"No, I can't."

"Why not?"

"Jenny's using it."

"What's she doing with our Vega?"

"Julian got sick, He was throwing up and running a fever. She had to rush him to his pediatrician at the clinic. What are neighbors for? Oscar's due back from Seattle any minute now with their car."

"Well, what am I supposed to do?"

"I don't know. What's all that racket I hear in the background?"

"What? Oh . . . some kinda contest or something. Listen, I don't feel like being trifled with today. I'm standing here with two bags fulla stuff, my feet are soaking wet, and my sinuses are starting to act up again. Now, I don't know if you wanna go through Thanksgiving this year or not, and I don't care. My interest is falling off fast. We can eat hot dogs and drink Kool-Aid far as I'm concerned, and —"

"Calm down, Durwood! Calm! Down! Don't go getting your blood pressure up. Why don't you just find one of those security officers, explain what's happening, and let him take it from there?"

"Talk to one of those goddamn rent-a-cops? What the hell do they know? I know where I parked the son of a bitch!"

"Durwood, I'm gonna hang up on your ass, you keep talking to me like that! If you don't trust the security cops, then call a real one, but I'll bet you anything the station wagon's right there in the parking lot."

"Now . . . Shit! . . . You know something, Dixie? I'm gonna tell you something. You're strange, *strange!* You are one strange, ridiculous, hard-to-tell-anything-to woman. You—"

Click.

He couldn't believe it. She'd hung up on him. Here he was trying to go along with this absurd national joke called Thanksgiving and she didn't have the decency to be of any help whatever, not even in an emergency. For a few slow seconds he found himself wishing for the old days, when his life had been built around business, practice, big games, play-offs, plane schedules, checking in and out of hotels, press interviews, and all the rest of it. His family appreciated him then. At least they didn't take him for granted. Dixie and the kids were happy to see him. He had status and felt needed and loved. It was so uncomplicated. If he had to play ball on Thanksgiving—or Christmas or New Year's or on their anniversary for that matter—it was no big deal. That was just that. No one got upset.

He leaned against the obnoxious telephone module, steaming leisurely. Something inside him had clicked too. He caught himself not caring whether he ever found the Ford again. It was becoming a pain in the ass anyway.

Still, he had to make some effort, go through the motions at least. Stuff was melting inside the grocery bags—frozen daiquiri mix and other juices, vegetables, ice cream. He'd have to pull himself together enough to make some kind of decision. The noisiness of the crowd around him made it hard to think.

A fat, graying, yellow-haired man in a sharp pinstripe suit, with an old-fashioned Adolphe Menjou boutonniere blooming from the lapel, had mounted a platform in the arcade Pavilion Room and, with both arms aloft, was trying to hush all the foolish-looking shoppers. While straining to locate a rent-a-cop at the fringes of the crowd, Durwood couldn't help overhearing and taking in the spectacle, the ceremony, whatever you wanted to call it. The fat man was announcing, as he thanked the participants, that there'd be only three winners of trips-for-two to exciting Reno, and absolutely no second prizes.

A perky little woman with red hair and freckles joined the man on stage. She was decked out in a spangled costume that Durwood had a hard time pinning down. Was she supposed to be a cheerleader, a tennis star, Wonder Woman, or what? He couldn't tell. She had skinny legs, large breasts, and a not-to-be-believed grin that might earn her a living in a cheap furniture-showroom commercial on some UHF channel.

Just as he caught sight of a security officer—a roly-poly black man who looked to be in his fifties—the redhead plunged one hand into an embroidered box and pulled out a slip of paper. She handed it to the fat man.

"Ladies and gentlemen, hold on to your hats and umbrellas . . . The first winner of an exciting two-day vacation in exotic Reno, Nevada . . . Mr. and Mrs. Salvatore P. Rinaldi of Daly City!" Like TV-trained cretins, the crowd broke into half-hearted applause. The fat man wanted to know if the Rinaldis were present. No, they weren't; they'd have to be notified by mail. The redhead dipped her hand in again to select Winner Number Two as Durwood collected his rain-soaked, crumpled bags and headed toward the officer, who, arms folded, was digging the show.

"And now Carol will select our next lucky winner . . ."

Heads turned the way they always did when Durwood made any kind of conspicuous showing at a public gathering. "Height makes might" was the way an old basketball teammate of his used to put it. He was right up behind the rent-a-cop now, tapping at his shoulder.

"... Estelle Yee of El Cerrito, California, is second to receive a fully paid United Merchants trip to fabulous Reno!"

The officer spun around, looking as if he'd just been rudely jarred from some cozy dream. "Uh, what can I do for you, sir?"

"My car's gone."

"Beg pardon?"

"My car . . . I parked it out here by Woolworth's, and now I can't find it. I think it might've been stolen."

"You're kidding!"

"Nope, honest. It's missing from the lot."

The cop took a tiny notebook and ballpoint pen from the shirt pocket of his dark blue uniform. "What kinda car is it?"

"A new Ford station wagon, yellow."

"License number?"

"WINNER."

"Run that by me again, brother."

"Spelled W-I-N-N-E-R. . ."

"Oh, I get it." The cop laughed as he stepped back to get a good look at Durwood. "Seem like I know you from someplace."

Durwood shrugged.

"You ever work at the post office? Or was it . . . I used to drive a little for United Parcel. You ever work for them?"

Another round of applause distracted them both momentarily.

"I know this might sound bad," said the cop, "what with your missing car and all, but it just so happen I put a few coupons into this sweepstakes thing myself and I'd kinda like to stick around and find out how I come out."

"No rush," Durwood told him, and by now he meant it.

The two men sized up one another. It wasn't easy for Durwood to keep from stooping a bit, the way he used to do, to make people who were shorter than himself feel at ease. They both focused on the platform, where the fat man was unfolding the last slip of paper that the redhead would hand him.

"Thank you for your patience, ladies and gentlemen. The third and final recipient of a free trip to romantic Reno izzzz . . . Mrs. Madeleine Knight of Dolores Street, right here in San Francisco!"

"Aw, shit!" The cop looked bugged.

Durwood was puzzled. "What?"

"Nothing," said the cop. "Excuse my French."

"No," said Durwood, "that wasn't what I meant." He raised one hand and, in a booming voice, called out to the man on stage. "What did you say the name was again?"

Theatrically, the fat man repeated the name Madeleine Knight. Durwood set down his bags and slapped a hand to his forehead.

"Somebody you know?" the rent-a-cop asked.

"Yeah, sort of—that's my old lady."

"Knight. . . Knight, hmm—" The cop chuckled as he snapped his fingers. "*That's* who you are . . . Durwood Knight. You the same one used to play guard with the Beanstalks? You *got* to be. Can't nobody else be running around here tall as you are, going by the same name. Hey, it's a pleasure to meet you, bruh! I been a fan of yours going all the way back to when you first got traded out here."

Not knowing what else to do, Durwood slumped while the pudgy security guard tried to shake his hand. "But . . . but what about my car?"

"Don't you worry 'bout a thing. We gonna get your car back for you."

"You are? How can you stand there saying that when we don't even know where it is?"

"C'mon, man, what's a Ford station to a celebrity like you? First you better run up there and claim your prize. These people out here at this shopping center is cheap. I know that for a fact. See, I work for 'em."

"The last thing I need right now is a free trip to Reno. There aren't any *free* trips to Reno. That's how come there is a Reno."

"Now, that's cute," said the cop, looking even more impressed. "I gotta remember that. But, like I say, you better go claim your prize right quick anyway, before they change they mind and snatch it back. I wouldn't put it past 'em."

"I didn't even know my wife had entered this thing."

"Sure wish mine was more like yours. I might as well be married to the vice squad, the way she steady be's on my case. Would you believe I still have to save up and sneak off to buy me a coupla Irish Sweepstakes tickets every year?"

Once again Durwood picked up his bags. Handing them to the guard, he said, "Watch these for me, would you? I'll be right back. By the way, what's your name?"

"Cholly," the cop grinned with obvious pride. "Cholly Banks. Hey, these bags is heavy!"

With windshield wipers thumping and the radio fixed on a country-western station, Cholly and Durwood cruised the whole shopping-mall parking lot in a car marked "Security Patrol."

"Well," said Cholly, "this the third time we done gone around this lot, and I ain't seen nothing even resemble that Ford of yours. Think the best thing for you to do would be to file a report with us and the regular police."

"I just don't believe this is happening to me." Durwood's eyes were growing watery.

"You sound a little stopped up," Cholly said consolingly. "I see you taking this thing kinda hard."

"It's my sinuses," Durwood tried to explain as he fingered the side of one nostril.

"Aw, listen, Durwood—if you don't mind my calling you that. It's just one of them things is all it is. It don't happen too often out here but, far as I know, we got a pretty good record of getting these cars back. Lemme ask you something."

"You always listen to this kinda music?" Durwood asked out of nowhere.

"Oh, hell yeah, I love it. Makes me homesick, though."

"I see," said Durwood.

"But you know that game y'all played against the Lakers when Abdul-Jabbar and them was kicking y'all's ass right up to the last period, and somehow or other—I had to go out to the fridge so I missed how it happen—you got aholda the ball and laid up some points that turnt the whole game around? Look like that inspired everybody else, and before anybody know what to expect, y'all'd done gone into that defense thing the Beanstalks so famous for and jived the Lakers into playing shaky."

"Yeah, I remember that game," said Durwood. "It was at the

Coliseum. We had to go into an extra period but ended up taking it by eight points. The crowd was ready to turn the place out."

"Aw, it was feeding time at the zoo. I got so excited, I up and kicked over a whole tall can of Colt 45. That's when I realized how great you was. I mean, you never was known for being no superstar or nothing like that, but for a guard you was tops. Push come to shove, you could always come through with some fast faking and dunking."

"Thanks, Cholly."

"I mean it, Woody, every word. Never did think you got the kinda credit you deserved. They couldn't box you out 'cause you kept moving, plus you was hell on them offensive rebounds."

"I really appreciate hearing that." Durwood's sinuses suddenly seemed to be clearing somewhat.

"You a Texan, right?"

"Born and bred in Carthage."

"Hell, I'm from Corpus Christi. Now, see, we nearbout next of kin."

As much as he was enjoying all of this stroking on Cholly's part, Durwood's bad head was about to crack open with petty details. He wanted it to be the weekend after Thanksgiving, when he could sleep late and vaguely remember what a bad dream all this had been. Already he could hear his grown son, whose flight was due in any minute now, laughing with him about it.

Cholly, checking the dashboard, said, "Hey, we almost empty! I better zip over to the Shell station and fill up. We ain't supposed to let these patrol specials run out, you know."

"But how do I get home?" asked Durwood.

"Uhmph, that do pose a problem, don't it? Tell you what. Since I'm already supposed to be out here helping you find your sheen, why don't I just run you over to where you live at. I can put down on my chart that the man had to get home some kinda way, and that'll explain the extra mileage."

"Much obliged," Durwood mumbled, borrowing a phrase that hadn't crossed his lips in he didn't know how long. It was from childhood. Then he remembered that you never said that until an act of kindness or politeness had been carried out. He wasn't so sure about Cholly driving him home, but he was even less certain about being home at all.

HOME WAS AN OLD four-bedroom, semi-Victorian house on Dolores Street in the Upper Mission. Durwood described it as semi-Victorian because the rich hippie landlady he'd bought it from had cut remodeling costs by having aluminum windows and fake wood paneling installed in rooms at the back of the house, where she must have figured passersby wouldn't notice. One of Durwood's rainy-day projects—provided he ever got back in the chips—was to have all of those phony touches ripped out and the original effect restored.

For the moment, and only for the moment, he was satisfied to be ringing the doorbell with his chin. Dixie, her hair in curlers, let him in. All she said was, "Come on in, Woody. I'm on the phone to Connecticut. Be sure and wipe your feet."

Most people, or so he had always heard, saw red when they were roundly outraged. Durwood saw violet, a whirling violet that was on its way to turning purple. The nerve of her! She hadn't even offered to hold the door open while he wiped his feet and wrestled with those goddamn bags.

He pushed the door shut with one knee and pried off his sneakers by the heels with his toes. His socks were still squishy, so he set the bags on the rug, peeled off each sock, and collected his load, checking to make sure that he wasn't leaving tracks as he balanced himself across the living room on his heels.

By the time he reached the tiled corridor leading to the kitchen, he experienced one of those flashes that his old buddy

Brewster called "deejay voo." Durwood knew that something unpleasant was going to take place before he could make it to the kitchen. Trembling, he strained to gain control of himself, blinking hard to make the violet go away.

He hadn't made it halfway down the hall before one of the rumpled, rain-soaked grocery sacks bottomed out on him. Liquor, wine, soda bottles, and glass jars went crashing to the floor every which way. The sound and sight of it jolted him so, that, for one microsecond, he stood wondering if the second bag had slipped involuntarily as well, or whether, out of alarm, he'd simply given up and let go of it. What did it matter now anyway?

Splattered eggs, vodka, Scotch, rum, gin, burgundy, chablis, club soda, tonic, ginger ale, and 7-Up gushed around his feet and along the corridor in fluid, glass-strewn puddles, merging with pickles, olives, cocktail onions, oysters, jelly, and half-melted ice cream. By now Durwood was seeing a whole lot more than purple. He was seeing $2.95, $1.79, $5.25, $9.95, $7.39, $6.75, $4.59, and avalanches of 89- and 65-cent buys sloshing around beneath him, literally trickled away.

Time stood still. Durwood took a deep breath to calm himself, but what his poor nostrils inhaled was so overwhelming that it cleared his aching sinuses completely. He had never had any trouble handling the kinds of tension that built up on the basketball court. In fact, he had always welcomed game-time emergencies, tight squeezes, impossible situations. But plain old ordinary everyday life, once it jumped off the track, had a way of throwing him for a hard loop every time.

He wanted to cry. No, he wanted to howl. Or maybe all he really wanted to do was grab Dixie, snatch all those rollers out of her hair, and throw her out the window. If she'd only helped him with those bags, none of this would've happened in the first goddamn place! He could hear her in the background, cackling into the kitchen phone all the way to Connecticut—another long-distance hen session he'd end up having to pay for—with her meddlesome mother, Nadine. As far as Durwood was concerned, Nadine needed to be locked up in a tower—the way those old kings used to do with their worrisome wives—or, at the very least, put away someplace where blunt instruments weren't allowed, where she could waddle around in a robe all day and eat soft foods.

While his blood pressure rose, he became aware of a peacefulness settling in—a kind of troubled inner quiet that often spread over him once he'd reached the end of some rope. Whenever that happened, there was nothing for him to do except slow down and take a good long look at himself trying to function in an unbearable situation that he was helpless to change. He sometimes experienced a similar sensation while writing out a check to the phone company.

Stepping over a box of cornmeal and a package of ground pork sausage, avoiding, as best he could, cutting his bare feet on shattered glass, he skillfully backed away from the mess. At least the turkey—$22.95—was intact. There wasn't much damage you could do to a dead turkey, short of taking a hatchet to it. Maybe the yams and squash would taste all the better for having soaked in wild booze and floor dust.

When Durwood remembered how many months and fights it had taken them to find it, he thanked God that Dixie's precious Persian rug had been spared. With that much to his credit, he slumped down into his favorite chair—a fat, funky, overstuffed one with a shape that Dixie still grumbled about whenever company was expected. By this time tomorrow, she'd be grumbling up a storm. Well, she could snort and snarl all she wanted for all he cared. She could do whatever the hell she pleased. She could go back to Bridgeport and stay there with Nadine. They deserved one another. He was sick of her ass, tired of all of them—Celia, Nissa, even Leon, whom he hadn't even seen for a year and who didn't have the courtesy to call and let them know what time his plane was coming in. What did they take him for anyway, an automatic money machine?

Good old Durwood, good old Woody, good old Daddy—he'll see us through, he'll make a way, don't worry!

He might not have been the chump of the century, and yet, as he sank back into his chair, his womb, to let numbness take over, that's exactly how he was beginning to feel—like an absolute fool sliding over the hill, like somebody's used-up doormat.

If he doesn't make this morning's flight by dawn, it's going to be curtains for him and the whole hurting team. What's going on? Nothing's making sense. He knows he set the alarm for four o'clock. He knows he has to somehow get up and function, no matter how much his back is troubling him. His head is an old, scrap-heap medicine ball left out in the rain with its stuffing coming out. He can't get his knees to move. Even his fingernails are smarting from scratching and digging into he can't remember what. He can't remember anything. That's the trouble. Or is it? Buzz. Click. Buzz. Click. The clock keeps sounding and he keeps turning it off, groaning for five more minutes of sleep. Like a man on fire with thirst in a desert who would give anything for even a mayonnaise jar of polluted tap water, he'd gladly pay a month's salary to be able to somehow make that plane in his sleep. It can't go on this way. He can see Dixie glowering at him from all the way across the country. Dixie see him? But she's in San Francisco, or is it Cleveland? One thing he knows for sure is that this is Chicago and they've got an afternoon game to play way up in Buffalo. He forces himself to sit up in bed. The effort practically cracks his back. He peers around the room in the half-dark. There's nothing but emptiness and locker-room musk. He can hear the coach and owner now— "Told you last time, Woody, you miss one more and you can kiss your contract good-bye. Getting a replacement for you won't be any big thing, you know!" What's the matter with him? Has all that missed sleep and years on the run finally caught up with him and socked him away? He feels like he's been mummified alive, strait-jacketed in bed sheets, and sweaty bed sheets at that. Why can't they put up in some first-class hotels for a change? Good talent needs good treatment. Or was he getting only what he deserved? And when was the last time he'd missed a team flight? That would have to be Cincinnati, when he was a college rookie, acting crazy, messing up, burning the candle at both ends and down along the seams as well. Well, this is it! He's got to pry himself loose from the bed before it turns into a tomb for real. Feeling every nerve in his body about to go snap, he places both arms at his side and, no longer caring what happens to his body, rolls himself as violently as he can across the bed. He's got to make something happen. Anything. Get going, Durwood! Change the picture and play it from there! Perched now at the bed's edge, straining, praying to feel himself fall to the floor, he discovers that, no matter how hard or how much he pushes and grunts, he won't be able to make the drop. Well, so much for that. There goes everything. There he lies, frozen, the victim of a circumstance he can't even begin to understand, much less combat. Painfully amazed and swimming in grime, he watches the rest of his life go swirling down a gigantic drain, like post-game, shower-washed sweat and grit. Even the clock seems to be giving him the razz as it buzzes again. He's so busy clutching his trembling thighs, for lack of anything better to hold on to, that he can't be bothered to turn the damn thing off. Besides, it's been fooling him all along by posing as a clock when actually—like he himself and everything around him—it's dying, melting like a painted memory, turning into something entirely different . . . But what? . . . He no longer can see well enough to tell . . . Is it his eyesight, or can time be reversing itself and curtaining what little light is left with absolute darkness, with a swish, with a wrinkle, with a—What is it he hears? . . .

Fluting and luting. Stoutly plucked chords, some of them melancholy, mixed with breathy flute accompaniment, resounded in his head, which felt hollow now, like a flesh-and-blood echo chamber. At first it seemed to be coming from far away, but before he could locate it spatially, the music had moved right in on top of him and, for good measure, was sweetened by a voice. It was a soothing, high-pitched voice that playfully, if not uncertainly, flexed itself as it captured his ear.

"And that's the way time goes," it sang, "and that's the way time goes . . ."

Durwood lifted his head and opened his eyes partway, just enough to squint down along his outstretched legs to where a girl with gentle features sat at his feet; rhythmically pulling at the nylon strings of a guitar as she intoned words scrawled on a scrap of paper resting in her lap. Behind her sat a muscular boy whom Durwood had never seen before in his life. He didn't notice how beautifully the boy was playing the flute so much as he did the gleaming ring in his left earlobe and the fact that the boy's thick, black hair gave every appearance of having been professionally straightened and curled.

"In the blink of an eye," the girl sang with a lilt, "we get born and we die, but that's the way time goes."

The voice belonged to Celia, Durwood's fifteen-year-old daughter. Durwood had chosen the name Celia because he loved its soft, liquid sound. And after all these years, he still enjoyed pronouncing it—*Celia, Ceee-lll-ya, Seee-uhhhl-ya, Seal-ya.* It was a name you could whisper in the dark and count on getting a tender response. Celia looked so pretty and fragile in her bright blouse and faded jeans that Durwood felt stupid, even guilty, about ever having spoken harshly to her, as he had done the night before. He and Celia were having their ups and downs of late, especially their downs.

"Well," Celia asked, laying her guitar aside, "what do you think?"

"I think I must've been dozing."

"We know that, Dad. I mean, about the song. How's it sound to you?"

"The song?" He wasn't sure he'd heard enough of it to say anything intelligent, so he only said what came easiest. "It sounds pretty good to me. There's something about it, though, that I'm still trying to piece together. The melody . . . isn't it sort of based on an old folk song?"

"Old folk song!" Celia looked hurt. Her brown eyes, which had been fully open until now, narrowed just enough to make Durwood realize that he hadn't said the right thing. "This song happens to be mine, Dad. I wrote it. I made it up. Moby and I worked out the arrangement together and thought we'd try it out on you to cheer you up a little."

"Cheer me up? About what?"

"About the car being stolen and that mess you made out there in the hallway."

"It took a long time to clean up, too, Mr. Knight," said Moby. "But we all pitched in and got the job done."

There was too much coming at Durwood for him to process in his groggy condition: Thanksgiving, a missing station wagon, something about a free trip to Reno, rain, darkness, an alarm clock, his aching back, fallen sacks of expensive groceries, Celia's song, pieces of dreams, and now this strange male youngster with funny hair, who, although unintroduced, was suddenly inside his very house, telling him about how long it had taken to clean up an accident that he'd fallen asleep to put out of his mind.

Turning to his daughter, Durwood said, "I don't believe I've had the pleasure of meeting your friend."

"Moby," she said, "I want you to meet my father."

"It's an honor to get to know you," said Moby, getting to his knees and sticking out his hand, which struck Durwood as being rather large for a flute player. "I grew up admiring you. I know you must hear this all the time, but you've always been someone I've looked up to."

Durwood shook Moby's hand and at the same time felt cheated that the boy hadn't come on rudely to him. At least that would've justified his natural inclination to dislike him. Right away he'd sized the boy up as being too streetwise and cute for any daughter of his to be hanging around with, but he could be wrong. He always went by hunches anyway, and the hunch that he got was that Moby—and what the hell kind of name was that in the first place?—had been knowing Celia too long for him not to have even heard his name mentioned before now.

Knowing he had to be casual, the way his father had been with him when he was Moby's age, Durwood tried his best to ease into the confrontation. "Celia," he said, "how long have you and Moby been knowing one another?"

"Since seventh grade," Celia began, "but musically we're just now beginning to get acquainted."

"I've only been playing for a year and a half," said Moby, breaking out in a scraggly, mustache-crested grin.

Durwood didn't even like Moby's teeth—the way they inched out crooked in front and the gaps between them. What a shame the boy's folks hadn't provided proper orthodontic care the way he had for Celia.

"You're pretty good on that thing," said Durwood, "for someone who just took it up."

"Thanks," said Moby. "I started out on clarinet in the school band, but they needed another flute, so I tried it out and liked it."

"Celia has an older brother, well, half-brother, technically, who's into woodwinds."

"Oh, yeah, Leon—he's great."

"So Celia's told you about him?"

"Sure, but I've heard him on a couple of albums, too, with different groups. His saxophone playing's something else. He's got a sound of his own on tenor, kinda loose and talky, you know. I don't know how he does it, but I could listen to him play all day."

Celia was beaming. "And he's gonna be here any minute now," she said. "I can't wait. You've gotta meet him, Moby. Maybe we'll all get to play together. Ooo, I can't wait!"

"I'm looking forward to it," said Moby.

"I wish he'd call and let us know when he's getting in," said Durwood as he stretched himself and, for the first time since waking, looked all around him. "Where's Nissa?"

"She went over to play with Peaches and them." With that, Celia paused, as she sometimes did, with her mouth hanging open. To Durwood she looked like a startled sleepwalker—long, lean, and not all there.

"Is there something you're trying to remember?" he asked.

"No, not really. I was just wondering what we're gonna do about the station wagon."

"There's not much more we can do right now. I've notified the police. I don't know how they stole it because I locked it like I always do. You know how careful I am about that stuff."

Turning to Moby, Celia said, "Dad's one of the biggest worriers I know, bar none."

Again Moby managed a big, snaggle-toothed grin. "Maybe he should've been traded to the San Francisco Worriers," he quipped.

"That's funny," said Durwood, not bothering to laugh.

"In fact," Celia went on, "what he really is, is paranoid."

"But it's easy to see how a man in your father's position would have to kinda look out for himself."

Durwood resented Celia's remark, partly because it was un-

17

necessary and all the more because it might be true. "Whoever ripped it off," he said, "had to be doing some pretty fast stepping, that's all I can say."

In one swift, elegant maneuver, Celia whisked herself smoothly from the floor up onto the arm of his chair. Perched there, as Moby looked away nervously, she placed both arms around Durwood and said, "I'm just glad you didn't get hurt. I'm happy you got home safely."

This was enough to melt anybody, especially an old softie like Durwood. The little kiss on the cheek she gave him, and the hug that followed, was the best thing to happen in days. What was it with fifteen-year-olds? The day before, they'd argued to the point of calling a moratorium on speaking with one another. Now she was not only his loving daughter, but also—going by the way she was acting—a friend who really seemed to care about what happened to him. Durwood was so moved that he wanted to sit right there and savor the moment for hours and hours. He might have done just that if Moby hadn't been in the room, or if they all hadn't heard the flap of Dixie's slippers in the hallway as she approached the living room.

"Celia," said Moby, "we're gonna be late." He was standing now with his flute packed away in its battered, black, hard leather case.

"Where you off to? asked Durwood.

"Disco roller-skating," Celia told him. "They've got a special discount going this afternoon, half off, at the Rolleradium." She slid from the arm rest and grabbed her guitar. "Dad, did you really like 'That's the Way Time Goes,' or were you just saying that?"

"I liked it, what I heard of it."

"You sure dream hard, Dad."

"What do you mean by that?"

"Nothing. I'm gonna make some changes in the lyrics and do a tape. See you later. Hey, you think Leon'll be here when I get back?"

And just like that, without waiting for an answer, the two teenagers were on their way—two peculiar young people Durwood was going to have to spend some time getting to know.

Just then Dixie reached the living room, looking strange with a sponge in one hand. Durwood found himself stiffening at her approach as he braced himself for the worst. Something was up. It wasn't like her to let him nap after what had happened in the hallway, let alone their car having been stolen. Suddenly aggravated all over again and practically twitching with suspicion, he sat up prepared to demolish the woman—as hard a day as he'd been having—if she so much as glanced at him the wrong way.

Durwood's suspicions were further aroused when he saw a tiny smile that could have been a smirk come to Dixie's lips as she rested the damp sponge on the coffee-tabled sports page from yesterday's *Examiner*.

"So you're up," she said, smoothing the frown on his forehead with hands that smelled of disinfectant. But just as he was clearing his throat to sound off, she lowered herself onto his lap and, gently fingering the nape of his neck, pulled his head down to where she could kiss him on the mouth. She tasted faintly of oranges. It made him wonder about his own waking breath.

He was so tired, though, of being on edge and on guard that he allowed himself to respond automatically by letting his tongue wiggle into her mouth to form what is known in France as an American kiss. A French athlete he'd met at college had told him that once, and Durwood still believed it. Steaming rather rapidly himself, he could feel Dixie's face heating up as she writhed against him and tightened her hold. What would the kids think if they could see their parents now? It was so unlike either of them to be carrying on this way in the middle of the afternoon, much less after what had just gone down.

Dixie was wearing an ankle-length cotton dress. He rubbed at the fabric covering her thigh, then pillowed the back of her head with his sticky palm. That's when he touched something hard and not very tender.

"Sorry about the curlers," she said in her tiniest voice.

"Baby," he whispered, "you know I still love you, but I'm still trying to figure out what this is all about."

Dixie laughed. "There's nothing to figure out."

"There isn't? The wagon's gone, tomorrow's dinner's been sabotaged . . . and I still have to pick up Leon at the airport."

"You can cross Leon off your list."

"You mean he finally called and said he wasn't coming?"

"Nope, he called up and announced he's been in town for a couple of days already."

"Where the hell is he?"

"Berkeley."

"What's he doing over there?"

"Something about a . . . a gig. He said he'd explain."

"How'd he sound?"

"Like he always does—vague, like Leon, I guess."

"But why didn't he let us know?"

Dixie shrugged and got to her feet. "I wouldn't lose any sleep over it."

"But it's rude of him to treat us that way."

"Of course it's rude, but I don't feel like talking about it. I'm tired of dealing with negative crap. I'm calling a truce, okay? Now, why don't you go upstairs, get into something comfortable, and finish out your nap? All the kids're out for the afternoon, I'm fixing to go grocery shopping, and the house'll be nice and quiet."

"Tell me, Dixie," Durwood asked pointblank. "How come you're being so nice to me all of a sudden?"

They were both standing now. She put her arms around him again and pressed close to him. "Woody, you know I love you. I know all the changes you've been through today, yesterday, and the day before that. I just want you to relax a little, get some rest. We can talk tonight, okay?"

"You gonna take a taxi to do your grocery shopping, or what?"

"There you go with that negative stuff again. No, I'm not taking a taxi. Jenny just got back with the Vega."

Durwood squeezed his wife again and said, "There's something else I've been meaning to tell you."

"What's that, honey?"

He fingered his chin. "Can't think of it right now, but it's important."

"Bad news or good news?"

"I can't remember. I'm sorry. My head's still muddled."

"Then do us all a favor and get some rest. Tomorrow's gonna be strenuous, and there's still a lot to be done."

"But . . . aren't you even mad at me, I mean, just a little?"

"Mad, no. Pissed off, plenty!"

"It isn't my fault the car got stolen. The grocery bags were soaking wet and—"

"Durwood, how many times do I have to tell you I'm not in the mood for any negative bullshit this afternoon? Just because you're dumb doesn't necessarily mean you have to be deaf besides. What's done is done. We can split hairs later if you're still in the mood."

"Hey, one more thing," he asked as she was turning to leave. "Who is this Moby character Celia's been seeing?"

Dixie patted him on the behind and said, "Moby's a sweet kid. Very precocious . . . at least, I think so. He lives with his father in the Mission. I told you about him."

"You did? When?"

"A couple of times, but you never heard a word I said, which is typical, don't you think?"

"Now, wait a minute, Dix. I never heard the boy's name in this house before, and now here you come telling me how sweet and precocious he's supposed to be. I don't understand."

"But I do," she said and kissed him on the cheek. "Sorry, but if I don't get going now, Thanksgiving'll be ruined, and we wouldn't want that to happen, would we?"

Durwood still couldn't believe that any of this was happening to him, not even for a minute.

In bed that night, full of pizza, chablis, and Pepto-Bismol, Durwood felt more relaxed than he had in weeks. That little extra sleep in the afternoon had worked wonders. Their new king-sized waterbed, still a novelty to him, had been worth every nickel of inflated credit-card investment. He floated in it with the lights down low, half-watching some Hollywood movie on cable TV—a lavish film set in the 1920s about a handsome outcast who'd made all his money illegitimately, gangster style, and who was straining to get to this married woman named Daisy who lived down the way. Durwood had trouble following it because his mind was on a lot of other things. He did recognize Robert Redford, though, and wondered what a good-looking actor like him was doing in a turkey like this. Having spent many years in show biz himself, he knew the answer to that one.

Durwood rarely watched anything on television, movies notwithstanding, from beginning to end. His favorite way of relating to the tube was to cut right into the middle of whatever happened to be on and to tune out or change channels before it was over. He must have watched a thousand shows that way. For some reason, he derived great pleasure from snapping on the set to find a story in full progress before his eyes. He usually had no idea of how it began and didn't give a hoot about how it might play out. All that mattered were the images—images that he could weave his own dreams into any which way. It was something like nibbling snack food—he didn't care to fill up on any one item.

As soon as Dixie climbed into bed, all negligee and fragrance, off went the set and out went the light. With the kind of money Wilt Chamberlain made, or even a fraction of it, Durwood, too, could have pressed a button to make the roof slide back while he lay on his back in bed. He and his love could gaze at the heavens—one star at a time if they so pleased—or, better yet, pitch woo while enjoying the rain that was falling. Now, that would be class!

He remembered the times he'd played in Seattle, where rain had been a backdrop for his moodiness. He liked to believe that he did his best thinking in wet weather. This notion went all the way back to his Texas childhood, when his heart would light up at the sight and smell of an approaching summer storm.

Dixie, whose tempo was faster than his, got him into a complicated kiss that wouldn't stop. He cornered her in it while maneuvering both of them into position for other kinds of foolishness that they loved acting out without shame. The name of the game was mutual surrender between two seasoned adults who were more than consenting. And contrary to all social evidence and appearance, it still wasn't what you'd call a spectator sport.

Coming down, drifting back into separate realms, Durwood found himself thinking about the way he'd felt when Dixie had described to him in detail how she'd felt the first time they had held each other naked.

Years ago, having slipped away from a big party in Oakland given by Beanstalk trainer Brewster Day, both of them looped on good champagne, they had necked and wrestled in his polyethylene apartment to Oscar Peterson's "Canadiana Suite" playing over and over again with the speakers turned way down low. It had been one of those too-good-to-be-true nights—in a word, crazy—when everybody was happily hustling everybody else at the party and gypsying off to wherever people drift once the party is over for them. He and Dixie had been among the last to leave.

Dixie—a bonafide Army brat who had grown up in places like Heidelberg, Okinawa, Panama City, and Fort Dix—was doing post-graduate work in library science at UC Berkeley, and he had just been traded to the Beanstalks from Cleveland. New York had got her hooks into him long before that, but that was before he'd aged. He was trying to remember the days when it finally got to be 3 A.M. in the Passionate Era, when making sense—to say nothing of love or war—just plain didn't count. That night, in the warm and windy October darkness, they had clicked by finding that they wanted to be with each other all the time. And now here they were, still together on what was technically Thanksgiving in a tough year that Durwood would just as soon forget as account for, his first year—would you believe, his first season?—away from playing pro ball.

Still, it meant something—he wasn't sure what—after all this time to be on halfway decent terms with this sweating woman, his wife—part mother, part adversary.

Stretched out face to face, Dixie's scratchy toes reached only as far as his knees. She was perspiring like fresh fruit taken from a refrigerator and allowed to languish at room temperature—a sweet funk, delightful, that surrounded him softly.

"Now," she said, "can you remember what it was you had to tell me?"

Tweezering a short and curly hair from his tongue with fingers, he savored the way she was holding him as he said, "Yeah, we won a trip to Reno."

Tickled, Dixie sat up. "C'mon, you mean that little contest they were running out at the shopping center? How'd you find out?"

"I was there."

"When?"

"This morning. I called you, remember?"

"But why didn't you tell me about it then?"

"It hadn't happened yet."

"You were there at the drawing?"

"What is this, a deposition?"

"Why, that's wonderful!" She pulled the covers up over them and kissed him again. All of this sudden affection was beginning to wear on Durwood. "When can we leave?"

"I don't know what the catches are yet. They handed me this envelope. It's in my jacket pocket."

"Oh, Woody, I'm so happy! Something told me to enter that contest!"

"And something tells me there's gotta be a big fat glaring clause in it someplace that we don't know about yet."

"Now, really, there you go again, dwelling on the negative. You've been doing too much of that lately."

"Some of it might have to do with finances, baby. Money. *Muh-knee*. It isn't like the old days when all I had to do was stay in shape, sign on the dotted line every couple seasons, and get out there and play B-ball. We're out here now on our precious own. We're hustling."

"Hustling," she whispered and made a face as if she'd just bitten into a prickly pear. "You know how much I hate that term."

"Would you like it better if I called it by some other name?

Okay, take our accountant, Geller—what was it he called it? Oh, yeah, he's got a Yiddish word for it—*schvitzing*. What say we call it *schvitzing*?"

"Anything but hustling. Hustling always makes me think of . . . you know . . . dirty people, unsavory types."

"You mean, like politicians, housing developers, rich surgeons, and—"

"You know what I mean," she snapped.

Durwood was quiet for a long time before asking, "How come all of a sudden I'm finding out about all kinds of things nobody ever bothered telling me about before?"

"Like what?"

"Well, like this contest you just won. Or what about this little flute-playing clown with his hair gassed and the earring that Celia's been running around with?"

"Here we come back to poor little Richard Mobley again."

"Poor little Richard Mobley, is that his name?"

"Yes, that's his name. What do you need to know about him?" asked Dixie. "What pisses me off about you is all those years when you'd be home for a couple days—or even during the off season—I'd tell you things and tell you things, and you never heard a word I said. I don't understand that. I mean, you were always out there someplace in another world."

With no warning, Durwood began sliding his hands down around Dixie's hips and thighs, alternately smoothing the flesh there and squeezing.

"I'll tell you about Moby," Dixie said, "but first I want you to know I'm too tired now to be lying up here making out with you all night. One or two more times is about all I can manage."

The shallowest of belly laughs rose up past Durwood's throat. He actually had been looking forward to falling asleep.

"What's so funny about that?" asked Dixie as she nuzzled her lips into the ticklish crook of his neck.

4

SOMEWHERE IN THE MIDDLE of the night, long before morning, Durwood got up with so much on his mind that he had to make a special effort to calm his thoughts long enough to slip into something comfortable without making a sound. Down the hallway he tiptoed, past the girls' rooms and down the stairs, not stopping until he reached what was known in his house as Daddy's Room. There he clicked on the light.

Insomnia was new to Durwood. Throughout his nerve-twisting career, going all the way back to college days, he'd rarely known a sleepless night. It had only been during the past six months—since retirement and taking up a new way of life—that he'd been troubled with unwanted wakefulness. He refused to take sleeping pills or tranquilizers. Downers, like uppers, always left him feeling drained. In the end, they weren't worth it.

He had been reading and clipping articles on insomnia from newspapers and magazines and had assembled a hefty file on the subject. Remedies, however, seemed to boil down to two schools of thought: those authorities who advised rolling with sleeplessness by either reading or otherwise exercising the mind, and those who prescribed exotic variations on the old sheep count.

Durwood dealt with insomnia by puttering in his studio, his den, his goof-off quarters. Unless something specific was terrorizing his brain, he usually could bank on being back in bed asleep, or almost asleep, within an hour and a half. There was always the danger, however, of sinking into a sleep so light as to make him dream that he was awake. Insomnia experts had a medical term for it, but Durwood called it Scare Time.

While up, he thought about his life and about life. To keep his mind off money, the family, the future, and failure, he reread his old scrapbooks of clippings and pored over boxes of interesting mail, or he reviewed and polished his trophies and plaques.

He loved these mementos and souvenirs, right on down to old fan letters. When all else failed, he would divert himself by listening to records, jazz mostly, through a very lightweight stereo headset, an old birthday gift from his son. There was plenty in that busy room of his, plastered with signed photos and framed keepsakes, to keep him enthralled for hours.

For my man Woody, a funky workhorse & the hottest guard ever & a favorite from way back.
Rick (Barry)

Hey Durwood you're tops! Don't forget Houston where they cheer for a "touchdown" everytime you make a basket. Glad you 'ppreciate Jimi Hendrix much as I do.
Jimmy Walker
(Kansas City–Omaha Kings)

Dear Editor:
   Thanks for the informative article on Durwood Knight, basketball's finest and hardest-working guard ("Durwood Knight: Poetry in Constant Motion," November). Having followed Knight's career from college days in Cincinnati to the NBA to the ABA, I can say that I've never seen a player scuffle so consistently as he does. The high and mighty critics might get off calling Woody a "gunner" but, to this fan anyway, he is one wizard of a hustler who earns his keep game after game, season after season. Someone like Walt Frazier can lollygag around the court for half of every game and win praise for being "cool" while Knight remains an underrated veteran. Just for the record, could you print his career statistics? I'll bet he stacks up more than favorably with Charlie Scott.
Chris Moskowitz, Miami, Fla.

Dear Durwood,
   I'm a senior at USC who is writing a paper on you for my Ethnic Studies Colloquium. I also do a little modeling, nothing fancy. Just for small independent agencies here in the L.A. area. My measurements are 36-24-36 and I try to keep in shape by playing tennis and swimming (see the enclosed snapshot). Next month I turn 21. I think you're terrific and I would like very much to conduct an interview with you when I come up to visit my cousin in San Francisco which will be in 2 weeks. I know you're busy but it really would help me out. Maybe in some small way I could return the favor. I know you're a married man with one's pick of the ladies, however I am a

"now" woman, modern discreet and unusual. As you probably can tell I have a slight *"thing"* for you, academically that is . . . (smile) . . . and would appreciate your answering as soon as you can.

Your devoted fan,
Darlene Pratt
(213) 732-1173

This last spicy item—inked in ballpoint on lilac-colored, perfumed stationery—had been forwarded to him from Beanstalk headquarters three days ago. It still made him grin. He had received letters like it before, lots of them, and he always liked to savor them secretly before dictating some polite, noncommittal reply. He still wasn't sure what to do with this one. The girl in the glossy picture with practically nothing on reminded him of Dixie—the way she used to look in her bikini-wearing days—but the face, which was cute, even striking in a Mediterranean sort of way, lacked any of the character that attracted him to women closer to his own age.

While sniffing the note and reaching for its envelope, Durwood's attention was drawn to an enlarged black-and-white photograph of Wilt Chamberlain that rested on his desk. Wilt always seemed to be grinning back at him. Taken many years ago in Philadelphia, Wilt's home town, where they had hung out together one night with a couple of other players at a downtown pinball and amusement parlor, the portrait bore a sprawling inscription dashed off in Chamberlain's own hand:

Woody, when it comes to playing basketball you can come early and stay late, but you still can't shoot a penny arcade rifle worth a damn. Oh well, we can't all be perfect like The Kid!

Best always,
Wilt

And then, as crazy as it might seem, there was the natural hunger of wanting to have been elsewhere during all those years it had taken to assemble his precious keepsakes. What else would he have done? What else could he have done? Did Willie Mays feel this way? Miles Davis? And what about old movie stars, former presidents, and dictators in exile? What could be running through their been-there minds at this solemn hour if they, too, were up, like him, looking at the world through uncolored glasses?

Who was he kidding? He knew it wasn't the same. Those people were set; he wasn't. They moved in another world while he still had to contend with this one. He still had to sweat putting Celia and Nissa through college, keep up the notes on his Dolores Street sanctuary, build up a retail record outlet with his old trainer pal Brewster, maintain his sanity in the face of the holiday onslaught, and somehow, as if that weren't enough, figure out what he was going to do with the rest of his life.

He put a record on the turntable, plugged in the earphones, and lay back on the sofa bed to listen to "Night Train" by Jimmy Forrest, a tune that had been hot around the time he was beginning to pay attention to what the grown people around him were really all about and up to. He saw his father as a philosopher, a dyed-in-the-wool barbershop intellectual. Artie Knight, *Artemius* Knight, his neck hunched over some customer's head as he slaps on hot lather with a brush, allows it to stand and do its beard-softening job while he gets busy buzzing his clippers around the man's ears. Unlike your pedestrian order of barbers, the man was an artiste; there was nothing mechanical about him. He had style. For one thing, he never started in at the same spot on every head he worked. Most barbers had a favorite opening: above the ear, the nape of the neck, the front or top or side of the head. Durwood's father first had to size up the individual customer—and customers to him were always clients—before he'd even pick up his clippers. Artie might even tell a particular prospect right off the bat that he didn't really need a haircut, just a shape-up or a shave. People seemed to like that, or, rather, they liked the idea that here was someone who wasn't out to nick them.

Artemius Knight did that for close to half a century, then retired and said, "You get to the place where you need to sit back and look at what you've been doing for a living all your life. That's when you see not only what it's taken out of you but also what it's taught you about life."

It made Durwood glad to remember those words. He also imagined how his mother would react if she could see him now, totally grown, a year from turning forty, sprawled out across the sofa bed with a thin blanket covering him, picturing himself as the man playing the heated saxophone he was listening to, jubilating about the righteousness of simply feeling good. Every grown person he'd heard talk about "Night Train" had said something like, "It just makes me feel good!"

But as it always must, the tune ended. Other LP selections took its place. All Durwood wanted was to go on feeling good, the way he had when he was just beginning to play ball professionally with others, some of whom would become friends, who, outside of the fun of playing the game itself, were as lost and vague about what they were doing in the business as he was.

The business was nothing but the blues, to be sure, but what in the world did you do once the record was over?

That was when Durwood let himself get relaxed enough to drift off into Scare Time.

"Knock knock."

He was gone away, absent, not home.

"Knock knock."

Sometimes it was painful for him to have to come back from delicious nowhere.

"Daddy! Didn't you hear me? I said 'knock knock'!"

"Who's there?" Durwood groaned, aching with sleep.

"Duane."

He cocked one eye open, then two, and slowly tried to make sense of Nissa in Star Wars pajamas, leaning over him, breathing into his face. Apple juice. Her hair was a mess. She sounded stuffed up. Her nose was running.

"Uh . . . Duane who?"

"Duane who?" Nissa giggled. "Did you say 'Duane who'?"
"Yeah. Okay, Duane who?"
"Duane the tub, I'm dwowning!"

Oh, his little girl was triumphant now, beside herself with laughter as she leaped on top of him. She was getting too big to be bouncing around on his midsection. Gradually it sank in that he had fallen asleep on the sofa bed in his study. He also was becoming aware of a thumping sound, muffled and rhythmic, like a heartbeat, coming from he didn't know where. Was it his heart? He placed a hand to his chest. No, maybe it was Nissa's.

"Shhh," he told her.
"Why?"
"I hear a funny noise. Is it your heart beating?"

They both got quiet and listened.

"It isn't my insides making that sound, Daddy, but . . . but now I can hear it too." Suddenly her eyes grew large. "Daddy, do you think it could be a bomb or something?"

"A bomb?"

"Sure, a time bomb. There was this policeman on the news, and they showed how he and these other policemens and firemens and people found this bomb in this lady's house that was ticking like a clock and . . . and you know what they did, Daddy?"

"What did they do, sweetheart?"

"They took a . . . took a . . . What do you call those things again?"

"What things, dear?"

"You know, those things like you got in your tool chest . . . A pliers? You turn things with 'em."

"Oh, you mean a screwdriver."

"That's it, a screwdriver. They took a screwdriver and untook it all apart and made it so it wasn't gonna go off and blow the lady's house up and everything. You think that's what maybe we're hearing now?" Nissa clamped her tiny arms around his neck. "Ooo, Daddy, I'm scared!"

"There's no reason in the world to be frightened," Durwood assured her, sitting up.

"Well, what can we do?"

"We can start by using our ears. Let's listen real hard. You go over there and listen, and I'll see what I can make out on this side of the room."

"Betcha if Celia was here she'd know where it was coming from. Celia can hear anything. Can I go wake her up?"

"No, let Celia sleep. Let's just listen around."

Nissa broke out into a huge, chortling grin. "We'll make it like a game. Okay, Daddy?"

Durwood cocked his head this way and that while Nissa crawled around the rug. He watched her follow the long cord that ran from the stereo amp to the middle of the floor. She picked up the headset, pushed it to one ear, then fastened it over her head.

"Daddy!" she cried. "It's coming from here! Listen!"

When Durwood got down on all fours and sat on the floor with his daughter to listen, he realized right away what the problem was. Laughing out loud, he said, "Well, I'll just be! How dumb can you get?"

"That's what it was, Daddy, wasn't it?" Nissa pointed toward the turntable. "The record was over and you forgot to take the needle off. Ah ha ha, Daddy—" She broke into singsong. "You for-*got* to take the *neee*-dle off, for-*got* to take the *neee*-dle off! . . ."

After disengaging the stylus from a Johnny Hartman/John Coltrane album and clicking off the amplifier, Durwood plucked a Kleenex from the box on his desk and sat down cross-legged to wipe Nissa's nose. "Blow into this," he said.

"I can't."

"What do you mean you can't?"

"I just can't."

"You can at least try."

"Oh, all right." Nissa took one inhale after another through her stuffed-up nose. "See, Daddy, it isn't working, see?"

"Honey, you don't breathe *in* to blow your nose, you breathe *out!*"

"Then show me."

"Like this," Durwood said, lifting her hand to his nostrils. "Feel how I can make air come out of my nose without even opening my mouth? Just by breathing out . . . like this. Can you feel it?"

"Yes, it feels warm."

"Now, here, you try it."

Ignoring the tissue, Nissa placed her nose against the back of sleepy Durwood's hand and, after several feeble tries, finally succeeded in letting loose a blast that left his wrist smothered in mucus.

"Dog-*gone*," he told her, snatching his hand away, "you're supposed to do it in the Kleenex, not in my hand!"

His reaction was so strong and his gesture so abrupt that it frightened poor Nissa, whose face was clouding. "I'm sorry, Dad. That's the first time I ever could do it."

"It's all right, sweetheart." Durwood was loosening up now, laughing as he tissued his arm and hand. "When you grow up into a beautiful woman and start charming the world, I can say I knew you when you didn't even know how to blow your nose."

Nissa, innocent and perplexed, asked, "But what does that mean? Will people even know what you're talking about?"

Durwood laughed harder, then hugged her and said, "Yes, they'll know what I'm talking about, but I do believe that you're coming down with a plain old common cold."

"What's the difference?"

"The difference between what, Nissa?"

"A common cold and a regular cold."

While Durwood was getting his answer together, Nissa was busy checking out his blanket, pillow, and robe.

"Hey," she whined, "how come you're sleeping down here again instead of upstairs with Mommy?"

"Because it's Thanksgiving, my sweet little angel, and your daddy's got to go take care of some outside chores."

"What does that mean?"

"I gotta run."

"Daddy, would you fix me a peanut-butter-and-banana sandwich before you go? I'm starving."

WHEN HE WAS SAILING, when he was moving physically, everything was more than mellow. There was no word for it. Things were just the way they were supposed to be, mellow *plus*, and that was that.

You sailed, you ran, you ran away. You outdistanced others who were mostly extensions of yourself. You jumped back. You swung. You let yourself stop and you let yourself go.

You did it, whatever it was you wanted to do, or whatever your body told you to do. That was what it was all about, nothing else—letting your body do what it not only wanted but *had* to do, the same way it digested food, sweated, pushed, reflected, and slept. But the trick was in knowing how to act on inner signals. All it really was, was a balancing act. You flashed signals to your brain—which was every functioning inch of you—and you acted without thinking about whatever got flashed or bounced back. Like the centipede who froze in his tracks when asked which of its one hundred feet he put forth first, Durwood was only interested in results.

Durwood was running in Golden Gate Park, loving the way it looked and felt on an overcast holiday morning, and loving the way sweat was pouring out of him, making his sweatsuit earn its name. He felt as if he could keep this up forever, trotting out of the park down 19th Avenue, all the way to the Bayshore Freeway, then south to Redwood City, San Jose, Monterey via the Coast Highway, cutting back in to Bakersfield, L.A., San Diego, Tijuana, Mazatlan, Guadalajara, Mexico City, galloping straight into Guatemala and Panama. There was no limit to how far he felt he could run this morning. Nearly forty years old and still going strong, still in tiptop shape, sleek as a dolphin, strong as a buffalo, chugger up mountains and racer into valleys, with gravity and Olympics-sized crowds pulling for him.

He was circling the park for the second time, enjoying the crisp morning chill that still surrounded everything as he wound past the Japanese Tea Garden, the de Young Museum, Steinhart Aquarium, and Morrison Planetarium in the Hall of Science. Scenes unreeled in his sweating head, a few of them fuzzy but most of them as clear and about as graspable as quicksilver.

In one scene, he's running cross-country. It's high school and he's a Texas All-State finalist bearing down for the big home stretch, dreaming of medals, honors, points, scholarship offers to faraway colleges; dreaming of winning his parents' approval at last. Coretha Rawlins will be there just beyond the finish line, ready to greet him with a desperate hug, ready to open her lips to him. How about that? A basketball *and* track star! You can't do much better than that! You can't do much better than that unless you own the team you're star of, right? They're going to have to give him all the keys to all the cities everywhere.

What Durwood heard toward the end of his run was the clipclop of horse hooves coming up behind him. Over his shoulder he saw a blue-suited mounted policeman who, dollar to a donut, was trying to overtake him. At first he paid it no attention, but as the hoofbeats drew closer he found himself slowing his pace and growing vaguely antsy, like a law-abiding motorist who's about to be pulled over by the Highway Patrol and can't quite figure out why.

"Excuse me!" the officer shouted, tugging at reins as he rode up beside Durwood.

Durwood's heart was still racing, but in a fractured second he'd managed to compose himself, although he was still very much on guard. "Did I do something illegal?"

The officer reached inside his coat, took out a pad of paper, and smiled. "I knew there wasn't any easier way to approach you," he said, "so I just had to stop you."

"May I ask what for?"

"Aren't you Durwood Knight, the basketball star?"

"The *ex*-basketball performer, yes."

The policeman was delighted. "I thought so. A couple of my partners said they'd seen you out here running in the morning. I just got assigned here, but when I saw you whizzing along, I said to myself, 'Now, that's got to be him!' Hope I didn't break your stride."

"No problem."

"You know, you're somebody I've admired since high school."

"Is that right?"

"Sure is. I played a little varsity ball myself, but I never was a hotshot. Say, I'd appreciate it if you could give me your autograph." He handed Durwood the pen and pad.

"It would be my pleasure." Still dripping with sweat, Durwood was picturing himself exuding all the coolness and urbane aplomb of a suave junior senator. "To whom should I inscribe this?"

"Oh, you can just make it out to me—Jack Vandemeer. My kids'll get a big kick out of it."

"What are their names?"

Officer Vandemeer told him, and Durwood worked all five kids' names into his lengthy inscription.

"Can't tell you how much this means to me, Mr. Knight. You'll pardon me, I hope, for saying so, but I think the Bay Area Beanstalks are a joke, the way they're playing these days anyway. But before you stepped down I thought they were the hottest new team to come along in years."

"Hey, thanks. It's always good to get feedback from the fans."

"I mean that. Say, I don't see too much about you in the papers anymore. What're you up to now?"

"How's that?"

"Are you in line for a coaching position, a sportscasting slot, or, you know, how're you making your living these days?"

"I'm going into business."

"Great! What kind?"

"The record business."

"Oh, you're going to start singing, like Joe Frazier did there for a while."

"Nope, retail." Durwood was anxious to finish his morning run. "Knight and Day, the Record Setters. Remember that. We're opening the parent store on Divisadero late in January."

"Going to stock Country Western?"

"Sure, that and disco, rock, pop, soul, and jazz—plenty of jazz—and maybe a little classical too. We're also gonna have eight-track and cassette, inexpensive accessories and software, all the trimmings, without merging into big-time stereo outletting, you get me. Keep it basic, fun, and real. Knight and Day."

"I'll be sure and tell all my friends about it and drop by myself. Say, I know you have to get back to your workout. Listen, if there's any way I can help you out, just let me know."

"I'll do that."

"I'm in the book. Jack Vandemeer on McCoppin Street. It's listed under John, but friends call me Jack."

The two men shook hands.

Officer Vandemeer trotted off into the morning and left Durwood standing there, feeling perplexed. What kind of favor would he ever need from a uniformed autograph hound on horseback?

He finished the last mile of his run, feeling satisfied and knowing that this probably would be the easiest leg of his Thanksgiving journey.

THE LATE MEAL THAT MORNING was one of those off-day free-for-alls where everybody got up at a different time and ate whatever they felt like eating.

Durwood, who was capable of eating virtually anything at any time, got back from the park and heated himself leftover split-pea soup while Dixie scrambled eggs, made toast, and poured juice. Nervous about Thanksgiving, she talked about how she was going to cut back on sausage, oysters, eggs, and butter in this year's cornbread stuffing.

"Getting money-conscious again," said Durwood. "I'm glad to hear that."

"Getting health-conscious," Dixie corrected him. "I don't want it to be a lethal concoction. All that cholesterol's bad for you. Everybody in this family's subject to fall dead any day now."

"My grandmama back in Texas ate rich food all her life," said Durwood, "and she lived to see ninety."

"All well and good, but those old people back then worked so hard and kept so active that their arteries didn't have time to harden."

"Maybe so, maybe so," he mumbled, "but I hope the dressing turns out good. You know that's my favorite part of the meal."

"One of your favorites," she said, elbowing his belly playfully.

"I'm still in good shape," he barked automatically. "I'm always gonna keep in shape."

"Honestly, Durwood, I was just joking. Relax."

"I'd really like to do that. You know, relax. But it isn't the easiest thing to do in this house."

"Aw, relax, Dad," said Nissa. "It's easy."

"Oh, yeah?"

"Sure, you just take a deep breath—like this—and let it back out and relax."

While they were laughing over Nissa's remark and digging in, Celia appeared with a heaping plate of raspberry yogurt, apple slices, and skimmed milk. As he watched her sit down at the breakfast-nook table, Durwood came close to choking on a mouthful of soup.

Celia was wearing a pastel nightgown so flimsy that the dark bra and panties she had on underneath could be seen through it. His first impulse was to reach across the table, take hold of her generous ear, and twist it maliciously until she groaned with pain, the way his grandmother used to do to him. Why in the hell would she do such a thing? Lately the girl had become so unpredictable that he guessed it best to check himself, at least until he could get her off someplace by herself and try to talk to her.

It was Dixie who calmly reached across the table and touched Celia's hand. "And how are you this morning, Celia Knight?"

Ignoring her mother as she leaned in Durwood's direction, Celia said, "Hey, Dad, can I talk to you sometime today?"

"Sure, is there something the matter?"
"I need to talk with you. It's important."
"Well, if it's so important," Dixie cut in, "then maybe you need to be talking with both of us."
"No hard feelings, Mother, but—"
"Oh," said Dixie, "so we're back into calling me 'Mother' again?"

All of this led to a round of brief but intense eye contact, telepathic to a T, between Mother and Dad, who had been busy, on the side, boning up to prepare themselves for dealing with the ups and downs of the pubescent personality. Dixie had a stack of books about it by the bed and was always dipping into them. Durwood, who always would have some of the stubborn country Texan in him, had trouble taking any kind of theory about child-rearing seriously. But one point hit home. He had to hand it to the so-called specialists when they talked about how you should never confront an adolescent one-on-one, especially not a fifteen-year-old like Celia. You had to be roundabout. You had to be sneaky. You had to be, well, you had to be cool. They were too goddamn disturbed and guilt-ridden and volatile to tackle head-on. Somehow you had to remain aloof and distant, yet concerned and available.

"I've got a call to make," Durwood told Celia casually as he could, "and then we can go out for a walk."
"A walk!" Nissa squealed, wiping her nose on her sleeve. "I wanna go with you!"
"Well, that's just too damn bad!"
"Celia, watch your mouth!" Durwood warned.

Dixie shot Celia her nastiest, fed-up look. She was about to open fire on the girl when Durwood, eager to head off a new headache, placed his arm around Dixie and, in a low voice, explained to Nissa that she'd have to stay home.
"But why, Daddy?"
"Because you're coming down with a cold."
Nissa broke out into little-girl tears.

Having long ago perceived that this soap opera would go on and on for as long as you cared to stick around and participate in it, Durwood wisely excused himself and ducked upstairs.

A child's voice answered just as Durwood was about to hang up the phone. "Is Corky there?" he asked.

"Just a minute." The kid let the receiver fall into what sounded to Durwood like a crate of lead pipe fittings.

"Corky" was Corky Ski, a nervous buddy of his who was still playing as a guard with the Beanstalks. His real name was Jorge Szymanski, but, being a smooth-talking all-American boy with a flair for publicity, he had legally shortened his last name and allowed his first to stand the way most people ended up pronouncing it anyway.

"Hello," Corky said, sounding rushed.

"Corky, how are you? This is Woody."

"Woody! Say, blood, what's going on?"

"Didn't think I'd catch you. I thought you might be up in Portland by now for tomorrow night's game."

"Leaving in about fifty minutes, Wood. What can I do for you?"

"When're you coming back to town?"

"Day after tomorrow . . . Man, do you ever sound wiped!"

"I do?"

"Wound real tight. It must be the holidays. I know the feeling. Why so glum?"

"Well, I've got good reason to be. Listen, Corky, any chance we can get together for coffee or something when you get back into town?"

"I'll take a rain check on the coffee—you know I never touch the stuff—but that 'or something' part sounds pretty good."

"Whatever's your pleasure. I guess what I really need is a few hours away from all these women. They're making me dizzy."

"Like I always said, Wood, we male parents of female children gotta form some kinda lobby."

"I was thinking about your daughter, the oldest one—what's her name?"

"Jill. What about her?"

"All that trouble you were having with her a couple seasons back. I remember all those changes she was putting you through."

"Don't say it," said Corky, "let me guess. The shoe's on the other foot now, right?"

Durwood laughed. "Did you ever get the urge to just haul off and bash her or choke her when she was messing you around like that?"

"Believe me, I know what you're going through."

"How's Jill doing now?"

"That's a tough one to deal with, Woody, but she's okay, I guess. She's in junior college now and on some kind of a man-hating kick. We still have to work pretty hard to keep the clan together around here. But, c'mon, man, I got five women scheming against me. You only got three."

"But you seem to be so tight with your family, and I guess I'm still corny enough to go for that."

"You'd be surprised to know what goes on backstage."

"No, I wouldn't. You forget my whole life's being lived backstage these days."

"You on top of it yet?"

"On top of a powder keg. Do I sound like I'm on top of anything? I'd hate to tell you what's gone down around here just in the last twenty-four hours."

"Well, that's . . . that's—" Corky's voice broke off abruptly. Somebody had picked up an extension and begun dialing. "Is that on your end or mine?" he asked.

"I don't know for sure," Durwood drawled, "but what say we find out?" Pursing his lips, he whistled into the mouthpiece as shrilly as he could.

Whoever had been there vanished with a click.

"As I was saying," Corky resumed, "that's what scares the pee outta me."

"What're you talking about?"

"I'm talking about what's happening to you right now. What happens when you get outta the business."

"You're always telling me how you hate pro ball."

"Sure, I hate it, but I love hating it. You're out there now in that other world I don't know a thing about."

"Raise up, Corky, don't go rubbing it in!"

"Listen, Wood, I must needs exit. I know where you're com-

ing from, and I'll give you a ring as soon as I'm back—and we'll do it."
"D'Annunzio still giving you guys a hard time about team morale?"
"Not in the last couple weeks. We been winning."
"I know . . . Good luck in Portland. I always liked that town. I kinda wish I was flying up there with you."
"Well, you can sub for me any Thanksgiving you want. I always figure the pilots and crews are more susceptible to getting hung over and blowing it on holidays. I'd rather stay home and do the turkey show."
"Good luck anyway, Corky. I'll peep in at you on the tube if I get a chance."
"Such alumnus devotion! Make sure your TV's in color so you can check out this breathtaking tan I picked up last week in Miami."
"It'll keep," said Durwood, chuckling as he noticed how relieved he felt, if only momentarily, to be carrying on this kind of knuckleheaded jive again.

On the way back from their midday stroll through the Mission District, Celia led Durwood through the little park near home. She tugged him by the hand toward a sunlit bench at the edge of the playground area.
"Since there's practically nobody here but us," she said, "why don't we sit and cool our heels awhile?"
Durwood was nervous. From years of being on the move and away from the home scene, he no longer was always sure how to talk to his kids—which tone of voice to use, or how far to push a topic, particularly when it got touchy.
"Well?" he said finally.
Celia turned and trained her dark, doleful eyes up at his—those jeweled portals to her troubled soul. What threw people off about Celia—what threw him off anyway—was that you could never tell simply by looking at her what kind of mood she might be in. Those fiery eyes, pug nose, generous mouth, soft cheekbones, and the black hair that framed her long face in fluffy curls—none of it looked anything but innocent to Durwood. Innocent, attractive, and vulnerable—very vulnerable.

"Do you have any ideas," she asked, "about what Mom wants for Christmas?"

Suddenly Durwood was all smiles. "So that's what the big mystery's about," he said, relaxing at once. "And what's the big rush over Christmas anyway? We're barely into Thanksgiving."

"But, Dad, it'll be here before you know it. Patsy's already done all of her Christmas shopping."

"She has?"

"Sure, you know what she's like. The whole family's that way."

"What way?"

"Now, *really*, Dad. You know the Matsons always have to be the first ones on the block to do anything. Remember how Patsy's mom was the first person we knew to actually own a Cuisinart, and Mom wanted one so bad she—"

"She was ready to rush out and charge one, but I made her wait until her birthday. All the bread I laid out for that gadget and she still complains about fixing meals."

"I don't care to get into all that," Celia said tactfully. "I just wondered if you thought Mom might like a necklace. There's a man downtown sells jewelry on the street that he makes himself. I saw this necklace. Would you come look at it with me and tell me what you think?"

"Where'd you say this fellow was?"

"Right on the street, Union Square. He's interesting, too, and his stuff isn't all that expensive."

"How much is the necklace you're talking about?"

"Fifty dollars. Is that too much? I've got about a hundred and fifty saved up, but I have to buy for you and Nissa too—and Patsy and I are exchanging gifts this year."

"Is that all?"

"How do you mean?"

"You aren't buying presents for anyone else?"

"Like who?"

"Like for any boyfriends?"

Celia giggled and batted her eyelids quizzically. "Since when do I have a boyfriend that I'd be buying a Christmas present for?"

"Oh, I don't know. This young man you've been practicing with—Moby—looks to me like you get along pretty well."

"So just because we get along doesn't mean we have to be going together."

"Well, you're popular at school and all that. There isn't anything wrong with your dating somebody, just so your mother and I get a chance to meet him and know who he is."

"Daddy, I don't understand."

Remembering how much his touch had meant when she was seven and eight, Durwood took a chance and stroked her soft cheek with the back of his hand. When Celia lowered her eyes and smiled, he said, "You probably think I'm prying, and I probably am, but all I'm trying to do is get to know you better."

"What do you need to know?"

"Who you are. What you're doing when you aren't with us. How your mind's working these days. You're gonna be seeing a lot more of me than you have in the past. You're a big girl now, almost a woman, *almost*. I need to know what's going on inside you."

Celia surprised Durwood by caressing his arm with both hands as she pressed her face into the upper sleeve of his rumpled, hooded sweatshirt. "Daddy," she blurted out suddenly, "I'm scared."

Alarmed, he eased an arm around her shoulders, the way he might have done a girlfriend at the movies on a first date or, going way back, to console a high school teammate who'd been walloped on the court during a practice session.

"Scared of what, dear?"

"I don't know. Just scared. I get that way sometimes. Lately it's been happening a lot."

Durwood, being Durwood, immediately began to think the worst. Was she pregnant? Hadn't Dixie told her about birth control?

"What's wrong?" he asked, blowing his cool. "What kind of trouble are you in?"

"Trouble? What're you talking about? I'm not in any trouble. I'm just worried about the future, our whole family's future."

Durwood wasn't certain that it was all right to feel relieved yet, so he said, "The future? I don't get it. The future's taking care of itself right now, Celia."

"Daddy, you don't even know what I mean, do you? Do you? I'm talking about the fact that we really don't have any future, do we? You really haven't been earning much of anything since you stopped playing ball."

"I did okay with my summer clinics and workshops."

"But you've always done those between seasons in the summer. It's that real steady income that matters, and you won't be able to count on that now."

"Aren't you still a little young to be worrying about stuff like that? I'm not exactly what you'd call idle these days."

"Oh, I'm happy about the record shop you and Mr. Day are gonna open. It's a great idea, but do you really think it's gonna make it with the state of the economy being what it is today? I mean, the average person is too involved with basics—like, you know, power shortages and inflation—to have much money left over for buying records."

"I see you've been doing your homework," he said, beaming. "I also see you've been talking with your mother."

"I wish you'd give me credit for having a few ideas of my own sometimes. I'm old enough to see the reality of some of what's going down."

When Durwood used to carry her strapped to him in an infant-sized backpack, he never dreamed that she would one day be talking to him this way, much less on a traditional holiday that was supposed to be festive. All he could think to say was, "We should get together more often, Celia, and just say what's on our minds."

"I already know what's on your mind."

"I'll bet you do."

"You're saying that to be sarcastic, but I'm serious. You think I'm sleeping around, don't you? You'd like to know if I am and who I'm doing it with."

"I'd simply like to get back on a friendly, man-to-man—I mean, person-to-person—basis with you. In other words, I'm here, I'm available, and I care about what happens to you."

"I'm okay, Dad."

"Are you? Hey, I know in some ways I'm hard to deal with, but I'm still your father and I love you. Fathers are going out of style, you know."

"Well, I care about you and Mom enough to not wanna throw any money away on a gift she might not even want."

"Just let me know when you're ready to go down and look at that necklace and I'll be happy to come with you."

When he squeezed her shoulder, Celia said, "Please be nice to Moby when he comes around. He isn't my boyfriend. We do think a lot alike, though, like about music. He thinks I'm a good songwriter."

Picking up the feeler, Durwood was honestly able to say, "I think you've got talent, kid. What you gonna be when you grow up?"

"The same as I am now," Celia said, rolling her eyes at him, "except wiser and richer and a lot more famous."

"Will you still know us when all that happens?"

"Maybe. It's hard to say." She stood up and put her hand in his and pretended to be hoisting him to his feet. "What if I turned out to be the first woman to play with the Utah Jazz? How'd you like that?"

"Tell you," he said as he rose with a sigh, "I don't think I'd mind that at all."

"You wouldn't?"

"Nope, just as long as you didn't marry one of 'em."

As they walked home, Durwood felt short-changed, uneasy about their little outing. He should have brought up the see-through nightgown nonsense. On the other hand, it was such a cloudy, brisk afternoon that it made him feel warm inside even to be on speaking terms with his daughter. At least some ice had been broken. You don't rush these matters. Recalling the torture that Corky had gone through with his promiscuous, pill-head daughter Jill, Durwood had sense enough to know how to leave well enough alone. Perhaps, as a father, there was still hope for him. If only he could back-step through time and make up for the way he had neglected the fifteen-year-old Leon, his son by another woman—Coretha—the first one he'd ever slept with who had meant anything to him.

"By the way," Durwood said as they turned up Dolores Street, "I haven't bottomed out yet."

"How's that, Dad?"

"Come depression, recession, or whatever's around the corner, I'm not about to let you guys starve or go on relief. Just trust me."

"I want to."

"You've got to—for as long as you're living with me anyway. Now, if you can find someplace better to go, then that's another story."

Stopping all at once in her tracks, Celia grinned and, turning to Durwood, said, "Race you to the front steps! On your mark . . . Get set . . ."

And while he stood in place, waiting for her to say "Go," she took off up the hill toward their house. It was all he could do to try and keep up with her, huffing all the way and coming in second—a very close second, but second all the same.

THE FIRST ONE TO NOTICE anything funny was Brewster Day. "I woulda sworn," he told his girlfriend Mitzi, "I heard a saxophone coming from someplace just now."

It was getting to be nighttime, the other end of Thanksgiving, and they were all stuffed, sitting around the fire Durwood had built, listening to Celia sing and play the guitar. The girl was good and she knew it. Although she excelled at performing her own original songs, she also enjoyed—hambone that she was—doing standards, folk tunes, trendy pop material, and occasional blues. Her style was breezy, direct, and remarkably listenable for someone who was mostly self-taught and who had barely turned fifteen. Sometimes Durwood grew a little jealous as he watched and listened to her fingering chords—simple and modern—all up and down the neck and make cute little single-string runs, as she was doing now, in the fashion of jazz-in-amber. He held back on telling her how accomplished she was because he wasn't crazy about encouraging her to perform. Two show-biz people in one family, he thought, was easily more than enough.

When, during a lull, Brewster made another remark about hearing a saxophone, Nissa said, "Shhhh!" and they all stopped chatting while she crept across the living room and out into the vestibule to the front door.

"It's coming from out on the porch!" Nissa cried.

Durwood hurried to the window, took hold of the drapes, and, parting them, looked out and began shaking his head. "Well, well, well," he laughed, "do tell!"

"Who in the world is it?" asked Dixie, jumping up from her cozy floor pillow.

"It's Leon," said Durwood.

"I knew it!" Celia shouted. "I knew it! And he was right in tune with me too."

Durwood flung open the door, and, sure enough, there stood long, lanky Leon, almost as tall as his father, in an Army-surplus rain poncho and wide-brimmed hat, a padded vinyl horn case slung over one shoulder, the white plastic horn still at his lips. Instead of saying hello, he sounded a gutsy blues figure in the lower register and walked in with a triumphant grin.

"Happy Thanksgiving, everybody! Sorry to be so tardy on the Sacred Bird Day, but you know how it is . . . I got hung up."

"Yeah, and you hung us up too," said Durwood, who, in spite of Leon's rude entrance, was happy to lay eyes on his only son again.

They shook hands, embraced, and stood sizing up one another while the rest of the family quickly moved in on the new arrival. Even Brewster and Mitzi approached Leon with tickled politeness. There were handshakes and hugs all around, and more hugs, and more handshakes.

"You had dinner yet?" asked Dixie, who seemed to be reviewing Leon's appearance from some private new angle. "I can heat you up some turkey and ham and dressing and whatever else is left."

"You know I stays hungry, Dixie, but you can skip the meat this time around."

"Skip the meat?" As a worshipper of protein from the Year One, Durwood was concerned. "What do you mean, 'Skip the meat'?"

"No offense," said Leon, who still had Celia clinging to his arm. "It's just I went on this vegetarian diet in August after the band got back from Europe and Japan, and I'm still on it." Turning to Dixie, he added for her sake, "Hey, listen, it's safe. I wouldn't mind tasting a little bit of your turkey, but please, could you leave off the pork? And please don't bother heating it up."

Durwood had to admit that he no longer knew his son well enough anymore to know right off if he was witnessing a change of heart or only a change of mind. The kid looked healthy to him. He couldn't wait to get him out onto a gym floor to find out how he was functioning at the age of twenty-two without benefit of meat.

Celia looked enthralled. "I've been waiting," she said, "to hear about your travels. You gotta tell me all about it!"

"Japan?" said Brewster, who looked to be every bit as excited as Celia. "I'd like to hear about that place." Brewster was now Durwood's business partner, a former Beanstalk staffer with a mind, if you could call it that, of his own. To Durwood, he was an enigma, one of a kind, who nevertheless had winning ways. His job had been to bandage the players' ankles and attend to their sprains and bruises. He had been something between a trainer and some kind of mop-up team shrink. Eagerly, Brewster maneuvered Mitzi to his side. "This is my friend Mitzi," he proclaimed, "and she's from Tokyo."

"Is that so?" remarked Leon, who—from where Durwood stood at least—seemed to be beaming for Mitzi and nobody else.

"I understand you can make a lotta money in that town if you know how to bow right and don't get too uppity." Having said that, Brewster stepped back, looking as if it were Mitzi's turn now to translate.

"Europe and Japan," said Dixie, putting on her nostalgic face, "you're talking about where I grew up. Did you get to Germany?"

"That was our first stop. We played all over the place—Munich, Berlin, Düsseldorf—for two weeks."

"I spent my childhood on an Army base in Heidelberg. Uh, *Wie geht es Ihnen?*"

"I'm fine, thanks, but that doesn't mean I know any German."

"I was born in Heidelberg," Dixie went on, "and stayed there for eight years before we moved to Japan."

"What I would like to know," said Durwood, still holding in his gut from the meal, "is what are you trying to prove by not notifying anybody you were in town and showing up here way after dinner like this?"

"Dad, can I explain all that to you tomorrow?"

It had to be okay. Already it was pushing ten. Durwood had a headache from eating and drinking and talking too much. Had anybody asked him six months ago, when he'd first retired, if he ever wanted to check back into any of those old, funky, make-do hotels or motels he'd spent his whole adult life in between and after games, he would have said, "Hell no!"

But that was exactly what he wished he were doing at that moment. There'd be no family hassles to cope with, no property to maintain or worry about up close, and nothing complicated to think about except how to get from now into the future, financially, just the way Celia had been putting it to him. During those old road days, though, it seemed there was no immediate problem that he couldn't solve by thinking hard for a minute and then picking up the phone. It was almost like wanting to be back working the old NBA circuit in the days when Skeeter Moss—a hard-playing dunker and then some—would fake an early-morning wake-up call with the motel operator that would result in Durwood and the rest of the Beanstalks being jarred from their sleep at some ungodly hour in a city whose name they weren't always sure of.

It sure was going to be nice having another man around the house for a few days.

Durwood watched Leon dribble the ball down-court and toss a few lay-ups. They hadn't played around this way together in years. In fact, Durwood got more of a kick out of this physical approach to getting reacquainted than when they simply talked. The big drawback, of course, was that he couldn't always tell from his movements what Leon was thinking.

When Leon was ten, it thrilled Durwood to hear him talk about becoming an athlete like his dad. He loved giving the boy inside tips and pointers on playing all kinds of sports. But by ninth grade Leon had gotten sidetracked into music, and there he stayed. Durwood always thought that he'd have made a better-than-average athlete; he had the build, stamina, and coordination, and he performed smoothly under pressure. True, Leon had never been one to suffer much pain—which was prerequisite to becoming a great athlete—but, with time, that might have changed. That he lacked drive and didn't seem to be particularly competitive, well, that got to Durwood. It worried him. That had to be a trait he inherited from Coretha, his mother. All the same, Durwood still could be proud of the fact that Leon was a loner like himself.

"You know why a lotta your shots aren't making it?" Durwood moved in on Leon and tapped the ball. "Check this." While Leon looked on, he dashed through some jump shots, chest shots, hooks, lay-ups, a couple of overheads, and one remarkable free throw, bringing almost all of them off expertly.

Leon looked impressed. "Hey, Pops, you're a pro from way back, but I never knew you were so hot at just plain shooting. How come Rick Barry and Frazier and Baylor got all the credit?"

"And all the money too!" Durwood yelled, not cracking a smile. "All that is, is flash. It's one thing to showboat and clown when it's just me and a buddy or two. It's a different story when you got umpteen vicious hardlegs coming at you and crowding you so close you don't even have room to poot, much less fake, pass, or shoot."

"I see what you mean. It's the Zen principle."

"The *what* principle?"

"Never mind," said Leon, "it isn't important. What you're saying is that a pressure situation's another matter entirely."

"Absolutely. It's like those lab-controlled experiments we used to have to do in college. Like, I've always been a good shot. I could do that before I ever knew the first thing about running or handling the ball. I was born with the touch, but it's taken me years to keep cool enough to use it when the heat's on. What I wanted to show you is something I hipped you to a long time ago, when you were in junior high back in New York."

"Something basic, I bet."

"That's right—the seams, remember?" Durwood held up the ball with both hands for Leon to see. "You gotta keep your fingertips on these seams. That's the only way you're gonna get that good backspin you need."

"Well, awwwwriiight," said Leon, "now I remember. Honest, Pops, everything you ever taught me's still imbedded in my brain someplace. You gotta remember I been fingering saxophones and flutes for so long now that it's hard to get back into how a basketball's supposed to feel."

"That's easy to understand, but here, give it another try." He tossed the ball back hard and watched how Leon caught it. "Great! You didn't forget what I told you about *that*."

Careful to follow his father's instructions, Leon promptly lobbed in two hooks and a two-handed chest shot that no one could have said was pure luck. Like every proud coach he'd ever known, Durwood was gloating.

The rest of the session was fast and practically wordless. Durwood and Leon did what they'd come to this private gymnasium to do, which was to work up a sweat and an appetite. For the most part, all they were doing was playing a little elegant, indoor alleyball. Leon seemed to be having fun, enjoying himself and not really caring about technique or precision. It took Durwood a while to relax and overcome his professional instincts. Once he did, they had a ball.

Showered, dressed, and feeling good, they stepped out into a late-morning drizzle and were crossing the street to Leon's Fiat when Durwood said, "Wait!"
"Huh?"
"Look!"
"What is it, Pops?"
Durwood pointed. "That yellow car parked at the corner."
"You mean, the station wagon? What about it?"
"It's mine, the one that I told you got stolen."
"It is?" Leon scratched his head. "Looks pretty beat-up to me. I thought you told me it was new."
"Son of a bitch!" Durwood growled and bit his lower lip. "Will you just look at that!"
"What's your car doing here?" asked Leon.
"That's what I intend to find out."
The hood looked as if somebody had taken a sledge hammer to it. The doors were unlocked. Durwood and Leon climbed inside. The first thing Durwood noticed was that the cassette tape deck was missing.
Leon sniffed and turned up his nose. "Smells like somebody's been smoking grass in here too," he said. "And not all that long ago either."
Sure enough, when they pulled out the ashtray, which was crammed with butts—and none of the Knights smoked anything—they found a freshly abandoned roach still smoldering, causing Durwood to cough and sputter. The car was littered with half-crushed malt liquor cans and girlie magazines.
Durwood found his key, turned it in the ignition, and gunned the engine. The gas needle floated just beyond empty.
"Funny people," Leon observed, "whoever it is."
"Funny and cheap," said Durwood. "I stood in line half an hour to fill this tank."
"What do you think we should do, Pops?"
"Why don't we wait around for a while and see who turns up?"
"You mean, wait right here?"
"No, in your car."
Leon had to think for a second. "That's fine with me, only I

hope nothing happens to that Fiat. I rented it without taking out any collision or personal-injury insurance."

"Why would you go and do a fool thing like that?"

"Trying to save a few bucks."

Durwood shook his head. "Just like your mother, that's just like Coretha."

They staked out the scene from the Fiat, which was parked three cars behind Durwood's on the same side of the street. Leon sat in the driver's seat, where he clicked on the radio and scanned the dial until he came across a station playing Chinese opera.

Durwood, who had slid the front passenger seat back as far as it would go to make room for his legs, said, "Don't tell me you like to listen to that stuff?"

"Sure, it's different. That's what I like about the Bay Area. You guys got so much going that you never know what you're gonna run into."

"Tell me about it, Leon."

"No, really, you don't get this kind of cultural mix back East so much. Pops, you know, I'm finding out you can learn from everything. I fell in love with Japanese classical music while we were over there—the koto and all those instruments. Okay, it sounds a little peculiar at first, but after you get used to it you can hear where that culture's coming from. The more you listen, the more you hear. Silence—now that's something the Japanese really know how to use."

"You don't say? Well, they must know how to use a whole lotta things because they've got all the money tied up right now—them and the Arabs and the Germans. You gotta hear Grandpa Artie talk about it. As hard as he fought in World War II."

"Yeah," Leon went on, failing to pick up Durwood's cue, "and, like, you take the Chinese . . . They've got these modes you can transpose a dozen different ways. I'm talking about there's anything from sixty to eighty-four different keys in Chinese music. Now, can you imagine that?"

"You're way over my head," said Durwood. "Back when I was studying trumpet, I always thought the twelve keys we got over here were about five too many."

A flute gasped. A female voice intoned a soft, mournfully low note that quavered before breaking up into quickly chopped, singsong syllables. A succession of little cymbals sounded, topped off with the crashing of one large cymbal. It all sounded pretty spooky to Durwood, who didn't even care for traditional Western opera; who, in fact, had a hard time dealing with the aging jazz avant-garde.

"I know I'm reactionary," Durwood said, trying his best not to sound defensive, "but I still like a solid beat and a good, strong melody you can still remember after the music's stopped."

Leon laughed as he studied the look on his father's face. Durwood had no idea what he saw there—some kind of wistfulness perhaps. "That," said Leon, "is what Cab Calloway called bebop when Dizzy Gillespie first started playing it in his band."

"What was that?"

"Chinese music. Cab said, 'Don't be playing that damn Chinese music in my band!' And the rest is history."

"Well," said Durwood, "I'm history too."

Leon got quiet before asking, "How long did you play, Pops?"

"Up through high school," said Durwood, softening. "Sometimes I'm sorry I ever gave it up."

"Well, why did you?"

"Couldn't do everything, you know. It was either music or sports. I had to work after school too. That didn't leave me much extra time. Life's pretty short. I mean, it's a monster. It doesn't feel that way when you're still your age, but sooner or later you gotta figure out what it is you do best, then pretty much stick to that one thing. I always knew I could play ball, so I opted for that. I had my doubts about playing trumpet." He gave Leon's shoulder a gentle squeeze. "Glad somebody in the family turned out to be a musician."

"Sounds to me like Celia's headed in that direction too. I think she's got a lot going for her. She really should take lessons."

"You think she's good, huh?"

"She's better than good, Pops. She's gifted. Haven't you noticed?"

"What do you think about her personality?"

"Well . . . she's moody, I know, but what Gemini isn't? For the record, I think I have to disqualify myself as an objective character witness when it comes to Ceel, Pops, because she kinda worships me a little. I mean, it makes me nervous. She's sensitive as hell, and I think you and Dixie have got to be really careful how you deal with her."

"You heard her friend Moby play flute?"

"Moby? Who's that?"

"I guess you haven't met him yet."

"Well, remember I just now got here. I—"

Suddenly Leon sat straight up. As suddenly as he had snapped the radio on, he turned it off and said, "Hey, get a load of that!" He was peering through the windshield at a curious pair that had just appeared at that very moment from out of nowhere. The two were ambling toward the station wagon. "Pops, you think that's them?"

All Durwood saw when he turned to look was a chubby little old lady wearing dark glasses and a bright yellow, hooded raincoat and carrying a white cane. Leading her by the arm was a tallish young woman wearing boots and a rumpled trench coat and holding an umbrella over both of them.

"Now, hold on," said Durwood as he leaned forward and strained to see through the mist that was fogging the windshield. "Better turn your wipers on. I wanna make sure I'm seeing what I think I'm seeing."

Once Leon got the wipers to flapping, Durwood had no trouble whatever seeing quite clearly that the younger woman was, indeed, helping her senior friend into the car, into *his* poor, stolen, damaged, violated Ford wagon. The very spectacle of it was throwing him for a loop, yet he couldn't keep his eyes off what he still couldn't believe he was seeing.

"Now, this is interesting," said Leon.

"You must be thinking what I'm thinking."

"Maybe. Like, are they gonna hot-wire it, or what?"

"Which is exactly what I'm waiting to find out."

"So what do we do once they start up?"

"We follow them."

"We do? All right, and then what?"

"See where they go and then call the police."

For some reason, Leon broke out laughing.

"What's so funny?" Durwood wanted to know.

"What's so funny," said Leon between chuckles, "is I come all the way out here to play a two-night gig and see you guys and end up in some kinda ludicrous 'Streets of San Francisco' television escapade."

"Well, you can write a tune about it after you get back to New York. But right now it's serious and for real, and I intend to find out for myself what the hell's going on."

They both watched and, rolling down their windows, listened as the younger woman—having by now gotten her companion seated—slammed the passenger door shut. They couldn't make out what she did after she walked around and climbed in behind the wheel, but there was no mistaking the sickly wheeze and roar of the engine turning over.

"Damn thing needs a tune-up bad," said Durwood. "Hey, let's get moving!"

"Pops, I was just thinking. Maybe we should've repossessed the thing while we had the chance. We still can. Hell, one of 'em's blind."

"I thought about that, but it's too late now. She's pulling out, hurry up."

Leon lost no time in getting the rent-a-car going. They trailed the Ford through heavy traffic along the waterfront all the way to Bay Street and Columbus Avenue, where it turned into the busy Tower Records parking lot, then nosed its way into a tight spot and stopped. Leon had to double-park on Columbus in a dangerous lane with the motor idling.

The tall woman got out and rushed inside the store, whose hugeness, fluorescence, and year-round crowds had always provoked Durwood, even when he himself had, on occasion, been part of the crowd.

"Now what do we do?" asked Leon.

"Shhh, I'm trying to think . . . We can go over and quiz the old lady, or we can bust inside and jack up her friend, or—"

"This is all so strange," said Leon, who was clearly out of his element.

"I'd sure like to get my tape player back," said Durwood.

"Took me half a day to install that sucker—with Brewster's help."

"I'll do whatever you say, Pops."

"Tell you what . . . Pull up behind 'em and block my car so they can't back out."

It took some maneuvering, but Leon managed to do precisely that.

Durwood got out and approached the Ford. How absurd, he was thinking, to be going through this. For the first time ever, he found himself wishing that he had a gun, a pool cue, a big stick, anything comforting. No telling how crazy these fools might turn out to be. If push came to shove, he could always get nasty, kamikaze nasty, but surely he could handle a little old blind lady and her daughter, if she was her daughter, without having to raise a finger. He rapped on the car window, which the old lady opened at once.

"Yes, sir?"

"Lady, this machine happens to belong to me. Now, I don't know what you're doing in it or how you and your friend got ahold of it, but it's mine, understand? And I want it back. Right now."

"Sir, I don't know what you're talking about."

"Madame, stealing a car is still a felony, even here in California, and I do intend to put whoever it was stole this one from me down up *under* the jail."

"I'm sorry. I don't know who you are. My niece borrowed this car from her boyfriend to drive me home. I couldn't even tell you what it looks like, you wanna know the truth." And, having said that, she genially lowered her shades so that Durwood could see that she was, unquestionably, blind.

This confused him. He hadn't expected her to be so civil. While he stood trying to get his next move together, Leon let out a blast on the Fiat horn. Durwood jerked around in time to catch a black-and-white S.F.P.D. squad car, with whirling red lights, pulling into the lot.

One of the officers stuck his head out the window and shouted to Leon. "Hey," he said, "you can't block all the rest of these cars like that!"

Just as Leon, with a studied smile and the waving of arms,

was summoning the squad car over, Durwood saw the blind lady's niece walk out of Tower Records. There was a man with her. He was broad-shouldered, thick-necked, and wore a waist-length leather coat and bell-bottom jeans. He was surly-looking, too, with his shaved head and under-the-chin beard with no mustache. For some reason, though, he looked familiar to Durwood, who felt as if he'd seen the man before, in a dream maybe. Lately Durwood seemed to be getting as much out of his dream life as he did his waking life; events and impressions got mixed up. There was something about the eyes, the mouth, the cute toughness of this joker that set something off inside him, that clicked.

Carrying red-lettered, yellow packages and oblivious to everything except their own conversation, the pair moved with their heads lowered against the rain toward Durwood's car.

Leon, all hands and mouth, was still explaining the situation to the two policemen. Durwood leaned in close to the old lady and whispered, "Listen, I want you to get real quiet. If you do, we'll have this little mix-up straightened out in no time."

"Please," cried the lady, "explain this to me. What you gonna do? You gonna hurt me? I don't get any of this. You aren't one of those leftover Cuba skyjackers, are you?"

"Just take it easy, ma'am."

Freaking out, the woman grabbed her cane and began poking it frantically at Durwood's face through the window opening. He managed to get a firm enough hold on it to yank it from her.

"You—You asshole!" she screamed. She was shaking all over. "You got malice in your heart, don't you? You gonna hurt Bobbi and Trip, I know it! But I ain't gon' let you. I'll . . . I'll scream, that's what I'll do!"

She had shouted the names Bobbi and Trip so loudly that the approaching couple froze in their tracks.

"Awww, shit!" Trip hollered, spinning around. "What the hell kinda trick you done put us in now? Run, goddamn it, run!"

Panicked, they took off running. Bobbi darted—rather mindlessly, Durwood thought—across Bay Street, jeopardizing her life as she weaved her way through fast-moving traffic. Cars squealed to a halt. Horns blared. Uptight drivers poked their heads out of windows and called her everything but a child of God.

Trip was sneakier. Right away, he split off from Bobbi at the corner and casually walked across Columbus along Bay while the light was still conveniently green, attracting the attention of no one but Durwood, who never took his eyes off him.

As Durwood was taking off after the young man, racing right past the cops and Leon, he heard one of the men in uniform say, "Hey, are you—?"

"Woody Knight," his partner said with a smug, gap-toothed grin.

"Excuse me," Durwood shouted over his shoulder, "but could you keep an eye on the old lady?"

Now it was Durwood's turn to do some tricky snake-hipping. He whizzed across the intersection on a red light. Trip had reached midblock by now, but Durwood knew well what his long legs were capable of doing when he was riled up and wired on nerve. He had to give Trip credit, though; the boy was no slouch, not by a long shot. Trip could haul ass with the best of them, but Durwood could tell that the fat package Trip was clutching was becoming a burden. Other people on the sidewalk either scurried and scrambled out of Durwood's way or stopped to gawk at him.

Durwood shifted into a higher gear. It was only a matter of a few yards now. He was determined, whatever it took, to nail this creep.

Glancing back, pop-eyed, gritting his teeth, Trip did something Durwood never could have anticipated. He slowed down, spun around, and, grunting, hurled the Tower Records package straight at Durwood's head, flinging it edgewise, Frisbee style, with both hands and with all his might.

The package struck Durwood on the side of the neck. The pain was so tremendous that he thought he'd been shot. He groaned as he wobbled off-balance and collided with a party of umbrella-toting, raincoated nuns. Horrified, outraged, the sisters, as they were sent scattering, shrieked and jabbered away in French while trying to step around all the record albums spilling out of the bag onto the watery sidewalk.

Two youngsters in pullover knit caps who were jaywalking

across Bay Street broke out in raucous delight as they raced to the scene, got down on their knees, and started scooping up LPs. "Hot damn, Willie," one said to the other, "lookit all these al-blums! Get all you can—we can dry 'em off later!"

Police sirens were reddening the chilled, soggy air. Durwood was only vaguely aware that their wails were growing louder. He could barely move his wounded neck now, and his hearing seemed about to go out on him. Everything around him, except what had to be done, was getting blotted out in a hurry.

When Trip turned the corner, disappearing momentarily, Durwood made a silent, grudgeful vow—as unnecessary as it was frantic—to make this bastard pay for all the wrong he and his family ever had been dealt.

Rounding the corner, Durwood again caught sight of his moving target. Trip was zigzagging across to the opposite side of the street, this time through traffic that was relatively light. For Durwood, he was as good as caught. It didn't matter that two squad cars were moving in now to ease the chase. It no longer mattered that he might very well end up being paralyzed for life from the neck up. His silly tape player no longer mattered, nor did all the funny feelings he'd been going through since retiring from pro sports. He was going to muscle himself a living Christmas present, and do it in advance!

During one of those odd moments that only a mathematician devoted to the study of probability theory or queues might be able to explain, the street was suddenly free of oncoming traffic. Durwood, motored by sheer will, finally got his talons into Trip—was that the name he'd heard?—and knocked him to the pavement in the middle of the street. Right away, Durwood was on top of him, digging his knees into Trip's back and twisting his arm in a brutal hammer lock, enjoying the pain he was causing. But as much as he wanted to harm this joker—bash his head in, karate chop his neck—common sense told him that he'd best be cool. It was bad enough having to put up with the indignity of the situation. He didn't need an assault charge piled on top of that. Cruelly, he kept twisting the groaning man's arm as—over and over again, through clenched teeth, under his broken breath—he said, "Thank you, thank you, thank you, God . . . if there is a God!"

One pair of policemen, covered by reinforcements, rushed in, handcuffed the suspect's wrists behind him, and stood him firmly on his feet. When Durwood saw tears come to Trip's eyes and noticed, while the cops were frisking him, how young a man he was, his thoughts shifted to his own children, to Leon, and he had to swallow hard to keep from making a spectacle of himself.

Trip wouldn't answer any of the questions put to him. The police were only too pleased to listen to Durwood's side of the story. He told them about the shopping center, the report he'd filed, how he and his son had come across the stolen car accidentally. He told them about and described Bobbi and her blind aunt, who were, so he was told, already in custody. He also told them about the missing cassette player and how his neck was killing him.

"You intend to press charges, Mr. Knight?"

"Is rain wet?" he answered, brushing himself off. "Hell, I'm like everybody else I know when it comes to this stuff. I'm no liberal."

Somehow, while he was being shoved into the back seat of a squad car, the suspect managed to get close enough to Durwood to spit on him.

HE FELT CONFINED, absolutely pent up. Having to wear a neck brace was bad enough, but being cooped up this way in Brewster's mobile home—even for the length of a brief business conference—qualified as cruel and unusual punishment. A man Durwood's size needed room to stretch.

"And that's the bottom line," Brewster was saying. "Insurance is a bitch, I know, but on top of everything else we have to take out good theft and burglary insurance or we might as well pack it all in right now and dissolve the partnership."

Durwood, as he tried to make sense of what Brewster was telling him, was doing his best to ignore all the neatly rubberbanded stacks of bills—fives, tens, twenties—that lined the top edge of the sofa back. "But why theft *and* burglary?" he asked.

"Because . . . Okay, say some screwball comes into our shop on a stick-up and starts shooting up the place. Now, I'm not saying this'll happen, but suppose it did. Then we'd both be personally liable for anything that went down in there, and if any customers happened to get hurt in the process, we'd just be shit out of luck."

"Maybe that's a chance we have to take. I mean, we could both get gunned down too."

"Slow down," said Brewster. "Let's break this down some. Now, this partnership means a lot to me. I love making money. I'm in this for the bread. I even go for the gamble that's connected with any kind of business, but I'm no fool. I'm definitely for eliminating unnecessary risks. We can't afford to take any dumb chances."

A cold wind was whipping through the trailer. It made Durwood's neck ache. He got up from his chair and slid one of the aluminum windows shut. Brewster was a fresh air freak, but he didn't seem to mind. Stacked along the window ledge were little piles of fifties and one-hundred-dollar bills.

"So, Wood," Brewster continued, "I think we need to take out this CDDD policy."

"CDDD? What does that stand for?"

"Stands for Comprehensive Dishonesty, Disappearance, and Destruction. That's the best kind of policy. Covers pretty much everything for a small business like ours. And, you know, even *that* isn't going to be all that easy to manage since our shop is situated near what's known as a red circle zone."

The tangible idea of being part owner of a hip record store still excited Durwood, even though precise business details put him to sleep. He wasn't used to making quick decisions off the basketball court. In the past, most business decisions had been made for him. Brewster was the one with a head for figures, the one whose practical know-how Durwood was counting on to keep Knight and Day functioning and solvent on a day-to-day basis. Even if it did, in some ways, leave him feeling inadequate and vulnerable, he knew he would have to rely on Brewster.

"Let me mull all that over for a day or two," said Durwood.

"What's there to mull over?" asked Brewster. "We've got no choice. I've thought it through already. I've been in retail before, and I know the danger of going into it underinsured. That's almost as bad as going in undercapitalized."

"All right," said Durwood, slowly but finally. "I suppose I can go along with that. We'll have to move a lotta records to stay on top of the overhead and outlay and still make money, won't we?"

"You catch on fast, Wood." Brewster shook his head, stood up, poked his hands in his pockets, and walked to the window. What he saw outside caused him to shake his head again.

"So do you think we can make a go of it?" asked Durwood. "I've been reading about this oil crisis and the petroleum situation. They predict that the effect on the record industry might be tremendous. The record companies have been worried about declining sales. They're cutting back on personnel."

"I know about that, Wood, but if you do your homework and check out what happens during most recessions and depressions, especially the last Great Depression in this country, you find out that entertainment's one of the last things most people give up. Books, records, movies, booze—they still sell no matter how hard times get."

"So how come you keep shaking your head?"

"Come over here," said Brewster. "I want you to look at something."

What Brewster pointed out was an approaching band of rough-looking juveniles on mopeds who had suddenly and brazenly roared through the gates of Mobile Village. They were buzzing around the grounds, looking menacing in an indifferent sort of way—a threat to Brewster's glorified trailer court, a South San Francisco hideaway off Highway 280, which had been officially proclaimed the World's Most Beautiful Freeway.

"Mark my word," said Brewster, "those dipshits are up to no good."

"Urban blight," was all Durwood could say as he remembered yesterday, Tower Records, the chase, his throbbing neck.

"Correction," said his partner, "sub-urban blight." Brewster's lips were curling into a nasty little smile that was really a snarl. "You know, man, there's a generation coming along that's . . . that's . . ."

". . . That's worse than ours."

Brewster was tickled. "You said it, I didn't. What they are is crazy and depraved, and they scare the shit out of me! The only good thing I can say for them is they make me glad I never had any kids. And when you stop and look at how they grew up—drinking, on dope, violence, corruption, and all that do-your-own-thing crap—then what can you say? Now, you watch and see if this won't be the generation that'll turn this country fascist fast. Speaking of which, how's your case coming along with that punk you nailed the other day?"

Durwood looked away and rubbed at his neck brace. "It's all bogged down in legal procedure for the time being. The arraignment's next week, but you know how the law is around here. Punishing anybody's old-fashioned. It bores me to even have to talk about it. I can't even afford the time it's gonna take to settle this mess. One thing I do know, though. I know I've seen that clown's face before, but I can't put my finger on where."

"It'll all come back, don't worry," said Brewster as he took a wad of floppy one-dollar bills from his pocket and began peeling them off, laying them on the window ledge next to the fifties and hundreds.

Still mystified, Durwood thought of asking what that was all about, but all he did was look at Brewster. He had learned long ago that it was sometimes best to leave people the hell alone and not question their eccentricities, particularly if you liked them.

"So it's okay with you if I go ahead and sign us up for the CDDD?"

"Go on ahead and do whatever's right," said Durwood. "But tell me, Brew, do you really like living out here like this? I mean, in a trailer?"

"Mobile home, Wood; we call them mobile homes. Wouldn't live anyplace else. Not only do I like it, but the price is right.

Excuse me a minute, would you?" Brewster shoved the window open and stuck his head outside. "Hey!" he shouted. "Yeah, I'm talking to you, punks! Get the fuck away from here before I call the law on your ass! The sign says 'No Trespassing,' or can't you read? Illiterate bastards!"

As he studied all the photographs of basketball players, himself included, lined up on Brewster's wall, Durwood—who was about to keel over with claustrophobia at this point—concluded that the only way to live in a place like this was to get yourself reduced to picture-frame size.

"Sorry, man," he said, unbuttoning his coat, "but I gotta get outside and breathe me some air."

Brewster placed the last dollar bill on top of the pile, which he shaped into a tidy little stack. Obviously pleased with himself now, he turned to Durwood and, stifling a yawn, proclaimed, "Well, that's that. Let's get back across town."

If Durwood didn't know better, he might have sworn that his balding partner, who stood a little under five-feet-ten and was trim for a man of forty-five, was amused by his attack of physical discomfort.

It was one of those delicious mornings that always took him by surprise when they happened along. Dixie was off at a meeting that had something to do with getting the arts and sports restored to the public education curriculum. Celia and Nissa were at school. For a few unscheduled hours, Durwood had the entire house to himself.

He didn't know what to do, or, rather, there was so much he should have been doing that he didn't feel like doing anything. He should have been talking with Gail Díaz, his lawyer. He should have been answering his mail. Among the letters that stuck in his head was one from an old acquaintance, Chuck Rourke, querying him about his plans for the future. The Shriners Hospital for Crippled Children wanted him to know they were looking forward to the little pep talk he'd be giving the kids soon. An old college professor, a fan of long standing who had taught him geography back in Cincinnati, was on her last cancerous legs and wanted to know how he was doing. *Who's Who in Sports* wanted him to update his entry. He had a new idea for the shop that he needed to try out on Brewster. There was an electronics shop he had to stop by to check out a sale that excited him. And then there was a certain limousine service he still had to call.

Durwood found the last of the turkey in the refrigerator and made himself a sandwich, dashing on all the Tabasco sauce he wanted without having to answer to Dixie about it. Turkey was still, as far as he was concerned, the blandest of holiday foods and certainly one of the most overrated. After four days running, he was turkeyed out.

While he sat munching in the breakfast nook, trying to make up his mind about where to begin, he picked up the newspaper. Lying on the table underneath it was a book whose cover caught his eye. Depicted on the shiny, hardbound cover was a bright, colorful arrangement of tangled vines encircling a title that intrigued him: *The Wisdom of a Fool*. Durwood idly opened the book to the first page and saw Celia's name neatly printed there in a fancy, calligraphic hand. It made him smile when he reflected on how good she was at so many things. Then he flipped the pages from back to front and was surprised to notice that all the pages of the last third of the book were blank and that the rest of it was jam-packed with that same careful printing of Celia's.

Must be some kind of a notebook, he thought, and set the volume aside. The peppery effect of the hot sauce was beginning to get to him. Sweat stood out in beads on his forehead and around the sides of his nostrils. He dabbed at his face with a paper napkin, then picked up the book again. Since childhood, Durwood had loved to read while he ate. On the road, he used to scan the papers, the sports magazines, or a good paperback someone had recommended. As a kid, it had been cereal boxes or milk cartons or ingredients listings on the labels of jars. With the family around, he rarely got to do it anymore at mealtime. This time he cracked the book open at random and, out of sheer curiosity, started to read.

The musician in me wants to turn away from all that isn't sound, that isn't solid. There isn't much that's solid about the way things look. When I look at my family it all seems so hopeless and I want to make myself invisible and disappear into the way a song sounds. In MS. MAGAZINE *where they featured this article on what women think is erotic, Alice Walker (who is a writer) wrote that "For me the most erotic thing in the world—next to sex itself—is jazz. There's a real mellow kind of jazz that's just like fingers up your spine—and so healthy." I can relate to that a whole lot.*

Durwood looked up, impressed, fascinated, but feeling a little like an ass to be reading Celia's thoughts. What was this stuff supposed to be? It didn't exactly look like a diary, but was that what it was? He polished off the first half of his sandwich and, making certain his fingers weren't greasy, skipped ahead a few pages.

Moby's got the magic and the magic's in me. It hurts to hear the way he talks about his mother when he calls her all those bad names that his father (who drinks too much) must be putting into his head. Good thing he's got his uncles and his aunts and his cousins to relate to. I met one of his older cousins once, however I didn't like him. All he talked about is "burning" people. He said that when times get hard he's going to get him a big truck and drive around to rich folks' homes when they aren't home and collect what he's got coming to him. Poor Moby, sometimes I wish I could be his mother. His real mother ran off with a friend of his father's and they moved to Minneapolis. When his dad's stoned girlfriend stays overnite they make Moby sleep out on the couch. But he's got his music the same as me and the music is magic. When we kiss it's like two melodies running counterpoint. That time we went to see the light show (Laserium) at Morrison Planetarium and he touched me in the dark and I trembled when his hand moved up to touch mine. I wanted to. . .

Dreading what might be in store if he read on, Durwood looked up from the page. So, this really was some kind of private diary after all. But why in the world would Celia leave it lying around where anybody might pick it up?

Durwood remembered the time in seventh grade when he'd written a rather foolish letter—which he'd never intended to deliver—to some girl in his homeroom class. Her name was Aileen Conroy. His brother Clarence had gotten hold of it somehow and had showed it to a couple of the guys. From there, word of the letter got out and gradually came to the attention of his folks. Poor Durwood had taken such a ribbing that for years he was tight-lipped around his family and close friends on the subject of girls. It wasn't until he met Coretha Rawlins in high school that he opened up a little, and then only after his mother had let on that she knew what was happening.

He bit into his sandwich again, but it no longer tasted the same. What should he do? He opened the newspaper and tried to concentrate on the football and basketball write-ups. Pictures registered, but the words were a blur. He got up and went to the kitchen wall phone, dialed, and took care of his business with the limousine service. When he tried ringing Brewster at the shop, all he got was a busy signal. Well, it was now high time he settled down at his desk in the study and got a couple of letters out of the way. He cleared his plate and glass from the table, washed them quickly at the sink, and stacked them in the rack to dry.

All the while, Celia's book seemed to be glowing like aurora borealis where he'd left it open, face down, on the table. Now, that didn't look right. Hadn't he better close the book and slip it back under the paper the way he'd found it? Nervous, he lifted *The Wisdom of a Fool* and turned it over. The cover still blew him away. Was Celia supposed to be the fool, or was he? As much as he tried—and he was practically trembling by now—he couldn't bring himself to snap the book shut and leave it alone. It was as if he were possessed by some invisible gremlin who urged him to leaf through those pages one more time—to run, as it were, another spot check. Hell, he'd already glimpsed more than he'd cared to. One more peek wouldn't do any harm.

This time Durwood turned directly to the last filled-in page, before the book went blank, and studied a felt-pen nude that Celia had sketched and colored in lightly with crayon. This tiny caricature, in all its frontal nakedness, bore remarkable resemblance to the girl who had drawn it. She was standing on top of a column of words printed in such small characters that it hurt Durwood's eyes to read it.

The new me that's moving into my body right now isn't me at all and yet feels like it's more me than the me I thought I was. She doesn't have a name so I'll just call her Woman. But if I call her Woman then why not by her whole name which would have to be Woman Hood as in Robin Hood and what she steals from me is only what I (the old me that's evaporating away) let her have and gladly like Patsy says about her virginity that she was ready to give it up gladly. This new me has one thing it wants to be and that is to be free. Of me. Of thee I sing oh mother and father of the me that's fading away. To stay. Woman Hood is beautiful and powerful. She takes from the young and gives to the old. All the gold she gets she holds like a cold good-bye to every/body who thought they owned the old me. This new me belongs to no/body but me and I can share and I can merge this new (no) body with whoever I want to. Dear Woman Hood you're only a flowing red lady (ugh!) robbing the cradle of all my chaotic and cacophonic yesterdays.

 Whew! Durwood closed Celia's book. He'd have to think about this last passage. His impulse was to feel resentful. To think that he'd brought this child into the world—nourished, encouraged, and provided for her—and now here she was muttering behind his back about how free and independent she was becoming while still sitting on her ass at home. The nerve! The unfairness! Why, when he was her age, he was working part-time on weekdays after school, full-time on Saturdays, running track, and learning how to handle himself on a basketball court. Nobody ever pampered him!
 But, when he stopped and thought about it, all that had been long ago and far away in a little Texas town that had changed so much since he'd grown up and left, it might as well have been in New Zealand. He wasn't even permitted to have such thoughts when he was fifteen, much less put anything like them down on paper. Anyway, he wasn't a girl and had never had a sister. Maybe it was different with females. Or was that just his deep-seated sexism, as Dixie put it, coming out again? Besides, he wasn't supposed to be violating Celia's privacy this way in the first place.
 Well, he'd have to give it all a good thinking-over.
 While Durwood was thinking about it, he got busy putting

the breakfast nook back in order. Just as he was headed for Daddy's Room at last, the telephone rang. It was Corky Ski.

"I'm back in town. You free this evening?"

"Man, am I ever glad to hear from you! No, I'm not free. Well, it's complicated. Maybe you can help me work something out."

IT WAS DIXIE'S SECOND champagne cocktail. She was enjoying it so much and putting it away so shamelessly that Durwood, still at work on his first, started wondering about her again.

"You decided what you're having?" Dixie asked, going over the menu for the third time.

"How come you gotta know what I'm having?" Durwood said this, knowing that there was no possible rejoinder. It was something they always went through—one husband and one wife equaling, with the passing of years, a reasonably predictable third party. It was a routine, a number as predictable as the gradual softening of table butter.

Whatever they each ended up ordering, he could count on her asking for a helping of his meal, offering some of hers in return. There must have been a thousand routines between them that played like that. Once you'd been married for as long as they'd been, you got so you knew them by heart. There were entire areas and periods in their relationship that he didn't dare touch on unless he was drunk or righteously outraged. There were phrases, expressions, catchwords, places, and people's names that he kept to himself. There were ongoing hassles that he avoided bringing up since he knew all too well beforehand how they would go from start to grunt.

"I'm worried about Celia," Dixie said out of nowhere.

"So what else is new?"

"No, really, Woody. I'm worried about her deep down. I heard her talking on the phone with Moby the other night. I didn't mean to eavesdrop, but . . . Well, I did just happen to pick up the extension, and there they were, laughing and snickering and carrying on."

"Carrying on about what?"

"Sex," said Dixie.

Sex. His ears were on fire. Dixie now had his full attention. Out of the corner of one eye, he saw the loose-jointed, boyish-haired waitress looming nearby.

"What about sex?"

"He was telling her how pretty she was and how he liked the way she turned him on and how they ought to get together over the holidays or something."

"And what was Celia saying?"

"She was giggling and going along with it, lapping it up, talking about how much she liked him."

"Kids," said Durwood, smiling, for some reason pretending to be balanced and calm. He knew, of course, that there was a side to Dixie that soaked up any kind of gossipy speculation.

"Kids," she said, "maybe so, but they don't stay that way for long. They sure weren't talking the way kids did when I was her age."

"But, honeybunch, I've just been all up and down that road."

"You have? And what'd you find?"

"I saw how boys and girls are gonna try and get to know one another whether we like it or not."

"Well, I wasn't even thinking about boys when I was her age."

"What were you thinking about?"

"Going home."

"Going home? Where were you guys stationed when you were fifteen?"

"We were living in Hamburg, Germany."

"Well, I was thinking plenty about girls by then, but I was cool about it."

When the waitress appeared, Durwood ordered veal piccata and a salad with green goddess dressing. Dixie was still hemming and hawing, trying to make up her mind. "Bring her the calamari," he said. "We'll probably end up trading off anyway."

Dixie didn't object, but she did squint her eyes at him and cut them at the tizzied waitress before agreeing. Once the waitress had taken off, she said, "You didn't have to keep staring at her like that."

"Like what?"

"You know what I mean. You were . . ." She lowered her voice and glanced around. "You were sizing up her boobs and drooling over her butt . . . and everything."

"I was?"

"Don't bullshit me, Durwood. I was watching you."

"Maybe if you paid more attention to the menu instead of me, you wouldn't have to have me order for you."

"You stupid, ignorant, pitiful men are all alike. Just flash a little leg and cleavage at you and you're all ass."

"I could say something about you women, but you've heard it all before."

Dixie made out like she was pouting, but Durwood could tell that this, too, was part of the performance. Anything to keep him on his husbandly toes, slightly off-center, tensed. It was funny, really. Knowing that there was no way they were going to enjoy a peaceful meal if he pursued the subject, he scrapped it completely by resorting to laughter, saying, "Baby, it's your birthday. Let's try and enjoy it, okay? Now, getting back to Celia, I kinda think what with all that stuff you told me about how smart and short-changed he was and needed attention, I kinda thought behind all that you'd know by now how serious this thing between them was."

"I'd like to think that too," said Dixie, burping elegantly and draining the last of her cocktail. "Depends on what you mean by 'serious.' It's hard for me to even talk about the weather with Celia without her getting grudgeful or defensive or paranoid. I think she'd rather be relating to you. But if she *is* fooling around, I want her to know about protecting herself. She started her period summer before last, you know."

"So you told me."

"Doesn't any of this shake you up? I mean, you are her father.

Haven't you been keeping up with the statistics on teenage pregnancy lately? It's on the rise. The girls, they don't care. They act like having a baby out of wedlock's organic or something." Dixie was munching on cocktail ice now. "I can't blame them for not wanting to take the pill, not with all that bad press it's been getting. But we should look into getting her fitted for a diaphragm."

"Before you go getting all worked up, maybe we oughtta first find out if she's been having intercourse with anyone yet. Tell you the truth, I'm more worried about Celia than I am her sex life."

"What do you mean?"

"She's got me upset, and I intend to do something about it. But let's don't jump the gun. First things first. It's Friday and it's also your birthday. That combination doesn't happen every day. We're lucky to have Leon home with the kids. Now, let's try to enjoy our dinner, take in a show, and get a little loose for a change."

"I'll try," said Dixie, settling back in her chair. "I'm sorry, dear, you're right. I can't seem to get over this . . . I can't believe I'm thirty-five."

"Thirty-five and looking good. I wouldn't mind being thirty-five again myself. Turning forty's all right, though. A great age to start getting down to business. The day I turned thirty—remember?—it took me so long to get used to it, the next thing I knew I was thirty-three."

The waitress arrived with their orders. This time Durwood went to great lengths to avoid even so much as glancing at her. With strained exaggeration, he kept his eyes trained on the candlelit portion of red tablecloth in front of him and only allowed himself to look up after she said, "Enjoy!" and was gone.

"Hey!" said Dixie.

"What's the matter now?"

"She gave me yours."

"What's it matter? Dig in. The plates're too hot to pick up now anyway. I'll split this calamari with you, and you can save me some of my veal."

"One more thing," said Dixie.

"For crying out loud, what?"

She leaned forward and lowered her voice. "You overdid it that time, don't you think? I don't mind you looking, just don't gawk."

Zippily salting and peppering his food, Durwood said, "You can't win. You just can't win." He forked up a mouthful and, munching heartily, added, "You think we'll ever learn to communicate peaceably?"

"Not when you talk with your mouth full. You know all that salt's no good for your blood pressure, and black pepper isn't the easiest thing to digest. You really don't expect me to share your overseasoned food, do you?"

"Oh, shut the fuck up!" he mumbled.

"What did you say?"

"I said, 'Eat up.'"

Was nothing safe from the reaches of Mama Don't Allow? Durwood was wondering whether to tell Dixie about Celia's diary when he remembered to look out of the enormous picture window beside them. There was San Francisco Bay, looking turbulent and cold, with a raggedy, time-eaten moon floating overhead.

Durwood poured wine and lifted his glass to Dixie's. "Well, happy birthday, Madeleine."

Dixie, whose maiden name had been Madeleine Dixon, smiled and said, "Thank you, dear," then pressed her knee up against her husband's under the table.

First things first, he thought to himself again. This wasn't the time to bring up Little Ms. Woman Hood.

WHEN HE SAW THEM COMING OUT of the restaurant, the white-haired chauffeur got out of the limousine, pulled on his cap, and hurried around to curbside to hold the rear door open for them.

"Good evening," he said, "and a very happy birthday to you, Madame. I trust you enjoyed your dinner."

"We did," said Durwood, eager to check out Dixie's reaction to this little touch. "We did, indeed." Already he himself was knocked out by the driver's natty, dark uniform and the way the indigo Lincoln Continental was gleaming in the street light. He had always loved those scenes in old black-and-white Hollywood movies.

"I don't believe you, Durwood," said Dixie as she climbed inside. "I just can't believe how crazy you are." She was all grins, however.

While the Lincoln was purring through traffic, Durwood found it easy to say, "Now do you see why I insisted on taking a taxi to the restaurant?"

Dixie nodded that she understood, then shook her head in disbelief. Durwood could only guess at what was going through her head. How dumb and extravagant, she must have been thinking, to be squandering all this money on a hired car—just to be cute—when they could just as easily have taken the Vega or even the wagon. But he also could read that sparkle in her eye that told him how much she was enjoying every minute of it.

The driver pulled up in front of the Mocambo, a nightclub on Polk. "I do hope that you enjoy the show," he said with flat politeness as he held the door for them. "You would like for me to be here for you at eleven, correct?"

"Make it eleven-thirty," Durwood told him, consulting his beat-up Bulova self-winder.

The chauffeur took a look at his own expensive electronic digital watch and said, "Eleven-thirty it is, sir."

As Durwood had expected, the Mocambo impressed Dixie, who, to put it mildly, seemed satisfied and tickled too. There wasn't a hatcheck girl or roving photographer, but the place had all the charm and quiet class he thought a real nightclub should have. Chic, urbane, and tastefully laid out, it was the perfect setting to catch a veteran like Johnny Hartman—a handsome, brown-skinned singer whose range and repertoire were stunning. His performance was so moving, in fact, that Dixie, during the course of one ballad, put down her drink and whispered to Durwood, "I can't understand why he isn't rich and famous."

"Like me," said Durwood.

"But, Woody, you *are* famous."

"Not as famous as that giraffe over there."

"What giraffe?"

With a nod, Durwood indicated that Nate Thurmond was present, slouched a few tables away, nursing a Heineken, lost in the music.

"Hey," said Dixie, looking pleased, "he does get around, doesn't he? I don't think I've seen him since we ate at his restaurant. We have to get him back over to the house for dinner sometime."

Durwood shushed her and said, "Why don't we let the man finish up his song in peace?"

When the set was over and they had paid up and were leaving, who should run into them at the door but Big Nate himself, looking every bit the sport he was, in a sharp, navy blue suit and turtleneck.

"Woody! Dixie! I didn't know you guys were hip to Johnny Hartman! Isn't he something?"

"He's great," said Durwood, shaking Nate's hand, "but not as great as this fine little mama of mine here who's celebrating her birthday."

Nate swooped Dixie up into his lengthy arms and said, "I'd still like to get you on the payroll to cook at my joint. You don't think that's sexist, do you? Happy birthday, sugar, and many happy returns. What is it, your twenty-first?"

"Close," said Dixie with a wink. "It's my twenty-second."

"Well, man," said Durwood, "I see you're still ugly."

"Maybe so, but not half as ugly as you are. Tell me, have you ever thought about applying for an ugly grant? Just think. You could do a project on, say, Ugliness: Its Evolution and Practical Application. I got a lawyer friend could help you write the proposal."

"I'm ready to give that a whirl, but only under one condition."

"Which is?"

"Which is you'd have to provide me with some firsthand research material, *aye-eee*, in the form of a few pictures of yourself. I'd need some from your babyhood on up through and including your alleged adulthood. Plus, you'd have to write me a signed endorsement."

"What kind of signed endorsement?"

"Oh, something along the order of, let's see . . . 'I can't think of anybody more qualified to explore the topic of ugliness than Durwood Knight, that is, with the possible exception of myself.'"

"Funny," said Nate, smiling as he turned toward the door. "Funny, but fallacious."

"When," asked Dixie, "can we get you over to the house again?"

"Anytime at all," he said. "Just give me a ring and if I'm not there leave a message with my answering service. I'll get right back to you. I'd like to hear what you're doing with the rest of your life. That's a heavy one, isn't it?"

Durwood shook Nate's hand warmly and said, "Any and all advice from somebody who's been there will be duly considered. In other words, help!"

"I should've known something was up," said Dixie. They were back hanging out in the Lincoln. "You've been playing that album Hartman cut with Coltrane for days. I love it. Hey, you're gonna be more famous than Nate, you know."

"Oh, yeah, and how's that gonna happen?"

"When you start making headlines on the financial page. I can just see it now—'Woody Knight Files for Bankruptcy.'"

"Keep it up, baby, and by this time tomorrow I'll have kicked mucho ass."

Dixie snuggled close to Durwood, smelling delicious, lovely, and drunk. He pulled her face around to his and kissed her on the mouth, dry-tongued at first, then juicy, slobbering, as he slid his tongue against hers. He knew by then that he had to be half-lit, but he got a rise out of seeing Dixie in this condition for a change.

"Excuse me," said the chauffeur. "Do we take a left or a right at the intersection?"

"Left," said Durwood, stupidly indignant. He'd never thought about it much before, this business of being driven around. Now that he was charged up and ready to tell the driver to carry them someplace where they could be alone, he wondered how all the jet-setters and Beautiful People put up with this sneaky invasion of privacy, where you lived in the public armpit, or certainly in the nostrils, of anyone who happened to be standing close to you.

DURWOOD, AS IT TURNED OUT, hadn't known the first thing about being in an armpit—public or otherwise—until he and Dixie set foot inside Boogie Your Boodie Off, the hottest new straight discotheque in town. If cigarette smoking really was declining, you couldn't prove it by the carbon monoxide and nicotine clouds that hung like smog over this vacuum-packed room. There was barely space enough to stand in, much less dance.

"Why didn't you tell me we were going dancing?" Dixie was growing excited all over again. "I would've worn something different."

"You're beautiful, sugar, just like you are."

They paid for tickets, visited the bar, then squeezed onto the floor. It only took a few choruses of a Donna Summer number for Durwood to realize how tricky it was to disco with a twisted neckbone. He wasn't crazy, either, about the way a lot of people were staring at him, as if he were some kind of freak or as if they knew him.

On the matter of tallness, Durwood stood moot. Being tall often had been something of an embarrassment for him unless he was working. Nobody but Dixie and Brewster believed it, but he'd spent a good deal of his life feeling like some talented cousin who the rest of the family could do without unless it was show time. Being on a dance floor brought on that feeling again. For some reason, he was thinking about poor Jackie Wilson, a singer he loved, who had come out with "Lonely Teardrops" and a string of million-selling hits years ago. He used to play Jackie's records in the locker room before games for good luck. Recently, he'd read where Jackie was a vegetable now, literally withdrawn into the fetal position, unable to speak, spoon-fed on baby food and wasting away in some New Jersey institution. Right now it was easy for him to imagine himself in Jackie Wilson's shoes.

It was pushing midnight, time for all the true city slickers to get down and show their natural behinds. The crowd was cutting up and cavorting so hard that Durwood, who couldn't and didn't want to keep up, knew he was going to have to go someplace and sit down with his stiff-necked self. He just wasn't connecting with all this sweat and gyration. The beat was too booming, the melody too meager.

What this really is, he thought, is possession music, trance-inducing zombie sound. All these semi-fried, electrified Punches and Judies had been caged up and locked down in jobs at home or work all week, storing up what some shrink might call "malignant energy." Since they weren't Haitians or Brazilians or Holy Rollers plugged into Voodoo or Macumba or the Holy Ghost, getting loose at Boogie Your Boodie Off was the readiest and safest way for them to exorcise or, in any case, exercise their demons.

That was cool with Durwood, but couldn't the management program some slow numbers too? He was waiting for something to come on that would give him and Dixie a chance to drag each other around the floor while they got tender.

"How come they don't put on a George Benson ballad?" he yelled, hoping Dixie could hear. "Why don't they play Leon Russell doing 'Song for You' or that Tune Weavers record from the fifties—'Happy, Happy Birthday, Baby'—or something with feeling? All this motion music is making me nauseous!"

Dixie didn't answer. She couldn't hear him.

Rubbing up against the backs of his legs was a finger-popping young woman who looked Filipino. She stood flailing her arms, hardly lifting her feet off the floor, but wiggling around in such a way that her tightly trousered bottom kept bumping against Durwood. Even though it didn't bother him, he couldn't relax and groove with it either. What did bother him was that he could no longer tell who Dixie was supposed to be dancing with. Was she dancing with him or with that tall, red-headed woman close by in boots and rolled-up jeans? Or was she dancing with someone he thought might be the redhead's partner—a sleek-looking dude with processed hair who was dressed in a cream-colored suit? This particular young blood was one of at least a dozen others who were out on the floor doing Barry White imitations.

None of this seemed to be bothering Dixie one bit.

"Sweetheart," Durwood said when the second tune ended, "I'm just about disco'd out."

"What's the matter, Woody, your neck still giving you trouble?"

"Either that, or I'm getting old and out of shape fast." He said this with a fraudulent chuckle, but he meant every syllable of it.

"I heard *that*," Dixie laughed, accompanying him as far as the bar. "If you're ready to go home, honey, I guess I'm game."

"That's up to you. You're the birthday girl."

"Well, if you don't mind, I wouldn't mind getting back out there and shaking 'em down some more."

"Who with?"

"Nobody in particular. I'm just having fun."

"Then have fun then. I'll be right over there at the bar having me some coffee."

"You're upset, aren't you?"

"Upset? Why in the hell should I be upset? I just can't cut it on the floor, that's all."

Dixie, in her burgundy dress with dark, wet moons at the underarms and her matching head scarf, was beginning to sweat. Tossing her head, she sprinkled him, then blew him a toothsome kiss that made him want to lunge for her.

He broke away, turning his back on the dancers, and sized up the bartender, an earthy-looking woman sneaking up on thirty whose breasts were cantaloupes and whose face was salty in a sweet sort of way. She wore her chocolate hair in a bun piled on top of her nightwise head.

"And what's it going to be this time, Mr. Knight, same thing?"

"Just coffee this time, thank you."

"Cream and sugar?"

"Black, thank you. You know me?"

"Who doesn't?" He thought he saw her pout, then smile, in rapid succession as she pushed a cocktail napkin and ballpoint pen toward him. "Would you do me the honor?"

Durwood had no choice but to scribble out a greeting and sign his name.

Sliding the coffee cup in front of him, the woman batted her slick, black eyelashes and flashed one of those primordial female looks, seemingly from out of nowhere, that was capable of momentarily stunning a male into remembering things about himself and his nature that all his conditioning, if he wasn't a brute, had trained him to repress. In the same instant, he connected with her green eye shadow, which brought to mind his old Beanstalk uniform and the way it looked on color TV.

"An autograph for an autograph," the bartender said mysteriously, quickly jotting down her own name and phone number on another Boogie Your Boodie Off napkin. "I do some freelance writing on the side—for magazines and places—and I'd love to do a piece on you, a profile if you're agreeable."

"But I'm just a retired private citizen now."

"That," she told him with a gleam in her eye, "would be my angle."

He watched her fold his autograph and tuck it into the freckly cleavage of her low-cut working blouse. He hadn't been hit on this brazenly in years.

"I'm free days," she added, "and I'm off Mondays and Tuesdays. I hope you'll think about it."

"I appreciate your interest," he said.

One long, hot swallow of coffee was all it took to jolt him. Normally, he stayed away from the stuff, but tonight he seemed to need that caffeine rush. From somewhere behind the bar, he thought he heard a telephone jangle. While the bartender was answering, he picked up her napkin and looked at the name. Audrey Spain.

Suddenly the phone was being handed to him and Audrey was saying, "I don't believe this, but it's for you!"

"It is? Well, what do you know? Hey, thanks. Hello?"

"Durwood, it's Corky. I can't believe I actually gotcha!"

"The music's so loud I'm not sure I'm hearing right. That you, Corky?"

"Sure is. What's happening, buddy?"

"How come you're telephoning? I thought you and Janet were gonna put in a surprise appearance tonight."

"We got car troubles, man. The radiator's overheating. I'm scared to risk driving down to the city."

"Well, I'm sorry to hear that, but I'm glad you called anyway. Dixie didn't know you were supposed to be here."

"You guys having a good time?"

"Dixie sure seems to be enjoying herself. My damn neck's killing me."

"I hope you haven't written us off, Woody. We will surprise her, but it's gonna have to be postponed, I'm afraid. Say, can I wish her a happy birthday?"

"That—" said Durwood, looking around, "—that won't be easy. I can't see Dixie right now. She's out on the floor."

"Well, listen. Tell her me and Janet send our best. You take care of yourself, pal. Get old Brewster to give you one of his special liniment rubdowns. I'll be talking with you soon."

"Right. Well, good night, Corky. I appreciate your calling."

"No problem. Catch you later."

Durwood hung up and looked over to thank the bartender, but she was busy drawing draughts of beer for a fat, thirsty-looking couple plopped down at midbar. He gulped more coffee and spun around on the groaning stool, ready now to start worming his way back into the crowd.

Durwood found Dixie wiggling in a loose embrace with her gum-chewing partner. They were shuffling around in very slow motion to "What's Your Name?" by Don and Juan, a golden oldie from the fifties.

Durwood hated the fifties—his fifties anyway. His memory of them was of tough, vulnerable years, sad like Texas light on a winter Sunday, late in the afternoon, when he'd sit sulking at the desk in his dead brother Clarence's room off the backyard. While trying to get around to homework he should have had ready days earlier, he'd absently study the sleeping fig-tree limbs outside the window and shudder at how old and hopeless they looked.

"I'm cutting in, Dix, if you don't mind. This is supposed to be *our* dance."

"You her old man or something?" asked the loose-jointed man she was leaning against, becoming self-conscious now.

"Or something," said Durwood, ready, if necessary, to squeeze this clown's head in like a balloon. The way Dixie was bucking her eyes made him feel like snatching her around some too. When you got right down to it, it was Dixie's birthday they were supposed to be celebrating. All he was doing was trying to make her feel good.

"Well," said her dancing partner as he sized up Durwood and the situation, "I ain't about to come between no dude and his old lady!" And, with that, he slunk away gravely in the direction of a pulsating blonde with a catatonic leer who was got up in roller-skating garb.

"That poor thing," Dixie observed with contempt, "is definitely hot to trot—with her funny-looking behind."

"All well and good," said Durwood, "but what in the hell's the matter with you, Miss Madeleine?" That Madeleine dig always hit home.

Uncentered now, he caught himself feeling all kinds of things, most of them funky in the aboriginal sense. His shirt was clinging to his chest. Dixie was flowering with humidity like some rare hothouse orchid, pleasingly pungent to him, unlike the stickiness of his own body.

The two of them—warmed by mutual body heat, her moist hand locked into his—junior-high-schooled it around the floor, doing their best to ignore what anybody else was doing.

IT WAS WELL PAST TWO WHEN they finally got in. Durwood got ready for bed before tiptoeing down to his study to get Dixie her presents. There he found Leon, still in his clothes, crashed on the sofa bed and still clutching his flute. Gently, he pried the instrument from Leon's fingers and covered him with a blanket. All the while, he was savoring what few memories he'd treasured of tucking this boy in and giving him fatherly kisses on the cheek in the days when Leon was still only a few hundred nights old. A teenager then, Durwood was now sort of an absentee dad about to turn forty with a son who already was more than half his own age.

How could that be?

What a cheat time was to have beaten him out of being around to watch Leon grow up day by day. Stopped in his slippered tracks, with a lump in his throat, he fondly studied Leon's peaceful, boyish face in the soft light slanting in from the hallway. To think that he'd fallen asleep practicing, and in Durwood's room.

Durwood lugged the two ribbon-bowed packages up the stairs and through the hallway past the girls' rooms. He heard Celia groan and mutter in her sleep as he trudged by, but he was tired and too eager to open the birthday boxes to stop and give what he thought he was hearing any real attention.

By now, Dixie was more than technically wiped, and feeling

pretty damn good about it. She sat on the edge of their enormous bed, stretching and yawning, naked except for a sheer raspberry bra.

"Isn't it nice," she was saying, "not having to drive the babysitter home?"

"Well, Miss Cool-Whip Sherbet of Nineteen-Whatever, I can go one better than that. It also means I ain't got to make all that small talk while I'm driving the babysitter home while I'm figuring up how many hours we owe for, not to mention the tip. Also—" and here he squashed his voice in, gleefully grunting what followed, "we can go straight to sleep without me having to explain to you what the sitter was like and what all we talked about."

"Mmmm, sleep, yum," sighed Dixie. "You'd never imagine what's on my mind, what I wouldn't mind doing."

"What *I'm* gonna do is give you your birthday present. It comes in three parts."

"What I wanna do to you . . ." she giggled. "Birthday present! Heyyyy! I'd just about forgot—"

In his karate-style robe and Birkenstock sandals, Durwood looked deadly serious as he hefted both packages onto the bed so that they lay between Dixie and himself. Slowly he began peeling the gift wrap from the smaller box.

"You tickle me," cracked Dixie as she fell back against the pillow and slapped his backside, "all the time easing the paper off my presents like that. Why don't you just rip it off? How come you gotta be so . . .?"

"Meticulous?"

"Get outta here with meticulous! Now, what was it this girlfriend of mine used to say back in Germany?" Dixie rolled her eyes around and snickered. That's when Durwood realized how drunk she really was. "Oh yeah, now I remember. She used to say, '*Die Wurst ist fertig.*' And that's about how I'm feeling right now. I want you to push back my hair and whisper in my ear, 'Dixie,' no, 'Madeleine, *meine frau, die Wurst ist fertig!*'"

"Sorry, but I don't know that language. All I know is there's such a thing as dramatic presentation." Durwood was glowing as he neatly undid the last Scotch-taped panel of paper. He pulled the styrofoam packing case from the box and unsnapped its lid. "Here, I want you to feast your bloodshot eyes on this! You know what it is?"

"Honestly, Woody, it's tomorrow already. I'm in no mood to be playing guessing games."

He folded back the packing case lid and brought out a smooth formidable-looking video camera. Impressed with its lightness, Durwood loved the way it felt in his hands. His eyes watched Dixie checking out all the lenses, cable, and other accessories. She looked about as polite as anyone in her condition could, but she didn't seem comfortable.

"A video camera," she commented. "It's awfully pretty, Durwood, but what am I supposed to do with it?"

"Hold on," he said frantically. "It goes with—just a second—with . . . It goes with this." He ripped the wrap from the other box, the chunky one, and sat back gloating as though he'd just snatched the veil from a little piece of sculpture he'd been knocking out evenings after work in the garage—something along the order of Rodin's *The Thinker,* or the Statue of Liberty.

"And what's that?" she asked.

For one thin sliver of a moment, he felt like leaping across the bed and pummeling her. A sturdy piece of metal pipe wrapped in Turkish towel would've done the job without leaving any incriminating bruises.

"Maybe I'm wasting my time," said Durwood. "Are you interested in any of this, or what?"

"Really, what kind of question is that? I'm your wife, your old lady. Isn't that what the man at the disco called me? I love you. Come whisper something delicious in my ear. Come to bed, and we'll examine all this . . . all this wonderful equipment . . . in the morning, when my head is better."

If he'd had a few more drinks, he might've forgiven her instead of pressing on. "Ever hear tell of a Betamax?"

"Sounds like a Jewish fraternity, but I know what it is for real. I've seen the ads."

"Oh?"

"Sure, it lets you tape all the shows you missed while you were out and play them back at your convenience, like phone messages."

"Well, I never thought about it in those terms, but—"

"Darling, I think it's great. We can make home movies of the kids growing up and of us. How can I thank you?"

What? Here he'd gone and laid out close to a grand and a half buying luxurious media gear for this woman, and here she was, drunk of course, but coming on, well, tactful, polite, a little too polite for him. Technically, there wasn't anything wrong with her reaction, but there wasn't anything right about it either.

"You're disappointed," she said. "Aren't you?"

"Now, why would you say that?"

"Aha, I knew it! I can tell by the look on your face. You're upset about me, my reaction. I hope all this didn't set us back too much."

Durwood shrugged, rose, and began repacking everything.

"Maybe it's because I'm a woman, huh?"

"How's that?"

"You probably don't think I appreciate hardware like this the way a man would. But I still get plenty use from that miniature tape machine you gave me last Christmas. Celia does too. In fact, I taped the meeting we had yesterday at the PTA, and you know what?"

"What?"

"I listened to it back and think I argued pretty damn persuasive for getting sports and music back in the schools around here. Don't mean to toot my own horn, but I betcha I'd be a bitch in a courtroom."

"I'll tell that to Gail. She might have to send for you to be a witness in this stolen car bullshit."

"Me, a witness? I wasn't even on the scene when all that stuff happened."

"Never mind," Durwood said, knowing for certain now that her mind was, indeed, on other things, to say nothing of her hands. He felt them sliding under the hem of his karate robe. He was right on the verge of asking about the goose bumps on her arms when they heard somebody scream.

16

THE SECOND SCREAM REACHED their ears while Durwood was racing down the hall. He rushed into Celia's room and snapped on the light. Celia was sitting up in bed, her lips moving rapidly. Her wide-open eyes were glazed like a sleepwalker's, and there was a terrible expression on her face. Her hands flew up in front of her mouth, then down around her shoulders as she hugged herself, shivering like a naked skater on ice about to take a spill.

"Sweetheart," he cried, "are you okay? Can you hear me?"

Durwood sat by Celia and threw his arms around her, straining to steady her, to be reassuring. She continued to buck and jerk like one of those frightened baby calves on his grandmother's farm that he and his cousins would sneak off and ride when no one was looking.

"She all right?" asked Dixie as she wobbled into the room, half-dressed now and tearful.

"Don't know yet," said Durwood, still rocking Celia in his arms. "Celia, honey, it's Daddy . . . Everything's fine now . . . Mommy and Daddy are here with you . . . Wake up, darling, you've been having a bad dream." The motion seemed to be having a steadying effect.

Celia squinted, then blinked, as she clung fast to him. Tears were streaming down her cheeks. "Daddy, where am I? Wh-what's going on?"

Dixie crouched on the floor by the side of the bed and wrapped her arms around Celia's waist.

"You're at home in your room, that's where you are. Mom and I heard you scream, so we came running to see what the matter was."

"I—I was screaming?"

"Yes, dear," said Dixie. "What on earth were you dreaming about, anyway?"

89

"I can't remember." Celia looked distressed. "Honest, I can't remember."

"Just relax," said Dixie, "and get hold of yourself. It'll all come back."

"Honest, Mom, I . . ." Again Durwood watched Celia's sleep-creased face go through another transformation—from disturbed wakefulness to gentle alarm—as she shook her head slowly, pulled away from him, and, with folded arms, leaned back against the upright pillow. "I . . . I think it might've been something about . . . something about a monster." She said this and sighed, but he could tell that she was still far from feeling relieved.

"What kinda monster?" asked Dixie.

"Hard to describe." Celia scratched her head through matted hair. "It wasn't like the kind of monster you see with your eyes, that scares you by the way it looks. It was more like . . . more like a feeling than a thing. You know? Does that make any sense?"

"No," said Dixie, "not exactly."

"Makes perfect sense to me," said Durwood. "I have dreams like that all the time."

"You do?" said Dixie, getting up and taking a seat at the foot of the bed.

"Sure," he said. "They used to involve stuff like was my contract gonna be renewed. Now I dream about money, credit, insurance, cars, Christmas, our future, and all like that."

"You never told me about any of those dreams, Woody. My mother used to say there was wisdom in dreams."

"Well, any fool can dream," he said. "Maybe Nadine's right. Maybe all dreams are is the wisdom of a fool. That's how they leave me feeling sometimes."

"I don't know if I like the implications of that," said Dixie.

"What a funny thing to say," said Celia, staring straight at her father. "This thing, whatever it was, was after me." She was practically smiling now. "It was like this huge presence, really dark, you know, and I was trying to outthink it because, you see, in the dream I could make it leave me alone if I thought hard enough, but . . . but it was like I was running out of thought power 'cause I was scared. And the scareder I got, the more it kept closing in on me, trying to suffocate me. I knew if I didn't get away in time it was gonna spread all around and all over me and squash me to death, and—"

"Forget it, Celia," said Durwood. "Please! You don't have to torture yourself like this. It's all over now. Why don't you try to get back to sleep and dream about something good this time."

"Well, I wouldn't mind hearing about it all the way through," said Dixie.

"How come, Mom?"

"I don't know. Maybe because telling dreams, even if they're bad, is good for you, I think. At least you get them out of your system when you tell them to someone else, somebody who cares about you or even somebody neutral."

"That's your mother's opinion, honey, not mine. I keep most of my stupid dreams to myself."

"So I'm finding out," said Dixie, cutting her eyes at him. "If you're all of a sudden telling this much, it makes me wonder what else you dream that you aren't telling about."

"All I know," said Celia, who was bright-eyed now, "is there was this monster in the shape of a big feeling, if you could call it a shape, and it was evil. It was scary and it was evil, that's all."

"Celia," said Durwood, tucking her back in, "it's all over now, whatever it was. Get yourself some sleep. Tomorrow's Saturday and you can stay in bed as long as you like."

"Wait," said Dixie, getting up. "I need to check something." She pressed the back of her wrist to Celia's forehead. "Well, you are damp, but I don't think you're running a fever."

"I feel better now," said Celia as she curled back up under the covers. "Sorry I had to go and cause all that commotion. Good night."

For Durwood, consolation lay in no longer having to get the girl up in the middle of the night to go pee. He and Dixie still had to take turns doing that with Nissa.

"She worries me," said Dixie, who was curled up again herself. Durwood could feel his wife's warm belly snuggled against his back. "She's too young."

"Too young for what?"

"Too young to be having dreams like that."

"How old you think you have to be to have bad dreams?"

"That isn't what I mean. Her description of that so-called monster . . . She said it was more like a feeling or an idea or something."

"So? You've forgotten what it's like being her age, Dixie."

"And I suppose you haven't."

"Nope."

"What was all that talk back there about you having nightmares?"

"I never said I had nightmares. All I said was I have those kinds of dreams all the time. There's a difference."

"You mean, you're really that uptight about things?"

"I'm still the breadwinner in this house."

"I can get a job, you know. My library science M.A.'s still good."

"Maybe so, but you forget it's been a long time since you've hit the job market in this area."

"They're still building libraries and opening schools. People are still reading books."

"No, I mean the Bay Area. Baby, do you have any idea how many Ph.D.'s are out here driving taxis and pumping gas?"

"Can't be all that many pumping gas anymore. Anyway, you're talking about English majors and humanities people. Library science graduates are always in demand, all over the country."

"What makes you think so?"

"My friend Fleeta's been getting nothing but offers and promotions, and we graduated together from U.C. Berkeley."

"But sweetheart, that was years ago. I'm talking about right now. Jobs are hard to come by, believe me. You haven't been out there."

"Oh, and I suppose you have?"

Durwood, as he sniffed his wife's breath, did a slow, mental double-take and remembered that she'd been out dining and drinking and dancing and was, in fact, for all intents and purposes, still inebriated. Once he'd gotten this straight in his head, he had little trouble figuring out what not to say.

"I'm a man without a future, Dixie. You should know that by now."

Durwood felt Dixie's arms closing in around him as she kissed, or, rather, mouthed, the soft part of his shoulder.

"Woody, now, I hate to have to be saying this again, but all those years when the season would be over and you had a little time to play around with . . . How many times did I tell you to stop signing up for all those dumb basketball clinics and camps and learn to do something else?"

"What was so dumb about that? We needed the money, didn't we?"

"You could've gone back to school, or trained for some other profession. Look at Lincoln Rucker and Bolo Harris—they'll make a killing in real estate. Look at Skeeter Moss with his Datsun dealership. You could've gotten into something lucrative, too, where you sold your brain instead of always selling your body—in season and off season. But would you listen to me? Hell, no, you knew everything."

"I knew enough to do what I had to do. We bought the station wagon. You had to have the kitchen remodeled and get that three-thousand-dollar Persian rug. Our trip to Jamaica cost money, just like the trip to Connecticut where we did our millionaire act and picked up everybody's tab. Celia's got beautiful teeth now, and do you know why? Because I paid for braces and dental work all those years. Getting a nest egg together to go into business costs money. Christmas costs money. Breathing costs money. Everything we do costs—"

"That's enough, Durwood. I don't need to hear anymore. It's late. We've had a hard day. All I know is I told you way back when we first got married that . . ."

And here Durwood found himself doing the old husbandly fade-out, as he liked to call it. He simply turned to another channel and tuned into another program. Long ago he'd figured out that this was the only way to survive any kind of business, including monkey business, whether it was related to sports or opening a shop or marriage.

He slipped away inside himself to a place where he lay on his back with hands behind his head on a private patch of grass, looking up at the sky, where he could listen to himself saying, "You marry somebody and you not only marry the way they look or think or behave, but all the ways they understand you, make love with you, love you, and hate your simple ass. You marry changeability itself; the way she keeps or doesn't keep house; her hopes, illusions, ignorance, fears, and weaknesses. And you marry the very gleam in her great-great-great-grandfather's eye when he sat on the bank of a river on a warm afternoon in some faraway and forgotten millennium and, letting his peasant thoughts drift with the current, dreamed about glory and pondered the nature of dynasties."

Generations later, here Dixie and he lay, and the complexity of it all was making him sleepy. What was all this about? He'd never been a superstar, not even a little star in his business. He'd always been a trouper, a good soldier, a hard worker. Now he was going to try his hand at merchandising, something else he might fail at while somehow keeping afloat. It was an old dream of his, like learning to play the trumpet convincingly or stumbling across a big, gray canvas sack full of hundred-dollar bills dropped out of a bank-heist getaway truck.

"Baby," he settled on saying, "everything you say is true, but what you forget is I'm not exactly an old man yet. We've got a lotta bread tied up in this shop, and that's a long ways from interviewing for welfare or food stamps."

"Oh, Woody, I'm sorry. I really am." She pulled his face around and kissed him on the mouth. "I get off on these tangents and don't know when to quit. Thank you for all that birthday love."

"Birthday love? What a way to put it."

"Good night, dear."

"Hey, I gotta tell you, Celia wants me to go downtown with her to look at some Christmas things."

"Good. You need to spend more time with her. She's getting to be pretty sensitive about that."

"Okay."

"And I meant it, Wood, what I said about getting a job."

"Well, you go on ahead and do that, but remember, somebody's gotta be around to look after Nissa."

"Ohhh, Nissa," Dixie hissed, sitting up. "Do you mind getting her up tonight, darling? It's getting so she's too heavy for me." She pinched Durwood playfully on the leg as he twisted out

of bed. "And when you get back," she said, "I've got a little treat in store for you."
"When I get back, I won't be in any mood for treats. Nissa's probably already peed by now, and anyway, I got a headache."
"But it's still sort of my birthday. Don't I even get a wish?"
"Sure, I'll give you a wish. I wish you would shut your eyes and go to sleep like somebody with some sense."

Somewhere in another world, wombed in darkness, that bell is ringing again. Except for an urge to rip the son of a bitch out of the wall, Durwood is almost succeeding in ignoring it. Sleep is upon him like refrigerated fog, cooling him out so smoothly that, for a measureless space of time, he gets to feel what it's like being in a movie and sitting out there in the theater, watching it at the same time.
But Dixie, poor thing, fumbles around in the dark and answers the bell.
"Uh, who is this? Hello? . . ."
Durwood is striding in slow, instant-replay motion straight toward the basket, dribbling like a machine. He's what, twelve years old? But the same age as now at the same time.
"Hello . . ."
He's got the basket all to himself. Up he leaps, lifted by his long arms, and—
"Is there anyone there? . . ."
—dunks the ball right in to score. The ball bounces back into his magic hands, hands he would've happily sent off for if he'd ever seen them advertised in the back of some magazine. The fuzzy Opposition is moving in on him like locusts, coming at him from every point in space. He makes a fast pass to Corky, who, sweating like a race horse, attempts a frantic hook shot. Corky misses, but the ball falls into Durwood's hands on the rebound, and making the tip-in is like slicing a piece of cake.
"Would you please say something? . . ."
And then it happens. Some joker from the Opposition tries to knee him from behind. He whirls around and, with no time to think, splits this fool right in the jib. Blood comes coursing out

the boy's nose, and Durwood, feeling rotten, grows lightheaded, totters, and asks to be taken out of the game.

"Goddamn it!" he hears Dixie saying. "It's the middle of the night, and I'm in no mood to be played with!"

The dream snaps in two. Dixie's voice has somehow sawed clean through it.

"Might be somebody calling from back East," he blurts out, "with a bad connection."

"Okay," she says, "one more time . . . Hello! . . . Can you hear me? . . . Hello? . . ."

Her slamming down the receiver did it. Durwood sat up in bed, totally awake.

"Who was that?" he asked, still stupefied.

"Sure wish I knew. They wouldn't say anything. And I could tell they weren't calling me from all that far away either."

"Strange. That hasn't happened in a long time."

"Strange is right, but strange at this time of night is scary and pisses me off."

"Well, just one of those things."

"I hope so," Dixie huffed.

Durwood listened to Dixie pulling the covers back up around herself, then lay back down to see what happened next in the dream.

"All this is happening," he heard himself saying, "because I read her diary."

"Whose diary?"

"Celia's."

"She doesn't even have a diary. Now, would you keep quiet so I can concentrate on all that wonderful rest I was getting?"

Durwood was jealous of Dixie as he settled on his side and faked slumber in the dark, trying to get a handle on everything he'd just dreamed and half-dreamed.

BREWSTER AND MITZI WERE in good moods when Durwood stopped by the shop the following noon. They were munching on the remains of a take-out order of sushi and teriyaki chicken from the Japanese restaurant around the corner, and gloating over the brand-new cash register that had just been installed.

"Made in Japan," Brewster was saying. "Isn't it beautiful? This thing'll do just about everything except sell the merchandise, and it might even do that. I haven't finished reading the directions yet."

"It sure is costing us enough," said Durwood as he glanced around the half-finished shop, wondering how long it was really going to be before Knight and Day Record Setters staged its grand opening.

"Mitzi here's been teaching me some Japanese," said Brewster, "but I'm gonna have to learn me some Arabic too. That's what's happening, you know. The whole world order is changing."

"Changing, nothing!" said Durwood. "It's done changed! There's a bunch of rich Arabs trying to buy the Beanstalks from D'Annunzio right now, haven't you heard?"

"Oh, I read about that, yes," said Mitzi, "but I thought they were from Iran, no?"

"An Eye-ranian's the same as an A-rab," said Brewster. "They all come from the same part of the world."

"Oh, no," said Mitzi, who looked like a shy, tiny princess in her bright kimono. It was the first time Durwood had seen her in anything but Western clothing, mostly sweaters and slacks. "You are, I'm afraid, mistaken about that. The Iranians insist that they are not Arabs."

"Well," said Brewster, licking teriyaki sauce from his fingers, "they sure coulda fooled the hell outta me."

Durwood punched a button on the new register for fun and said, "Mitzi knows what she's talking about, Brewster." He grinned like a child when the empty cash drawer came whizzing out at him. "And they aren't really in the same part of the world."

"But their money's coming from the same source, isn't it?"

"Listen, Brewster, that's about the same as saying that Texans are Arabs too."

"Hell, they just might be before this thing is over. I don't wanna get into all that. If you and Mitzi say the Persians aren't A-rabs, then that's good enough for me. The only point I'm trying to make is that the money done got funny. The change got strange a long time ago, and these greenback dollars of ours—don't care how many safeguards the president comes up with against inflation—they just ain't getting it like they used to. Me, I wanna be where the action is. After Mitzi gets through schooling me in Japanese and I get a little Arabic under my belt, then look out, 'cause I'll be ready for Freddy!"

"I have heard that!" said Mitzi with a smile.

"No, baby, you got it wrong again. What you say is, 'I heard that!'" Brewster turned to Durwood. "See, I've been trying to bring her up-to-date with her English too."

"You still think we picked the right machine?" asked Durwood as he gazed into the sheen of the sleek, shiny register as if it were capable of ringing up prophecies.

"This dandy little device here," said Brewster, glowing, "is a monster. Once we get it programmed right, it's gonna help us cut way down on paper work and inventory problems by telling us exactly what we've sold, how many, and when. And the thing I like about it is it's so smooth and quiet and . . . and perfect, like Mitzi."

"I love to see you both so happy," said Mitzi, her politely pleasant face relaxing into a rare, unguarded smile bordering on spontaneous laughter. She, too, pressed a few keys on the machine and looked delighted when it purred and beeped and whirred in response.

Brewster bent over and kissed her on the forehead.

"How much longer are the carpenters gonna be?" asked Durwood, seeing how uneasy his partner's public display of affection was making Mitzi. He not only wanted to change the subject, he wanted to know what was going on.

"The best way to find that out," said Brewster, "would be for you to ask them. They're both out on a lunch break right now."

"A lunch break, or a dope break?"

"Hey, Wood, listen up. You know as well as I do that those guys do good work, real good work. So they're leftover hippies, so what? It's bargain labor. I don't care what they do in their free time, just so long as they get our work done. Do you know how much bread we've saved? Thousands, my man, thousands of inferior U.S. dollars!"

Durwood had to admit that he was happy with the shelving, cabinetry, and paneling that the carpenters had built to his and Brewster's specifications. "Say, Brew, I've been meaning to talk with you about an idea I have."

"Is it new, is it unique, will it make us more money?"

"I don't know about all that, but I think it's pretty good."

"Well, let's put it on the turntable and see if it plays."

"Corny," said Durwood, "but I'll tell it to you anyway."

"What does it mean, this 'corny'?" asked Mitzi.

After giving it some thought, Durwood told her, "Corny is how we describe something that's been done or said so much that it isn't funny anymore."

"So," she asked, "does corny always refer to some manner of funny joking or a humor?"

"I'll run it down to you later, baby," Brewster said impatiently. "Right now I'd like to hear what Durwood's got up his sleeve."

Mitzi shook her inky tresses and shrugged. "I will never understand more than only half of what it is, about which you are speaking."

"My idea's simple," said Durwood. "How about, instead of just laying in records and tapes and musical stuff, we also stock a few sports-related items as a sideline."

"Like what?"

"*Sports Illustrated, Basketball Digest, The Racing News*, books. And maybe some action posters of outstanding players, sweatshirts, T-shirts, even a few of these jogger's radios they've got out now, and—"

"Hey, great, great!" Brewster's eyes were doubling in size. "That's a wild idea. I love it. I can hear the promo coming over the air right now—'You'll also find at Knight and Day a fine selection of quality sports publications and other paraphernalia and memorabilia at reasonable prices, yada-yada-yada.' Hot dog! Woody, you're a genius! We'll clean up! That's some clever merchandising. It fits right in with the shop's theme too."

"The theme's what got me to thinking about it."

"What is it for, this jogger radio?" asked Mitzi.

"It's a radio," said Durwood, "that you wear around your neck so you can listen while you're running."

"But why will joggers want them? To jog, as you say, is to wish to be quiet inside one's head, yes?"

"Mitzi," said Brewster, "you ask too many questions. The theory behind all this is to make some bread. Now, we'd better get busy and finish cataloging these new album shipments."

"I'll help out too," said Durwood. "Nothing I like better than fooling around with records."

"One hopes so," said Mitzi, "because now you are within the market."

Puzzled, Durwood looked over at her. After giving what she'd said some thought, he shook his head and said, "That's okay, Mitzi. I think I know what you meant. I'm in the business, right?"

"Yes," she said with a little blush and a huge smile. "That is it precisely."

As he was parking in his driveway on Dolores Street later that afternoon, dead set on getting right to work on the talk he would be giving at the Shriners Hospital, Durwood saw Moby sitting on the front steps, reading a book.

Well, well—maybe he was finally going to have a chance to get a look at this youngster close up, one-on-one. All he had to remember was to take his time, proceed coolly, and not jump to any hasty conclusions until he'd checked him out.

Durwood got out of the wagon, locked it, and, gripping his attaché case and moving as jauntily as he could, climbed the hilly incline toward the porch, proud of his height as he examined the boy.

"Afternoon, Moby," he said in a firm voice. "You're looking awfully studious."

Moby looked up with a pleasant expression. Dressed in jeans, plaid shirt, and a puffy, insulated vest, the early December wind swishing his doctored curls around, he got to his feet. Using his finger as a bookmark, he cleared his throat, crammed his free hand in one of his vest pockets, and said, "Hi, Mr. Knight. I was just sitting here waiting for Celia to get home. We're supposed to go over some numbers."

"Some numbers?"

"Some tunes."

"You guys really get a kick out of playing together, don't you?"

"I know I do. Celia's more of a perfectionist than me. Everything's gotta be just right for her or she gets uptight."

"You don't have to tell me. I'm her old man. I have to live with her. What's that book you got there?"

"Oh, this?" said Moby, blinking at the beat-up paperback he was clutching as if it were some kind of embarrassing stain on his trousers that he would rather hide. "It's just the *Guinness Book of World Records.*"

"Hey, I keep hearing about that thing, but somehow I never seem to get around to sitting down and reading it."

"Well," said Moby, scratching his head uneasily, "you don't actually read it. You just sorta flip around in it until you flash on something interesting; then you sit back and really check it out, you know, soak it up and memorize it so you can go out and quote it and blow people's minds."

"I see," said Durwood as he put down his briefcase, pulled up his trouser legs, and lowered himself onto the top porch step. "When I was a kid—and this was way before your time—I used to get all worked up over something called 'Ripley's Believe It or Not.' You probably never heard of that. It used to be in the funny papers."

"Was it anything like that 'Believe It or Nuts' you see in old *Mad* collections?"

"The same idea, I think, except what you saw in *Mad* magazine was a take-off on the original Ripley stuff."

"I think I know what you mean. Like, they'd say where there's this woman way off in Polynesia or someplace that's got seven toes on each foot, and all seven of her children were born the same way, and then all of her granchildren'd pop up with the seven of spades on their foreheads for birthmarks."

"You got it," said Durwood, who couldn't help laughing, "but it was all on the level. I never have forgotten this man named Edicoe Needles who Ripley wrote up. He was a black man from Detroit who used to eat something like sixty pork chops and then follow that up with twenty-five peach and blueberry pies. One Thanksgiving he put away three turkeys, three hundred raw eggs, and ten cups of black coffee. If I have one cup of black coffee, I'm ready to start scratching paint off the walls."

"You're joking," said Moby.

"About Edicoe Needles or my one cup of coffee?"

"About the three hundred raw eggs. Shoot, I mean, Just looking at a raw egg makes me sick to my stomach."

"What's your favorite food, Moby? What do you like to eat?"

Moby rested the book on top of his battered flute case and smiled as he looked away thoughtfully. "Well, I don't know. I like lots of things."

"For instance."

"Oh, I like chili, home fries, spaghetti, barbecue, Chinese food, Mexican food, and—"

"Mexican food? Anything in particular?"

"Enchiladas, tacos, bean burritos, refried beans."

"So you're a bean man, eh? I'm crazy about 'em myself. Is somebody in your family Chicano or something?"

"Yes," said Moby. "My mother. She's from Albuquerque, New Mexico, and my dad likes to tell people he's from South America."

"Is he really?"

"Sure, he's from Knoxville, Tennessee. That's South in America, right? But he left there when he joined the service and went to Korea, just like my mother left Albuquerque and came here to California when she was little."

"Did she just leave by herself, or what?"

"No, the whole family moved to Bakersfield and then up to Richmond to work in the shipyards."

"Your mother must be interesting. I've been in New Mexico a

lot, playing ball mostly, but I never really knew anybody well that's from there."

"I hardly ever see her anymore." Moby's eyes turned away again. His nose wrinkled as he fingered it nervously along one side. Rapidly and absent-mindedly, he picked up the book and let his thumb flit across the page edges. Studying him, Durwood thought about those Big Little Books, as they were called, that he'd loved as a child, with their animated cartoon inserts in the upper corners of pages that you'd flip to see the pictures move.

"Doesn't your mom live with you?" he asked.

"No, not anymore."

"Then who do you live with?"

"Just my dad, mostly."

"You don't have any brothers or sisters?"

"I've got a half-sister somewhere, but I never met her."

It was obvious that Moby really didn't want to talk about any of this, yet Durwood felt he had to keep the banter going in order to put the boy at ease. He really wanted to get to know him, and there seemed to be so little time. What could he ask him now? How was he going to break the ice? He glanced again at the *Guinness Book of World Records* and asked, "You mind if I have a look at that?"

"Not at all, Mr. Knight. Here, you wanna borrow it? They got a lotta basketball statistics in there you might be interested in."

"Is that right? Say, why don't you quiz me a little and see how I do. It's so hard to keep up once you're out of the game."

"Aw, c'mon," said Moby reluctantly, "you probably know everything about the sport."

"No, really—try me, test me out, just for the heck of it."

"You sure you want me to do that?"

"Absolutely. Go ahead."

Still looking a little embarrassed, Moby thumbed around until he located a section near the back of the book; then, scooting away slightly so that Durwood couldn't see what he was reading, he cleared his throat and asked, "Okay, can you tell me the name of the man who shot the greatest number of accurate free throws?"

"Oh, that's easy," said Durwood, chuckling to himself. "I thought you were gonna hit me with a toughie."

Moby was smiling politely, but Durwood could tell that the boy was looking at him as if he didn't believe him. "Well, who was it, then, and how many free throws did he score?"

Durwood put on a big show of looking distressed by deliberately furrowing his brow and touching fingertips to his forehead as though he were lost in contemplation. Finally, he said, "That would have to be none other than Ted St. Martin. The year was 1976, and he was giving a goal-shooting demonstration. As I recall, he sunk something like two thousand free throws in a row."

Moby's tight little smile erupted into a gap-toothed grin. "Not bad," he said. "Actually, it was two thousand and thirty-six."

"I know it was way up there someplace. All right, hit me again."

"Who's the tallest basketball player?"

"Male or female?"

"Oh, so now we get technical?"

"Professional or amateur?" Durwood knew that would rattle him.

"Okay, let's just say in the NBA."

"Tommy Burleson. Last I heard, he was seven-foot-four."

"And what about in the world?"

"The tallest one I know about is some dude out of China—can't think of his name—but he's close to eight feet."

"Can you narrow it down any closer than that?"

"Hmmm, well, I think he's around seven-foot-nine."

"Seven-foot-nine and three-quarters," snapped Moby. "And his name is . . . lemme see . . . His name is . . ." Moby stared hard at the print on the page and stammered out the name. "It's, uh, Moo . . . Tye . . . yeah . . . Choo. That how you say it?"

"Don't ask me. It's all I can do to pronounce vegetable chow yuk."

"Well, it's spelled M-u, T-i-e-h, C-h-u."

"Good. You got any more?"

"Sure," said Moby, turning the page. "Who's the rebound record-holder?"

"You can't be serious."

"I'm as serious as a heart attack."

"Ouch," said Durwood, clutching his chest and making a sour face, "don't say that! I'm getting to the age where that expression just isn't funny to me."

"Sorry, Mr. Knight."

"Aw, that's all right. But, to answer your question, to the best of my knowledge, the reigning rebound champion is still Wilt the Stilt. As a matter of fact, when you start talking about basketball, there really isn't too much he hasn't excelled at."

Moby shut the book and handed it back to Durwood. "Well," he said, shaking his head, "I don't think you'll be needing this to do any boning up on that subject. But there's plenty of other information in there."

"I'll bet."

"Can I ask you another question, Mr. Knight?"

"Anything you want. Shoot."

"Have you—" Moby's eyes were brightening now. "Have you ever met Wilt Chamberlain?"

"Sure."

"Really? Do you know him?"

"We've played together, hung out together, and even fought."

"You mean, fought, like, with your fists?"

Durwood laughed. "No, I mean, got mad with each other and cussed each other out."

"Over what?"

"Well, you see, Moby . . . Wilton Norman Chamberlain is a very funny guy. He can be funny ha-ha when he wants to be, but he's funny strange all the time."

"How so?"

"Oh, there're just these certain areas where he can get on your nerves—my nerves anyway. You take this thing he's got about being the hottest target shot around. I've been through that with him quite a few times now—once in Philly, several times in New York, plus a couple times right here in San Francisco. A few of us'll turn up in town at the same time, and if we happen to be between games, Wilt likes to haul us into some amusement arcade and show off what a good shot he is."

"Is he all that good?"

"Sure, he's good, but I'm no slouch myself. I could beat him hands down if he'd ever stop signifying and shut up. He goes in for a lotta razzing and wisecracking. That makes me nervous, so I fall down in my shots. One of these days, though, I'm gonna teach him a lesson!"

"I sure would like to meet him," said Moby, openly enthusiastic now. "I used to wanna grow up and be like him."

Durwood shook his head. "He'd be tickled to death to hear you say that. He's one of a kind, though, and maybe that's just as well. You play much basketball, Moby?"

"Not really. Me and a few buddies get together sometimes on Saturday mornings at the playground over at school and fool around."

"It's fun, isn't it?"

"It's something to do. Keeps me out of the house."

"I kinda get the feeling you don't like being at home."

"Aw, Mr. Knight, you'd never understand. I can't even practice my flute at the house without my dad getting upset."

"What does your father do for a living?"

"He works for this man at a used-car lot and retreads tires and stuff."

Just then Durwood saw Moby's face go sour as something in the yard caught his attention. The screeching and squawking of birds startled Durwood as he whisked his head around to the place where the youngster was staring, just in time to see a fat, chesty blue jay swooping down on what looked to be a baby sparrow. Moby jumped to his sneakered feet at once and rushed off down the steps to shoo the blue jay violently with flailing arms and cries, frightening both creatures.

"Goddamn blue jays!" Durwood heard him say. "Excuse me, Mr. Knight, but I can't stand 'em. All they are is a menace, those suckers! They're mean! You ever notice how they like to pick on littler birds?"

Durwood wasn't only startled by what had just happened; there was something about the way the wind was making Moby's hair shiver. His hair. Durwood had never liked Moby's hair, which looked as if cats had been sucking on it. What if he were to get rid of that hair? For a twinkling, he pictured Moby skinheaded—a teenage Mr. Clean. Something was beginning to register that made Durwood uncomfortable, but he had no idea what that something was. Before he had time to give it further thought, his feelings drifted into a brand-new moment that found him becoming aware of Celia and her girlfriend Patsy Watson strolling up the sidewalk. Patsy had always reminded him of Tina Rawlins, Coretha's younger sister. She was tall like Coretha but not as shapely. Like Tina, Patsy was wiry and pretty in a pinched sort of way. She and Celia both had that certain look about them that older girls seemed to exude when they teamed up in pairs. For Durwood, it was almost as if they were already planning in secret the kind of woman each was going to become.

"Hi, Moby! Hi, Dad!" Celia called out, shifting her books and waving. "Sorry I'm late!"

Patsy, wearing what might very well have been a Dior head scarf, which fitted her like a helmet, nodded directly at Durwood and said, "Hello, Mr. Knight. You guys gonna do a little dance for us?"

Celia said good-bye to Patsy and climbed toward the porch. "Moby," she said, "I'm sorry to hang you up, but I thought I told you I had to stay through sixth period today."

"I thought that's what you said," Moby told her, "but I wasn't too sure. Anyway, I like your neighborhood. Your dad and I even got a chance to talk."

"Well, it's about time."

"Maybe Moby can come to dinner sometime," said Durwood.

"Hey, that'd be a treat, Mr. Knight."

Durwood watched for Celia's reaction, but when he saw that she was taking it all in stride, he said, "Tell me, what did Patsy mean when she asked if we were gonna do a little dance for you guys?"

Celia's hand shot up to cover her embarrassed smile. "I get so ticked off with Patsy when she pulls those numbers. She's so uncool. She'll say the first thing that comes into her head."

"But what did she mean?"

"Yeah," said Moby, "I wondered about that too."

"Oh, from the corner we saw you out there in the yard jumping up and down and swinging your arms around, that's all. Now that you bring it up, what *were* you doing?"

Moby shot Durwood a sidewise glance. "I was showing your dad how to conduct an orchestra."

"Aw, c'mon, get outta here!" said Celia, playfully pretending to push him away.

Durwood noticed, though, that Celia's hand had rested on Moby's chest for just a fraction of a second too long, as though she might have let it linger there if Durwood hadn't been in the picture. He noticed, too, that he was getting tired out from playing these little games with Moby and Celia. Or was he only playing games with himself? And now that he thought about it, was any of the stuff he thought he was seeing really happening that way? Maybe he was just making it all up—seeing what he wanted to see, or needed to see. In any case, his sinuses had started to itch again.

"Daddy," Celia asked, "after Moby and I get through practicing, would you go downtown with me to check out that necklace I told you about?"

"What necklace?"

"For Christmas, remember?"

"Not today, honey. I have to be in court in the morning, and right now I gotta write out this talk for the kids at the Shriners."

"I thought you were giving up all that," said Celia, who was definitely disappointed.

"Don't worry, we'll do it soon." Durwood picked up his briefcase and Moby's book, then reached in his pocket for the front door key. "Say, Moby," he called, turning to face them again. "You sure you don't have any brothers or relatives?"

"Relatives, yes . . . Brothers, no . . . not that I know of."

"Daddy, what a strange thing to ask."

"I guess that makes me strange," said Durwood, "but wait until you live to get as old as I am. You'll be strange too. I can guarantee you that. You two better get your practicing done before Dixie gets back with Nissa. You know how hard-headed your sister can be."

"Don't worry," said Celia, "I can always lock my door."

"Now, I don't know about that."

And Durwood meant what he said. He definitely did not like the idea of Celia and Moby in Celia's room by themselves, much less with the door locked. But the first thing he did when he got to his study was to hang out a "Do Not Disturb" sign that he'd picked up at some hotel; then he locked the door, sat down in his thronely leather chair, and almost breathed freely.

TWENTY-FOUR HOURS LATER, Durwood was tooling along Geary Boulevard fresh from the arraignment, during which Gail Díaz, his attorney, had told him not to worry about a thing. Driving past the Japan Trade Center made him think of Mu Tieh-Chu, the world's tallest basketball player, and what a fuss the sports press had made over him when his Chinese team had played against some Japanese All-Stars.

It was right about then that Durwood got the uncomfortable feeling that he was being followed. From the time he'd pulled out of the parking lot near the courthouse, he had been vaguely noticing in his rear-view mirror that a dirty white Chevy van with rubberized bumpers appeared to be taking every turn he took. It was a chilling hunch, a little like the sinking feeling he used to experience in his playing days whenever he realized that his performance averages had been slipping for longer than a mere couple of games.

He tried to control his paranoid notion by thinking about the arraignment, which had irritated him. He hated courtrooms and legal procedures. The defendant, Charles Triplett and his sullen band of cronies and rooters, or whoever they were, had behaved as if they might be conspiring to assassinate Durwood. Gail Díaz had urged him to ignore them, explaining that it wasn't unusual for someone in his position to feel uneasy. As a law student, Gail had worked for a couple of summers assisting Beanstalk owner Frank D'Annunzio's attorney as a case researcher. Durwood, who had always been impressed with Gail's sharpness and confidence, kept in touch and hired her as his personal lawyer once she got going on her own. Gail had told him that it wasn't necessary for him to be present at the arraignment, but Durwood had insisted on being there just the same. The dragginess of all the other cases they had to suffer through before Trip was hauled in had sabotaged his plan to arrive early for the three o'clock charity appearance at the hospital, which was way out on 19th Avenue.

With images of Trip still blazing in his mind, Durwood came to Fulton Street, which bordered on Golden Gate Park. He looked in his rear-view mirror. Sure enough, the van was still there, two cars in back of his. He scurried into the left-hand lane. As soon as it was able to, the van did likewise.

A moment before the signal flashed red at 25th Avenue and Fulton, Durwood managed an urgent left in time to stab his way into a line of traffic that was cutting through the park. The van was left trapped at the red light in the turn lane.

So far, so good. Even should it turn out that he wasn't being tailed, this spur-of-the-moment maneuver ought to give him enough of a lead to shake his worries for good.

Durwood crept along in the winding lanes of stop-and-start traffic, relaxing somewhat, trying to enjoy the greenery, the spicy fragrance of eucalyptus trees, and the coolness of the thinly overcast midafternoon light. It wasn't like early morning, when he felt like the park was his personal property, but it was still a winner. One of these days, once he got the shop off the ground and everything going his way, he was going to take the whole family on a slow drive up the coast through Oregon and Washington, camping out at state parks, then all the way to British Columbia. It was hard to believe that they'd never done that. Life was too short to be dwelling on ugliness and bullshit all the time. How pleasant his hospital appearance was going to be—moving among innocent kids who happened to be physically handicapped, instead of wasting time in court with twisted adults with crippled minds who didn't know the meaning of common decency.

Music, that's what he needed! Some good old, soothing, easy-listening music. The bastards still hadn't come up with his cassette player, but he still had his radio. When he reached to punch it on, he noticed that he was practically out of gas again. Talk about a bummer! What if there was a line? He'd be late for his talk. Recalling that he was low on cash, he knew that he'd better start looking for a Chevron station, where his gasoline credit card would save him. He saw one two blocks ahead when he rolled out of the park onto 19th Avenue.

Luck was still with him. The green flag was out, and, thank God, there wasn't a line. He felt blessed.

Ordinarily Durwood headed straight for the mini-service pumps to save a few pennies, but today, feeling safely beyond the pinch, feeling like Durwood Knight, sports pro, he pulled up to the full-service island and told the blue-capped girl with red hair, green eyes, and grease-smudged cheeks that he wanted a fill-up. And would she check the oil and water, please?

"For sure," she said, grinning at him with teeth that reminded him of the jack-o-lantern he'd helped Nissa carve at Halloween.

"Excuse me, but where's the restroom?"

"On the side in back," the girl told him, continuing to gawk while she pointed, "but you gotta use the key."

"The key?"

"It's inside the station hanging on a hook by the Coke machine. We keep it in there to keep the junkies and perverts out."

When Durwood came back out, the attendant was skimming the last of the scuzz from the rear window. "Did you have a good time?" she asked, wiping the dripping squeegee on her tight trouser legs.

Suspecting her of being some kind of cretin, he ignored the remark and went into the pocket of his blue denim suit—an outfit that Dixie had told him was corny and passé, but one he thought kids might still be able to relate to—and whipped out his shiny, patriotic-colored charge card.

"Just a sec'," the girl mumbled and, turning, smiled as she gestured toward a vehicle that was just beginning to nose its way into the pump area. "Be right with you, Choo Choo!" she shouted.

Durwood stepped back and looked at the driver, a fat man with a snaggly chin beard. He had on a dark turtleneck sweater and was wearing a golfing cap turned backwards that rested like an afterthought on top of pink plastic curlers. Watching the man chomp on a toothpick while he bopped his chunky head up and down to jaunty classical music turned up real loud, Durwood felt himself growing dizzy.

He did a double-take, then a triple-take. He stepped around the island to where he could make out the license plate on this Chevy van, the same one that had been trailing him. "WE GONE" was how the license read. With jumpy, bloodshot eyes, the driver spun around to glare at him. Durwood glared back like a method actor, drawing his lips taut across his teeth and shaking his head dramatically from side to side.

Durwood thought he saw the joker flinch and then try to cover it with a sickly grin, but he could have been imagining that too. To be on the safe side, he kept up his stare, determined to memorize the features: the flat, flaring nostrils, the caterpillar-like eyebrows, the mouselike teeth, and, most of all, the man's enormous roll of frowning forehead, which gave the effect of everything, all of his features, being crammed into the bottom of his face. The man looked like something a hostile caricaturist might have drawn or, better yet, dashed off with drooling contempt. Durwood didn't give a damn what the dude thought of his staring. He could handle himself, plus he knew that he would never forget that face.

But still, he could be wrong about having been followed. It was best to keep cool. Dixie was right. He did have a bad habit of getting worked up too easily over the wrongest things. He got back into his wagon, signed for the gas, and rolled down both windows before starting the engine.

"Everything was fine under the hood," the girl told Durwood. "I feel like I know you."

"It's probably mutual," he cracked.

"Well, enjoy what's left of your day."

Durwood nodded and opened the glove compartment, pretending to be busy with papers there, pretending to be fidgeting, but all he really was trying to do was stall for a while with his eyes and ears wide open.

The station attendant hustled over to the fat man's van, saying, "Heyyy, Choo Choo, what's been happening? Ain't seen you around here in a coupla weeks. Where you been, on vacation?"

"You know me, baby, I stays on vacation."

"Fill it up with super?"

"We can start with that."

"What else you need?" she giggled. "Some oil?"

The craziness of how it was looking was getting to Durwood. If anyone had told him ten years ago that the time would come when he'd be watching some man propped up behind a wheel with his hair up in curlers, while a girl—pumpkin teeth aside—was getting ready to pump him gas, he might have laughed it off as science fiction.

"Now, Nonie, you know good and well what else I need. You heard that record. It was on all the stations."

"What record?"

"'Give It Up,'" he sang, "by Marvin Gaye."

"Give up what?" She was blushing through oil-smeared cheeks.

"Give up this little menial gig," he told her with a wink and a flourish, "and come work for me."

"And qualify for food stamps, right?"

"Food stamps, shit! Make you some real money, that's what. I can sense that deep down in the lovely recesses of your mind that you want to."

"You never give up, do you?" she said. "What do you take me for, one of those dumb college broads?" She giggled again and pulled out the gas hose.

"Ooo, be careful now," groaned Choo Choo. "I won't have nobody messin up my tank. Just had me a new one put in from where this chump at the Shell station poked a hole in it with one of these silly new kinda thingamajigs that's supposed to keep you from toppin off. See, now, I shoulda pumped it myself. And, baby, I know how to service it real slow and considerate-like. I wouldn't go rammin it in too quick. Real gentle, now that's more my style. You know, ease it in with a feelin and wiggle it around to the place where you got a good suction seal, and then, and *then*, that's when you can clamp down, if you follow me,

Nonie, where you go to chokin up on it real snug and tight and feel all that natural gasoline go to trickling up inside."

Fuel was spilling all over the concrete while the station attendant, still red in the face, stood holding the hose with her mouth hanging open. She turned, probably out of nervousness, and peered at Durwood. "Need anything else, sir?"

"No," he mumbled, acting as if he were hitching his seat belt. "Just getting myself together."

Durwood drove away feeling perfectly free to proceed to his gig without having to worry about being shadowed.

"Choo Choo," he said aloud to himself as he roared off down 19th. "Choo Choo . . . WE GONE . . . Get outta here!"

THERE MUST HAVE BEEN over thirty kids waiting in wheelchairs, on crutches, and sitting up in beds. They greeted Durwood with friendly applause, hurrahs, and eager smiles as Mr. Josephs, a senior official, led him onto the ward.

"As you all know," Mr. Josephs announced, "we tend to be partial to football players here at Shriners, but we do think it's a good policy to mix it up from time to time. And so today we are fortunate to have such a celebrated basketball star as Durwood Knight honor us with his presence. I don't think I need to bore you by citing all of Mr. Knight's many credits. There are a great many fans of his right here on the ward this afternoon, myself included . . . "

Despite the informality of the occasion, Durwood felt himself tensing. All those notes he'd made seemed superfluous now as he looked around him. What in the world was he going to say to these poor youngsters? He knew from his preliminary exchange of letters with Mr. Josephs that most of them suffered from some form of orthopedic handicap. Others were victims of severe burns or had been crippled by cerebral palsy. There was a sprinkling of polio patients from outside the country, remote places where the Salk vaccine hadn't yet become widely available. Surveying their faces and bodies, he knew the best thing to do would be to speak off the cuff. He swallowed hard to steady the lump in his throat and the butterflies in his belly.

". . . So I'll turn you over now to Durwood Knight, who's going to talk a little about what's like to be a professional athlete and also answer any questions you might have for him. Mr. Knight, it's all yours."

"Please, all of you . . . It's Durwood while I'm here."

Mr. Josephs, adjusting his tie, smiled courteously and made a correction. "Well, take it away, Durwood."

"Thank you," said Durwood, standing now at the head of the room, still uneasy, but striving to keep his head moving so as to make eye contact with everybody there.

The children ranged in age from tiny tot to about fifteen. What kinds of things could he possibly touch on that would reach all of them? That banjo-picking comedian Steve Martin had been right on the money when he'd quipped that the banjo was probably the only thing that could have saved Nixon. Durwood wished he had a banjo or a guitar in his hands right now—some comforting prop to clutch while he gathered his scattered thoughts.

"I'd like to talk this afternoon," he began, "about things that make you feel good. You don't have to be in tiptop physical condition to feel good. I feel good right now just being here with you. You know why? Because I've lived long enough and had enough experience to learn that being a professional athlete is something like selling lemonade."

He paused to let that part sink in while he was figuring out how to word whatever might follow in such a way as to make his message clear to the very youngest among them.

"When you sell lemonade," he continued, "you're selling water, some lemon juice, and a little sugar. But you're also selling something that's cold and refreshing to people who're thirsty on a hot day. Now, how is that like being a professional athlete? Well, I'll tell you. If you're an athlete—doesn't matter if you're playing basketball, football, baseball, soccer, hockey, or any team sport, and it doesn't matter if you're a tennis pro, a track star, a weight lifter, a wrestler, or even if you're Muhammad Ali—what you're selling is your body. You're selling your body and your skill. You're selling everything your body's been trained and programmed to do. And if you're a pro like I've been for most of my life, then you've got other things to think about."

Here Durwood stopped and looked around to see if everyone was following him thus far. Nobody looked confused.

"Say you decide to become an auto mechanic or a TV repair person or a carpenter or a bookkeeper or a cook or a doctor. Well, you go to school and get your training and learn your trade or profession. You get your skills down and start in working, and you're more or less set for the rest of your life. That's what you do if you *aren't* a professional athlete. Now, if you're a professional athlete, then you've got a problem. Nobody tells you that this *isn't* the type of vocation or profession that you can sit down and program and say, 'Hey, I'm gonna go to school and major in basketball.' Certainly, you aren't going to be running around a basketball court for the rest of your life. You've got, say, seventeen or eighteen years at the very most to get out there and do your play-for-pay thing. You get old. Your body runs down. You're being paid to perform, and yet that doesn't only mean playing ball. It also means taking all the punches, falls, sprains, and other accidents that're bound to come your way. You're out there. I mean, you're *out* there, physically, *fiscally*—and all fiscal means is for money—so it's like a job. You're performing for the public, and the public, quite naturally, wants a little excitement for its money."

"Excuse me," a seven-year-old on crutches broke in, raising his hand, "but how do we pay you for playing basketball for us when we're watching you on television?"

"Or listening to the game on my transistor?" asked another child, this one a dwarfed boy of indeterminate age with a distinctly foreign accent that Durwood took to be Asian.

This was what Durwood loved most about children: their unpretentious innocence; the way they came right out, unlike most adults, and asked directly about what they didn't understand.

"Well," he said, "you don't actually pay us when you watch a game on TV or listen to a radio broadcast. Advertisers pay the station to play their commercials along with the program, and then you're supposed to go out and buy what they're trying to sell you."

"Then how do you get paid?" asked the seven-year-old.

"We get paid by the people who own the team."

"But why?" asked the dwarfed youngster.

"Why?" Durwood had to think about that one. He decided to come back with the old answer-a-question-with-a-question dodge. "Why not?"

"No," said the dwarf, his voice taking on a decidedly ghetto tinge. "What I mean is how come they pay you to be playing something that most people who aren't crippled like we are can play for themselves?"

Thinking fast, Durwood said, "I can only guess, but maybe it's because people enjoy seeing something done well, even a sporting event. It gives them something they can dream about."

"Dream about?" a tall kid asked.

"Sure, isn't that what you do? I know I do. When I was a kid, I liked to watch Sugar Ray Robinson box, or Larry Dobie slam a home run, or Big Daddy Lipscomb or Night Train Lane run touchdowns, or good old Number 6, Bill Russell, do his thing with the Celtics. I mean, I wouldn't just be following it, I'd be right out there in the game with those people, playing right along with them in my imagination. That's all I mean by dreaming. It has to do with ideals. It's like when I'd go to the Saturday afternoon movies with my brother and our buddies back in Texas. When the good guys up there on the screen did something fantastic—say somebody would leap off a horse right onto the top of one of the bad guys' trucks while it was moving—then we'd cheer and stomp and whistle and go crazy. After we left the picture show, we'd go and try to act out a lot of that stuff ourselves, you know. We wouldn't really attempt to do anything too dangerous, but we *would* get off into pretending we were the heroes when we played."

Durwood figured he was off the hook when he looked around and saw how most of the kids were still with him.

"In other words," the dwarf shot back, "you're saying people will buy tickets to see stars perform because they wanna be a star, too, and so they can identify with somebody who's doing a good job of what they'd like to be doing?"

"Yes, exactly, that's all I'm saying."

"You mentioned Bill Russell," said a palsied kid in his early teens. "Do you think he could shoot as well as Bob Cousy?"

Durwood rubbed at his chin and said, "Whew, that's a toughie! I'm sure glad this isn't one of those television quiz shows with the clock ticking off seconds on me. Let me say this . . . Russell could shoot when he got a chance to, but his heaviest thing was his passing and rebounding. He ·could shoot, though. Now, Cooz could shoot too. The problem in comparing the two is that they both were originals, one-of-a-kind. Cooz didn't even get interested in playing the game until he was thirteen, late, coming from France like he did. But he had his own funny way of dribbling and passing, just like Bill did. They were both sensational. Shooting isn't everything in basketball. Blocking and passing count for a lot too. Cooz was probably the greatest passer in the history of the game, but Bill . . . he was just great, that's all. Look, when a team wins eleven out of thirteen play-offs because a particular player was on that team—and those of you who follow the game and keep up know that's what the Celtics did—then you can't chalk it up to just plain luck or accident."

The kid who had asked the question seemed content enough with that answer. Durwood was still nervous. He wanted to move on to other subjects and get to know the youngsters.

"One more thing," the dwarf asked. "How do you rate yourself in the history of basketball? Would you put yourself up there with Oscar Robertson and George Mikan?"

For subtle reasons, this question, which struck him as being innocent but painful, caused Durwood to picture his father, Artemius Knight, as he stood by his paneled shop mirror, surrounded by the tools of his trade. For the thousandth time in memory, Durwood watches him set down the scissors and comb, then pick up the cylindrical brush and dunk it in a waiting bowl of hot lather. His nostrils are filled with the smells of Lucky Tiger Hair Tonic, Mennen's After Shave, and Wildroot Cream Oil mixed with those of razored hair, hot coffee, tobacco smoke, and human breath. As usual, there's an argument going on that's growing fiercer by the minute. Foolish men are slapping down one- and five-dollar bets on where the two Joe Louis–Billy Cohn fights took place. Armed with greasy, well-thumbed almanacs and quick-reference books of every description, Durwood's dad—known as Artie to his patrons—is refereeing it all and also picking up a few bucks for himself on the side.

"That's a tough question," Durwood answered. "To be truthful, I wouldn't care to place myself up next to anybody but Durwood Knight, who played the game the best way he knew how and the only way he knew how—fair and square."

As had happened at the shopping center during the Reno drawing, the audience broke out in spontaneous, inexplicable applause. It was as if a shiny new car, Old Glory, or a Big Mac somehow had flashed into all of their TV minds at the same moment. Durwood didn't understand it at all. But, what the hell—why not take advantage of this surprise ovation by relaxing and enjoying the situation?

Durwood wound up his semi-formal talk and walked around the ward shaking hands, chatting, and signing autographs and the three new basketballs he had brought along to present to the hospital. The youngsters and Mr. Josephs seemed delighted.

"I don't have no questions about basketball," a little girl told him, "but I would like to ask a personal favor if you don't mind."

"Depends on how personal it is," said Durwood, squatting beside the girl's wheelchair and looking into her serious, dark eyes set in a round, brown face topped with tight Afro curls. He noticed that one of her arms was atrophied. With her good arm, she handed him a sealed manilla envelope.

"Would you read this when you get a chance and write to me?" she asked.

"What is it?"

"Just something I wrote. I'd like to get your reaction. I write a lot of stuff I don't show nobody."

"Oh, yeah? What kinds of things?"
"You'll see."
"Thanks. I promise to get back to you as soon as I can."
"I know how busy you are, but I'd really appreciate it if you could."
How could he say no to those big, brown, shiny eyes of hers?
To much all-around groaning, Mr. Josephs announced that time was up, then escorted Durwood out of the room.
"Do the boys and girls share the same ward, Mr. Josephs?"
"No, they flit back and forth during the day and get together whenever we have speakers. That young lady you just talked to—Midge McHenry—she's quite a character."
"How so?"
All Mr. Josephs did was raise his eyebrows and shake his head uncertainly as if that subject was far too complicated to go into right then. As they were entering the elevator, he said, "I can't thank you enough, Durwood, for giving us so much of your precious time. By the way, what are you up to these days? I'll bet you miss being out there in the public eye."
"I sure miss the steady income," replied Durwood, "but I'm happy, I guess. The rest of it's duck soup."
"Ah, duck soup," Mr. Josephs said fondly with a sparkle in his eye.
"Oh," Durwood went on, "maybe with a little pea soup mixed in for good measure."
Mr. Josephs consulted his watch and slapped Durwood on the back. "Well, Durwood," he said, "you're a regular, down-to-earth fellow and a credit to San Francisco. And on behalf of the Shriners, the kids, and myself, I'd like to wish you all the best in any new ventures you might undertake."
"Thank you, it's been a pleasure."
And on that note, the two men shook hands and wished one another the best of holidays.

On his way to the parking lot, Durwood got to thinking how lucky he was to have a family that was basically sound, physically anyway. What the hell was he worried about lately? Was it only Christmas? Or was it that he was beginning to believe he'd really be better off living by himself in some bachelor apartment? He could send off a fat check every month—the bigger chunk of his earnings—and buy back his bachelorhood like every other man he knew. There'd be dues to pay, for sure, but there'd be all the trappings of freedom: fun with a capital F, filled with friends and females; women scuffling to satisfy his every wish just because he was who he was. Or would it be because he'd been who he'd been? There just wouldn't be any room at all for somebody like Dixie saying, "How come you didn't take out the garbage?"

"I'M BEGINNING TO HATE THIS part of town," was the first thing Celia said a couple of days later when she and Durwood met as planned on the Stockton Street side of Macy's.
"How come?"
"Because it's dumb and creepy."
"Creepy I can understand, but dumb?"
"Sure, dumb. You got all these dumb people mixing with all these creeps. I mean, just look around and see for yourself."
"Well, if you say so, dear. Now, where's that man you told me about, the one with the jewelry he makes himself."
With her bookbag slung over one shoulder, Celia looped her arm in her father's and led him toward Union Square to a sidewalk table manned by a thin, bearded, elderly gentleman with skin the color of cordovan leather and a full head of salt-and-pepper frizz. Short and neat in flared jeans and a trim Navy-style pea coat, the vendor rolled up the copy of *Variety* he had been reading and stood at attention the moment he saw them approaching.
"May I help you?" he asked.
"Hi," said Celia, "remember me?"

"Why, yes, of course. You're the girl who was gonna bring your dad down to help you shop for a Christmas present for your mother."

"That's me, all right."

"And what a tall, handsome father you have, young lady. Sir, I design and manufacture myself all the articles you see here—and the sticker prices are final. I'm not into bargaining or bickering."

Durwood admired the man's forthrightness and arrogance. If he were in his mid- to late fifties—which was what Durwood estimated the fellow's age to be—and hustling on the streets, he, too, would've taken a firm stance. Dignity. A true street artist and craftsman. He liked that. After scanning the merchandise that was attractively laid out against a black velvet drop cloth, he turned to Celia.

"What was it you were thinking of getting?"

She bent over the table and said, "It was a necklace."

"I believe it was this one you had in mind," said the street merchant, holding up one of his silver-and-turquoise creations.

"Yes, yes, that's the one, Daddy. Isn't it neat?"

Durwood reached for the necklace, fondled it, examined it, then asked Celia to try it on.

"Be glad to," she said, "but I'll need a little help."

"Here," said the merchant, "allow me."

When, with precise, delicate fingers, the jewelry man had fastened the necklace into place at the base of her neck, Celia modeled it for Durwood, saying, "Well, what do you think?"

"Looks awfully good to me, Celia. I know Dixie'll be crazy about it. How much you say it was?"

"Just fifty dollars, Dad."

"Uhmmm, ahemmm." The merchant cleared his throat. "I'm afraid it's gonna cost you a bit more than that, sir."

"But the other day," said Celia, disturbed, "you told me I could have it for fifty."

"That was some time ago as I recall. Over the past few weeks I've been forced to adjust my prices."

"But why?" Celia asked, her smile collapsing. "You told me you'd hold it for me, and you said—"

"My apologies, young lady. I'm sorry. If I told you fifty

dollars—and I always keep my word—then that's all I'm gonna charge. But you should understand that the economic situation is changing all the time and that prices must be adjusted accordingly. Turquoise alone's gone up five bucks a nugget, and sterling silver hasn't been getting any cheaper."

Durwood, who was openly sympathetic to this little man, said, "Hold on, sweetheart."

"Hold on, nothing!"

"Shhh," said Durwood as he turned to the merchant. "And how much are you asking for it now?"

He watched the man's eyes dart down to the necklace and up to the darkening sky. It was beginning to sprinkle.

"I was asking seventy-five for it, but—"

"Seventy-five!" Celia shouted. "Why, that's a fifty-percent increase!"

"Calm down, calm down," Durwood urged, nudging her as gently as he could. "I think seventy-five dollars is a perfectly reasonable price to pay for an original piece of jewelry as well made as this."

"But, Daddy—"

"Never mind, Celia . . . Seventy-five it is then. Fair is fair." He pulled out his wallet and counted out the amount in cash. "We'll need a receipt."

"Not only will I give you a receipt, sir, but I'll give you my card as well." The merchant was delighted. He looked around up and down the block. "Unlike most street vendors, I take a personal interest in satisfying my customers." Smiling, he hurriedly wrapped the necklace in colored gift-wrap tissue and tied it with yarn. "You have any trouble with it, any trouble whatsoever, just ring me at home or at my studio and we can work out an exchange or refund. I even do repairs for a modest fee. All I ask is if it works out and your friends get interested, please direct 'em to me. I'd appreciate the business."

Celia still looked ruffled, but Durwood couldn't imagine why.

The serious-eyed merchant—whose card announced his name, or rather, his title, as Morgan Lyle II, Creative Jewelry Maker—filled out a form receipt, which he handed to Durwood along with a ten-dollar bill.

"Please accept this," he said.

"But I don't understand . . . What's it for?"

"For your trusting attitude and for your trouble, sir."

"But I thought we'd settled on seventy-five dollars."

"Yes, so we did, but to soothe my inner conscience for causing your lovely daughter so much discomfort, I'm *not* going to charge you any state tax—which at six-and-a-half percent would come to over four bucks. I'm also going to deduct an additional ten for making me feel good by your show of confidence in me and my work."

"Wow," Celia drawled sarcastically, "how decent of you!"

"It's been a privilege doing business with you," said Durwood, meaning every word, as he reached to shake the gentleman's hand. "It's rare these days, Mr. Lyle, to meet someone of your ethical caliber."

"I appreciate that, sir. I really do." Lyle was addressing Durwood but looking at Celia. "I didn't go into this business to make a fast buck. I went into it because I love the work. I like working with my hands. That gives me a lot of satisfaction, and I want the public to enjoy what I do. Now, if I'd only wanted to make money, I would've stayed in show biz. I used to do bit parts down there in Hollywood . . . in the old days."

"You mean, *you've* been in movies?" said Celia, all eyes now.

"Played in dozens of movies, been on the radio, and before that, on the stage. I was practically born on stage."

"What movies you been in?" Celia wanted to know.

"I'd tell you all about it, but it's starting to rain. And if I don't get my stuff packed and put away, then I really will be asking for trouble."

"Can't you even tell us the names of a couple of films? Some of them might be playing on television."

"Celia, be quiet and leave the man alone. Thanks again, Mr. Morgan."

"The name's Lyle, but that's all right. I've been called worse. I hope your mother enjoys her necklace, young lady—and, sir . . ."

"The name is Knight."

"I know who you are. Durwood Knight, right? I figured you'd just as soon be treated like regular, everyday folks now that you're in retirement."

"Well, I'm not exactly in retirement."

"Oh, I know that too. I was reading somewhere—maybe it was in Herb Caen's column—that you're going into another line of work, just like I chose to. May it prevail, and may you and your family enjoy a safe and sane Christmas and, as the saying goes, a prosperous New Year."

"You took the words out of my mouth," said Durwood as Celia gave him a disgusted look.

"All that stiff, formal talk," Celia was saying, "that you and that street seller were carrying on back there. Yuchhh!"

"Precious, as I've tried to tell you so many times, there's a time to be loose and relaxed and informal, and a time to be formal and for real and polite."

"But, Daddy, he was jiving you! He was putting you on, and you didn't even see it."

"What couldn't I see?" He was navigating his way through serious rain.

"You couldn't even see how he was trying to get out of the promise he made me. He promised he'd sell me this necklace for fifty bucks, and then—just because he saw how well-dressed and polite you were, and he knew who you were—he switched the price."

"*Switched* the price?"

"Sure, he figured he had him somebody who wouldn't mind paying more money for something that probably should've only been twenty or thirty dollars in the first place."

"That sounds good the way you say it, honey, but you're forgetting something."

"What?"

"He already had the necklace tagged at seventy-five by the time we got there."

"Well, sure, he knew we were coming. I told him I'd be back to have you take a look at the thing before I bought it. What I wanna know is how could you fall for anything that shaky?"

"Celia, the man was good to us."

"I don't understand you, Dad."

"I never thought you did."

"Well, I thought I did when I was little, but I'm not so sure about that now. You used to be this big hero of mine. I figured you could do no wrong. I was hypnotized by your image, I guess."

"And how have I changed?"

"I don't know. Maybe Mom is right."

"And what does *Mom* say?"

"She says you're too easygoing. You'd be a big star if you weren't. You'd be right up there with Bill Russell and all the greats. You never would push. You're too easy, a pushover. You trust everybody. When they gave you bad contracts, you didn't complain. Team owners would beat you out of money you knew you rightfully had coming, and you never even—"

"Shut the fuck up," said Durwood, swerving suddenly to avoid hitting a stray dog, a wet and tan husky, vaguely familiar.

"That's Mouka!" Celia was hysterical. "Dad, watch out!"

"Who?"

"Mouka, the Matsons' dog!"

"What the hell is he doing crossing the street in the rain? Why isn't he at home? Don't they take care of him?"

"You don't have to swear at me!" she cried.

"Who's swearing?" he yelled.

"You just swore at me. You said—"

"Never mind what I said. I just don't need you sitting here in this miserable car, telling me about all this goddamn hearsay you don't know shit about! Easygoing! Shit! You sound like some parrot your mother trained. Nobody lasts in the sports world for as long as I did by being easygoing. I worked my ass off, and let me tell you something else while I'm—"

"Daddy, would you please keep your eyes on the road?"

"You know," he bellowed on, "it just so happens you've been very protected, *very* protected. I've tried to raise you decent and shield you from the facts of life that you still aren't anywhere near being ready for. But now, since you're so goddamn brilliant and think you know everything—"

"I wish you'd stop using that kinda language!"

They were headed uphill on 16th Street now and barely making it. Durwood knew that the car needed work, but—considering all the discomfort and inconvenience it'd been causing him since Thanksgiving, and even before then—he had no intention of putting anything into it beyond gas, oil, and water.

"I'm sorry," he said suddenly. "I'll try and cool down. I didn't mean to lose my temper, and . . . and I'm sorry you've got this low opinion of me, even if it is all wrong. On the other hand, I'm glad you finally got around to coming right out and telling me to my face what's been on your mind."

"I didn't mean a word I said." Celia's voice was trembling.

"You expect me to believe that, don't you?" Durwood asked, reaching for a tissue in the glove compartment.

"Daddy, I *said* I didn't mean any of that stuff."

"If you didn't mean it, then why did you say it?"

"It was . . . I was just—" Celia blew her nose into the tissue Durwood handed her and helped herself to another one. "I just wonder sometimes how you really feel about us. I mean, you're always complaining. I get the idea you think you might've been better off if you'd never gotten married."

"Celia, what makes you think I don't care about you guys? I love you. Can't you see that?"

"Oh, I don't know . . . It's a feeling I get sometimes when I feel like we're a burden to you . . . Me, especially."

Durwood remembered his brother Clarence voicing the same complaint at the dinner table once. How old were they then? Eleven and thirteen? Twelve and fourteen? Clarence was looking depressed. When Pops asked him what the matter was, Clarence groaned that he didn't feel loved. Gertrude, their mother, pulled a long face; her eyes moistened. Durwood, in his rolled-up Levi's and sweatshirt, felt embarrassed because he couldn't see what Clarence was getting at. Artie Knight, however, seemed relieved that this question finally had come up. He leaned back in his high-backed chair at the head of the table and touched his napkin to his lips. When he took the napkin away, there was an odd twist to his mouth under that big Teddy Roosevelt mustache.

"If I didn't love you," Durwood told Celia, parroting what Pops had told Clarence that evening, "do you think I'd let you sit at our table and put away all that food every day?"

He paused to watch this sink in, but all Celia did was sigh and shake her head.

"If I didn't love you," Durwood went on, high on how he was sounding to himself now, "do you think I'd keep letting you run me down the way you seem to like doing? Would I be encouraging you in your music and studies? Do you think, if I didn't like marriage or want children, that I'd keep trying to maintain a household where you and Nissa and your mother feel comfortable? Dixie doesn't even have to work. You don't have to work. When I was your age, I was already working my second job—"

"I know," she said, "delivering groceries for Slim Clement's Grocery Store. And you saved your money, five dollars a week with tips, and with that money you bought a brand-new car, and—"

"I can do without your mocking me, young lady!"

"'Young lady,'" she whined. "Now you're sounding like that con man that sold you the necklace. 'Young lady,' yuchhh!"

"Listen, I don't wanna hear anything else about that man. You're too young to know that people like him aren't easy to come by anymore. All people care about now is making the biggest profit in the shortest time with the tiniest investment. That's what's the matter with the United States of America today. Everybody's looking to make a killing. They don't care how. They don't care about the meaning of it, or the quality or importance or value, none of that stuff. You take when I was a kid and we got the money together to go catch a pro sports game—we'd root for the home team and the home players every time. That meant something. Now they'll buy up a whole team and move it from one city to the next and think nothing of it. And the poor suckers that make up the team, they get shifted around from team to team and town to town like cattle. Roots? What is that? Team owners—most of 'em anyway; Frank was an exception—team owners, what'd they care about your home life? Your cute little family? Trying to set down roots someplace?"

"Which is why we had to move from Cleveland, then to San Francisco, and all my old friends got blown away."

"Right, you know what I'm talking about. But we haven't moved since, have we? And you know why? Because nasty, old, good-for-nothing Daddy wanted his family to stay put, that's why. I could've socked away a whole lot more money every year if I'd been willing to relocate back East again, but I didn't. You didn't know that, did you? I cared enough about the family to pass that up. Money wasn't everything. That's how come I don't want you saying anything else negative in my presence about Mr. Morgan."

"You mean, Mr. Lyle?"

"Don't interrupt me until I'm finished. I've got a deep gut feeling about him. I know he's a good man."

"A good man," said Celia, sniffing. "What does that mean?" She sniffed again. "Hey, what do I smell?"

"What's it smell like?"

At last they were turning onto Dolores, their street, with only two more blocks to go.

"Smells," she told him, "like something's burning."

Durwood rolled down the window. "I don't smell anything."

"Daddy, it's inside the car, not out there in the rain."

It was one of Durwood's sinus days. He couldn't smell worth a damn. Even so, he stiffened when he saw smoke coming from under the dashboard.

"Daddy!" Celia shrieked and grabbed his arm. "The car's on fire! It's gonna blow up!"

In his softest, smoothest, coolest voice, he said, "Sweetheart, let go of my arm. You're gonna cause me to have an accident."

"But the car's gonna explode!"

"It isn't gonna explode." Durwood was praying that they'd be able to make it as far as their driveway, a block away. The radio had gone out and his headlights were flickering. Celia's new tears and the tom-tom thump of his own heart made him decide not to chance it. He pulled over to the closest empty curb space and turned the ignition off fast.

Breathing out slowly, Durwood turned to Celia and said, "See, what'd I tell you? It didn't blow up, did it?"

"But it was going to."

"Going to and did are two different things."

"What do you think the problem is?"

"The electrical system. I never had it fixed."

"Why didn't you, Dad?"

"Now, with all the excitement we've been having around here, I'm entitled to overlook a few little things, aren't I?"

"Depends on what you mean by 'little things.' How're we gonna get to the house with it storming like this?"

"The same way people have been doing since time immemorial . . . We grab our belongings, open the door, and run like crazy!"

"Very funny," said Celia, still sulking with her arms folded.

"Glad you think so. I don't think it's funny at all. But maybe we should look at it from your point of view. Now, say, the car's blown up and wiped us both out. We're dead now, hobbling around heaven on crutches and—"

"C'mon, Dad, cut it out."

He grabbed the wrapped necklace, put it under his coat, and said, "Why don't you leave the bookbag here in the car overnight so your things don't get soaked?"

"But there's something in it I'll be needing."

"Homework?"

"Well, sort of. It's a notebook I'm keeping."

"For school?"

"No, for me—for nobody to read but me."

A chill passed over Durwood as he began looking around the floor in back for something Celia could wrap her bookbag in. He was relieved to see a discarded plastic sack with orange peels in it.

"Stick it in here," he said, "and let's go."

As they made the dash across the street and up the sidewalk toward their house, Durwood laughed when he realized how much fun he was having. But when he saw how tightly Celia was clutching the bulging sack to her bosom as she hustled along in the drenching rain beside him, he caught himself feeling like some kind of lightweight spy.

21

DIXIE, OF COURSE, WANTED TO KNOW why they were so soaked. Dinner was getting cold. The Vega wasn't doing so hot. The hot-water heater in the back hall was acting up again. The paper boy got fresh with her this afternoon when he came to collect for the month. Nissa was coming down with diarrhea. Jenny's husband, Oscar, just got laid off, and they both seemed to have a touch of some virus that's been going around; maybe it's the same thing Nissa had—anyway, they've been thinking of moving back down to San Bernardino to help manage the family chain of hardware stores. Corky Ski called. And a man from the IRS—could Durwood please return his call after dinner? Oh, yes, and speaking of calls, could he come to the phone right away? She almost forgot. Texas was on the line.

It was Artie Knight, Durwood's father. After a quick hello and how-are-things?—delivered in rich, throaty, Texas tones—he got right down to business. The last thing in the world he wanted to do was impose on Durwood and Dixie, but Mama wasn't in the best of shape and wanted badly to see the grandchildren. After all, since his retirement, Durwood wasn't traveling around the country playing ball the way he used to, and they didn't get to see him or Dixie or the kids much anymore. He and Mama didn't need money or anything like that, but—if it wasn't an inconvenience or an imposition—they *would* like to fly up and spend Christmas week with them.

Drenched and exhausted, Durwood stood at the kitchen wall phone not knowing what to say, wishing that his father had worked up to the subject gradually instead of hitting him with it pointblank in a very weak moment at the wrongest of times. He knew right off that Dixie wasn't going to go for it. He also knew that the last thing he needed at holiday time was house guests, even if they happened to be his own parents. It was worse than being under house arrest. Already he could feel himself being slowly smothered, jammed between a rock and a hard place—damned if he did and damned if he didn't.

On the other hand, the kids really did need to see more of their grandparents, his folks, his side of the family. They already had been overexposed, in his opinion, to Dixie's people and their stiff, saditty ways. Let Artie and Gertrude come right on! It would be tough, no denying that, but it would be a short, merciful visit that Mama and Pops probably would cherish. Somehow it all would work out, with effort, if he went ahead and said yes. Within seconds, these conflicting impulses that were sapping his already weary circuitry were resolved and translated into speech.

"Pops, we'd be delighted to have you. Just be sure to write and let us know when you plan to arrive so one of us can be at the airport to pick you up."

"That's good news for us, Woody. Hey, by the way, has the shop opened yet?"

"Not till the first of the year."

"Good, good. Maybe I'll be your first customer. Don't be shy about asking my advice on anything. Can't say I know much about the record business, but I did run a shop, don't forget, for forty-some years."

"Don't worry, Pops, I need all the advice I can get." He knew he was expected to ask to speak to Mama. Time and his condition were so pressing, though, that he slyly circumvented that little trap by saying, "Tell Mama I love her. I hope she and the doctors can keep that arthritis and diabetes under control. We'll take good care of both of you here. Tell Mama Dixie's just put dinner on the table and doesn't want it to get cold."

"Yeah, I know what you mean. Dixie told us she was waiting on y'all to get home so she could serve supper. I understand, so I'll sign off. Give everybody a great big hug and kiss for us. It'll be so good to see you again."

"Same here, Pops, same here. Good night."

Sullen, Celia didn't talk much at dinner. She ate more than she should have of Dixie's tamale pie and excused herself early.

"Aren't you going to stick around for dessert?" her mother asked.

"No," she pouted and pushed her chair back from the table dramatically. "I've already gorged myself on misery. I think I'd best go upstairs and contemplate."

"Contemplate?" said Durwood.

"You've been awfully moody this evening, dear," said Dixie. "Are you upset about anything in particular?"

"You can take that up with Daddy. Good evening."

Just before reaching the staircase, Celia paused and half-shouted, "That was a great meal, Mom. I hope there'll be enough for leftovers tomorrow. I love your tamale pie."

"You weren't eating like you were thinking about leftovers," said Durwood. "Better leave a note on the fridge so Leon'll know."

"I was talking to Mom, if you don't mind!"

"Well, e*xcuse* me!"

When she was gone, Dixie leaned across the table and asked Durwood, "Can you tell me what that was all about?"

"It's complicated, baby, very complicated. I think she's sore at me."

"What did you do?"

"I'm not sure. She's a hard little lady to please."

"So I've noticed, but what happened?"

"I'd rather not say."

"Have you hurt her feelings?"

"I'm always hurting her feelings. I say good morning to her and her feelings are hurt. I do her a favor and I hurt her feelings. I can't win."

"Can you be more specific?"

"No, I can't. We had an argument in the car on the way over here."

"What was it about?"

"I'm sorry, Dixie, but I can't tell you."

"And why not?"

"Because it's something between us. She'll be all right. Let her get a good night's sleep, then we'll start all over again. It's nothing to worry about."

Dixie didn't look as if she believed him, but all she said was, "Well, if you say so. Why don't you help me clear the table for dessert?"

"What is it tonight?"
"Spumoni and fresh fruit."
"And is there any cognac left?"
"I think so."
"I could use a swallow, maybe two."
"What's the matter with you?"
"Nothing that a few weeks on the road wouldn't cure."
"And what do you mean by that?" Dixie was on her feet now, like him, gathering plates, glasses, crumpled napkins, salt and pepper shakers.
"It don't mean a thing, Dixie, it don't mean a thing. Not much does anymore, you know."
"And what was your father talking about, Woody?"
"You'd be surprised."
"Betcha I wouldn't. Your folks are thinking of paying a visit, aren't they?"
"What seems to be the trouble with the hot-water heater?" he asked, partly to appear lighthearted and partly to change the subject.
"I'm right, aren't I? They'll be coming out to spend Christmas with us, won't they?"
"Can't we enjoy the rest of the meal? We've got the whole evening ahead of us to argue."
"I knew it had to be something like that, I just knew it!"
"Dixie, can we postpone this for the time being? I'm not up for it."
"All I can say is you better start getting up for it. They'll be here before you know it. And I don't intend to be spending all my precious time chauffeuring them around, either."
"*Your* precious time? What about *my* precious time? I know I don't count for much around here anymore. I only bust my ass to keep the bills paid."
"Now, here you come again with that suffering martyr stuff—which is one strong reason for my making the decision I did."
"What decision is that?"
"I'm applying to law school."
"You . . . You're what?"
"You heard me, I'm—"

There was a crash as the stack of plates Durwood had been holding slipped and shattered into thousands of pieces, which he would later—after taking a slug of brandy straight from the bottle—sweep up with a bad plastic broom into a dustpan and jiggle, load after load, into the overfed garbage pail shuttered under the sink.

"What is this?" Durwood asked. "A conspiracy?" They were all but argued out and laid out too. He was chugging the last of his brandy at bedside.

"And why does everything that happens around here have to be some kind of conspiracy with you?" Dixie was already half-asleep by now and about as appealing to Durwood in her saltiness as a freshly netted sea otter.

"Because that's what it is, that's why. There's always something going on to foul me up. Right now it just happens to be the Christmas Conspiracy. Happens every year without fail. I ducked it for the longest while I was out there playing ball, but now it's coming back home. It's bunching back up on me to make up for all that time I wasn't paying any real dues."

"You know what you are, Durwood Knight?" Dixie's fake laugh almost disgusted him. "You're crazy, that's what you are. You are crazy and you are drunk and I am sleepy. Good night."

"Okay, I'm crazy, okay. Yeah, maybe I am. Any responsible man is crazy these days if he just happens to believe that the best person to have at home looking after his kids is the mother of those kids."

"Really, Durwood. I never thought I'd hear that old corny line tumble out of your mouth. I knew all along that's what you must've been thinking, but I never thought I would hear you *say* it."

"We men suffer, too, you know," he added as he snapped off the lamp.

"Aren't you even going to brush your teeth?"

"I already brushed them."

"But you've got brandy all over your breath."

"So what? I wouldn't care if I had hair tonic on my breath. I'm not brushing my teeth anymore."

"Now, that's just what the dentist told you. Said you were

gonna fool around and mess up your gums again by not taking care of your mouth. You went and shelled out all that money for periodontic surgery for nothing."

"Hell, it's *my* money."

"We know, Durwood. We know it's *your* money. All we are is wards in your goddamn castle. Now, do you mind if I get a little sleep, sir, in this big hotel you're running?"

"Hotel is right!" he snapped, sitting up. "That's what I run, all right—a hotel. And not even a first-class hotel."

"Look, if you'd sit down for a minute and study the scene around here, you wouldn't keep saying dumb shit like that."

"What do you mean? I'm here all the time, it seems like to me."

"I know it might *seem* like that to you, but there's plenty going *right*—forget about what's *wrong*. You hurt my feelings when you distort things like that."

Dixie's voice was growing trembly, and, even in the dark, Durwood knew what her eyes must be doing. This wasn't going to be an easy one to wind down. Dixie had been right: he *was* drunk and digging it. Drunk and probably crazy—everybody else was!—and ready to settle into one long, sloppy harangue until she started to turn on the tears.

"I mean, it's nice that you're gonna try to make the shop work, but that's all you think about. That and feeling sorry for yourself all the time. You're either over there with Brewster and Mitzi getting the damn place together, or else you two are bouncing in and out of banks and insurance companies, begging and borrowing, or else you're jogging or at your attorney's or goofing off with Leon or complaining about the car or complaining about your neck, or—"

"Hold it, hold it! I don't need to hear about all that . . . Get to the point. I'd forgotten how bad my neck still hurts until you had to go and bring it up. Which reminds me, the car's in bad shape. It burnt out on us."

"Burnt out on you!" Now it was Dixie's turn to be alarmed.

"We managed to coast as close to the house as we could get, but Triple A's gonna have to come out and tow it to Ace Auto first thing in the morning. The electrical system's shot, and we're lucky to even be here."

"You mean to tell me you're just now getting around to telling me that? That's why that child was so edgy at dinner. It must've frightened her half to death!"

"I don't think that's what she was upset about."

"All I know is she was awful."

"We got into a heavy discussion."

"What about?"

"Nothing. Nothing I care to discuss now."

"You never want to discuss a goddamn thing. Where the hell have you gone to? Busy as you were, you used to be accessible and want to talk about things. What's happening to you? What did you and Celia fight about?"

"I never said we fought. I said we got into a heavy discussion. Nothing new. I'm too inadequate for her. I don't push hard enough. I'm a fool, a chump. She sounds like you."

"I've never said any of that about you."

"Oh, no?" Durwood could have lit into her here, mauled her with words and shouted her down, but he knew the moves too well by now to get himself into that play where nobody scored any points in the end. "Hey," he said, "good night."

"You peanut-headed fool!" Dixie whimpered and turned to cry into her pillow. Tears still tore him up.

"Listen, Dixie," he said, "we're both tired, okay? Just let me get some zzz's and wake up fresh and start all over again. The situation never looks as bad in the morning as it does in the middle of the night."

"You'll never appreciate me . . . and all I've been through for you . . . And your daughters need you, Durwood. You keep forgetting that."

Now, what did that mean? Why was she squeezing all of that in now? Maybe he was getting to be just a little bit dotty. Dixie might be right again. He needed to slow down and look at some of this stuff coming at him. Was he pushing too hard, not analyzing his moves enough? Yeah, he needed to kick back, right here in the middle of this holiday sabotage, and study what had been happening in slowed-motion instant replay.

Still sniffly, Dixie asked, "Do you think they can fix the car in time for us to take it to the Dickens Fair this weekend?"

"I don't know," Durwood grumbled. "I just hope they can fix

it before the weekend. I've got some hauling to do tomorrow that I'm gonna have to cancel."

"Hauling what?"

"Fixtures for the shop—electrical doodads."

"Well, you know, there's leaves and stuff stacked up in the backyard that's been there for weeks and need to be taken to the dump."

And with that, Dixie turned on her side, poking her warm behind squarely up against Durwood's full belly. He was glad when her quiet sobs evolved into a light snore that the guilty part of him couldn't help but translate as her saying, *Take some of your own medicine, you noisy, sleep-wrecking bastard!*

THAT MORNING, EVEN THOUGH THE RAIN had stopped, Durwood skipped his usual run, something he rarely did in passable weather. There was just too much to get done. He had to get the Ford to the mechanic, rent another car, make a trip across town for the electrical fixtures, and attend to several other details, including some Christmas shopping, that made his head hurt. He rode up front in the cab with the tow-truck driver while they hauled the car to the shop. The driver was surly and, unlike most strangers, unimpressed with Durwood's height or former profession.

"Oh, yeah, that's right," he said, snuffing out a cigarette in the dashboard ashtray, "you used to play guard with the Beanstalks, didn't you? Nothing personal, Mr. Knight, but I never cared much for the team myself. They forced it down our throats anyway, you know—the city did. The city put that one over on us, working in cahoots with the Chamber of Commerce and the sports tycoons. You ever read this guy Charles McCabe, writes for the *Chronicle*? Well, you check a column he did back here a week ago on that very subject. He really covers that action, used to be a sports commentator. We needed the Stalks like New Mexico needs sand. He was right on the money. I clipped it."

"What was it about the Stalks you didn't like?"

"What *was* it I *didn't* like? You talk as if it ain't still going on, Mr. Knight. Just because you quit playing for the fuckers don't mean they've gone outta business and packed up and left town. Where you been, man?"

"The shop's just around the corner here, in the middle of the block. You wanna make a left."

"Hey, I know where Ace Auto is. I haul a dozen cars a week to that joint, the arrogant shits!"

"So you don't like them either, eh?"

"Lookit, the trouble with the Stalks is they're all show and no guts. I mean, real guts, like the Warriors, the Nets, or the Jazz. Nothing personal, like I say, but I always thought you had too much class to be wasting your time with those clowns—Gene 'Genetic Action' Jones, Bunchy Holmes, Corky Ski, all those amateurs."

"Watch it," said Durwood, holding up an admonishing finger, "you're bad-rapping some of my best buddies, you know."

"Oh, I'm sure they're all nice, neat guys off the court, but they can't play basketball for shit."

"Aw, come on, they can't be that bad. Those guys've got records. Gene Jones still holds the Western Division record for career scoring."

"Like I say, Mr. Knight, I got no grudge against any of 'em outside of the fact that when you get 'em all together they just somehow lack that hard-playing heart I go for in the game. Of course, I'm a big collegiate fan myself. You catch that Stanford–USC game Friday night? Now, that was basketball."

"You really follow the game, don't you?"

"I keep up some. Working nights like I do sometimes doesn't help. Well, here we are. And you wanna know something? The worst thing that ever happened to you in your career, if you ask me—which I know you didn't—was to leave Cleveland. You didn't have to, did you?"

"For my family, yes, I had to."

"Oh, I see. You needed more bread, right? Well, I can understand that, but you should've been contracted out to some team with a little more pluck. Hey, did I give you your Triple A membership card back?"

Durwood patted his jacket pocket and opened the truck door. "Oh, yes, it's right here. Thanks for all the good cheer."

"Big deal," said the driver, getting out too. "Hope I didn't hurt your feelings, but I'm the kinda guy has to talk to people real straight, you know what I mean? What's the use of bullshitting you and you bullshitting me? There's enough of that stuff going on twenty-four hours around the clock."

"Gotcha," said Durwood, puzzled that he didn't feel at all upset.

For the first time, as he watched the driver walk around to lower and unhitch the Ford, Durwood noticed that this bullish little man had a game leg and wore an elevated shoe on that particular foot.

In a rented Dodge Dart, he drove directly to the store to make his call. Since Brewster and Mitzi hadn't arrived, he relaxed, glad for the chance to be alone in the place with nobody looking over his shoulder while he checked out the situation and thought about what really still needed to be done.

Like most tax-paying citizens, Durwood always became more than a little nervous when it came to the IRS. He didn't like them intruding into his life one bit, and especially not when tax time was still a good three months away. He understood that they weren't about to kick down his front door and come rushing into the house with guns ablazing, but he also cherished the idea of having as little to do with them as possible. What could they possibly be calling him about anyway? He had kept right on top of his quarterly estimate payments.

"I'm sorry, Mr. Knight," said the voice at his ear, a smooth, female, functionary voice, pleasant enough but quietly on edge. "I've checked our directory from A to Z. There's no Mr. Ketchum that works for Internal Revenue. Perhaps you've confused us with the State Franchise Tax Board. They're up in Sacramento, and the number there is—"

"Wait, he called my house yesterday while I was out, and my wife took the message. It said to phone a Mr. Ketchum at the Internal Revenue Service by no later than eleven-thirty this morning."

"But, sir, I've checked the directory, and there isn't anyone with a last name that even vaguely resembles Ketchum in it."

"But there must be some mistake."

"If you'd care to speak with my supervisor, her name is Beulah Martínez. I'd be happy to connect you with her."

"That won't be necessary. I believe you. All I'd like to know is who would call up and leave a message like that?"

"Sorry, Mr. Knight, but I can't help you there. It's that time of year again, as you know. Perhaps you have some friends who are playing a joke on you. Lots of people, like, you take your stand-up comedians, they think income tax and the IRS are funny."

"No, I don't think you're funny at all. And I don't think this joke—if it is a joke—is very funny either."

"Nor do I, Mr. Knight. There are other people waiting on other lines. Is there anything else I can do for you?"

"No, thank you."

Durwood hung up feeling stupid and uneasy. Was he beginning to, well, could it be that he was starting to slip, just a little maybe? He leaned back in his chair and poked his hands in his jean jacket, the same one he had worn on the afternoon of the Shriners Hospital visit. Of all things, he thought for a long time about Celia playing guitar and wanting to get a record made. He thought about Dixie and Nissa at home alone now—Dixie, with diarrhea and doctors on her mind.

Then he slipped, for a few heartbeats, into a warm, bathlike daydream of himself as SuperDad, the man who stays home and does nothing but look after the practical, emotional, and spiritual needs of his wife and children. SuperDad is concerned with nothing else. Somehow, in this flickering fantasy, rude first-of-the-month realities don't even come into the picture. Bills get paid by some angel—his old team owner, maybe—and they all mature and grow old and strong with long, leisurely, semi-annual vacations in the mountains or by the sea. They travel, too, whenever they feel the urge, without benefit of maids or governesses, and comfortably take in Lagos, Accra, Cairo, Rio de Janeiro, Tokyo, Kingston, Port-au-Prince, Amsterdam, Rome, Madrid, London.

Snapping back, Durwood found himself looking at all the sports posters stacked up on his office desk waiting to be hung on the walls out front. That was *his* idea, not Brewster's. Knight and Day was going to be classy, the coming thing: an offbeat little shop that stocked, not one, but two leisure-time items. It would be a way of distinguishing the place and, ultimately, further justifying its name. Yeah, he had plans for Knight and Day Record Setters. They were going to do all right, just fine, so long as he could keep believing in himself and Brewster and in what they were trying to do.

He leaned back, letting his mind wander this way in the luxurious emptiness of the store while his fingers fondled the edges of a fat chunk of paper inside one of his coat pockets. Curious, he pulled it out and saw that it was a sealed envelope—the one that the girl in the hospital ward had made him promise to open and read. Embarrassed that he had forgotten, he dropped it onto the desk in front of him and carefully peeled back the Scotch-taped flap. It was a letter written very neatly in a large hand, straight up and down, with little circles over each lower-case *i* and at the end of every sentence. He glanced at the opening—"Dear Mr. Durwood Knight"—and then flipped through the pages to see how long it ran on. The letter itself was only a page and a half; the rest looked like poems or something. Ever since the day he had gotten a note from some loon wishing him a bad fall that would lay him up for the rest of the season, he was ready for anything when it came to letters from the public.

Dear Mr. Durwood Knight,
  I have two requests but you don't have to take this too seriously since I know how busy you celebrities be.
  First I would like to dedicate these poems to you (all of them). You don't even have to answer me about them unless you feel like it. Please. Just read them.
  Second I would like to ask something unusual by way of that other request. My dream is to spend one Christmas Day in the home of somebody

successful such as yourself and your fabulous family. I know this might sound impossible and like I'm trying to force myself off on you for a Christmas meal but it isn't like that. It just so happens that my Dad who is all I got now that my Mother died is in the hospital himself this year. He got hurt real bad in a street accident in Richmond. My Uncle and Aunt who usually help him out taking care of me they have to be in L.A. for a big wedding. I could spend Christmas at the Shriners here but I know I would feel pretty lonesome if I did that.

You are probably asking yourself why I picked you and I know how bold I must seem like to you. I picked you because I know somehow deep down that you won't turn me down.

Honest I don't have much to offer in return but I hope you get to the poems soon and see how they go so you can form a reaction. Mr. Knight I know you are a kind man so I hope you don't just throw this in the waist basket along with the rest of your junk mail. I can't wait to hear from you soon.

Yours sincerely,
Midge Morningstar McHenry

Durwood was still pulling himself together and had gotten as far as the second of five poems when Brewster bounced in looking bewildered and harassed.

Brewster took one look at Durwood and said, "I don't know who's in worse shape, you or me. What's the matter, man? You look like you spent the night with a bedful of boogie women."

"You should talk. You kinda look like you've been taking boogie-man lessons yourself."

"I just spent the last hour trying to dig up some bread."

"But, Brewster, we've already borrowed more money for this thing than we can ever pay back. Don't you know when to stop?"

"Take it easy, Wood. I'm talking about some other money, some money that's mine."

"What money you talking about?"

"The bathroom money."

"Bathroom money? What bathroom money? What the hell are you talking about?"

"I had a hundred dollars in fives at the bottom of my laundry hamper, which I keep in the bathroom . . . and now it's gone."

"But why would anybody—" Durwood caught himself as he remembered all the times he'd absent-mindedly watched

Brewster play with paper money stashed along shelves behind books, tucked away in drawers, and even rolled up into clean pairs of socks. So why not at the bottom of the dirty-clothes basket?

"I took the bathroom apart, looked everywhere, and I still can't find it. Nobody's been in there but Mitzi, and I know she wouldn't be rummaging around in the dirty clothes. At least, I don't think she would."

They sized up one another. Durwood was the first one to laugh. "Tell me, Brewster, and you don't have to answer this if you don't want to, but—"

"But what?"

"No, forget it. I don't even wanna know."

For a moment, he thought that Brewster might come out and offer some explanation for his strange habits and behavior where cash money was concerned. But Brewster did no such thing. He walked over, stood behind Durwood, and looked over his shoulder at the pages in his hand.

"What's that?"

"A letter and some poems from a girl—she's probably around ten—at the Shriners."

"What's she talking about?"

"She wants to have Christmas dinner with me and my family."

"Oh, yeah? What's she look like?"

"How come you wanna know that?"

"Curious, Wood, just curious."

"Oh, she's brown-skinned and curly-haired with one bad arm."

"What's wrong with her arm?"

"Well, it's shriveled up, sort of."

"Oh, I see. Is she photogenic?"

"She's got a wonderful face—warm, cute, and very expressive. But what do you have to know all this for?"

"I don't know, Wood. It's just an angle, that's all. I've been trying to hit on some new public-relations angles for the store when we open up next month."

"Well, I certainly hope you aren't planning on using this child in connection with any publicity plans you might have. She's only a sad little girl with a physical handicap. I won't let you go exploiting her."

"Just being inquisitive, man. No harm in that, is there? By the way, are you gonna have her over for dinner like she wants you to?"

Durwood passed Brewster the letter to read for himself. There was something in him that got a small charge out of watching his partner's face go from smart-aleck curiosity to sincere concern as he scanned the curlicue handwriting.

"That's pretty heavy," said Brewster. "How's her poetry?"

"Heavier than the letter. She seems to know a lot for somebody her age."

"I was like that too."

"Like what?"

"Didn't you go through a thing when you were a kid where you had to be out of school for a long time—out sick, say, for a couple of months—and when you came back you knew a whole lot more than the other kids? You'd just plumb got smart. And you know how it happened? It happened when you kicked back and read what you wanted to read and watched what you wanted to watch; like, you looked at everything that was going on and put it all together—one, two, three. By the time you got back, you knew everything sort of by osmosis, and the rest of the kids couldn't figure you out. That was at Barrett Junior High, back in Philly."

"Yeah, there was a joker like that in my high school in Texas. He was out with the flu when that was a big thing, and then he came down with the measles on top of that—the last kid in public school to get the measles, and he came back a monster!"

"That's all I'm talking about. I'll bet this Midge McHenry is a monster too. You really oughtta think about tying her into a media stunt where she'd be our first customer and we'd have it video-taped where she's thanking you for that Christmas dinner and—"

"Just put it out of your mind, Brewster. I haven't even had time to really talk to the girl yet."

Thankfully, the phone rang. It was Mitzi.

THEY DIDN'T BOTHER COMING DRESSED in Victorian costume, but plenty of others did. As a compromise, however, Dixie, Celia, and even little Nissa had gotten themselves up in long dresses and shoulder shawls. It was a little like being on the set of a mammoth *David Copperfield* production that had gotten completely out of control.

Durwood, who hated mingling in crowds every bit as much as he loathed the savagery of Christmas, shuddered to think that he had postponed an informal luncheon with a big record wholesaler and a quiet Saturday-afternoon consultation with his lawyer to attend this bustling fair. As always, he kept rationalizing his participation in any of this hurly-burly by thinking, well, it's for the kids, it's for the kids!

"Do you know, Christmas is only two weeks away," said Dixie, "and we still haven't sent out a Christmas card?"

"I sent mine out," said Celia, "right after Thanksgiving."

"That's overdoing it, baby," said Dixie. "That's much too early."

"But it's over with, Mom."

"What are you driving at, Dixie?"

"What I'm driving at is there's a man over there selling the most tasteful cards I've seen in years—and I'd like to pick up about a hundred of them."

"And who's going to fill them out and address the envelopes this year?"

"We'll all take turns doing it. You can do some, I can do some, and Celia can do some. She's got such nice handwriting anyway."

"Flattery will get you nowhere," said Celia. "Like I said, I already sent out my cards. Why should I have to be punished for you guys being so slow?"

Nissa, whose eyes were all aglow, and who was holding her father's hand, said, "Daddy, can I have a balloon?"

Since it was such an innocuous request and had broken the gloomy turn the talk had taken, Durwood was only too eager to satisfy Nissa. While Celia and Dixie headed for the gaunt, terrier-haired greeting-card-seller's booth, Durwood rushed to buy his youngest her balloon.

The pink-cheeked blonde, dressed like Queen Victoria herself, pumped helium into the orange balloon Nissa selected, then tied its air end with string and the string to a small metal washer to keep the balloon from flying away. Nissa, overjoyed and grinning to show it, poked her ring finger into the hole. Seeing his child content made up for the outrageous price the balloon had cost Durwood.

Durwood caught up with the older females in time to find out that Celia wasn't all that crazy about the cards her mother had chosen.

"I'd like to do some last-minute personal shopping of my own," Celia announced in that haughty, grating way that made Durwood want to choke her. "Do you mind if I break off and do some private looking around?"

"Where do we meet up, and when?" asked Dixie.

"How about," said Durwood, "at the puppet show at three o'clock? Nissa will love that, and there's a place to eat close by."

"Solid," said Celia.

"What's this 'solid' stuff?" asked Dixie.

"Well, that's what Patsy's dad says all the time—and I like the way it sounds."

"Who do you still have to buy anything for?" Dixie wanted to know.

"For Moby."

"You got enough money?" asked Durwood.

"Moby isn't worth more than two or three dollars, and I've got that much."

"Will you be okay?"

"I'll be just fine, Mother. Just trust me, trust me for a change, all right?"

Durwood did a slow burn, but swatted Nissa's balloon to conceal it. He and Dixie watched their puzzling daughter amble off into the crowd.

"I've got a theory," Durwood said to Dixie.

"About what?" said Nissa.

"Why, Nissa," said Dixie, laughing, "you don't even know what a theory is."

"I do too, Mom. It's like an idea, isn't it?"

When Nissa first complained about how the washer was beginning to hurt her finger, her parents paid no attention. They were too busy getting caught up in the spectacle—and what a spectacle it was! Dixie was entranced with a display of Haitian folk art at a booth manned by a hefty black man in a Buckingham Palace guard outfit, while Durwood was across the way getting worked up into a lather over a shiny ingeniously designed stereo system that worked by remote control. The only thing that stopped him from plunking down the money for the system right then and there was his realization that he hadn't done any Christmas shopping yet for the rest of the family.

Durwood joined Dixie and Nissa in time to hear Nissa say, "My finger hurts. It really does."

"Then take the ring off, dear," said Dixie, obviously annoyed.

"But I can't. It won't budge."

"But did you try hard?" asked Durwood.

Nissa, whose eyes were growing watery, nodded to indicate that she had, indeed, been trying.

"Here, let me see it." Durwood knelt and took Nissa's left hand in his. Attempting to make a little game of it, he breathed softly on her fingers, made a funny face, and, in his tenderest voice, told her to take a deep breath and to count to ten.

"Daddy, how can I count while I'm holding my breath?"

"Never mind, just do it!"

"Hold your breath, dear," said Dixie. "Daddy'll take the ring off for you. I'll do the counting."

Nissa did as she was told. Durwood, working quickly and gently, tried to twist the washer off, but he couldn't get it to slip past the knuckle. The count was up, and Nissa was disappointed.

"What's wrong?" asked Dixie.

"Her finger's swollen up at the joint. I can't . . . well . . . it's hard to get off . . . just like she says."

"I told you, Daddy, I told you."

"Excuse me," said the Haitian folk-art salesman, a chunky, broad-faced man with a smile that, combined with his mustache, was winning. "I don't mean to get in your business, but you might want to take your little girl to the lavatory and rub some soap on her finger. That'll probably do the trick. I had that happen to a girl I knew once. Gave her a ring and changed my mind and couldn't get the sucker to come back off until I tried the soap trick. They got that slick, slimy gick here comes out of a dispenser. I'll betch any one of these paintings it'll work."

"Oh, thank you," said Durwood. "Nissa, Mommy's gonna take you to the bathroom."

"But I don't have to pee or make a B.M."

"Never mind, just go with her."

"Wait a minute," said Dixie, her eyes narrowing as she focused on the booth attendant, who wore a stick-on name tag that read: "Millard Chenault." "Mr. Chenault, did you mean that about . . . about the painting?"

"Hell, yeah . . . uh . . . excuse me. Yes, I did mean that. I'll . . ." Pausing, his face turned very serious as he thought about what he was about to risk. "Sure, absolutely. Come back here and tell me the soap solution doesn't work and you can pick a canvas, any canvas, and it'll be on the house, the house being *me* of course."

Dixie rushed off with Nissa, leaving Durwood to fake interest in the merchandise at hand. There was something about all of this so-called primitive art that got on his nerves. To begin with, he suspected the painters themselves of being brazen hustlers, although understandably so. The rice and flour sacks that many of the bright paintings were done on added to the hustling effect. Still, because he knew how poor and needy people were in Port-au-Prince and the Haitian countryside, he was toying with the idea of purchasing something cheap, one of those little canvases—no panoramic view of black and brown people planting greenery or picking fruit under a radiant, blue-skyed rainbow of sunshine, just a painting of a houngan alone with himself and the spirits.

"See anything you like?" asked Millard Chenault. "I know I don't have to tell you this, but Haiti was the first country in this hemisphere to revolt successfully and run the French out. It's a black country, brother, and even though the white people like to keep saying it's a dictatorship, well, at least it's *our* dictatorship for a change, if you know what I mean."

"Yeah, I know what you mean. It's like Uganda was."

"Now, wait a minute, sir. I'm only talking about this hemisphere—Haiti, not Africa. But when you think about it, Haiti's still got more African retentions, African-style living, than anyplace else in the West. It hasn't been watered down, you know. It's the real thing, brother. Say, don't you play basketball?"

Durwood wasn't ready to pick out *that* old thorn again. He said, "No, you're getting me confused with someone else."

"Oh, sorry."

When Dixie and Nissa got back, the washer was still on Nissa's finger. Nissa looked frightened, and her finger, though cleaner, looked redder and more swollen than ever to Durwood.

"It didn't work," Dixie said loudly, pretending to be talking to Durwood, but making certain Millard Chenault heard her every word.

"Now," said Chenault, "did you apply the soap and lubricate her finger real good?"

"I did better than that," said Dixie. "I smeared her whole hand *and* the washer with that gunk."

"Well," said Chenault, pursing his lips, "I've never been one to welch on a personal promise. Pick out a small painting you like and it's yours, anything within reason anyway. I really can't give away any of the bigger ones. My boss'd kill me."

Eyeing him fishily, Dixie said, "I was under the impression that you were the boss here."

"And that's correct."

"Then what do you mean, your boss would kill you?"

"I just might up and kill myself," he said, grinning sheepishly. "Perhaps you'd like to buy a painting as well . . . since the price is right."

Durwood could see that Dixie was pleased, but he was worried about Nissa and the whereabouts of her sister. Inspecting his daughter's tiny hand again, he noticed that the finger was growing inflamed at the crucial area. "Dixie," he said, "I think we should find out if there's a physician or first-aid person on duty that could help us."

Only too happy to direct their attention away from himself and his precious Haitian primitives, Chenault pointed eagerly toward the Cow Palace entrance and cleared his throat. "The first-aid station is right over there."

"Don't you go rushing off anyplace," said Dixie, eyeballing him and wagging her finger, "because I'm coming back for my painting."

They pushed through the dense, edgy crowd, Durwood moving so rapidly at one point to avoid being spotted that Dixie had to remind him that—unless he wanted to carry her on his back—Nissa simply couldn't hack the pace.

"Daddy, my legs aren't as long as yours!"

At last they found themselves in front of the only booth at the fair that wasn't decked out with cutesy-poo banners and theme-related trimmings. It vexed Durwood that the chesty, long-haired woman in attendance, whose eyes and teeth were big like Dixie's, was wearing a "Gay Is Here To Stay" button. They explained to her about the stuck washer. At first she repeated Chenault's soap trick, then tried using a little Vaseline. When that failed to work, the young woman wasted no time in suggesting that Nissa be taken to the emergency ward of San Francisco General, which happened to be right in the neighborhood.

"What's that?" Nissa asked.

"It's a very big hospital, dear," said Dixie.

Now Durwood really was beginning to come unglued. It was as if someone, malevolent and unknown, had put a mojo on him, a triple whammy, the real McCoy. "How're we gonna work this, Dix?"

"Simple. We'll bundle her up, hop in the car, drive her over there, and—"

"That isn't what I meant. Somebody's got to stay here and meet Celia, remember?"

"Oh, I see what you mean. Let's see . . ."

"Daddy can take me to the hospital, Mom, and you can stay and meet Celia."

"Oh? And why should Daddy be the one to take you to San Francisco General?"

"Because you like to shop and Daddy knows how to drive that shifty kinda car we rented."

Christmas, crowds, and hospitals—that was the triple whammy. Durwood's brother and grandmother both died in the same hospital in different Decembers. As they walked into the emergency ward, with its strong fluorescent lighting and heavy medicinal smell, memories the color of moonless nights in the piney woods were needling Durwood so rapidly and painfully that he lapsed without warning into immediate depression and, for a moment, thought he might have trouble breathing.

"What's wrong?" asked Nissa.

"Nothing, honey, I—"

"You feel sad, don't you? Don't worry, everything's gonna be all right."

"And . . . and how do you know that?"

"I just know, that's all."

Her sensitive toughness was a quality Nissa seemed to have been born with, and Durwood was proud of it. With some solid up-front guidance, he thought, this girl was going to get through this gangster-run world unscratched. Celia he wasn't so sure of, but Nissa was going to survive, flourish, and prosper.

Their wait among the pitiful casualties would have been a lot longer had it not been for a fat man whose wife had stabbed him in the foot with a butcher knife insisting, after conversing with them, that the little girl and her "sportsman" father go ahead of him.

"They know me pretty well around here," the man added, "cause me and Mattie takes turns comin in to get fixed up."

Once they were inside one of those little rooms where in no time they had Nissa sprawled face up on a papered table, Dr. Skolnick, a skinny man with a neat, professorial, graying goatee, said, "I want you to understand, Mr. Knight, that we're going to have to file it off. There's no other way. Your daughter's finger is too swollen now to do otherwise. I sent for Mr. Pappalardi, a very skillful paramedic who works with the police department, and he'll be here shortly."

"Why this particular person?"

"He's the best around for this sort of thing. He's sawed off quite a few handcuffs in his time, and he knows how to use that special tool. It's going to require some time, but you can help by sticking close by and reassuring your little girl that we aren't going to hurt her."

Swallowing hard, Durwood nodded his head slowly to indicate that he had no choice but to go along with it.

Nissa, trying to be brave but frightened to the point of near hysteria, cried and screamed as the man leaning over her from the back of her pillowed head sweated and sawed with his special file. While he worked, Durwood hovered over Nissa, holding her down, really, by the arms, talking to her, cracking jokes, nuzzling her plump little cheeks and neck with kisses and affection, tissuing beads of sweat from her tiny forehead. He felt as if he had betrayed her somehow.

"How can you let them do this to me, Daddy?"

"I know it seems like we're being mean, darling, but, honest to God, we're doing it all for you."

"You mean, you're hurting me for me? McDonald's does it all for you, too, but they don't go hurting people."

Nissa cried so much that she developed hiccups. Durwood actually was glad about that since it gave him something new to do. He could make a little game out of curing her.

After Mr. Pappalardi had filed halfway through the top edge of the washer, he turned to Dr. Skolnick and Durwood. "I'm switching tools now," he said. "This one's curved so I can get down in between her finger and the metal and saw from the center on up."

"The only problem here," Dr. Skolnick told Durwood, "is that since the blade is curved, the back of it—which is rounded and harmless, so don't worry—might sometimes press up against Nissa's finger and alarm her."

"You won't be scared one bit, will you, Nissa?"

"About what, Daddy?"

"About any of this."

"I'm gonna try. Will they be finished soon?"

"Very soon," said Mr. Pappalardi.

"Relatively soon anyway," said Dr. Skolnick.

"Daddy," Nissa asked, hiccupping between sobs, "what are they talking about?"

"Instead of that, angel, ask me what's black-and-white and has sixteen wheels."

"All right, what's black-and-white and has sixteen wheels?"

"You really want to know?"

"I asked you, didn't I, just like you told me to? So what's the answer?"

"A zebra on roller skates."

Giggling and whimpering, Nissa said, "Hey, that's pretty good . . . but how come sixteen wheels?"

"Well, how many wheels does a roller skate have?"

"Oh, I get it! A roller skate's got four wheels . . . and . . . and a zebra's got four legs . . . so four times four equals sixteen . . . right?"

"Congratulations," Durwood said with a smile as he pressed one forefinger to Nissa's damp forehead, "and for that you get a little gold star."

"Not bad, Dad. Now tell me another one."

Dr. Skolnick, who had been popping in and out of the room to check on things, injected Xylocaine into Nissa's finger. "Just a local anesthetic," he explained. "It doesn't last long, but it will enable Mr. Pappalardi here to work a little faster without worrying about hurting her."

"Feels like we've been here for hours, Daddy."

"I know what you mean, honey. It'll all be over soon, and you'll forget any of this ever happened."

"You're (*hiccup*) only saying that to make me (*hiccup*) feel better, aren't you?"

"Hold your breath and count to ten."

"Aw, Daddy, that old trick again? You know it never works."

"Try it anyway, hon."

She did. And when it failed to stop her from hiccupping, she tried it again.

"Boo!" Durwood shouted, so loudly, in fact, that it caused Mr. Pappalardi to jump. Even the young Filipino nurse, who had just stepped into the room to relieve Dr. Skolnick, froze in her tracks and grimaced. "Sorry," said Durwood, himself a little shaken.

Startled, Nissa could hardly talk at first, but finally she managed to say, "Daddy! . . . Why did you do that?"

"You'll see."

Durwood was glad when the nurse started sponging and washing away all the powdery, metallic filings from Nissa's tortured finger. It had taken a total of an hour and forty-three minutes, and he felt as if he'd lost a good fifteen pounds. But the washer was finally, triumphantly off, damn it!

"Congratulations, Nissa," said Mr. Pappalardi as he shook her damp hand. "You're a brave little girl."

"Hey," said Durwood, reaching into his pants pocket, "I'd just like to thank you, man." He pulled out a twenty-dollar bill and mashed it into Mr. Pappalardi's palm.

"What's this?"

"Just a little side tip. I think you deserve it."

"Oh, no, sir. I can't accept anything like that."

"Why not?"

"Because he doesn't want to share it with me," said the nurse.

Nissa sat up, looked at her finger, noticed the purple-brown ring where the washer had been, and asked, "Is this mark gonna be on my finger for the rest of my life?"

Durwood was so relieved that he became playful again. "Perhaps," he said.

"No fair," said the nurse. "No, it won't, dear."

"It'll be there for a long time," said Mr. Pappalardi. "But don't worry, it'll go away."

Nissa went straight for Durwood's neck with both arms and held on tight, crying for joy now. Durwood let himself choke up a little, swallowed hard, and grinned. The nurse and Mr. Pappalardi broke out into jubilant applause.

24

"Hey, that was pretty exciting," said Nissa, now that she was a hero and the center of attention.

Dixie was distraught. "Celia hasn't shown up yet. She's gotten lost. Something's happened."

"Mommy, the doctor said I was a brave little girl."

"And he's right, dear, you are. You really held up well. You should've been there, Dixie. You would've been real proud of her."

"I know, and I'm sorry that I couldn't be there, but somebody had to be here for Celia. Oh, Woody, what in the world could've happened to her?"

"Can we have her paged?"

"You mean, like on the loudspeaker, Daddy? Wowee, let's do that! That's fun. Remember that time at Great America when I got lost and they called my name over the speaker and that nice lady found me and took me where you were waiting?"

"That's a good idea," said Dixie.

"You guys wait here while I go take care of that; then maybe we can take turns walking around looking for her."

"Can I go with you, Dad? I wanna see how they do that."

"No, Nissa, Daddy's going to walk around some to see if he can find your sister, and you know how quickly you get tired of walking."

"Aw, but I won't get tired. I promise."

"No, you stay here with Mom. After we find Celia, then we can go back to the paging station and you can see how it works."

"Oh, all right."

Pushing his way through all manner of shoppers and gawkers and showoffs, Durwood finally was directed to the office area by a friendly old security guard who said that he would be glad to keep an eye out for a tall, fifteen-year-old girl in boots wearing a long dress, a navy blue coat, and a dark orange shawl.

"What can I do for you?" asked the sleepy-eyed Asian lady at the paging station. Durwood couldn't get over her powdered fru-fru wig.

"I've lost my daughter."

"What's her name?"

"Celia Knight."

"Where would you like her to meet you?"

"Over by where they have the puppet show."

"No sooner said than done, sir."

Consulting a chart and clicking on the public-address microphone, the lady's soft, musical voice was instantaneously heard throughout the Cow Palace.

"*Paging Celia Knight, paging Celia Knight. Will you please come to booth one thirty-two . . . Paging Celia Knight . . . Please come at once to booth one thirty-two. . . .*"

"Thanks," said Durwood.

"I'll repeat it two or three times if you like, say, every five minutes for the next fifteen. But let me know if she doesn't turn up. We can send security out looking for her."

"I'll do that. Thanks again."

"Hope you find her."

"I do too. It isn't like her to wander off that way without telling us first."

"Well, you know, it's that time of year. Anything can happen."

"I heard that."

For a moment, while pushing and moseying through the crowd, Durwood thought he caught a distant glimpse of Celia, with her back turned to him, watching a man demonstrate a glass-cutting device that instantly converted perfectly fine old bottles and jars into tacky-looking drinking utensils. But when he got close, it turned out to be a woman in her fifties.

At length, Durwood grew tired and, after giving the whole place a speedy going-over, went back to where he had left Dixie and Nissa.

"*—Celia Knight . . . Celia Knight, your father is looking for you . . . Please come to booth one thirty-two, the puppet show booth. . . .*"

The show had begun, and the area was crowded now with

parents and young children. Durwood's stomach was in knots, and Dixie looked as if she were about to scream. Taped-recorded selections from the *Nutcracker Suite* drifted from the little stage, where a lovable old puppet witch was busy luring Hansel and Gretel into her house made of sweets. Nissa was right up there in the front row, breathless and charmed.

"Well, what do we do now?" asked Dixie.

"I don't know. They'll send some of the security people around the floor to look for her."

"But you've already done that."

"Maybe she was in the ladies' room or something."

"But surely she would've heard the message over the P.A."

"I don't know, Dixie. I just don't know what could've gone wrong."

"Then maybe I should go look too."

"First go tell them to alert security."

"All right, but don't lose Nissa."

"No way in the world I'm gonna let her out of my sight."

As Durwood watched Dixie hurry away, his stomach fluttered and his heart began to swell with loving thoughts of Celia. Had there been such thing as a guilt detector, it would have registered a whopping response and started beeping like crazy when brought anywhere within a mile of where he stood now.

They were in the front office, where the head of security, a Mr. Chase, was saying, "All I can tell you for now, Mr. Knight, Mrs. Knight, is we've combed the place and still can't find the girl."

"Well, what do you suggest?" asked Dixie, frantic and hoarse.

Mr. Chase, who looked a little like Oliver Hardy of Laurel and Hardy, rested one hand on his enormous beer belly and slurped on a filterless cigarette. "You can stick around here and keep looking for your daughter until the fair closes. That's one way. Or you can let us get in touch with the San Francisco Police for you and file a missing-persons report. Either way it's hellish, I know, because you're dealing with time, and all you want is your little girl back right now."

"She isn't so little," said Nissa. "She's fifteen. Mom, do you think Celia's been kidnapped?"

"How dare you even think such a thing! Of course she hasn't been kidnapped. She's just . . . She's just—"

"Disappeared?" said Nissa.

"Disappeared," said Dixie, finally breaking down and crying. "Celia's gone and . . . and . . . there isn't anything we or anybody else can do about it."

"That's not true, dear," said Durwood as he cradled Dixie in his arms. "Mr. Chase here just told us what we might try doing."

"But he doesn't care. It isn't his child."

"Mrs. Knight," said Chase, his head so ensphered in tobacco smoke that he looked as if he were peering at them from a crystal ball that was slowly unclouding at a séance, "I'm in your corner. I know how you feel, and we're trying to help. In fact, we're doing the best we can."

"Well," sobbed Dixie, a basket case now, "the best you can do isn't good enough."

"Take it easy, baby," said Durwood. "You're getting too emotional."

"Getting too emotional? My own daughter's been kidnapped and all you can say is I'm getting too emotional! Well, what the hell am I supposed to do anyway, be calm and serene and meditate?"

"But, Mommy, you already said Celia hasn't been kidnapped. She just disappeared."

"Quiet, Nissa, this is just between us grownups."

"Why should I be quiet? She's my sister, isn't she?"

"I'm sorry," said Dixie. "I didn't mean that. Of course, she's your sister, and you should be allowed to . . . Mr. Chase, would you mind if I smoked one of your Lucky Strikes?"

"Oh, no, Mom, don't! You aren't gonna start smoking again, are you? You'll catch cancer, just wait and see!"

"It's okay," said Durwood. "Leave your mother alone. Smoking one cigarette isn't going to give her cancer."

"But she'll smoke another one, then another one, and then another one, and then she'll smoke another one, then—"

"Shut up!" Dixie snapped.

"Baby," said Durwood, "take it easy."

"Be my guest," said Mr. Chase as he thumped up a Lucky and handed Dixie the pack, looking relieved, almost cheerful, now that he could be of some immediate help. "They're pretty strong if you're used to filters. Maybe you'd like to sit down?"

"Thank you," said Dixie. She slipped out of Durwood's arms and collapsed with a groan into a leather-bottomed chair next to a floor-model ashtray that was brimming with nasty-looking butts and ashes.

Watching her light up and take that first draw was shattering. Durwood thought about all the propaganda, scare tactics, control programs, and one-step-at-a-time gimmicks and devices that had gone into curing Dixie of the habit. Sitting back now, smoke pouring from her beautiful, parted lips, she looked like a sophisticated college call girl titillated at the notion of becoming a porn star. But Durwood preferred seeing her smoke to hearing her bitch.

"It's getting late," Durwood announced. "Let's go home."

"What do you mean, go home?"

"Honey, what else is there for us to do now? We've been in this place for hours. It's been combed, every inch, and Celia's still missing. They can't find her, and Nissa's gotta get a good night's sleep."

"But I'm not even tired, Daddy."

"Then how come you keep yawning and rubbing your eyes?"

"Because there's something *in* my eye, that's why."

Dixie, drained and fearful, said, "I've got a better idea. Why don't I drive Nissa home and you stay here until they shut down?"

"And how do I get home?"

"You can take the bus, can't you? Well, I suppose you *could* take a taxi . . ."

"Do the buses still run at that time of night?"

"They do," said Mr. Chase, "but you might have to do some waiting. Where is it you live?"

"The Upper Mission."

"San Francisco, huh? Well, I'd drive you if I didn't happen to live down in Pacifica."

"And what if I do stick around here and she still doesn't turn up? What good is that gonna do anybody?"

"Honestly, Durwood, you just can't go abandoning Celia like

that. Anything could've happened to her, anything! Oh, Celia . . . My poor baby!"

"I'm *not* abandoning her! Look! . . . Oh, all right, all right, we'll do it your way. But I'm taking a cab home. I don't care what it costs. If it's okay with you, Mr. Chase, I *would* like to file a missing-persons report."

"No problem, Mr. Knight, no problem at all. We can take care of that right away if you like."

"Make it an all-points bulletin," said Nissa, whose sad excitement was as exasperating to Durwood as Dixie's depression and fright, to say nothing of his own uneasiness, which lay like a jagged chunk of meteorite still cooling in the pit of his stomach.

"An all-points bulletin it'll be," said Chase.

This brought a tiny smile to Nissa's lips as, following her mother's gentle command, she zipped up her blue nylon jacket and, making a face, pulled her woolen cap with its fuzzy ball on top down over her soft little ears.

"I need the car keys." Dixie held out her hand.

As Durwood handed them over, he got a look on his face that caused Mr. Chase to clear his throat and ask, "What's wrong now, Mr. Knight?"

"It's the shift," said Durwood.

"Come again, sir?"

"My wife can't drive a standard shift. Say, Dix, this isn't gonna work. We've come up with something else."

"You know," Dixie admitted, "I've been so knotted up that I wasn't even thinking on that level."

"Then what do we do if Mommy can't drive the shifty?"

"That's a good question," said Durwood.

"And I've got the answer," said Mr. Chase. "Why don't you three go on home and leave the investigating to us professionals?"

VIRTUALLY ASPHYXIATED, SMOKED OUT, and coughing like crazy at intervals to show it, Durwood sat up with Dixie and Leon at the dining-room table by the telephone long after Nissa had been put to bed.

"What are you trying to do?" he finally asked Dixie. "Make up for all those months you've been off tobacco?"

Looking irritated, helpless, Dixie mashed her cigarette out and turned to Leon. "What do you think we should do now?"

"I'm with Pops," said Leon. "What else is there for us to do except sweat it out? I swear, I've been through more traumatizing episodes relaxing with you guys for a few days than I go through in months on the road with the band." Leon had canceled a union-scale recording session scheduled for that night in order to stay home with them. Durwood loved him for that. "Actually," Leon went on, "it's been pretty interesting."

"Interesting?" said Dixie. "You find Celia's disappearance *interesting*?"

Never one to leave himself open to derision—not if he could head it off—Leon, if the tempo called for it, could talk the same way he could play—fast. "Yes, interesting," he said. "It's like being in a picture where you have to take sides, and, going by my deep feelings for both of you, I'm happy to be on what I *know* is the right side, the good guys' side. I only hope I can be of more than passive support."

Well! Durwood could see that this eloquent comeback was calculated to keep Dixie fixed right there in her chair, not batting an eye—smiling, in fact, as though she were the world's most flattered woman in distress. Leon's stock, in their estimation, was growing by leaps and bounds.

Nervously, they had been taking turns calling Celia's friends to find out what they could. Every one of the kids was shocked by the news and, to a person, promised to get back in touch the minute they heard from Celia. Since Moby's line had been registering a steady busy signal for hours, they still had him down—tentatively, of course—as their prime suspect, even though no one could yet articulate just what it was that Moby was supposed to be guilty of, if anything. It seemed to boil down to Dixie and Durwood, who really didn't know the boy, simply not trusting him on general principle. Under the circumstances, it just so happened that a two-hour busy signal smelled fishy to them, conjuring up just enough of an image of smoke in their jittery psyches to make them imagine where there might be fire.

Durwood was on the verge of lifting the receiver again to dial the operator and have an emergency check done on Moby's number when the phone rang. It startled the three of them so much that they let it get all the way to the fourth ring before Leon broke the spell and answered.

Durwood caught himself staring at Leon's face as he spoke and, looking across the table at Dixie, saw her doing the same.

"Hello . . . Yes, this is the Knight residence . . . Celia? . . ." Leon flashed a quick wink at his panicked audience, cleared his throat, and continued. "I'm sorry but . . . I'm afraid you can't speak with her at the moment . . . Well, no, she just isn't feeling well . . . No, it's nothing serious . . . She got up feeling funny this morning, and all day she's been under the weather, but—" He motioned strenuously for Durwood, Dixie, either one, to pick up the phone in the kitchen.

Durwood, armed with his portable cassette recorder and a little suction-cup device from Radio Shack for taping phone conversations—purchased but never used during the nuisance-call-in-the-middle-of-the-night phase—slipped quickly to the red wall phone in the kitchen, pressed the wire-tap gizmo to the earpiece, engaged the "Record" mechanism, and smoothly, quietly, uncradled the receiver. It occurred to him that he should have been taping everything that had gone down by telephone that night.

"Yes, that's right," he heard Leon saying, "she decided to turn in early. We're hoping she'll be all right by tomorrow."

"But you aren't Mr. Knight, are you'" asked the female voice at the other end.

"No, I'm just a house guest."

"Well, you certainly have a nice, soothing, low voice."
"Oh, thank you."
"What's your name?"
"My name?"
"Yes, you do have a name, don't you?"
"Uh, sure, it's . . . it's Lee."
"Just Lee?"
"Leon, actually."
"Oh, that's cute. Hope you don't mind my being nosey. I just like to have a name to go with voices I like."
"I see."
"Now, tell me what you look like."
Durwood couldn't believe it.
"First," said Leon, "tell me who you are."
"Martha Briggs," she giggled.
Durwood felt like a perfect fool, standing there in the kitchen in his socks, adjusting the level on his Panasonic recorder, which technically belonged to Celia. It was the machine she used when she sang and played guitar, made up songs, and interviewed herself.
"I'm around six-four, weigh two hundred pounds, and—"
"No, what do you really look like? Like, what color eyes do you have?"
"Brown."
"And your hair?"
"Blond."
"Really?"
"No, I was just joking. It's black."
"But is it curly or straight?"
"Curly."
"You mean real curly?"
"Yeah, real curly."
"Like, is it nappy?"
"Real nappy, baby, like a goatskin coat from Afghanistan. They bleach them things with urine, you know."
"They do?"
"Sure, and you better not get caught out in the rain with one."
"Ah, you're just putting me on."

"Nope, I'm putting the coat on *you*."
"Very funny."
"Hardly, but should I tell Celia you called?"
"Please do. Are you sure she can't come to the phone now? I mean, I really do have something important to tell her."
"Just hold on a minute," Leon said theatrically, then cupped his hand over the mouthpiece. "Celia!" he shouted. "Hey, Ceeeel-ya!"

While Leon was pretending to be summoning Celia, Durwood, wondering why the boy was wasting time this way, tuned in to sounds going on in the background at Martha's end—brisk soul music, disco, the Funkadelics, stuff Celia played sometimes.

"And so what's up?" asked Martha.
"The verdict is she can't come to the phone, just like I thought. She needs to stay in bed."
"She does?"
"Yep."
"Now, that *is* strange."
"And why do you say that?"
"Because it is—it's weird. Celia knew I was gonna call her around this time tonight. She went to the Dickens Fair with her folks this afternoon, right?"
"I think so," Leon said weakly, "but I don't know. Hey, all this is getting to be too much for me. I don't live here. Like I say, I'm just visiting. Maybe you'd better call back in the morning and talk with Celia herself. Better yet, why don't I have her call you? She have your number?"
"Yeah, but just in case, maybe you'd better write it down."
"Okay, spring it on me."
"It's seven-six-seven . . . two-six-seven-six."
"Got it, and I'll relay the message, Martha. Good night."
"Have a good one yourself, handsome," said Martha. "Maybe we'll meet up one of these times."

Durwood heard muffled giggling, then a click. He hung up and walked back into the dining room. Dixie was halfway finished smoking another Fact. The room smelled awful.

"Who's this Martha?" asked Durwood.
"Never heard of her," said Dixie.

"She sure sounded bold," said Leon, pulling at his beard. "Anyway, we got her number. We can always call her back."

Without making a sound, Dixie started to cry again. "The whole situation is about to make me sick," she sobbed. "All that phony play-acting you were doing, with Woody taping it and me sitting here ready to jump out of my skin."

Durwood went over to where Dixie sat and put his arms around her neck from behind. The back of her head was touching his knees. "You better take a hot bath and get some sleep," he told her. "It's going to be a long, cold night."

"But I can't sleep. I know I won't be able to."

"Then you'd better just lie down and try to rest."

"And what about Leon and you?"

"We'll probably be up and around. I thought we might take turns napping and listening for the phone."

"And the police," said Dixie. "Don't forget to keep calling them too."

"We won't forget a thing," said Leon. "How can we?"

"Maybe you should take a sleeping pill," Durwood called after Dixie as she headed up the stairs.

"Maybe," she answered flatly, "we'll see."

Durwood wished to God there was something he could do that made sense. Maybe, under the circumstances, he was being too hard on Dixie about smoking. He would try going easy on her, for a little while anyway. He figured that he ought to be trying to comfort her, reassure her, but he didn't know how. She was tense and freaked out, and that was that. Besides, he needed a little comforting himself. Confusion wasn't the word for what he felt. Maybe he was the one who should be taking the sleeping pill. To be knocked out, to be oblivious to pain, love, a wife, children, making a living, money, Christmas, hassles, details—that seemed more than appealing. The thought of it was downright heavenly at the moment.

But then he ducked back into the kitchen, grabbed the brandy bottle and a couple of glasses, and invited Leon to join him in the study for a drink and some relaxation, whatever that meant.

26

HARDLY AT EASE, THEY SAT watching television, or, rather, segments of Betamax tapes that Brewster had dug up and put together of some old games. It always made Durwood nervous to look back at video-taped images of himself doing what he had spent so much of his life doing automatically. It was nice having Leon around tonight, if only to get some idea of what it all looked like to a halfway objective bystander.

First they looked at highlights from a Beanstalks vs. Phoenix season opener from a couple of years back. Durwood had to hand it to himself for surviving that one because he had been fighting a bad cold, diagnosed as flu the following morning, and yet somehow performed almost flawlessly, particularly in defense situations. Then there was a Beanstalks vs. Lakers fiasco, a 95–77 disaster that he would just as soon forget. It had been the decisive game in keeping the Stalks out of the play-offs that year, his last.

"Hey, Pops, wake up and check yourself doing a one-on-one with Kareem. You don't come out looking bad either."

Durwood had been cat-napping. Brandy, strain, and fatigue finally were getting to him. He snapped back slowly, with the sound of the giddy game announcer's voice nipping at his ears—

"... clock shows two minutes and nine seconds remaining, with the Lakers rolling over the Stalks 91 to 72 ... The Stalks tonight have been trying to win it from the perimeter, and they haven't shot a good percentage ... Outlet pass to Knight ... Knight bluffs ... Jabbar is right there checking him ... Here's a pass to Gene 'Genetic Action' Jones ... Jones jumping ... thirty-foot set ... No good! ... It was sort of a set shot which he lunged into ... Jabbar intercedes ... It's out of bounds ... Jones is a wild man, goes for anything ... The Beanstalks seem to have gone clear out of sync now, including on the foul line. They haven't been that sharp tonight . . . Knight's been playing his best, only one reach-in foul . . . Beanstalks getting a little more speed generated now, but they still haven't been able to get shots to fall . . . The Lakers got twenty shots in the third quarter, the Stalks fourteen . . . There were ten Laker turnovers to the Beanstalks' two in that quarter . . . And it's just turning out to be one of those funny nights . . . A good night for Woody Knight, a crazy back-court night for the Stalks . . ."

—and then he blinked his tired eyes in time to see himself striding in to the foul line. It was funny to be looking at this clean, no-real-contact image and thinking about how he actually was feeling at the time.

"You know something, Pops?"

The ball was back in action now, zipping past him on its way to Jabbar, who faked, advanced, and got away with dunking a real sucker ball.

"You're a trouper, you know that?"

"Thanks, Leon."

"No, listen to me. You're like me. You aren't a club man. You work hard, as hard as anybody, but when the gang lets you down you go on about your business and do what you have to do."

"And what I have to do now is sleep."

"Then why don't you stretch out and get yourself a real nap. I'll be up for a while to handle the phone."

"That last girl's voice . . . What did she call herself? . . . Martha? She didn't sound quite real to me."

"How so?"

"Hard to say . . . Somehow it just struck me as a put-on of some kind. Hell, you're the musician. You're supposed to have ears for that kind of thing."

"Pops, you're being paranoid, but I can understand why."

"You're doggone right, I'm paranoid!"

"So why don't you just go to bed and give your mind and body some rest."

"It's no use, Leon. I know I wouldn't be able to sleep. I'd rather sit up here and doze on and off. I'll be okay."

"Anyway, we got her number."

"Whose number?"

"Martha's. I wrote it down. It's on the tape you sneaked."

"That's right. She did give us the number, didn't she? What say we call it?"

"But, Pops, it's late. It's pushing one-thirty in the morning."

"So what? This *is* an emergency, isn't it?"

"I suppose. Well, hold on. I left the pad with her number on it in the dining room."

While Leon was out of the room, Durwood sat on the sofa bed and looked nervously around him at all the sheet music, score paper, and offbeat books on religion, philosophy, nutrition, and poetry that had been drifting from Leon's room into the study. No wonder the boy was so calm. He had his music, his beliefs, his dietetic regimen, and yoga. All of that appealed strongly to Durwood, who, like everybody else, still was given to pondering the road he didn't travel. He envied his son.

For the briefest of moments, he turned toward the video screen in time to catch a glimpse of himself receiving a long pass, from the right side, from his Beanstalk teammate Billy Bohanon. He watched himself pick it up, drop it, back in with a dribble, try to get up the shot, but think better. Durwood fed Gene Jones, outside right, and as Jones—with Durwood ready to assist—tried to lay it up, he got hammered by Phoenix's MacNeil and had to go to the line.

"Here's the number, Pops."

"Tell it to me and I'll dial."

"Seven-six-seven . . . two-six-seven-six. What you gonna say when you get her?"

"Just want to ask her some questions. Like, who is she and how does she know Celia? That's all."

"Suit yourself," said Leon, who seated himself in a vaguely yoga-like position to watch Gene Jones lob in his first shot from the line.

Durwood finished dialing, listened for the connecting click, heard a short ring, then another click. At first he figured that Martha might have the phone hooked up to an answering machine to take after-hours calls, but he was rudely brought back down to reality when a feminine voice, as mechanical as they come, announced: "At the tone, the time will be one twenty-nine and fifty seconds . . ."

"What?" he screamed into the mouthpiece.

". . . The time is now one-thirty . . ."

"Something wrong?" asked Leon, looking up.

"You better believe something's wrong. We've been screwed!"

"How so?"

"You like saying that, don't you? 'How so?' Here, listen for yourself." Durwood handed Leon the receiver and watched his face as he placed it to his ear.

Leon's eyes grew big. "Wow, Pops! . . . I . . . I don't know what to say."

"Say what you've been saying all night—*how so? how so? how so?*"

Leon hung up the phone and said, "Aw, you're being unfair."

"Maybe I am." Durwood shook his head and breathed hard through his nostrils. "But I don't mean to be. I guess what I really wouldn't mind doing right now is getting me a pistol and shooting somebody."

"Who? Celia?"

"Don't be ridiculous. I could never hurt her, not knowingly, but I sure would like to give whoever she's with a good working-over."

"And how do you know she's with anybody? She could be out there all by herself."

"And what in the hell would she be doing? She doesn't even have a change of clothes, or a toothbrush, or any money that I know about."

"Listen, I know Celia. We dig each other. You know that. I've got a feeling she might be trying to tell all of us something by cutting out this way."

"Well, I fail to get the message—and what a dismal, bullshit way to communicate!"

"I know how you feel. Believe me, I feel just as hurt and pushed out as you and Dixie and Nissa, but I wouldn't start thinking about doing anything violent until I got the whole story."

"And how do we get that?"

"Just be patient. She'll call. I know she will."

"You willing to bet on it?"

"No."

"Why not, since you're so smug and sure of yourself?"

"Pops, I'm not being smug. I just have this strong intuition that Celia will be getting in touch. Besides, you taught me a long time ago that the best way to win a bet was not to place it in the first place."

"I said that?"

"Sure, way back, years ago. You told me that when I was eight years old the time you came to New York and took me and a buddy of mine, Dexter, out to Coney Island. We were on the midway and kept asking you for dimes to pitch in these little jars they had lined up, where for every coin that went in you got a Kewpie doll. You let us throw pennies instead of dimes, and, sure enough, we threw ten pennies apiece and missed every single time. Then you said, 'See, now, if those had been dimes we'd be two dollars in the hole. Now all you've lost is twenty cents, but if you hadn't thrown *that*, we'd still be two bucks ahead!' I never did forget that. In fact, you've saved me boocoos of bucks over the years."

Moved, Durwood sat on the floor next to Leon and, swinging an arm around his shoulder, said, "I hope Celia and Nissa come through this thing as safely as you did. I don't get to say this kind of thing too often, but . . . well, I'm proud of you."

"You've never told me that before, Pops, so I know you must mean it."

"Hello . . ."

"Hello . . ."

Leon had picked up on the first ring. Durwood muttered a separate hello in his sleep as soon as the ringing reached his ears.

"Yes," he heard Leon answer drowsily, "this is where Celia Knight lives . . . Oh, hi, Dixie . . . didn't know you were up there on the extension . . . I beg your pardon? . . . What was that? . . ."

"Who is it?" whispered Durwood.

Leon touched an index finger to his lips and pointed to the tape recorder. Durwood could tell by his bunched-up eyebrows that something strange was going on. Acting at once on Leon's signal, he hooked up the wire-tap thingamajig and clicked on the tape recorder.

Quietly, exasperated, with one hand clamped over the mouthpiece, Leon motioned him over. "They want you, Pops. Be careful. They're crazy."

They? Who was this *they*? With pieces of dream still teasing his head, Durwood grabbed the phone and, trying to calm himself and wake up at the same time, said, "What can I do for you?"

"Ask not what you can do for us, Mr. Knight, but what we can do for you."

"Who is this?"

"Aw, you fulla questions this morning, ain't you?"

"Is this some kind of prank?"

"Now, there you go, Mr. Knight—or do you mind if we call you Woody?"

"I don't want you calling me a damn thing until you can tell me who the hell you are!"

"Okay, Mr. Nobody, you wanna play it like that. But lemme just drop a little information on you before you go to talkin all outta your neck. To answer your question—no, this ain't no prank."

"Quit messing with me and get to the point!"

"I'll get right to the point, sir, in a minute. First, though, I gotta tell you something that might can help you. You can get as testy and as uppity with me as you like, but your pride ain't gonna do you no good. You need to take that pride of yours and leave it at the gas station."

"The gas station? Take what to the gas station? The hell're you talking about?"

"Take your pride to the gas station and have the mechanic there give it a good overhaul. We'll even pay for it, yuk yuk yuk . . ."

"You must be out of your mind! Listen, I've had enough of this. Either you tell me who you are and what you're calling about, or I'm hanging up."

"Wrong. That's where you're wrong again. You know why? Because we know where Celia is."

"Celia?"

"That's your daughter's name, isn't it?"

"Yes . . . Yes, that's . . . that's her name, but—"

"And you want her back, don't you?"

"You . . . You've got Celia?"

"I never said that. All I ever said was we know where she is."

"Wh-where is she? Come on, whoever you are, *tell* me!"

"Sorry, Woody—and I'm gonna call you that, whether you like it or not—but it don't work like that. I mean, for me to call up and tell you where you can find that sweet little girl of yours and then have you say thanks and go get her—like, you know, that just wouldn't make sense. You been around long enough to know don't nobody get somethin for nothin. That's bad business. Like Billy Preston says, 'Nothin from nothin leaves nothin.' So you gotta have somethin if you wanna *deal* with me."

It was chilly in the room. The thermostat was lowered at night to conserve heat, but sweat was pouring out of Durwood the way it did at half time. At the same time he felt as cold as ice and wiped his forehead on the sleeve of his robe.

Everything was swimming in ultraviolet light. Dixie's pitiful whimpering on the upstairs extension, before she hung up abruptly, was like an audible wound. Durwood felt as if his stomach were trying to digest a fish skeleton whole. Something—was it splinter or bone?—was caught in his throat.

"So what do you want me to do?"

"What do we want you to do? . . ."

The sassiness, the downright evilness of the voice at the other end—male, muscular, malevolent—made him think, for dark reasons, of the twentieth century and how unreasonable, no, how fucked up it was. He remembered the time his father, a sharecropper's son, had told him about the 1930s kidnapping of the Lindbergh baby. There he was, Charles Lindbergh, international aviation hero, the victim of instant fame. Durwood knew a little something about that. His father liked to cluck his tongue and say, "What if Bruno kidnapped you?"

And now here he was, Durwood Knight, an athlete of dubious achievement, with notoriety and publicity surrounding his name. Durwood Knight, under the gun and by now not above doing something crazy. Who was this new Bruno? And—

". . . 'What do you want me to do?' Hey, now, that's a fantastic line, Woody. I wouldn't mind gettin that one down on tape."

Having run out of things to say, Durwood steeled himself, looked at his watch, then over to Leon to see if the recorder was still working. Leon held up his thumb and forefinger curled in the shape of an O and nodded.

"You still there?" asked the voice.

"I'm listening," said Woody. "You're the one called me, remember?"

"Good, then I'll get right to the point."

"I wish you would. This is starting to get on my nerves."

"I'll bet. So tell me, you still drivin that station wagon?"

Durwood gulped and said, "That's correct."

" 'That's correct,' " the voice said sarcastically. "How proper! Anyway, maybe we can work out some kinda arrangement that everybody'd be happy with."

"What sort of arrangement?"

"A real simple one, Woody. All you have to do is bring your ride in for a safety inspection to a certain service station, and after we give it a good goin'-over, you get your daughter back. Now, don't that sound easy and sweet?"

"And where's this service station you're talking about?"

"Hey, that's pretty slick, Wood, but it just won't do. You ain't dealin with no fool, you know. Your move is to tell me if you agree to the deal."

"There's a problem."

"Tell me 'bout it?"

"The car isn't in my possession right now."

"And where is it?"

"It's in the shop. There was some work I needed to have done."

"So you can't make it tomorrow?"

"No way in hell. The shop's closed until Monday."

"Hmmm, let me think . . . It's already Sunday and . . . well, then I guess it's gonna have to be Sunday whether you like it or not."

The thought of Celia being mistreated in any way by this bastard and his cronies made Durwood wish he could trace the call so that he could find out where they were and do them severe bodily harm. He wanted to hold Celia again, the way he hadn't for too long now, and protect her from scum. There was no way they were going to get away with this. He still couldn't believe it was happening, but the knot in his gut reassured him that it was.

"You mean," he said, "you want me to get the car over to this place tomorrow?"

"So it's true what they say."

"C'mon, quit messing with me. This is serious!"

"Serious is right. I'm serious, too, Durwood Knight. You get that raggedy machine of yours over to where I'm gonna tell you, and that'll prove to me it's true what they say 'bout basketball players."

"Which is?"

"You people are s'posed to be smart, the smartest of athletes."

Already Durwood could feel his arm tightening against this joker's throat while he booted him from behind with one knee. What was it about that stupid car of his that was making these evil people—whoever they were—so willing to go out on a limb like this?

"Okay, so would you please tell me where I have to be, and when? Give me a time."

"Yep," the voice laughed, "it's true, all right. You guys ain't no dummies. I want you to listen and listen hard, and don't go gettin no funny ideas 'cause we're prepared to get down and get funky, if you know what I mean. You ready for this?"

"Just a second," said Durwood, scrambling around for a pencil and paper. He was so shaken, in fact, that he'd momentarily forgotten that the entire exchange, in all its foulness, was being etched and preserved in magnetized oxide.

"Drive your car over to 19th Avenue. We want you to be at the Scheherazade Chevron at ten in the morning. You got that?"

"But you didn't hear what I said . . . The car's in the shop. I—"

"Sorry, Woody, but, hey, that ain't my problem. You s'posed to have a high I.Q."

"Could you give it to me just one more time?" he asked.

There was no mistaking the rudeness of the click that he got for an answer.

"Hello!" he said anyway, crazed, bruised. "Hello! . . . Hello?"

Leon, in rapid succession, pressed the "stop" button on the machine, then pushed it into "rewind." "He hang up on you, Pops?"

"We're up against some cold-blooded mentalities," said Durwood as he picked up the receiver again and began dialing frantically.

"Who're you calling now?"

"Moby."

"Why him?"

"Because I think he's closer to Celia than we know."

Again, he got the same old busy signal and hung up with a slam.

"Leon, what's Moby's real name? I keep forgetting it."

"Isn't it Richard?"

"I think you're right, but what's his last name?"

"Mobley," said Leon, who was listening to the call being played back now with the sound turned low.

Durwood, with his whole world—past, present, and future—winding through his throbbing head, plopped open the phone book and rustled around in its middle pages until he found the right one. His sticky finger made a downward smudge of a column of print until it landed on a "Mobley, Paul" on Capp Street. It wasn't necessary to write down the address. He couldn't possibly forget it.

"Where's my sweatsuit?" he asked, jumping up.

"You're asking me?" said Leon. "I don't even live here."

"We'll get into that later."

Durwood remembered that all his jogging gear was hanging in the bedroom closet. Going upstairs would mean dealing with Dixie, and he knew that, under the circumstances, she would still be awake and dead set against him doing what he knew he had to do.

Grabbing the telephone directory once more, he sat back down and let his hand douse wandlike over the last of the white pages, but with no idea whatever of the name he was seeking.

"Leon," he said, "what do you call those things that aren't trucks but aren't station wagons either? Like, they're in between?"

"You mean, Land Rovers? Jeeps?"

"No, it starts with a *V*."

"Vans?"

"That's it! Thanks . . ."

Van . . . Vandemeer . . . John Vandemeer. Durwood found the number and wrote it down with a felt marker on a sheet of yellow legal-pad paper, which he handed to Leon.

"What's this?"

"I'm taking off. Call this man and tell him I've got an emergency and need his help."

"But why don't you call him yourself, right now?"

Leon was making perfect sense, of course, but Durwood was so eager to be on his way that he wasn't taking time to really think things out. Pure action was what the situation seemed to call for.

"You're right," he told Leon as he reached for his glass and the brandy bottle. "Would you do me a favor and dial the number?"

"Sure, Pops. Who is it anyway?"

"He's a mounted policeman I met in Golden Gate Park."

"Aha!" Leon cracked as he whirled up the digits. "Not only are we gonna have another car chase, but now we're getting into horseplay too—cowboy stuff. What next?"

"It isn't funny."

"I know, I know." Leon handed him the phone. "Here, it's ringing."

Durwood gulped down the shot of brandy he'd poured himself and, drumming his fingers on the edge of the mouthpiece, waited for someone to pick up at the other end.

"You'd better calm down and take it easy," said Leon, "or you're gonna blow it."

"I'm a mess, I know, but—"

"Hello," he heard a man's sleepy voice say.

"Jack Vandemeer?"

"Yes, sir."

"Mr. Vandemeer, this is Durwood Knight."

"Who?"

"Durwood Knight. We met in the park. I—"

"Oh, well I'll *be*," Vandemeer drawled with a singsong yawn. "Woody! How're you doing, buddy? Forgive me, I'm still half-asleep. It's my day off. We had a few people over last night, and I guess I must've tied one on. Whew! What time is it? What's up?"

"It's too late to be calling, I'm afraid, but I've got one hell of a mess going on over here and thought you could give me some advice."

"Anything for a pal. Why don't you hold on while I get a cigarette; then you can tell me all about it."

And that was exactly what Durwood did. He held on for dear life and then talked until it felt as if his sinuses were on fire.

CAPP STREET. AL CAPP. Li'l Abner. Daisy Mae. Years ago, Durwood and a carload of tipsy teammates had parked on Capp Street and walked to 16th near Mission to the old Follies Burlesk, now boarded up, to catch the show.

That night, a sweating, blond stripper who reminded him of Daisy Mae herself—and, for his money, no one drew women like Al Capp could— had lingered in the blue spotlight at the edge of the runway, by then down to nothing but bracelets and rings, and squirmed to the music as she ogled the audience, moaning Mae West style: "Hello out there, all you gorgeous Beanstalks! I like my men the way I love my coffee—creamy, steamy, and sweet in the morning . . . But at night I like it strong, hot, and black, if you know what I mean." When the men stopped giggling, grunting, and clearing their throats, she turned her back on them and, bending so that her flaxen-haired head hung upside-down between her long, country legs, said, "As you can see, I'm very, very flexible."

Now Durwood found himself on another Capp Street—not one that was just a street sign that he passed every day as he went about his business, but one that, for the moment, was as vital to him as breathing or staying awake, or having luckily thrown on a coat warm enough to keep the snappy night wind from chilling him to the bone.

The address he'd memorized belonged to one of those old, unstable-looking, squared-off structures, as common as painted stucco, with fire escapes jutting out of them every which way like iron-handled grips. The last thing in the world he'd want would be to find himself trapped inside such a crackerbox when the Big Earthquake finally hit.

There was a peculiar feel to this part of the Mission, especially at such a desolate hour. Even though he lived only a few blocks away, higher up the hill in relative comfort, Durwood recognized that feeling at once for what it was. And what it was, what it meant for him, was connected intimately with the sadness of the poor neighborhood in which he'd passed his nervous childhood, except that this was a tiny city, a *barrio,* of poor people within a city, and a flashy, fabled city at that, not the small-town poor that he had grown up knowing. Other than that, the feel of the block was as familiar and as deep-seated to him as the urge to urinate.

In fact, there was a man taking a leak, quite openly, at the curb behind an exhausted VW Rabbit parked in front of the house next door to where he was headed. Two women sat fondling one another in the front seat with the car door wide open. Durwood saw them coming out of an open-mouthed kiss as he passed, right away gathering that the peeing man and the women all must be together.

Well, that's none of my business, he thought, but all the same, crisis or no, he found himself slowing his gait ever so slightly to pick up on whatever it was they might be putting down.

Presently the man zipped his trousers and stumbled back toward the VW door, which, along with the front end, had been severely smashed. To tell the truth, the three people themselves looked more than a little demolished. The man, who wore a cowboy hat with clumps of dark hair spilling out beneath it, stood watching his companions while he fumbled in the chest pocket of the long, polyurethane coat he was wearing. When he found his eyeglasses, he clamped them on and said, "Goddamn it, Jo, what'd I tell you 'bout that shit! Luisa's comin' with *me*!"

"The hell she is!" Jo told him in a hoarse, drunken drawl. "This scrumptious little Aztec angel is mine tonight, all mine!"

Durwood couldn't really make out Jo all that well, except to glimpse that she had chestnut hair and sounded as if she might know a little something about the martial arts. As for Luisa, who was leaning back in her seat with one leg poked out of the car, her booted foot resting on the curb, he could see that she was a real, if slightly drunken, prize all right—a birdlike beauty with a shaggy, black mane.

"Hey," said the cowboy, getting loud as he wobbled and fell against the side of the car, "that AC/DC babble don't convert so good around here, you know. You better back up on your function button, bitch, and hit it right!"

"Chhhsss!" Luisa hissed with a finger to her lips. "How come all thees fighting and bad words? Ay theenk we con all work eet out, okeh?"

Not only didn't Durwood have time to stick around to see how they were going to "work eet out," he just plain wasn't interested. Maybe that loudmouth tow-truck driver had been right after all. Maybe he should have stayed in Cleveland.

The buzzer didn't work, so Durwood rapped on the door, concentrating with his other mind on what Dixie would be saying by now and on what kinds of phone calls they might be getting at the house. There was an outside chance that Celia might even call. If only this were one of his bad dreams that'd gone too far. But no, his knuckles striking the hardwood door felt terribly real, and every time he knocked, flakes of paint cracked off and fell to the porch for good.

"Just a minute!" he heard someone from the other side say.

After listening to the clicking and sliding of more locks than he could count, the door opened just enough for him to get a whiff of something that was burning.

"Paul, is that you?" a young voice asked.

"No, Moby, it's me—Celia's father."

"Mr. Knight?"

"Listen, I know this is ridiculous, my turning up here at this time of night, but I gotta talk to you."

Moby's head appeared in the sliver of doorway to get a closer look, then Durwood heard him unclick what must have been the last of the chains before the door was pulled back wide enough for him to get a full-length view of the boy in sweatshirt and pajama bottoms. He was clutching a metal spatula and staring with bulging eyes.

"Come on in."

"I really am sorry about this," Durwood told Moby as he stepped across the threshold. Except for a light that shone at the distant end of the long, shotgun-style flat, it was pitch-black inside.

"You're lucky I even heard you knock," said Moby. "I was out in the kitchen with the radio going."

"You mean . . . you're here by yourself?"

"Yeah, but I thought you might be my old man coming home early."

"Early?"

"He's supposed to be staying over in Richmond at a friend's till tomorrow afternoon."

"Oh, I see."

"Come on back, Mr. Knight, I'm fixing myself a sandwich. You hungry?"

"What kind is it?"

"Well, it was gonna be a B. L. T.—bacon, lettuce, and tomato—but now it might turn out to be a B. B. L. T. 'cause I went and let the bacon burn."

Durwood followed Moby through a couple of darkened rooms into the tiny, cramped kitchen, which was rolling in smoke. On the little gas stove sat a smoldering frying pan with a fire underneath it turned so high that flames were licking up around its edges. Grease was spattering all over the place.

"Better make that a B.B.B.L.T.," said Durwood.

"I beg your pardon?"

"A badly burnt bacon, lettuce, and tomato sandwich."

As Moby rushed to the stove with his spatula, Durwood fanned a cloud of smoke from his face and coughed, then coughed again. "Moby, I'm afraid I'm gonna have to (*cough*) come right out with it (*cough*) . . . if you don't mind. Celia's disappeared."

"Disappeared?" Moby was trying his damnedest to scoop up the bacon ashes with the spatula.

"Look, Moby, I'm not the type to go getting into other people's business, but don't you think that flame oughtta be turned down?"

"Gotcha!" said Moby. He twisted the gas knob on the stove to lower the flame. "Now, what was it you were saying about Celia?"

"Actually, you might as well turn the thing all the way off now."

Moby followed Durwood's advice, then said, "Okay, what's all this about Celia?"

"She's gone, that's what." Durwood's eyes were watering. He wiped them with the back of his hand and coughed some more. "We went to the Dickens Fair this afternoon. She went over to do some looking around on her own and then—" He snapped his fingers. "And then she was gone, just like that!"

"Oh, my God!" Moby shouted. "Owwwch!" He dropped the spatula and grabbed his left hand with his right and started sucking on his fingers.

Durwood did a half-spin and spotted the sink. Dashing to it, he turned on the cold water full force and said, "Here, stick your hand under the faucet; then put some butter on it."

"But all we got is margarine."

"It's okay, that'll do."

"What're you talking about with this 'Celia disappeared stuff?"

"I mean it. She's been kidnapped."

"Kidnapped!"

Now water was splashing all over both of them as Moby held his hand in the hard-running stream.

"That's enough!" cried Durwood. "Turn the water off!"

Then, feeling a desperate need for oxygen, he parted the stiff lace curtains that hung behind the sink and, struggling with all his strength, forced the window open to let out some of the smoke.

"Great!" said Moby. "We've been trying to get that thing cracked for years. How'd you manage to do that, Mr. Knight?"

By the time he and Moby were sitting across from one another in rickety wooden chairs at the ramshackle table covered with an oilcloth that used to be checkered, Durwood finally began to see that he was going to have to be blunter than blunt. He realized this while he was mentally shaving Moby's hair from his head and, in real life, rubbing a cube of Saffola all over the boy's crisply toasted fingers.

"But why didn't you call me?" Moby was asking.

"We did, but your line was busy."

"It was? Oh, that's right. I forgot. I took it off the hook so Luisa wouldn't call and go waking me up."

"Luisa?" Durwood could hardly bring himself to say the name. "Is that your father's girlfriend?"

"Nope," said Moby with an unguarded grin. "She lives in the neighborhood. Mexican. I mean, straight outta Sonora. She likes to stop by when she doesn't see my old man's car parked out front, or Annie's. Annie's his regular. I can't stand her either."

"There's something I have to know," Durwood said, looking deep into the eyes of this awkward adolescent, his daughter's friend.

"I'm shocked about Celia," said Moby, "but I'm not surprised."

"You aren't, eh?"

"No, not really. She's been acting so strange these past couple of weeks, I knew she was bound to do something crazy."

"And you don't have any idea where she might be?"

Moby shook his head, picked up a scrap of charred bacon from the skillet, blew on it, and popped it into his mouth. An open loaf of bread lay on the table in front of them, its white slices spilling out beside a yellowish-pink tomato, a wilted head of iceberg lettuce, and Moby's shiny flute.

Finally, Durwood no longer could play the role of Mr. Cool

and keep biting his tongue. Moby's obvious resemblance to Trip, Charles Triplett, was growing more painful by the minute. The time had come for him to be cold and direct.

"Do you know anybody named Charles Triplett?"

"Sure," said Moby, sitting up straight, "he's my cousin. Why?"

"Does he go by any kinda nickname?"

"Well, most people that know him pretty good call him Little Trip. They call his stepfather Big Trip."

"Are you in touch with him?"

"Not especially. See, it's like I told you that time we were waiting for Celia—those're the cousins I don't too much care for."

"What is it about them you don't like?"

Moby wolfed down more cremated bacon bits and said, "Well, in the first place, Trip and his brother Josh are older than me, and when I was little they used to sorta bully me around. There's just these bad feelings between us that run way back, you understand. Now, Trip, from the time he was nine, I've been told, he's always been in trouble."

"What kinda trouble?"

"Oh, you know—stealing stuff and running games on people. He always thought he was slick and shouldn't have to work. He's the one I meant when I was telling you about this relative of mine says he's gonna get him a big truck and go around ripping off rich folks when times get hard. You remember me telling you that?"

"Yes, I do, but what I can't get over is how much you guys look alike. I mean, Trip's older and all that, yet you've both got the same nose and cheeks and forehead and—"

"People say that, but I never could see it myself. Well, maybe a little bit. He took his stepfather's last name, but his real father and mine were twins, you know. Maybe that's got something to do with it. How come you're so interested in him anyway?"

"There's something I'm trying to figure out. You knew my car got stolen, didn't you?"

"Celia told me that, yes."

"And did she ever tell you who it was that did it?"

"No, all she said was you and Leon got into some kinda chase with the thief and he messed up your neck, but you dusted him, right? That's when you started wearing the neck brace."

"That's right," said Durwood, tugging at the brace, "and I sure will be glad when it's time to take it off."

"So Trip was the one you tangled with." Moby frowned and shook his head again. "He's my cousin, Mr. Knight, flesh and blood, I guess. But, like I say, I don't have all that much to do with him."

"When was the last time you saw him?"

"Now, let's see . . . Me and Paul stopped by there—hmmm, now, when was it? . . . "

"Who is this Paul you keep bringing up?"

"That's my old man."

"You always call him by his first name?"

"Ever since I can remember. He and my Aunt Sophie and my other uncle in Richmond, they all call my grandfolks by their first names."

"I see, and when did you and your father last visit Trip?"

"Well, you see, we did go by the house to visit. We went there to see his mother, my Aunt Sophie, who was sick and just outta the hospital. But the way it turned out was somebody heard me talking about how I knew you guys and was a friend of your daughter's and—"

"Excuse me, Moby . . . You're saying my name came up?"

"Right—and Little Trip overheard it, and his jaws got tight behind it."

"How come? I mean, so what if you and Celia are classmates?"

"That's hard to explain, Mr. Knight. I wondered about it myself. Like, for years I've been wondering about it. See, the Tripletts and the Mobleys, they've always had this thing going about how we think we're better than they are. Paul's always been kinda on the independent side, you understand, and after he married my mother—with her being a Mexican, well, pretty much Mexican anyway—then they never really could accept that. It's like Josh and Trip and them were always getting on my case about how I thought I was cute 'cause I got good hair."

"And did they ask you where I lived?"

Moby helped himself to a slice of bread and, folding it in half, took a thoughtful bite out of the middle. "No. No, nothing like that ever came up. I just remember he was pissed—uh, sorry, Mr. Knight, I meant to say ticked off."

Durwood could feel his eyelids growing heavy. He knew it was because he needed rest, but the brandy and all that leftover smoke in the room weren't helping him either. It was as if an army of sub-microscopic men bearing torches were marching through his nasal passages.

"You got any coffee around here?" he asked.

"We got some decaffeinated, I think. That's all Paul likes to drink besides grapefruit juice and liquor. Want me to make you a cup?"

"No, I'd better do it myself. But first let me ask you this. As far as you know, Celia's never met Trip or any of your cousins, has she?"

"The only other person she's ever met in my family is Paul."

"Oh?"

"Yeah, we got off the bus together and I was walking her home after school when my old man happened to be driving up Valencia. He honked; then he pulled over and I introduced 'em."

"Where's your father keep his coffee?" Durwood asked, looking around the dingy kitchen with its peeling ceiling and cupboards with barely hinged doors.

Moby got up from his chair and said, "Here, I'll get it for you."

Durwood watched the boy cross to a nearby shelf, then cleared his throat and made another wild stab. "One more thing," he said. "You don't happen to know anybody named Choo Choo, do you?"

Moby turned around and, grinning loosely, set the almost empty jar of instant decaf on the table. "C'mere, Mr. Knight, I wanna show you something."

Once again, with his heart pounding, Durwood followed as the boy led him through the dark around a corner to another room. When the door was opened and the light snapped on, he saw Moby's unmade, floor-mattress bed. A disassembled tenspeed bicycle took up one corner. Stacked along one wall were produce crates holding a few record albums, some tape cassettes, a grimy basketball, school books and notebooks, a messy pile of sheet music, and an even messier scattering of magazines, most of them wrinkly and soiled—*People*, *TV Guide*, *Guitar Player*, *Low Rider*, *Senior Scholastic*, *Playboy*, *Nuestro*, and something called *Wet*.

"Over there," he said, licking bacon grease from his fingers and pointing.

Durwood turned to look and, sure enough, pasted to another wall was a festive collage made up mostly of pictures that had been clipped from magazines and newspapers and arranged in a doughnut shape with a cutely lettered "RAT OWN!" spray-painted in the center.

When he got closer, Durwood noticed a cut-out of Celia that once had been part of a school-paper article titled "High School Women Speak Out." Next to it was a picture of Leon culled from some music publication, and then came a large color photo of Durwood himself, a Sunday supplement action shot from some long-forgotten profile on the Stalks. The three images were rubbing shoulders and crammed in with what easily could have been hundreds of pictures of other people, most of them unfamiliar. But Durwood did recognize a few: Meryl Streep, Sugar Ray Moore, Mr. Peanut, James Earl Jones, Stevie Wonder, Telly Savalas, César Chávez, Eddie Palmieri, O.J. Simpson, Richard Nixon shaking hands with Duke Ellington, Jimmy Carter surrounded by jazz greats at the White House, Bill Walton, Jack Johnson, Shirley Temple Black in Ghanaian ceremonial dress, Bill "Bojangles" Robinson, King Tut, flutists Hubert Laws and Jean-Pierre Rampal.

"I'm impressed," Durwood told Moby, "but I'm afraid I don't understand what it was you brought me in here to see."

Moby positioned himself in front of Durwood and, using his pinky so as not to get grease on the collage, indicated a tiny newspaper picture of a short-haired man in a track outfit. He was sweating and had a bearded chin.

Durwood had to bend down in order to really see it. "Well, I just don't believe it," he said, moving in as close as he could. "Where'd you get this, Moby?"

"That's him, isn't it?"

"It sure as hell is, but how come it's up here?"

"He's got long hair now and drives a van, right?"

"That's the one I'm talking about."

"Everybody at school knows Choo Choo, Mr. Knight."

Durwood wasn't feeling well. He had to get away from this sad apartment.

"I still don't get it," he said wearily. "Don't be so hard on me. Moby. It's late, you know, and I'm a middle-aged man. You gotta slow up and break things down for me real simple so I can get some idea of what you're trying to tell me."

Moby nodded and, fingering his lower lip, said, "That picture of Choo Choo I put in the collage comes from an old school yearbook. It's from when he made All-City doing the high jump. All this happened way before me and Celia's time. He was hot stuff then, and people still talk about it, but the reason why everybody at school knows him is 'cause he still likes to come and hang around after classes let out and try to hit on girls."

"Interesting—and what's this young man's real name?"

"Bell . . . Cedric Bell. And let me tell you, he's out of his mind!"

"I can believe that."

"What're you gonna do, Mr. Knight?"

"What do you think? I intend to try and get my daughter back."

Bam! Durwood didn't know if it was the words themselves or the way he said them, or merely that the time finally had come for something to give. All he knew was that suddenly he saw that goofy, teenage look on Moby's face dissolve into something else—something serious. It was as if a blindfold had been lifted from Moby's eyes and plugs from his big, country-looking Eisenhower ears.

"Is there anything I can do to help?" Moby asked.

"I'm sure there is, but I just don't happen to know yet what. If Celia calls, would you phone our house and give us any information you get?"

"Sure. I feel real bad about what's happened." Moby sat down on his bed with his head in his hands. "I'm still having trouble believing Trip's got anything to do with this. Somehow it just isn't like him, you know. He's basically a coward. Stealing a car, yes—I can see him doing that or burning somebody in a deal. But I don't believe he'd have the nerve to actually go out and kidnap anybody."

"She talked to you lately about running away or anything like that?"

"Celia's real strange, Mr. Knight. I don't think you even know how strange she can be."

"I'm ready to learn."

"She's got a good imagination." Moby took a deep breath and exhaled with a hiss. "She'll make up something in her head, in her imagination, you know, and then swear it was true, like it really went down. Am I making sense?"

"I guess."

"It works when she's writing songs and stuff, though. I mean, Celia can put words to tunes so that you'd swear she'd lived out the stories her own self. It's amazing. I hope nothing bad happens to her."

Durwood yawned and, stretching his neck by rotating it slowly, walked over and sat down beside Moby on the disheveled bed. Now, how should he put this? How could he ask it so Moby wouldn't think he was prying or being nosey?

"You don't really know her all that well, do you?"

Moby swallowed and said, "Mr. Knight . . . I know you're her father and all that, but I'd give anything to be able to get her to lighten up on the music sometime and all that intense playacting she's into so we could just talk and get acquainted like, well, you know, like two young adults that aren't in a hurry to try and prove something."

"Prove what?"

Moby hunched over and drew up his legs. Durwood distinctly caught some kind of faraway cry in his voice when he heard him say, "I wish I knew. I'm crazy about her—as a person, you understand—but the only one she really seems to open up to is Patsy."

"Thanks for your time, Moby. I'm sorry to come barging in on you like this."

"Aw, that's okay. It gets kinda lonely when Paul takes off like this. Much as I hate it a lot when he and Annie are around, it's kinda nice to have company sometimes too. You ever feel like that?"

"Plenty," said Durwood, getting up and brushing himself off.

"You want me to call my Aunt Sophie and find out if she knows anything?"

"Wouldn't hurt," said Durwood. "It wouldn't hurt one drop, just so you call the house if anything turns up you think we oughtta know."

Moby stood up too, and this time Durwood could plainly see that the boy was upset.

"I'll kill 'em, Mr. Knight," he said in a trembly voice. "Whoever it is that's messing over Celia, I'll kill 'em—even if it's Trip or Choo Choo or whoever it is!"

Durwood placed his hand on Moby's shoulder and told him, "You don't have to go killing anybody yet. Just keep in touch, okay?"

"You self-centered son of a bitch!"

There wasn't much he could do now except concentrate on getting them there safely.

"I'm crying my heart out and so scared I can't even move, and you have the gall to go taking off without even bothering to tell me where you're going. That took a lotta nerve, Durwood. You don't give a shit about me or Nissa or Celia or anybody else. All you care about is yourself and how you're gonna look if any of this gets in the papers. And you know what?"

Why say anything when a grunt would suffice?

"I hate you, that's what!"

They were headed down Mission toward 6th Street, where

Durwood would make a right turn and cut over to Howard. Another left after that would put him right in front of Ace Auto at midblock.

"The least you can do is respond," said Dixie. Her eyes were puffy, and all that hostile cigarette smoke she was breathing out that he had to breathe in was making him sick to his stomach.

Durwood rolled down his window.

"What's the matter with you?" Dixie barked. "I'm already freezing!"

"So what am I supposed to do?" Durwood said finally. "Burn up in here with the heat turned on and choke to death too?"

"Oh, my poor, pitiful angel," Dixie whimpered. "If we ever do get you back, I promise I'll never yell at you again. I won't even get mad or upset when you sass me or don't do what I ask you."

"Aw, for Pete's sake, Dixie, would you knock it off! You know damn well you're gonna get sore at her again. That's just the way life is. How in the world can you care for somebody and not get angry with them every once in a while?"

"Would you mind your own business? I wasn't even talking to you."

Durwood pulled up behind the big car ahead of him that was stopped at the red light, then glowered at Dixie and made a production out of looking around in the back seat of the Dodge.

"Well, I don't see anybody else in here but us," he said. "So I guess it must be me you're talking to, or else you're talking to—"

"Pay attention! The light's green."

Durwood let his foot off the brake and got ready to go, wondering why the car in front of him hadn't budged. The driver probably was daydreaming. He honked.

"What's his problem?" asked Dixie. "Blow your horn again."

Durwood let out a long blast. Still nothing. He rolled down the glass and stuck his head out into windblown darkness. "Hey, move it!"

This time when the car failed to move, Durwood—who was very much in the mood to knock somebody's block off, anybody's—unbuckled his seat belt.

"Be careful now," said Dixie. "No telling what people are up to this hour of night."

"Night, nothing. It's about to turn daylight."

"Durwood, *please!* Why don't we just drive around him?"

Wired and ready, Durwood jumped out, slammed the door, and Muhammad Ali'd his way up to the door of the idling Cadillac, which was painted robin's-egg blue.

"What's the matter here?" he shouted. "You blind and deaf or something?"

He became quiet when he got close enough to see that there was something pathetic about the way the driver—a stout, red-headed woman with smeared eye makeup and lipstick—was positioned. Her hands were clutching the steering wheel, but the rest of her was slumped back in the seat. Long hair spilling over the headrest, she wore an expensive trench coat that was unbuttoned enough from the top down to allow him to see that all she had on underneath was black panties and a bra that heaved with every throaty breath she took. In fact, Durwood caught himself wondering if he sounded as terrible as that when he snored. Since her gold-filled mouth was opened as wide as the window was, he didn't have to lean down too close to get a powerful whiff of all that sweet wine or whatever it was she was broadcasting.

"What's *his* story?" Dixie wanted to know as soon as Durwood was back in the Dodge and gearing up to roar on around the stalled Cadillac.

"It isn't a he," he told her, laughing for the first time in days—laughing so hard, in fact, that he drove straight through the intersection, forgetting to make his right turn.

What he expected to hear was Dixie screaming at him. Instead, she mashed her cigarette in the ashtray and slid her tobacco-drenched body over next to him.

"This is too damn complicated for me," she said softly. "I just hope it works out. I hope nobody gets hurt."

"Nobody's gonna get hurt, sweetheart." Dixie was near enough now for him to bend his head and kiss her neck. "You know, I read that clipping you gave me about fifteen-year-olds and how the last thing in the world they want is to be seen with their parents. Hell, I can understand that. But these changes Celia's putting us through are a little on the cruel and unusual side, wouldn't you say?"

Dixie smoothed his thigh with the flat of her hand and, in a wavering voice, said, "Yes, I agree wholeheartedly, but who's to say how much of it's her fault?"

One look at Whitman Price, head honcho at Ace Auto, was sufficient reminder to Durwood of how much he detested all the smug, gum-chewing car-repair predators he had brushed with in life, who, with clipboard and ballpoint pen at the ready, almost inevitably ended up treating him like the helplessly naive bumpkin he was whenever he found himself on their turf and at their mercy. It was, after all, their rules he had to play by, and the name of this game was Gotcha!

Whit, as he liked to be called, was no exception—not even on a cold Sunday morning, bundled up in a leather jacket and porkpie hat instead of his customary blue coveralls. As he guided Durwood with cautioning gestures into the lighted, high-ceilinged garage, his square, leathery face looked creased with annoyance almost to the point of cracking.

"C'mon," he boomed, "come up some more . . . Attaboy . . . Easy now . . . You're okay on this side . . . Pull it on up . . . little bit more . . . Stop!"

Brewster was there already, looking like a longshoreman in his turtleneck sweater, Pendleton shirt, and thick knit cap pulled down over his ears. He moseyed over to the driver's side of the car and stuck his sleepy head in the window. "I'm really sorry you have to go through all this, Woody," he said. "I know how you and Dixie must feel."

"It's pretty bad, Brewster," she said, "but we appreciate your getting out of bed and coming down here."

Brewster shrugged. "Big deal. What're friends for if they can't help out at a time like this?"

"Did a guy named Vandemeer turn up yet?" Durwood was asking just as Whit Price came over and stood behind Brewster.

"No, who's that?"

"He's a policeman."

"So you've already alerted the cops."

"Well, sort of. I told him about it, and he knows the score. I really didn't wanna bring in the police officially until we had a chance to go over the station wagon ourselves and see if we find anything."

"One hell of a situation you're into here, Mr. Knight. I don't think I'd wanna be in your shoes."

"I don't even care to be in my shoes," Durwood said as he got out and opened the door for Dixie.

"Mr. Price—"

"Please, it's Whit."

"As you like. Whit, this is my wife, Dixie. She thought the searching might go a lot faster if she was along to help."

"Pleased to meetcha, Mrs. Knight. Well, the more the merrier, I guess."

"Maybe between the four of us," said Dixie, "we can give it a thorough going-over."

"I hope so," said Whit. "My daughter's in the hospital about to give birth, and I'd kinda like to get over there soon to keep my wife company in the waiting room."

"Oh, how wonderful!" said Dixie. "Is it your first grandchild?"

"Nope," he said with toothsome pride, "it'll be muh seventh if everything goes like it oughtta."

"Congratulations!" said Brewster. "Seven grandchildren! Then you must have quite a few children of your own."

"Just three," said Price. "All girls. The one that's just now gone into labor ain't even married yet."

"That seems to be the style nowadays," said Dixie.

"Who you telling? Amanda—well, we call her Mandy, you know—she's sixteen years old, so guess who's gonna be looking after that young'un of hers?" He shook his head in disgust and made a clucking sound with his tongue. "Not much me or her mother can do about it now. Makes me sick to my stomach to see the way the country's going to hell in a handbasket."

"My father used to say that very same thing," said Durwood. "I guess it's been headed that way for a long time now."

"Maybe so," said Price. "Maybe you're right. But I betcha if we'da stayed back in Tulsa like I started to do, and shoulda done, all this wouldna happened. California's too hard on kids.

They grow up too fast and pick up too many of these no-count, soft-headed, liberal ideas. You can't tell 'em anything."

"Heh," Brewster chuckled, "I heard that!"

"You should talk," said Dixie. "You don't even have any kids."

"That may be so, but I still have to deal with them. There's a little rat pack turns up at the neighborhood where I live that I had to get told day before yesterday. I ended up threatening to take a pool cue to one of the little bastards, come talking back to me and using all that goddamn profanity they get off television."

"Look here," said Price, growing excited, "they ain't even gotta look at TV. They can get it right outta the newspaper. Hell, they print stuff right in the family paper now that'd make my sanctified grandfolks roll right over in their graves, God bless 'em!"

"Listen," said Durwood, "I know things are terrible all over, but if we don't get down to business, ten o'clock'll be here before we know it, and—"

"I'm with you," said Price. "Your station wagon's right over here. Follow me."

Durwood walked in front alongside Whitman Price while Dixie and Brewster trailed behind.

"By the way," said Durwood, "did you get that electrical problem figured out?"

"Sure did, Mr. Knight. Took me and the guys a whole afternoon to get at it too. You're looking at a couple hundred bucks in labor alone, but, seeing as how I'm a fan and all, we decided that seventy-five plus tax was a pretty fair figure to hit you with. How's that sit with you?"

"Thanks," said Durwood. What else could he say? "I appreciate the break."

"Aw, don't mention it, Woody. It is all right if I call you Woody, isn't it? You *have* been coming in here for well over a year now."

"Yeah, ever since this lemon I bought went off warranty."

Price ignored the remark and said instead, "Well, I suppose the best way to go about this is for each one of us to concentrate on a different parta this machine."

"I'll go over the inside," said Dixie. "I'm good at searching out sneaky little places like that."

"Good," said Durwood, "and I'll get busy on the trunk and back."

Brewster snickered. "You guys're too obvious-minded for me. Let me under the hood. That's where I think I'd stash anything if I was trying to smuggle it past somebody."

Whitman Price stood looking left out. "I guess that leaves me to go down on my back on the dolly to look around up under this thing, huh? Well, if it comes to that, I'll do it. But I think I'm gonna start out helping Woody go over the back end. By the way, what is it we're looking for?"

"That's a good question," said Brewster.

"Well, I'll make it easy for you," Durwood shouted as he swung open the tailgate. "Just keep an eye peeled for anything unusual that looks like it might be valuable."

Vaguely in agreement as to what that meant, the four of them—edgy to a person at that unholy hour and armed with wrenches, pliers, screwdrivers, and other tools that Whitman Price provided—set about their tasks energetically. They pulled out the back seat, peeled back carpeting, got down under the dashboard, took the air filter and fuse box apart, examined the stereo speakers, and hauled out a worn, unfamiliar-looking spare tire, a jack, and an air pump Durwood thoughtfully had stocked along with other essential extras. Given his recent sour luck with electrical systems, he was now even thinking of laying in a fire extinguisher—just in case.

"Whew," Dixie grunted at one point, "I never knew there were so many places to hide things in a car!"

After they had been at it for close to an hour, an S.F.P.D. patrol car nosed its way into the shed.

At that very moment, Durwood and Price, both of them greasier now than they had intended to get, came out from under the station wagon. Durwood was still so peeved about the substitute spare tire he'd found with its balloon-thin tread that, on seeing Jack Vandemeer climb out of the police car, he let fly a frustrated "Shit!" and gave the tire, the sparest of spares, a nasty kick. He might have been thinking about the way he used to send a football sailing when he was a kid, or he might have been thinking about kicking in Trip's or Choo Choo's head, or maybe nothing at all. In any event, he didn't like the sound the tire made. He turned to Whitman Price and asked, "Did you hear that?"

"Hear what?"

"That sound the spare made just now when I kicked it?"

"You wanna know the truth," said Price, pausing to look up with a Phillips-head screwdriver clutched in one hand, "I was so busy getting this damn taillight back on and worrying about Mandy I wasn't paying attention to much else. What was it you heard?"

Durwood stood the tire up and, straddling it, bent over and rapped along its muddy side with his knuckles while he slowly revolved it. When he came to a spot that reverberated peculiarly, he became very excited. He bounced the ugly tire, then rolled it a ways across the dusty cement floor.

Whitman Price, who was watching closely now, said, "Hey, that sucker *is* wobbly, all right. I can testify to *that!*"

That was when Jack Vandemeer, with eyes as red as the devil's shining out of his puffy face, shuffled into the picture and said, "How's it going, sport? Bet you won't be getting in your Golden Gate Park jog this morning, will you?"

Durwood was so wrapped up in why the spare tire was acting the way it was that he barely acknowledged Vandemeer's presence. All he said was, "Oh, hi, Jack. I think we might be onto something. Could you hand me that tire iron over there? This tire's so old it's fused to the rim."

Vandemeer blinked and knitted his brow as though wondering if he were in the right place, then turned to scan the floor for the tire iron Durwood had asked him to get.

"It's right there," said Price, pointing.

Durwood happened to catch an eyeful of the policeman as he made his way around the side of the car and stooped to pick up the tool. For the first time he noticed how bowlegged Vandemeer was.

"What do you think you got there, fellas?" he asked as he

watched Price stand on the tire while Durwood pried off the rim.

"Can't say yet," Price told him, "but me and Mr. Knight here noticed it was wobbling something terrible, kinda like it might have something lodged up inside it."

"If it does," said Vandemeer, "then that's a real ambitious ruse. I got a cousin works for the Border Patrol down in San Diego, and, man, you oughtta see some of the stunts people pull to smuggle stuff over the border. Even just a gallon of Bacardi. You wouldn't believe it!"

"Betcha I would," said Durwood, who couldn't pry the rim off, and was looking for something sharp.

"What do you need?" Price asked him.

"You wouldn't have a knife or a blade of any kind, would you?"

Price snickered. "What, you mean you don't carry one?"

"What's that supposed to mean?" said Durwood, getting to his feet with a deliberate scowl.

"Oh, nothing. I—I was just making a little joke." Price was rubbing uneasily at his wrinkly neck.

"Well, don't go making them around me, hear? I don't play that 'All in the Family' bullshit!" Durwood was enjoying watching the old mechanic squirm.

"Sorry, Mr. Knight," he said. "No harm done."

"Here you go," said Brewster as he joined them with Dixie. "I got a switchblade. Will that do?"

Durwood tried to keep from cracking a smile as Brewster handed him the long, thin, pushbutton knife.

"I *keep* me a knife," said Brewster. "No telling when you might have to be cutting on something or somebody."

"Listen," said Vandemeer, "before you slice that thing up, there's something I have to tell you, Woody."

"What is it?"

"I went ahead and had a check run on that license plate like you asked me to do. 'WE GONE,' right?"

"Yeah, and what'd you find out?"

"Turns out," said Vandemeer, suddenly covering his mouth to

cough. It sounded to Durwood like the dry, rough hack of a nicotine fiend. "Excuse me, but it turns out that this particular vehicle's registered to somebody by the name of Cedric Bell. The latest legal address we have for him is over in the Western Addition. Does that mean anything?"

"It does now," Durwood told him, "but it wouldn't have meant a thing three hours ago."

"Do you know this person?" asked Dixie.

"He's the one I told you about—the one who was following me that afternoon on my way to the Shriners Hospital."

"But I don't understand," said Dixie. "How did you find out his name?"

"Moby told me."

Dixie's mouth flew open. She planted her hands firmly on her hips and stared at Durwood. "Do you mean to tell me little Moby's in cahoots with these people! I want you to tell me the truth, Durwood. Is he mixed up in this?"

"No, not really."

"Well, what the—"

"Baby, would you hold off while I take care of this? There'll be plenty of time to explain later on."

Durwood flicked the button with his thumb and watched the lethal-looking blade shoot out—gleaming, erect, and ready for action. He plunged the upper edge of the blade into the tire and, careful to keep his fingers out of the way, began slashing away at the tread-bare rubber in quick little crisscross motions.

"I'm surprised you'd keep a spare that raggedy," said Brewster.

"Are you kidding?" said Durwood. "I had a brand-new spare that came with the car before it got stolen. Those punks switched it on me. I never would've noticed it if they hadn't."

At last, having survived the advice of everyone present, Durwood was able to get a good look up inside the tire. All eyes were trained on him as he reached in with his blackened hands to do some feeling around and see what turned up, if anything. By now he was feeling raw inside, all chewed out except for a hint of a tingle somewhere in his belly.

"Well?" Brewster said impatiently, yawning.

Vandemeer fetched a pack of cigarettes from his pocket and waved it around. Dixie was the only one who reached for one.

Just then, Durwood's knuckles brushed up against something soft and keen-edged that felt dry and mushy when he pressed it. He tugged at it, breaking the adhesive that secured it to the tire's interior, and yanked whatever it was out into the light.

Whitman Price's eyes looked as if they were going to pop. Jack Vandemeer's hand was trembling as he flicked his Bic and held the flame to the tip end of Dixie's cigarette, which dangled from her lowered lip as though it had been cemented there with Krazy Glue.

"Well, I'll be goddamned!" Brewster remarked, releasing a slow, high-pitched whistle through his teeth that sounded like a siren winding down.

Dixie said, "Would somebody tell me what all the fuss is about?"

29

IN THE CLUTTER OF WHITMAN PRICE'S little office, fluorescent-lit and dingy, they all gathered around the corroded metal desk where Vandemeer was seated, inspecting the powdery contents of the plump, plastic Ziploc bag Durwood had recovered. In the raw, demeaning glare of light, the stoop-shouldered policeman looked totally shot and hung over—in a word, awful. By comparison, Brewster—who leaned anxiously over Vandemeer's shoulder, wide-eyed—looked fit and well-groomed, and Brewster Day, to Durwood's way of thinking, had never been anybody's fashion plate.

Vandemeer pinched up a portion of the powder and rubbed it between his fingers, which he then sniffed thoughtfully.

"What do you think it is?" asked Durwood.

Inhaling once more, this time more vigorously, Vandemeer shrugged and licked his thumb and forefinger. "Still hard to tell," he answered, throwing his head back and shivering slightly. "Tell you, I really don't know that much about these things. We can turn it over to my Uncle Rudolph—he works in the lab at the narcotics bureau."

"Sounds to me kinda like your whole family's in the police business," said Durwood.

"Not really," said Vandemeer, touching his hand to his nose again. "My grandfather did twenty years for bootlegging, and I've got another uncle was a swindler."

"Is that so?" Dixie commented cryptically as she took hold of Durwood's arm.

"And why do you ask, Mrs. Knight?"

"Oh, nothing. I just find it interesting, that's all. My mother's got a theory about that."

"Your mother?" said Durwood. "What's Nadine got to do with this?"

"Not much, I don't guess, except she's got this thing about how cops and crooks are connected up. The way she explains it, it's sort of a symbiotic relationship."

"What's that mean?" asked Price. "I never got as far as college, like you folks did."

"Means they need one another," said Durwood. "And that's okay about your education because I bet you make more money than all of us put together in this auto-repair racket."

"Like hell I do," Price shot back indignantly. "Maybe more than Officer Vandemeer here, but nowhere near as much as you basketball and sports people."

Much to Durwood's embarrassment, Dixie snickered and came out with one of her evil cackles. "A lot you know, Mr. Whitman Price! You don't know the half of it!"

"Hey," yelled Brewster, reaching for a chair, "this is getting on my nerves! We're supposed to be attending to the business at hand, and the business at hand is for somebody to identify just what it is we've come up with, right?"

Everyone nodded—everyone, that is, except Jack Vandemeer,

whose tight face was loosening as he helped himself to another healthy sample pinch from the plastic bag.

"Brewster's right," said Durwood. "I've got less than four hours before I lock horns with those creeps. I sure as hell don't want Celia to get hurt, so I have to know what I'm doing. The first thing I need to know is what is it we've got here. It's gotta be worth a lotta money."

Dixie turned to him and said, "Then why don't you let this gentleman call the law and let them handle the situation?"

"Because," said Durwood, "we can't afford to mess up. They told me over the phone not to pull anything funny. These kids sound like they're crazy, honey. If anything happens to Celia, I—"

Brewster pulled his chair up beside Vandemeer's and grabbed the first piece of paper he saw lying on the desk.

"What're you doing?" Price asked him, alarmed. "That happens to be an important invoice we have to send out tomorrow morning."

"Don't worry," said Brewster, "I'm not gonna hurt it. All I wanna do is test out this stuff for myself. If you'll just give me a chance, I think I might can tell you what it is."

They all watched while Brewster carefully picked up the bag and shook out some of the powder onto the sheet of paper. He snapped on the gooseneck lamp, and Durwood saw the white substance take on a shiny, crystalline appearance.

Brewster held out his hand. "Woody, I need my switchblade back."

Durwood handed him the knife, which Brewster used to scrape the crystals into four neat little lines.

"What the hell's he up to?" Price wanted to know.

Vandemeer shushed him and said, "I believe the fella knows what he's doing."

Durwood couldn't help nudging Dixie as they all looked on in amazement when Brewster wiggled around in his seat and took off one of his fancy-looking work boots. He pushed one hand up inside the boot and brought out a plastic sandwich bag containing three or four fifties and a couple of crisp one-hundred-dollar bills.

"Are those real?" Price asked.

"They sure look it to me," said Vandemeer, whose eyes were getting back some of their whiteness and whose uneven teeth were showing in the peaceful grin that seemed to be frozen on his reddening face.

Diligently rolling one of the hundred-dollar bills into a tight little tube, Brewster hunched himself over the desk; then, holding the money like a straw to one nostril, he touched the free end to the bottom of one of the powdery rows and, inhaling mightily, proceeded to snort his way upward until it had vanished. He then sat up briefly to catch his breath before plunging forward again, sucking the next line up into his other nostril.

"Now, tell me what you call that," Vandemeer asked sincerely as his glance moved back and forth between Brewster's face and the two remaining lines.

"I don't know what *you* call it," said Brewster, heaving with mirth as he batted his eyes and brushed his nose against the back of one hand, "but *I* call it cocaine. And it's some pretty good shit—I mean, it's some high-quality medication, if you ask me." He looked around himself, trying now to appear objective and aloof. "Of course, I'm like you, Officer. I'm no expert, you understand. All I know about it is what I read in the papers and see on TV."

"Well," Vandemeer went on, "I've never personally been in on any of the really big narcotics arrests, but from just looking at what we've got here I'd say this stuff must have a street value of anywhere from a hundred grand to a quarter of a million dollars, depending on how it's cut."

"A quarter of a million dollars!" yelled Dixie. "Our daughter's worth more than any quarter of a million dollars!"

"I know that, Mrs. Knight. That's why, as an officer of the law, I think we'd better make certain about our findings before we go endangering little Amelia's life."

"Her name is Celia," said Durwood, "and she isn't all that little. Now, what do you propose we do? We don't have forever."

Officer Vandemeer smiled at Brewster and reached for his rolled-up hundred-dollar bill.

"Uh-uh!" Brewster muttered gruffly. "This is *my* crutch! Use your own bread!"

"Well, we do have to be sure," Vandemeer said feebly as he peeled off a five from a tiny wad of money that he pulled at once from his pocket. In no time at all, he had rolled it up and was bent over the desk.

"Hey, man!" Brewster was protesting. "That's our evidence you're horning up!"

Vandemeer mumbled something unintelligible as he worked on the last line Brewster had measured, but he never looked up.

Suddenly Brewster reached out, grabbed the Ziploc bag, and pressed it shut at its wedged seams. "Listen," he said, "this is important. I've got an idea, but I need to have a word with Durwood—alone."

"Alone, nothing!" cried Dixie. "I'm in on this thing, too, the same as Woody. You must be outta your mind!"

"Not quite," said Brewster. Clutching the bag, he stood up and walked to where Dixie was still clinging to Durwood's arm.

"Bunch of fucking drug addicts!" Whitman Price snarled. He rushed toward the desk and snatched the coke-sprinkled paper right out from under Vandemeer's nose. "Get out of here, all of you!" he bellowed. "It's getting to be too weird in here for me! I opened up this place this morning outta the kindness of my heart. Next thing you know, you're gonna be whipping out hypodermics and poking needles in your arms, and I'm gonna end up getting my license pulled. Out! You hear me? Everybody, out!"

"Say, take it easy, Whit." Vandemeer was on his feet now, seemingly full of energy and fight. "You're forgetting something. I'm still the Man around here. I'm not about to bust anybody or pull their license." He spoke calmly and apparently with enough reassurance to quiet the old mechanic. At least his words seemed to take some of the bristle out of Price's resentment. "As a matter of fact, your cooperation in this case has been of singular importance. We law-enforcement officers take pride in citizens like yourself."

As he looked on, Durwood was thinking, well, this was *those* people's business. He turned to Brewster, who was showing Dixie his most serious face. "Dix," Brewster was saying, "this'll only take a minute. I don't want you to get any more upset than you already are, so why don't you let me speak with Durwood—just the two of us—outside the office?"

"What do you have to say that I'm not supposed to hear?"

"It isn't anything that you aren't supposed to hear. It's just something I just now thought of that might help us get Celia back faster."

Dixie, with nothing but stress and distress showing in her eyes, looked at Durwood in a way that made him understand that she was leaving the decision to him.

He hugged her around the waist and said, "Just give us a moment, honey. I don't know what he's got up his sleeve either, but it'd better be good."

Dixie bit at her lip and got out a smoke.

"I don't go for the idea one bit," said Durwood.

He and Brewster were out by the station wagon, talking low, as Durwood's grandmother used to call it, and grabbing quick glances over their shoulders.

"But don't you see how there's no way we can lose?"

"I'm sorry, Brewster, but it sounds tacky to me, real tacky, and dangerous too."

"Woody, ain't you found out yet that it takes nerve to live? I mean, you talk about dangerous! This crap you and Dixie are caught up in now isn't exactly what I'd call the National Safety Council."

"Maybe not, but I'm not about to get into fooling around with trying to sell dope."

"Look, you don't have to get directly involved yourself."

"What do you mean?"

"I mean, I could unload it. I know a few people, respectable people like us, we could unload it on. We don't have much time to be hemming and hawing, you know. I'm talking about I could drop this stuff on these people and *boom!*—just like that—we could walk away from it clean and split maybe forty to fifty grand apiece. Do you know how much capital that is? We could really do up the shop then and hold out for a *long* time."

Little flecks of violet were beginning to get in the way when

Durwood stopped and looked Brewster directly in the face. He wished he hadn't heard what he'd heard.

"Brewster," he said, controlling himself, "we've been friends for how long now?"

"Ever since you got traded to San Francisco—six years now."

"Right. And have you ever known me to ever do anything I didn't wanna do?"

"Never, but this is different. You see—"

"I see nothing, goddamn it! You're asking me to throw everything I believe in out the window and turn this thing into some shitty-ass get-rich-quick scam that I don't want dick to do with! I always knew how much you liked money, but I never thought things would come to this!"

Brewster sat down on the hood of the station wagon, undid the precious bag, and stared down into it longingly. It was as if he were on a sinking raft and having one last look at a cherished possession that he knew was going to have to be thrown overboard sooner or later.

To Durwood he looked like a greedy little boy, a child—like Nissa when she came home from making her Halloween rounds. He recalled the way Nissa had looked after setting her paper sack full of goodies on the kitchen table. It was too much for the girl. She kept dipping down into all those lollipops, candy bars, bubble gum, Saran-wrapped cookies, and little packlets of raisins and nuts, and plucking out the apples, the oranges, and the shiny coins. He and Dixie ended up having to threaten to take away her TV-watching privileges for a week in order to get Nissa to turn her swag over to them and get into her pajamas.

But what did you say to a grown man—a big, old, rusty-looking man who had been a comfort to him, his most dependable friend, during that long stretch he'd served with the Beanstalks; a man who had been more than just the team trainer? Brewster—himself a one-time "jackleg boxer," as he put it—had done a hell of a lot more than just bandage the guys' injuries, give rubdowns, dispense medication, and man the whirlpool machinery. You could talk to him about things, practically anything—team problems, personal problems, even about the loneliness that went with being on the road—and

Brewster would listen thoughtfully and offer careful, solid advice.

That kind of openness and warmth—friendship, really—had come to mean almost everything to Durwood when he was living in and out of jet-coach cabins, buses, limousines, taxis, motels, locker rooms, and shower stalls. What a fucked-up way to live! He'd spent most of his time getting to and from places that had become blurred with the years. In between, he did what he had been trained to do, hired to do—what, in the end, his fast-expiring contracts stipulated that he *had* to do: *Play ball! Perform, goddamn it!* And God help you if you didn't put on a good enough show—which invariably meant winning—to excite the fans, or, worse, the almighty management. The heat never let up. *It isn't whether you win or lose, but how you play the game.* He sometimes thought about that old chestnut that coaches had been dropping on kids, himself included, for how many generations? Where had it come from? Maybe that was true in some distant land, but certainly not here in the United States, which, as far as he was concerned, was a head-knocking, competitive society if ever there was one.

Aw, Brewster, Brewster! Durwood wanted so much for their friendship to last. A part of him longed now to be in a locker room after a tough win, waiting for Brewster to hand him an Empirin.

The faraway ring of a telephone overpowered the buzzing in Durwood's head. Panicked, he stared at his watch, then at Brewster.

"Listen, Wood," Brewster was saying, "I really didn't mean to freak you out. Guess I'm a little stoned and got carried away."

"I guess you did," Durwood allowed, "but there's no way I can get behind what you're proposing. Now, you can call me corny or square or anything you want to, but—"

"Forget it, huh? It was just an idea I had. I mean, everybody's hustling dope—the CIA, revolutionaries, everybody. But if it don't sit right with you, then okay, let's forget it. Is that a deal?"

Durwood heard the phone stop ringing and turned toward the office. "I never heard a word you said," he replied. "As a matter of fact, you never said it."

Brewster worked up a relieved, crooked smile and slid down from the hood of the station wagon.

"I'm going back in there," Durwood said over his shoulder. "That might be Leon calling."

"Mandy's just gone into labor," Whitman Price announced as he hung up the receiver. "Sorry, but I gotta close up shop now. The wife wants me to get over to the hospital."

"Is the father of the child gonna be there?" Dixie asked him.

Price blinked at her curiously. "Afraid not," he said. "He's in the Navy."

Fatigue was beginning to get to Durwood. Everything was looking different, feeling different. The glaring light, the stuffiness of Price's tiny office, the fact that they were all assembled in this tight little space because of a terrible reality—all of it was wearing him down. He needed something.

"You got a coffee-maker around this place?" he asked.

"Sure do, Mr. Knight, but I'm afraid we're gonna have to wrap things up." Price handed him the keys to the Ford wagon. "I'm giving you guys ten minutes to clear out."

"But we still have to get our act together," said Durwood.

"Well, all I can say is you'd better get it together fast and take it the hell outta here. That little baby that's waiting to get born can't wait, and neither can I."

Officer Vandemeer, who had been busy brushing the dust from the desk top into a business envelope, turned and looked directly at Durwood. "Look here," he said, very much the policeman again, "it's time to straighten up and do this thing right."

"And what do you suggest?" asked Durwood.

"I spoke with the captain at the precinct," he replied. "He's sending out a plainclothes unit. The idea is for us to return the evidence to its original hiding place, go through with the rendezvous, and take our chances. We'll stake out the service station and try to figure out a way to cover you without being seen while you're there talking the deal over with them to get Delia back."

"You're not very bright, are you?" said Dixie, getting right up in Vandemeer's face.

"I beg your pardon."

"It's Celia, not Delia. *Please* won't you make an effort to get it straight?"

"Forgive me," said Vandemeer. "It's a Sunday morning, it's my day off, and I'm lucky to be getting my faculties back. It's been a hard weekend."

"It's been a hard decade for us," said Dixie. "That's why I plan to go back to school and become a lawyer. Lawyers run the land, and lawyers run the government. I hate the way the land's being governed, so the way I see it is to join 'em."

"Interesting," said Vandemeer, "but we've gotta get our tails in gear and move."

"You're forgetting all those shreds out there," Durwood told him.

"What shreds?"

"The ones from that spare tire I cut up to get at what you call the 'evidence.'"

"Hmmm," said Vandemeer with a sneeze. "That means we've got a problem, don't we? By the way, where's that buddy of yours?"

They looked around at one another. Price started buttoning his coat and clicking off lights. Vandemeer brushed himself off and slipped the envelope into a coat pocket. Durwood walked over and stood behind Dixie, wrapping his arms around her and bending his head to her ear.

"I think I'd better get you back home," Durwood whispered.

"I think you should too," Dixie answered, "before I finish coming apart."

"The only problem," he went on, "is how am I gonna drive you and meet with these cops too? And somebody's gotta drive the rent-a-car."

With shining eyes, and looking conspicuously defensive, Brewster stepped into the musty office with the "evidence" held out in front of him. It dangled there from the tips of his fingers like a fat, white mouse held up by the tail. "Did anybody miss me?" he asked.

Durwood drove Dixie to Dolores Street in the station wagon while Brewster trailed them in the rented Dodge. On the way there it turned daylight and started drizzling again.

"When all this is over," Durwood found himself telling Dixie, "things are gonna be different between us."

Dixie squeezed his hand as he pulled up in front of their house.

"You'll never hear me complain again about anything. I mean, about anything at all. I'm so lucky to have you guys around to love me. What a goddamn fool I've been, worrying about money and bills and growing old and the future. What does any of that mean when it comes right down to having Celia back?"

"Please don't talk like that," said Dixie. "You asked me not to, so I'm asking you not to. It just scares me to be here by myself with Nissa while you're crosstown caught up in all that monkey business."

"Leon'll be with you."

Dixie took out a cigarette, looked at it, then put it back in the pack in her purse.

While Brewster parked the Dodge in the driveway, Durwood leaned to kiss Dixie on the corner of her mouth. When, with a flick, she softly pried his lips open with the tip of her tongue, which tasted faintly of nicotine, he took her damp hand, the one that had been squeezing his, and pulled it down between the insides of his thighs. It disturbed him that he could be feeling such emotions when he hadn't slept since yesterday and, for days it seemed, had been on the verge of murdering somebody.

Dixie gave him another kind of squeeze there—a gentle one—and got out of the car.

On the porch, they kissed again in front of Leon, who opened the door.

"Be careful," Dixie said. "This is real life now, not basketball. You don't have to go showing off. I want Celia back here safe."

Leon, by now looking as if a truck had run over him, yanked his father into the vestibule. "You want me to come with you?" he asked.

"No."

"But, Pops, this is crazy. Anything's liable to go down."

"You stay here with Dixie and look after her and Nissa. I'm supposed to turn up all by myself, remember?"

"Well, I've been chanting for you."

"Don't you mean *praying* for him?" said Dixie.

"No, chanting. I've been trying to get you past this thing with some kinda spiritual protection."

"I'm glad you're here," Durwood told him. "I'm just glad you're around, son. I—I don't know how else to put it."

"*Whiplash was suffered by twenty-six people when a man claiming to be the devil hijacked a roller coaster!*

Durwood was doing the driving again. He cocked his head toward Brewster and said, "Do you mind? I wish you'd turn to another station. This one's depressing."

"It's just this comedy record show," said Brewster. "I listen to it every morning."

"Don't care what it is. I don't need it!"

"All right, I'll find a music station . . . But you know, Woody . . . I've been giving this situation a whole lotta thought. In fact, when you called me and I was getting dressed to come over here, I thought to myself how dumb it was to jump on this scene without being prepared."

They were approaching Ace Auto territory again, where Durwood already could imagine all the changes they were going to have to go through—getting the car ready, shifting the dope to another spare tire, and listening to all that yak from his official, plainclothes protectors. Why was life so jammed up with the unnecessary? He was perfectly capable of self-destructing all by himself, without any outside help.

"Yeah," he told Brewster, "I don't know about taking on these monkeys like this."

Brewster casually dipped one hand inside his Pendleton shirt. He brought out something cold and laid it in Durwood's lap.

"Hey, what you got there?"

"Nothing much. Just a little afterthought. We used to call 'em two-dollar Saturday-night specials when I was coming up. I keep a couple of 'em around the crib. They're snug and reliable, plus they do the job."

Durwood picked up the pistol while trying to steer with his other hand. The feel of it scared the hell out of him. "Now, wait a minute! What am I supposed to do with this, Brew?"

"That's really none of my business, friend. It just occurred to me, like I was saying, that you might be needing a little technology on hand just in case all that muscle of yours should suddenly prove, uh, inadequate."

Durwood handed the gun back. "You're still high on that stuff, aren't you?"

"Well, I must confess that I'm feeling no pain. C'mon, Woody, don't be no fool. Just tuck it in your belt under your coat. The cops aren't about to go searching you."

"Is it loaded?"

"Sure is. But don't worry, the safety's on. I'll show you how to disengage it. It's simple. Why don't you pull off to the side for a second."

"No, man. That's one more headache I don't need right now. I can handle myself. Besides, it'd be just my luck to go reaching for that damn thing and end up shooting my own leg off or something."

"Nothing'll go wrong if you do what I tell you. Woody, I'm warning you . . . People have been known to get blown away behind this dope traffic and —"

"Uh-uh, Brewster, you hold on to it. I mean, I appreciate your concern and all that, but let's wait and see what the law's got up its sleeve. Anyway, just a little while ago you were only too willing to get both our lives jeopardized in a dope deal. Aw, forget it. We've been down that street already. Would you please put that thing away? It makes me nervous."

Brewster reached under his shirt again and came out empty-handed. Looking slightly rejected, he began twisting away at the radio knob. "Okay," he said, "just trying to be helpful. It's *your* daughter."

"*And in other news,*" they heard a calm female voice declare, "*a missing-persons report has been filed with the San Francisco police by former Bay Area Beanstalk basketball guard Durwood 'Woody' Knight, whose fifteen-year-old daughter Celia disappeared late yesterday afternoon while the family was visiting the annual Dickens Christmas Fair at the Cow Palace. Details are still hazy as of this hour, but KCBS will be broadcasting a complete description of the missing teenage girl, along with an update, just as soon as further information is made available. . . .*"

"Aw, shit!"

"I couldn't have expressed it any better myself," said Brewster as he settled back in his seat and folded his arms. "Just let me know if you change your mind."

"About what?"

"About this," Brewster told him, patting at the lump under his shirt.

Up ahead, through the windshield, Durwood saw the patrol cars, all four of them, parked in front of Ace Auto. And there stood Jack Vandemeer, gesturing wildly as he, presumably, explained something to a gray-haired man in a business suit and trench coat.

"Betcha anything," Brewster giggled, "that cop buddy of yours didn't tell 'em how much of that stuff he snorted."

Durwood, as he pulled to the curb, failed to see the humor of this or, for that matter, anything else. He did notice, though, that his hands were trembling when he reached to take the keys from the ignition.

Brewster noticed it too—Durwood could tell from the sober look that all at once came into his face. He watched his partner pull the knit cap from his head and rest it against his belly; then, to keep Brewster from noticing that he had registered Brewster's reaction, he looked away quickly and opened the door.

"Mind if I leave my cap in your glove compartment?" Brewster asked as Durwood was getting out. "My head's starting to get a little heated up."

"Go ahead, but I don't get it. Your car's parked right over there across the street. Why would you wanna—?"

Brewster winked at him and added in a low voice, "If the shit gets outta hand, just reach for my cap in the glove compartment."

"What?"

"The glove compartment, Woody. I'm putting it in the glove compartment, okay? That's all you need to know."

When the light bulb went on in Durwood's head and he understood what Brewster was muttering, it was too late for him to do anything about it. Already the gray-haired man, clutching a black satchel, was walking toward him with Vandemeer and another uniformed officer at his side. "Mr. Knight," the man said, flashing his walleted badge, "I'm Lieutenant Oakley Sparrow. Sorry we have to meet under such grave circumstances, but I think we need to talk over a little strategy before you go out to that service station."

"You won't believe this, Woody," Vandemeer blurted out, "but we already have a tail on Cedric Bell. Turns out the clown's got a CB rig hooked up in his van, and we've been doing a little intercepting."

"That'll do, Vandemeer," the lieutenant cut in, his blue eyes vivid in his chalky, round face with its salt-and-pepper brows. "I'll do the talking and explaining, if you don't mind."

IT WAS SUPERSONIC WEATHER—chilly and bright gray, the way he remembered Seattle. Rain was coming down in dribs and drabs along 19th Avenue as Durwood made his way south—alone now,—to the Scheherazade Chevron, as he'd been instructed. He tried to go over Lieutenant Sparrow's complicated moves in his head, but it wasn't easy. The tension was terrible. Just knowing, however, that the police would be watching his residence and that Trip's and Choo Choo's places were under close surveillance took some of the edge off—not much, but enough to give him just enough mental elbow room to hold himself together.

Elbow room. Something clicked. Just the phrase itself conjured up fizzly image-feelings of himself in the back court, psychically pinned to the wall and knowing that nothing short of magic would help him salvage the game. Elbow room, inches, borrowed space to maneuver in while he prayed for that moment when telepathy—Brewster's "deejay voo" or whatever name you gave it—would take over, and, suddenly, as if on cue, everything would flow into place as all the guys on the floor tuned in to one another. During such extraordinary moments, he would feel himself and all the players around him—teammates and opposition—heating up while, at the same time, his perceptions would be cooling to the point where it seemed that he was both watching and acting in a slow-motion movie of the game played backwards—a movie he'd already seen so many times before that he knew it intimately, frame by frame. He could sense precisely where Corky, Lincoln, Gene, Skeeter, and Bolo were going to be before they'd even gotten there. Every move—if only for a spell—every pass, fake, and turn would feel predetermined, orchestrated like a musical score, counterpointed, with every note and beat and nuance in place, right there where and when it was supposed to happen. Aw, what sweet interludes! A piece of cake. Whenever that happened—and, granted, it wasn't often—he had no doubt about there being such a thing as a patron saint of basketball players. Hadn't he himself been blessed at times with a backstage connection to the Source, a two-way cable to the Ace? If only this were true in these unregulated, everyday emergencies he had to put up with. But then, there was nothing "everyday" about what he found himself up against now.

Durwood motored carefully past Irving, Judah, and Lawton Streets. It was just before Noriega that he saw the red-white-and-blue Chevron station. Pulling in, he also saw that it was the very same service station he had been so pleased to happen upon that harried afternoon on his way to the Shriners Hospital.

And sure enough, when he checked out the sign that hung

above the office entrance, it plainly spelled out in plastic display letters: "Scheherazade Chevron—Nadir Adib Naheen, Proprietor." Durwood looked around for the redheaded girl with the funny teeth, but the only attendant on duty was an underweight blond boy, very clean cut, who was busy squeegeeing the scuzz from the windshield of a dark, aggressive-looking Lincoln Continental that hogged one side of the full-service island. He missed the girl whose presence might have injected a smidgen of familiarity that he would have welcomed just then.

His watch told him it was 9:45. Technically, he was early. What if they didn't show up? What if this was only a gag they were playing out at his expense? His stomach tightened as he pulled up, without thinking, to one of the mini-service pumps. Where was it all supposed to take place? Surely not right here on station property? Just who and what was he supposed to be on the lookout for?

Durwood got out of the car, straining to act as natural as he could, and unhitched the hose from a pump. This act in itself, a common enough ritual, gave him a chance to do some more looking around. As he did so, he took his time unscrewing the Ford's gas cap.

Across 19th Avenue, two unmarked cars, which Durwood assumed to be those of plainclothesmen, were parking. But what if they weren't able to get over to the station in time should anything go wrong? Go wrong? What could go wrong? Tentativeness was making him a little crazy. With sticky hands he cautiously nosed the beak of the rubber-collared hose down into his fuel tank. He wasn't sure that he even needed gas. What he did know was that if he didn't penetrate that opening at just the right angle for a snug fit, he was apt to spill some of the extortionate gasoline or else poke a hole in the tank as he already had done once. When he clicked up the lever to activate the pump, nothing happened. He tried it again, repeatedly fingering the trigger on the hose. Still nothing. He turned in the direction of the yellow-haired attendant, who was still busy filling the imposing Lincoln. What a gas guzzler! The boy waved to him.

"Sorry, mister," he yelled, "but that pump isn't working. I

217

haven't had time to put up a sign yet. Try the other one, why don'cha? But don't tell anyone I let you pump it yourself!"

That was fine as far as Durwood was concerned. The more time to kill and to steel himself, the better.

While he was backing up the wagon to another pump, Durwood got a glimpse of a bright orange Audi sedan easing past the station, creeping by jerkily, uncertainly, as if the driver were trying to make up his mind whether to pull in or move on. The only other orange Audi that Durwood knew anything about belonged to . . . He leaned forward and squinted through the misty drizzle. Well, what do you know, it *was* Brewster. Why, that zonked-out fool! This wasn't in the script. Why the hell would he deliberately turn up now to make things more complicated than they had to be? Brewster beeped lightly and waved before disappearing around the corner.

Durwood wiped the moisture from his forehead, unable to tell if it was drops of rain or sweat. He watched the attendant walk around to the front of the Lincoln and stand there, twirling his dirty red rag, waiting for the hood to pop.

Grudgingly pumping five dollars' worth of gas, Durwood tried to peek over inside the Lincoln. The unlowered windows were made of such highly tinted glass, however, that all he could make out were the shadowy outlines of a driver and a couple of back-seat passengers. He figured it had to be some kind of chauffeured limousine, perhaps on its way to the airport. At heart, he was halfway thinking about Dixie and how much she had enjoyed being carted around in luxury on her birthday night. It felt as though all that had happened months ago in some distant, uncalendared year that belonged to the Good Old Days. What had he been so worried about, so rushed and steamed up about? If only he could turn back the clock a week or two—one day would do—and pay more attention to Celia.

It was the slow passing of a marked patrol car that made him jump, causing the gas cap that he was twisting back in place to slip from his hands and fall to the asphalt with a clank. But the prowl car cruised right on past the station down the avenue, leaving him more in the dark than ever, with his nerves on fire, wondering what was going to come down. And when?

By then it was 9:55. Five minutes to go. Durwood couldn't believe the boy was still busy with the Lincoln. He checked to see if the plainclothes men's cars were still parked across the way. He felt vaguely reassured when he saw that they were. The plan called for them to remain in radio contact with other police units scattered throughout the neighborhood, supposedly on alert. At a given signal, when Durwood tugged at his neck brace a certain way, they all would converge on the station and block the driveway exits and entrances. The plan was simple-minded, risky even, but he'd had no choice but to go along with it. Lieutenant Sparrow had assured him that his men knew precisely what they were doing, that they were professionals who knew perfectly well how to overcome and disarm would-be assailants in such potentially violent situations. As for Durwood, he was of the opinion that even though he was a professional athlete, *that* didn't necessarily enable him to call the shots in any basketball game he played.

But here they all were, waiting, fumbling, and sticking it out. Time might not have been ticking by as quickly as he would like, but it was moving.

"Be with you in a sec," the attendant shouted at him. He finally was shutting the hood of the Lincoln. Even though Durwood was secretly thankful that it had taken forever for the limousine to get serviced, it nevertheless vexed him deep down to be reminded again of how little weight his piece of Ford wagon carried and how far down the pecking order he placed when it came to status and clout in the power-bent world of automobiles. Then, too, his being a mini-service customer probably didn't help any.

Durwood was fidgeting with his charge card and musing on this when the van—a sure-enough Chevy, rinsed off now but with the same "WE GONE" plates—came sputtering in from the street and squawked to a makeshift halt at the edge of the garage area, over by the public telephone booths. It was pretty much the kind of entrance Durwood had been expecting, and yet he still wasn't ready for it.

From where he stood, in the middle of an island, Durwood watched as Choo Choo left the motor chattering and got out on the driver's side. He was wearing a cheap, stiff, transparent raincoat and nothing on his head. This surprised Durwood since the youngster had wavy, black, glistening hair falling in loopy curls to his neck. You'd think he'd want to keep his perm from "going back." Puffing a pipe, he kept pulling up his stiff looking Levi's, which hit him just below his big belly. They seemed to be held in place, more or less anyway, by one of those fat, big-buckled belts from days gone by. Choo Choo took the pipe—one of those Sherlock Holmes numbers with a curved stem and oval bowl—out of his mouth and motioned with it.

From the other side of the van stepped a man who Durwood—at first glance, that is—couldn't recall having seen before, but as he studied the two, still at a safe distance, it struck him that the second party wasn't a stranger after all. In spite of the round eyeglasses, the oversized woolen flea-market coat, and all that soft, frizzy hair spiraling out from his head and down around his ears, the face was nobody else's but Trip's. And he looked absolutely giddy and harebrained.

The panic was on, but Durwood felt calm, uneasily so, as he wiggled his toes inside his damp sneakers, eager to see just how this ugly little scene was going to play. If it got too nasty, he still had plenty of time to grab Brewster's loaded knit cap from the glove compartment. He stood fast by the car door and watched. His heart was beating normally, not pounding the way it did before or after a game. He was psyched up now—no jitters, no fatigue—and ready for anything that might come crashing down around him.

Then a strange thing happened. Instead of approaching him or waving him to come to them, Choo Choo and Trip went into a whispering huddle; then Trip climbed back inside the van and slammed the door behind him. Choo Choo ducked into one of the telephone stalls and, looking over his shoulder, lifted the receiver.

Just as the station attendant was slack-butting his way over to process Durwood's charge transaction, the phone went off in the Chevron office.

"Now, that's just what I need," the boy said with shoulder-hunching resignation. "Probably my boss. Excuse me again, mister. I really wouldn't blame you if you just up and drove off."

"Take your time."

The boy hustled off, answered the phone, then came back out the door and hollered, "Hey, your name Knight?"

"Yeah?"

"Well, there's a call for you from somebody says it's some kind of emergency."

Durwood, who was ready to tug like crazy at his neck brace the minute he knew Celia was going to be safe, could almost appreciate the bit of cleverness he was witnessing. At least he had to give Choo Choo credit for having a certain amount of nitwit charm.

"Okay," he heard Choo Choo say as soon as he got the receiver up to this ear, "we got your daughter."

"Where is she?"

"We want you to walk back real slow to your ride and take the spare tire out. You got that? Sit it right there by the pump where you're parked."

"All right, and then what? Where's Celia?"

"I ain't got time for chitchattin and socializin, Woody. First do what I tell you, then come back to the phone."

Durwood wasn't so calm that he didn't feel the chill that was creeping up his back. He came right out of the station office, walked casually to the wagon, opened up the back, and took out the spare, praying that they wouldn't look at it too closely. He leaned it on edge beside the pump and walked directly back to the telephone without so much as looking over his shoulder.

"Sir," the attendant called after him, "you wanna sign for this?"

No sooner had Durwood picked the receiver back up than he saw Trip come dashing out of the van and across the lot toward the mini-service island. There he picked up the tire, shook it, and, grinning to himself, was about to start rolling it straight back to the van when the rear door of the Lincoln sprang open and a young woman stepped out. She was very light-skinned, practically albino, with long, snowy hair. In her gloved hand was a gun that was aimed directly at Trip.

Durwood dropped the receiver and let it dangle by its cord, then, with his mouth wide open, stepped back outside. This was something he had to see for himself.

"Let go of that tire," the woman said very clearly, "or get ready to let go of your life!"

Trip froze in his tracks. The tire rolled to a wobbly collapse.

A suntanned man in a cream-colored suit, wearing shades with mirror lenses, got out from the other side of the Lincoln and calmly walked over and picked up the spare. While the woman steadied her aim, never taking her eyes off Trip, her lanky accomplice—street dapper, to say the least—reached their car just as the trunk flew up. He dropped the tire in, slammed the trunk, and scrambled back inside the car.

All of Durwood's cool had melted by now. He wanted his daughter back, goddamn it!

At the very moment that Choo Choo, looking terror-struck, slammed the van door after jumping back inside and gunned the motor, Durwood saw Trip stumble and fall face forward onto the oily cement. He couldn't figure it. Had a shot gone off, or did he trip, or what? The only thing filling his ears now was a girl's scream—that chilling, bad-dream scream of Celia's all over again. Where was it coming from? "Daddy, Daddy, Daddy!" she cried. Durwood cocked his head. "Help, Daddy! Help me, please!" He heard banging, bumping, the pounding of fists, and the horrible slap-smacking of opened, flat hands against hollowed-out steel.

The van! He had to get to the van and stop Choo Choo!

Totally freaked, but wired for high voltage, Durwood grabbed the edges of his neck brace and tugged away like a maniac. Across 19th Avenue, unmarked cars started up at once, and, way off down the block, he thought he heard sirens, but none of that mattered any longer.

What mattered was getting Celia safely out of the back of that van, which was backing up at full speed now, about to gear up for a scorching getaway. Durwood thought about rushing out and throwing himself in its path but quickly changed his mind. Push having come to shove, Choo Choo didn't seem to give a shit about his fallen partner. Trip still was sprawled right there on the asphalt with his teeth clenched and his face screwed up, clutching the back of one thigh, while the attendant, suddenly the color of a youthful radish, hurried toward him.

As for the fancy Lincoln, which now looked spiderishly

deadly to Durwood, it was quietly slipping clean out of the picture. Whoever was driving had been clever enough to click on the emergency flashers just for the well-calculated hell of it.

Durwood was looking at Choo Choo's face through the windshield—the way he was sweating, the wicked set of his jaw with the pipe clamped in it, his bulging eyes. The sucker was scared! Then he heard Celia scream again, this time above the sharp grinding of gears. Torrents of filthy smoke jetted from the van's tailpipe with a pungent roar that made Durwood cough and caused the bewildered attendant to look in that direction, waving his red rag frantically.

"This fella's been hurt!" he shouted. "He's bleeding. Could you give me a hand?"

"Don't touch him!" yelled Durwood. "You might make it worse. Help is on the way!"

"What's going on? What're you talking about?"

There wasn't time to explain. It was hard enough to think, much less hear. The wail of sirens was everywhere. The van wasn't going to stay stuck forever. Durwood had to do something crazy—and fast.

Spotting an unopened can of motor oil perched on a gas pump by the station wagon, Durwood made a dash, swooped it up, took dead aim, and, gripping its sides as if it were a football, sent the container hurtling and spinning toward the van with all his might.

Shhhooommff!

The Chevy was just beginning to lunge forward when the missile smashed into the windshield, making a hole in the glass. Oil went splattering every which way. Unable to see in front of him, Choo Choo slipped into second and plowed ahead anyway. The blond attendant hopped onto the island, and, for a moment, Durwood thought the van was going to run right over Trip. But somehow Trip managed to roll himself to safety. The wig was sliding off his head, his smudgy face a snarl of pain and resentment. Durwood saw his mouth curl just as the van, which was picking up speed, swerved and then, with a screech, crashed sidelong into his poor, tortured station wagon.

"Goddd-daaammmn!" the attendant shouted.

Without so much as blinking, Durwood darted—it felt like

he'd sprouted wings and flown—to the passenger side of the stalled van. He snatched open the door and dove across the seat. Blind now to anything except the need to save Celia, he didn't give a damn which part of this jackass he grabbed, just so long as he connected with something—a leg, an ankle, an arm, his neck, an ear, *something!* What he got hold of, though, was Choo Choo's wrist, which he proceeded to wring as if it were the wet end of a mop.

"The fuck you think you doin?" Choo Choo yammered, breathing out smoke and at the same time whisking the lighted pipe from his mouth to dump hot ashes onto Durwood's face. Durwood ducked and felt the coals sprinkle down the back of his neck brace, searing the skin there, but all he could do was hold tight to Choo Choo's wrist and twist and twist. He smelled foam rubber burning. Choo Choo was bopping him in the head with the bowl end of the pipe. Durwood held fast and, with his free arm, swung as hard as he could at the whiskered face.

"Daddy, get me out of here!"

"In a minute," Durwood grunted as the stem of the pipe came dangerously close to poking out his eye. That made him angrier. Still holding fast, he hoisted himself up onto the seat and, struggling, shoved all his weight against Choo Choo. The door on the driver's side fell open. Finding himself at keen advantage now, Choo Choo took a swing and cracked Durwood on the side of the face. Durwood felt the sting of his cheek being torn. Then Choo Choo jerked his twisted arm up high and slammed Durwood's wrist down against the steering wheel with such force that Durwood felt a jagged tingle shoot all the way up past his elbow like an electrical jolt. His hold was broken.

Choo Choo leaped out and, slamming the van door behind him, snake-hipped his way around the demolished Ford wagon and jumped clean across the mini-service island.

"Stop him, somebody!" Trip cried out. "Motherfucker ain't nothin but a goddamn rip-off, shine-on artist!"

Durwood got a flash. The cap-wrapped pistol in his glove compartment—that would do the trick! If only he could get to it! But the passenger side of the Ford was so badly wrecked he knew he'd never get the door open in time. There was nothing left to do but haul ass. He took off running.

Just when it looked as if Choo Choo was going to make it off the lot, two cars—one unmarked, the other a regular squad car—squealed into the driveway and up over the curb onto the sidewalk, bringing him up short. The place was crawling with cops, Durwood noticed, now that he'd put his own life on the line. Some of them were brandishing their mean-looking police specials.

"My daughter!" he shouted, catching his breath. "She's in the back of the van. Get her out!"

His neck felt taped on and his arm still throbbed, but here he stood, one-on-one with Choo Choo at last, zigzagging back and forth. The joker had nerve. He snatched the pipe from his mouth, spat, and hurled it at Durwood, missing by inches.

Lieutenant Sparrow, bristling and red-faced, leaned out the window of the nearest unmarked car. He, too, was clutching a gun. Damn, thought Durwood, everybody's got one of those things but me!

"Don't move!" barked Sparrow. "Don't move or I'll—"

"No you won't either," Choo Choo snapped, cutting him off. "You might slip up and hit your boy here."

"Better not test me," yelled Sparrow. "I'll blast your ass straight back to your roots!"

"Fuck you, peckerwood!" Panicked, Choo Choo turned on his heels anyway, but ducked to the ground when the lieutenant shot up into the soggy air.

The report was still echoing in Durwood's ears as he threw himself on top of the fool and got him in a stranglehold. He couldn't tell whose heart was thumping—his or Choo Choo's—as he mashed his thumbs tight against the young man's Adam's apple. Choo Choo gagged and grabbed a bunch of Durwood's coat, but his grip gradually weakened and his hands fell away. And Durwood, sinking farther and farther away from himself, squeezed and squeezed and squeezed.

He was far away now, in a country where landscape, feeling, and thought were sponged up completely, soaking in warm ultraviolet light. There was no such thing as sound, motion, memory, or time. Only soft, peaceful nothingness; the slow pull of violet air swimming all around him, darkly lit, sloshing, lulling; the way life must be like down under the sea.

Durwood felt his head wobble, weightless on his body. His thoughtless head was nine-tenths helium, a dream balloon about to float up into endless purple haze. No longer tied to gravity, his body—if, indeed, he had a body—kept stretching to relink itself to his airy head and drift up through layers of pressure pools to freedom.

Lazily, he ascended the spectrum. Color unfolded. Violet—ultramarine indigo—blue—green—yellow—orange—red—and finally, as he listened to himself breathing again, he inhaled the color of now. Gray. Chilled grayness—the ghost-colored remains of his steaming breath, which hovered like a tiny cloud between his hot face and Choo Choo's down there on the wet, Sunday-morning sidewalk, where everything his nostrils registered smelled like gasoline.

"Woody?"

They were still trying to pull him off Choo Choo. A small crowd was gathering.

"Woody, listen to me . . . I think you better get up now."

It was Brewster's voice he heard, but what was he trying to tell him?

"I think you better get up and walk around some. It's okay. You can get up and go home. I'll drive you."

Durwood looked up and, sure enough, there was Brewster standing over him, a very weak smile on his face. Several policemen, including Jack Vandemeer and Lieutenant Sparrow, were hovering up there with him.

"What happened?" asked Durwood. "Did . . . did I . . . I didn't choke him to death, did I?"

"Well," said Brewster, "not quite. I'm no lawyer, but I'd say you came pretty close just now to setting yourself up for a manslaughter charge."

"Involuntary manslaughter," Lieutenant Sparrow said authoritatively. "Mr. Knight, we've got everything under control. Please step back so we can apprehend the suspect and get him booked."

"What happened?"

"What happened," said Vandemeer, "was you sort of got a hard-on for this, uh, gentleman here and went out on us."

"That'll do," said Sparrow, pushing Vandemeer aside and, with Brewster's help, pulling Durwood to his feet.

"You sure the kid's all right?"

Choo Choo lay with his eyes shut, but one look at the way his chest was heaving reassured Durwood that the bastard hadn't croaked.

"Don't worry," said Brewster, "he'll live. And I got some good news."

"What's that?"

"I took down the license number of that Lincoln before it got away. I would've been here sooner except I couldn't find a parking space. They got some kinda neighborhood Christmas fair going on around here."

Durwood adjusted his clothing and said, "Don't go talking to me about Christmas fairs. I think I've had it."

"Told you it was gonna get heavy, didn't I?" Brewster seemed almost gleeful. "But that Lincoln—it was too conspicuous to pass up. I checked out the plates the minute I drove past the station. See, you're from the country, but I'm from the city—South Philly—and it's the most natural thing in the world for me to get a fix on something like that. I'd do that as quick as I'd chomp down on a hoagie."

"I don't understand," said Durwood. "Why would you pay attention to a Lincoln parked at a gas pump?"

"Heh," said Brewster with an eager chuckle. "See, they were parked . . . Well, anyway, I saw the car parked up the street while I was waiting on a red light. I saw this funny-acting woman coming out the drugstore, looking like the Ice Queen, flashing all that fine leg and boodie; then, when she was getting back in the car, I just happened to peep this slick-looking dude hand her a gun before they shut the door."

"You saw all that?" asked Vandemeer.

"We'll get to that later," said Sparrow, more irate than ever. "Let's book these two rascals and get on with it."

"Where's Trip?" asked Durwood. Sparrow pointed, and Durwood looked across the way to see his old adversary with the shaved head being escorted in handcuffs to a black-and-white squad car.

"As you can see," said Sparrow, "we've got him in custody, and your daughter's safe and sound."

"Celia? Where is she?"

"I'm right here, Dad." Her voice was trembling.

"I'm afraid it isn't over yet," Sparrow went on. "There's still quite a bit of questioning to be done. We haven't established her role yet in all of this."

"Role?" said Brewster. "What role? The girl was kidnapped!"

Sparrow was implacable. "You know that," he said, "and maybe I'm ready to buy that too. It just so happens I believe it. But we've still got procedure to deal with. The law says we've got to question her."

None of this mattered a bit to Durwood when he turned around and saw Celia again—eye to eye, father to daughter. She looked even more tired than he felt. She looked absolutely deranged, unhealthy, bruised, and her face looked pinched, much older somehow, as though she'd aged ten years in a day. But it didn't matter. She was so beautiful that it made him quiver. Nothing mattered but the realness of Celia being here in the flesh, his own flesh and blood.

Whatever it was that had kept Durwood from swallowing rose up past his sinuses into his eyes and overflowed. He smothered Celia, staleness and all, in his arms, then lowered his damp, gritty cheek to hers.

DURWOOD WOKE UP HURTING IN THE upstairs bedroom. He must have slept deeply because he couldn't recall a single dream, not even a flicker of one. All he remembered was total exhaustion and the zombielike sense of relief he'd felt once he and Brewster had delivered Celia safely into her mother's arms.

He remembered the way they both had cried and carried on to the point where even poor little Nissa had been affected. Beyond that, except for some mention of getting Celia into a hot bath all he could recollect clearly was the soothing patter of rain on the roof and the delicious swish of loquat leaves against the window by the bed upon which he had undressed and collapsed.

Lying there now in nothing but his briefs, he still felt numb and mystified. What in the world had happened? What had he done to deserve all this? He stuck one leg over the edge of the bed, partially committing himself to getting up, but at the same time pulled the covers up around him and turned on his side just to see how sleepy he still might be.

When Dixie tiptoed in, wearing nothing but a terry cloth robe, he closed his eyes again for the hell of it and pretended to be zonked. She sat down on her side of the mattress, leaned over and kissed him on the cheek, then shook him.

"Woody," she whispered, "it's almost eight o'clock."

When he didn't move, she shook him again, this time tracing her finger along his neck and jaw and twirling it gently inside his ear. It tickled, but he managed to play dead.

"Baby," she said louder this time, "aren't you getting hungry?"

When he still wouldn't budge, she let go, and he felt her sit up and heard her sigh. Unable to resist peeking a little, he squinted slightly and cut his eyes just enough to see her pull back the covers and kick off her slippers. She rolled into bed and, inching over, put her arms around him. He liked the towelish feel of the terry cloth against his chest and neck.

They lay that way for a while, saying nothing, while Dixie's warm hands slid over his body. Durwood was just about to break out into a stretch and start groaning when Dixie, with no warning, tickled him full force under the arms and around his lower belly. No longer able to control himself, he brought his long legs up and quivered, laughing out loud.

"Okay," Durwood giggled, "quit it. Just stop and I'll get up."

"You don't have to," Dixie laughed. "Everybody downstairs is talking about going out for pizza, and we thought you might like to join us."

Turning to face her, Durwood said, "You sure don't look like you're ready to go anyplace but back to bed."

"Very perceptive, but I can be ready in no time."

"Is Celia up?"

"Up and starving."

"You talk with her yet?"

"A little bit. She's hard to talk to, for me anyway. And the phone keeps ringing. I pulled the plug up here so you wouldn't be disturbed."

"Who's been calling?"

"Who hasn't? We might have to get an answering service for a few days. All that stuff about the kidnapping's in the news now. The cops have been calling, reporters, guys from the team, D'Annunzio, Patsy, Moby, and somebody named Audrey Spain."

"Great, that's exactly what I didn't want." Durwood yawned and sat up. "How come you're going out for dinner?"

"Oh, I don't know. Leon and I've been cooped up here all day and thought it might be a good thing to get some fresh air. Nissa's pretty antsy too. You know how she gets when it's raining."

Durwood reached for his shirt, sniffed it, and said, "I can't put this back on. Maybe I'd better shower and change."

"Can I ask you something?" asked Dixie from her pillow.

"What?"

"Who's Audrey Spain?"

He thought about it fuzzily and said, "The name sounds vaguely familiar, but I can't seem to place it right now. Why?"

Dixie shrugged. "I don't know. She sounded goofy."

"Goofy?"

"Yeah, like she was high or had a speech defect or something. You can't remember what she does or where you met? I mean, she carried on like you were old friends."

Durwood rubbed at his cheek where a scab had formed and worked his neck and shoulder muscles around in circles. His body felt as if it had been danced and stomped on.

"Still hurt?" asked Dixie.

"Baby, I'm so tired of being racked up, I don't know what to do! You'd think I was a defensive quarterback."

"Want me to give you a massage?"

"Thanks, maybe later. I just refuse to put that goddamn brace around my neck anymore."

Dixie sat up and touched his shoulder. "Looks like you got burned on the back of your neck."

"Well, it feels like my whole body's been barbecued."

"Here," she said, slipping out of bed, "let me get some Neosporin and Band-Aids and sponge your cuts with alcohol."

"What'd Celia say happened?"

"She says it was rough, but she doesn't wanna talk about it in front of Nissa."

"So when do we get a report? I mean, the girl's only put us through the roughest couple days I've ever been through."

"Give her a chance to rest up and catch her breath. It'll all come out."

Durwood threw on his karate robe and started toward the bathroom with Dixie warm on his heels. "I've got an idea," he said, pushing on the light. "Why don't you and Nissa and Leon go out to eat and leave us here."

"But that won't work, Durwood. Celia's ravenous."

"Sure, it'll work. I don't think she's got any business being out in this weather so soon. Me neither. Besides, there's some ground beef in the fridge, isn't there?"

"If Leon hasn't eaten it."

"Leon? He's a vegetarian."

"That's what he says, but I could've sworn somebody's been nipping off those cold cuts I put in there to make Nissa sandwiches with."

"Well, he couldn't have eaten all of it. There still oughtta be enough left to melt some Monterey jack on top of and make cheeseburgers. I think that's what I'll do. I don't feel like pizza. I'd just as soon stay here."

Dixie turned on the hot water and held a face cloth under the stream. "You think you can get her talking, don't you?"

Durwood leaned forward, studying the cut on his face in the mirror. "That fool Choo Choo really messed me over some, didn't he?"

"That's how come you wanna stay here, isn't it?"

Dixie wrung out the cloth and handed it to him. It was hot and damp. Durwood pressed it to his wounded cheek.

"I wouldn't mind giving it a try . . . if it's all right with you."

"Suit yourself," said Dixie, "but don't go forcing her to do anything. She's still pretty tired and turned around."

"Ah, that stings, but it feels good." Durwood wet the rag some more and held it against the back of his neck. "Don't worry, I'll take care of it."

"How do you feel?"

He splashed water all over his face and said, "All wrung out, like this rag here. How about all that doctoring you were gonna do on me?"

"Here, hold still," said Dixie, sliding open the door to the medicine cabinet.

The hamburger was right there on the middle shelf where Durwood had seen it last. He hadn't had the nerve to tell Dixie that he was the one who'd been sneaking Nissa's sandwich meat. He broiled patties and heated a can of beans. They sat at the kitchen table, where he watched Celia douse her burgers and beans with ketchup, then wolf them down like a famished tigress.

"They didn't feed you too well, huh?"

Celia shook her head and munched. "I couldn't eat any of that nasty old food they were pushing at me."

"Oh, like what?"

"I don't know . . . Stuff they'd go out for . . . Fish and chips and things. I just couldn't work up an appetite."

"Where were you?"

"I'm not sure."

"How's that? Were you blindfolded?"

"No . . . Well, yes . . . part of the time, but only when they really didn't want me to see something."

Celia averted her eyes. There was a thin ring of ketchup around her lips, which she wiped at with her little finger and licked off.

"Celia."

"Yes, Dad."

"Honey, could you look at me?"

With her head lowered, Celia tore off another chunk of cheeseburger and glanced up at Durwood.

"Celia, I don't mean to be a pain in the ass or pry. But this has been quite an ordeal, wouldn't you say? Now, the police are going to be questioning you, and everybody'll be talking about it. Don't you think it might be a good idea for you to go back and start at the beginning and tell me what happened? You don't have to go into all that much detail if you aren't up to it. I know you're worn out. I'm wrecked myself. Could you just give me some idea of what happened after we saw you last at the Dickens Fair?"

"Dad, can I finish eating first?"

"Then can we talk?"

"Yes, yes, I promise."

Durwood removed the patty from his bun, cranked pepper on the remaining tomato, lettuce, and red onion, then spread on more mayonnaise and bit in. The meat, with its toasted crust of bubbly cheese, looked and smelled good, yet he didn't feel like eating it. He was thirstier than he was hungry. Upending a full tumbler of ginger ale, he didn't stop until he had smacked the last drop.

For the first time, Celia gave her father a long, amused look as he set the glass down. "Wow, Daddy, you were really thirsty, weren't you?"

"Hey!" he said, honing right in on her momentary warmth. "After supper, why don't I make a fire and we can curl up in the front room and have some sherbet like we used to. What do you say? We can watch a movie on television or something."

Celia held a forkful of beans midway between her plate and her opened mouth and smiled like the child her father had almost forgotten.

Durwood poured them both more ginger ale and held up his tumbler. "I love you, you know. I really never knew how much until yesterday."

"Oh, Daddy," Celia whimpered and let her fork drop, reaching across the table.

Durwood didn't even flinch when her nervous fingers, fumbling for his, smeared ketchup and grease all over the sleeve of his fresh, clean shirt. Taking hold of her slippery hand, he stared

233

past the moistness of her sad, brown eyes clear down into something very beautiful and frightened that shone behind them, perhaps just beyond them.

"I'm sorry," she said suddenly, pulling back and picking up her fork again. "I—I don't know what to say."

Durwood watched Celia munch another mouthful of beans half-heartedly. Something had changed. She was elsewhere. He wanted to be there with her and hear her describe what was really on her mind.

Getting up, Durwood walked around and stood behind his daughter's chair, resting his hands on her shoulders. "You go on ahead and finish up," he told her. "There's ice cream and sherbet in the freezer. Why don't you scoop us up a couple bowls and bring them to the living room. I'm gonna go build that fire."

The blazing oak fire, Durwood had to admit, was a gem. He felt very much the family man now, stretched out on Dixie's Persian rug in the flickering light of the snapping flames with Celia on cushions beside him. Except for the glimmer of the TV screen across the room, there was no other light in the room. He fingered the Band-Aid on his cheek and tried to get Celia's story straight.

"Now, let's see," he said. "You say you walked out of the Cow Palace, and then you—"

"No," she corrected him, "I was led out of the Cow Palace."

"And who was leading you?"

"Sidney."

"Who's he?"

"It's a she."

"Hmmm, women have just about taken over that name and gone with it, haven't they?"

"Sidney is Choo Choo's girlfriend."

"Girlfriend? So the rascal's got a girlfriend, huh?"

"Well, I don't know what else to call her. She isn't really his girlfriend. She's more like a . . . a business partner of some kind."

"A business partner?"

"See, Dad, both Choo Choo and Trip know all these girls and women they're always calling up and—"

"Tell me this, dear . . . Just how did this Sidney know you were gonna be at the Dickens Fair on Saturday? If you just tell me that, then maybe I can get the rest of what you've told me in perspective."

"I don't know how they knew, Daddy. They just *knew*. I mean, this woman came up to me and said, 'Celia Knight. Aren't you Celia Knight?' And when I told her I was, she said, 'C'mon, you're going with me.' I asked her where we were going and she just said, 'Don't worry, this'll only take a minute.'"

Durwood propped himself up on one elbow and stared directly into her eyes. Celia blinked and turned away, then cleared her throat.

"Dad," she said, making a sorrowful face, "I'm the one who got kidnapped. I know what happened, but I get so depressed remembering it I might get a few details jumbled up here and there."

Frankly, Durwood didn't give a hang about the factual small points that he was pressing Celia to clarify. All he truly cared about was the sound of what she was saying, the tone of her voice, and the way it wavered. Given her condition and the touchiness of the situation, he figured that the easiest way to go about this would be to somehow keep her relaxed and talking. His one big hope was that Dixie and the gang wouldn't come piling through the door and ruin everything.

"Okay," he said, once again straining to sound casual. "Forget about Sidney and how they knew about the fair. When you got outside, what happened then?"

"I told her, 'Hey, where're you taking me? What's going on? My folks're waiting for me back there.'"

"And what did she say?"

"She didn't say anything. She just kept nudging me and bumping me with her shoulder and saying stuff like, 'Shut up, you little bitch, and do like I tell you if you don't wanna get hurt!'"

"This Sidney said that?"

Celia nodded and licked the last of her sherbet from the spoon.

"Was she a big woman?"

"Not especially."

"You told me a few minutes ago that she was kinda on the large side and mannish-looking."

"I'm sorry. I must be getting her mixed up with a friend of hers I met later on. I didn't mean for it to jump off like that."

Jump off like that. Well, all right. He was getting old—older anyway. He grew up saying things like "strung out behind" and "My nose is open." So why not Celia's aggravating lingo? That must've been something she picked up over the weekend. He'd never heard her use the phrase before.

"So where did she take you?"

"To a car."

"Did you happen to notice what make it was?"

"It was a little brown car, beat-up and old with stuffing coming outta the upholstery. I think it was a Buick."

"But you aren't sure?"

"No."

"And who was driving the car?"

"A big, brown-skinned woman."

"You remember her name?"

"No, she never said anything."

"Was there anybody else in the car?"

"Nobody but the three of us."

"Did Sidney come up to you at the Cow Palace and introduce herself? I mean, did she say, 'My name is Sidney, and I've been assigned to push you around for the rest of the—'"

"Please, Dad, don't be facetious."

"Then how did you know her name was Sidney?"

"That's what Choo Choo called her."

"And when did he come into the picture?"

"He was waiting at this building they taken me to."

"*Took*, sweetheart, if you don't mind."

"All right, this building they *took* me to. It was a run-down apartment building way out in Hunters Point. I think Choo Choo either lived in the building or else knew somebody who lived there. Anyway, they pulled up around in back and Choo Choo was waiting there in his van."

"The same one from this morning?"

"That's right."

"And did he take you inside the building? Is that where you spent the night?"

"No, we just stayed there long enough for him to make some calls and work on his van. I remember him telling Sidney something was wrong with the transmission."

That part sounded plausible. If it hadn't been for the van's gear troubles at the Chevron station, no telling how all of this might have turned out. There was something central, essential, that was troubling Durwood, and he thought he had held off long enough in probing it.

"Celia, tell me, did you have any previous knowledge of this Choo Choo boy before you got involved in this?"

"Any previous knowledge? . . . "

With thinning patience, Durwood studied Celia's face, watched her eyes dart about the room as if distracted. She dragged the sleeve of her sweatshirt across her brow and, pursing her lips, sat up in her cross-legged, guitar-playing position.

"Any previous knowledge," she repeated feebly. "Like, how do you mean that, Dad?"

Maybe he was going about it all wrong after all. Maybe it was time to tackle this thing head-on and to forget about upsetting Celia or hurting her feelings.

"You still understand English, don't you?"

"Yes, but—"

"Yes, but nothing, Celia! Fine. I'll put it another way." He spoke slowly this time, with exaggerated softness and clarity. "Did you know Choo Choo before any of this happened?"

"You mean, before Hunters Point?"

Durwood didn't really want to hear it, or did he? There was nothing more pathetic or sickening than being lied to by a kid, especially one's own. He had never forgotten the pitiful spectacle of Leon—who must have been three at the time—with specks of chocolate on his hands and crumbs around his mouth, telling him that he hadn't gone and helped himself to a batch of chocolate-chip cookies that his mother, Coretha, had baked and left to cool on the kitchen counter. And now, years later, here was Celia being devious about something that was considerably more serious than cookie snatching. It was painful.

"Well," he went on, for better or worse, "did you know Choo Choo?"

"I, uh, I guess you could say, in a sense, that is, that . . . I sort of knew who he was."

Durwood pulled himself up, spooned himself some ice cream from the bowl, then smoothed Celia's hair with his hand. "Now, Celia," he said, "I want you to understand that I'm not just asking this for my own information. Do you realize that you're probably going to be questioned—and I mean questioned to death—by the police before all this is over?"

"Yes, I understand that."

"And do you also understand that I am not an attorney and this isn't a courtroom and you aren't sitting up there on anybody's witness stand?"

By the squint of her eyes and the way she was fidgeting with the flared hems of her jeans, he could tell she was on the verge of making them both miserable. What he couldn't figure out was why. Why couldn't she answer a very simple question that he had tried to put to her as gently as he could?

"I want a one-word answer. Yes or no. Now, did you know this Choo Choo?"

"Yes," she said finally in a quavering voice. "Yes, I did."

"How long *have* you known him?"

"Daddy, how come you're making such a big production out of this?"

Durwood tried to get control of himself. He looked down at his bowl and picked it up, feeling its cool ceramic underside and looking at the melting trickle of ice cream that remained. Then, with a grunt, he slung it at the fireplace. It shattered into pieces against the painted brick.

Celia screamed and jumped to her feet, lifting her hands to her face. "How come you did that?" she sobbed.

"How come you had to go and lie to me?"

"I didn't lie to you. I already told you I knew him."

He was close enough now to grab her, and that's just what he did. He grabbed Celia by the shoulders and shook her until he realized how much bigger than her he was. That was something Dixie was forever reminding him—how big he was, how strong he was, and how, if he wasn't careful, he could badly injure the children. "Daddy, you're hurting me," Celia whined. "Please don't do that. I'm sorry, I'm. . . I'm sorry!" The tears were flowing like gutter water now.

Durwood let go of her and stood back, swallowing hard to hold down the ache in his throat, the ache in himself. "I don't know what you're trying to pull, Celia. I don't even know what's going on in that heavy head of yours, but I do know this . . . I might've been away from you guys for a long, long time, but you can bet your little bottom that I'm back now. I mean, I'm back for good! And you know something else?"

Celia was shaking. He wanted to hold her and steady her, but the knot in his stomach wouldn't let him.

"I don't intend to kick back and let you or anybody else in this family try to slip any bullshit over on me! I'm surprised, I'm *shocked*, that you think you can do that to me. Your mother and me and a whole lotta other people—Leon and Nissa included—have been clawing up walls for the last twenty-four hours, worried about whether you were dead or alive. Kidnapped! That is serious. No way that isn't serious. You go out there, disappear on us, put us through pure hell, pure *hell*, and then come trying to suck up to me with the shallowest crap I ever had to sit still for. Do I look like I'm retarded? Do I?"

Celia's curdled face and the way she was shaking her head told Durwood more than he cared to know. She lunged for him and, throwing her arms around him with a shudder, said, "I didn't mean for it to turn out like this . . . I wasn't trying to hurt anybody . . . It was Choo Choo got me into this . . . When he kept coming on to me on the playground after school, and Moby'd get mad but wouldn't tell him to fuck off like he should've and—"

Durwood stared at her. She was crying and whimpering and sniffling so much that he was having a hard time understanding her words. What was it she was babbling through that runny nose of hers? He pushed her back down to rest on the floor cushions and handed her a paper napkin, but she wouldn't let go of him. She clung to his arm and kept touching his face, and, like someone still gripped in a post-hypnotic trance, she gazed at him fixedly and carried right on with her tear-choked chatter.

". . . See, it started as a joke, just a little prank between me and Choo Choo . . . I told him I wanted to do something crazy, and he said, 'Okay, why don't we let's do that, like, what you got in mind?' And . . . and I thought it'd be interesting to find out what'd happen if I was missing for a day, say, and you and Mom wouldn't know where I was . . . Then there'd be all this commotion and everybody would be looking for me, but I was gonna show up, be back home in no time, with no harm done . . . But . . . but Choo Choo and Trip and them, they tricked me, because they had all this dope they stole—or somebody stole—and they needed me to get it back so they could sell it and make thousands and thousands of dollars to buy all these clothes and cars and things to go to South America and buy some more dope . . . But the other dope, they had to get that back first . . . So they had to get in our car, because that's where it was hid, but Trip . . . Trip hates you . . . I couldn't stand to hear the way he talked about you . . . Neither could Choo Choo . . . They got in a fight, and, and—"

Blinking her swollen eyes, Celia broke off, sobbing, then broke down completely. She curled up on the cushions and buried her head in Durwood's lap.

The anger tightening his stomach seemed like nothing when pitted against the nameless change he was navigating now. Waves of urges and emotions—and pity was one of them—flashed and sputtered throughout his body, like shooting stars with a sting. For a moment, he thought he'd no longer be able to breathe the oak-smoked air in this shadowy, sad room. He cuddled his daughter, tentatively at first, then helplessly. And, feeling the lurch and heave of her back, fragile under his touch, he bent and pressed his lips to the sticky, wet edge of her face and swallowed again, tasting salt.

The phone rang. Durwood let it ring. There was no one out there he wanted to hear from. It stopped, then rang again. Celia continued to cry and mutter muffled words into his lap.

Rain fell. The fire crackled and popped. Across the room, in some other world, his boy Clint Eastwood was just completing a daring leap onto the roof of a speeding school bus when the screen went white and Santa Claus came on, bearing glad tidings and avalanches of Coca-Cola in bottles and cans, surrounded by falling snowflakes, bundled-up children with shiny sleds, and all the seasonal trimmings.

Just then Durwood heard the front door push open and Nissa bounding inside.

"Hey, we're back, you guys," she sang, "and we brung you some pizza! Daddy! Celia! Is anybody home?"

Later that night, with both girls in bed, Durwood sat up watching television with Leon and Dixie, telling them what had happened. Durwood was still shaken.

"I don't get it," said Dixie. "I always thought Celia was smarter than that. At least I thought she cared enough to keep from scaring us like that. I don't understand the child."

"I think I do," said Leon.

"Then would you explain it to me and Durwood?"

Leon turned to his father and said, "Well, it goes back to what I was telling you yesterday." He laughed. "Hard to believe it was just yesterday, isn't it? Anyway, I intend to get her off by herself as soon as I can and find out what I can. But my gut reaction, my intuition, is pretty much what it was from the beginning."

"And what does this sixth sense of yours tell you?" asked Durwood.

"It tells me that Celia's suffering from the same thing I was suffering from when I was her age. The only difference is her circumstances are a little bit different than mine were."

"Hold on," said Dixie, getting up to change channels. "The eleven o'clock news is about to come on."

"Who cares?" snapped Durwood. "This is more important. Tell me, Leon, what kind of suffering do you mean?"

Leon nestled back into his spot on the sofa and looked hard at Durwood, who was perched on the edge of his big, overstuffed chair, and leaning forward so as not to miss one word.

"It's like a sickness," Leon continued. "There's no name for it. I mean, at fifteen I was all screwed up. I was lonely. I felt rejected, inadequate, confused . . . I was all those things, and yet, deep down, I felt superior to most of the grownups I knew—except for my heroes, that is. You know who some of my heroes were. They were musicians—people like Lester, Bird, Miles, Art Tatum, Duke, Monk, Mingus, Coltrane, Sarah Vaughan, I could go on and on—but I didn't know any of those people personally. All I had to go by was the music they played. Beautiful music. They were safe heroes to have because to me they were superhuman. My other big hero was you, Pops."

Uneasy about what Leon might say next, Durwood settled back and watched Dixie bend, on her way back to the sofa, and pick up a fragment of the bowl that he'd smashed. She promptly held it out to him in her open hand and grimaced, shaking her head.

"Go on, I'm listening," he told Leon.

"Well, I worshipped you. Maybe I didn't show it, but I did just the same. You were my father and you also were making it as a professional athlete. The kids at school looked up to me because of that. Practically everybody did. I wanted you to see and know how much I thought of you, but, since you also were my old man, it was tough. I mean, I sure couldn't come right out and say it. On the other hand, I was getting another side of you too—a side the public never knew about. I didn't put you down, like Coretha did sometimes. I guess she had a right to, being my mother and all. But there was a part of me, I guess I'm trying to say, that couldn't stand you, Pops—and please understand that all this was going on inside me years ago. You know I don't feel that way now."

"So how come Celia had to go and get herself kidnapped? Are you saying she feels the same way you used to feel about me?"

"Yes and no. You see, I had my music and I was a boy, and I don't care what they're saying nowadays, boys and girls are emotionally different. I really believe that."

"They aren't only emotionally different," said Dixie, grinning slyly.

"You know what I mean. I was used to hardly ever seeing you or being around you. Coretha had other men friends, and a couple of them—one in particular—gave me some of the kind of attention I thought I should've been getting from you."

Durwood hung his head, then looked up and said, "As I've told you many a time, I'm not at all proud about how stupid I was in those days, Leon, and all I can do now is try to make it up to you. But—"

"That isn't necessary to say anymore, Pops. I understand perfectly now, believe me, but I'm one of the lucky ones. I was an only child, but I had my music and friends and plenty of other things I was interested in. If it hadn't been for the music, I don't think I would've ever gotten over. . . ."

"So what it boils down to," said Dixie, "is you were strong and a little on the unique side, right?"

"No," said Leon, who was talking now as much with his hands as with words. "What it boils down to is Celia's gotten a taste of what it's like to have a father who's around, physically anyway, but who still isn't available to her. Oh, hell!" he muttered, closing in on some invisible object with his long fingers. "I wish we all were telepathic the way human beings used to be, so we could just sit and broadcast pictures to one another. Words get in the way."

"I think I get what you're saying," said Durwood. "Don't worry, I'm not deaf . . . not yet anyway. Dixie, would you turn that thing down, *please!*"

"Hey, look!" said Leon.

Durwood turned his head in time to see an old publicity photo of himself on the TV screen.

"Where did they get—"

"Be quiet!" said Dixie. "I'm trying to hear!"

"San Francisco Police this morning, responding to a call for help, rushed to the scene of this service station and successfully subdued and apprehended two local men suspected of the Saturday-afternoon kidnapping of fifteen-year-old Celia Knight, the daughter of former Bay Area Beanstalk star Durwood 'Woody' Knight. . . ."

"Since when was I ever a star? I'm the one almost got myself killed out there, and here they go taking all the credit."

"Shhh!" said Dixie.

They were being treated to film footage of the Scheherazade Chevron station and a slow pan of the pump area. There was even a tight close-up of the blood left on the pavement where Trip had been felled. Two policemen in rain jackets were shown hunched over the red stain, pointing it out and looking as though they were engaged in grave analytical speculation.

"The two arrested were twenty-one-year-old Charles Triplett, Jr. of the Western Addition and twenty-two-year-old Cedric Bell of Hunters Point. While plainsclothes and marked police units led by Lieutenant Oakley Sparrow were closing in for the capture, one of the alleged kidnappers, Triplett—and that's his blood you're looking at now—suffered a bullet wound in the leg when an unidentified blonde woman reportedly fired on him from the back seat of a black Lincoln Continental—California license plate IOU 000—that had been parked at the scene but sped away before police closed in. A fellow officer of Sparrow's, Jack Vandemeer, who describes himself as an old pal of Woody Knight's, gave the Channel 6 News Posse the following account. . . . "

All at once, there stood Vandemeer with a mike thrust in front of his mouth, in full electronic splendor, and looking nothing like the man Durwood remembered. Oh, he looked like himself, all right, only the image seemed too smoothed out somehow, too well-rounded. In his snappy uniform, in brilliant color, Vandemeer resembled a character actor in a big-budget Hollywood movie and, with his somber expression, gave the appearance of being more all-American than Durwood ever could be, even if he were to deck himself out in an Uncle Sam suit tailored by Yves St. Laurent and assembled in the Republic of South Korea.

"Well, I got this call from Woody early Sunday. We're old pals. And he told me his daughter'd been kidnapped, and, in order to get her back, he had to deliver his car to the two suspects at a gas station. His car'd been stolen the day before Thanksgiving and later recovered, but apparently there was a sizable amount of high-quality cocaine with a street value totaling close to a quarter of a million bucks stashed in the spare tire. The suspects wanted that in exchange for Woody's daughter Delilah. . . . "

Dixie gulped and said, "The bastard still can't get Celia's name right, can he?"

"Turn the sucker off! I hate the way they dramatize and play-act that shit!"

"No, leave it on," Leon blurted. "It's interesting."

"I'm with Leon," said Dixie.

"What's so interesting about it? It's all wrong and slapped together, just like everything else I've ever heard about myself in the news. That isn't how it went. I was there. I got hurt." He peeled back his Band-Aid. "See that? That fool tried to split my jaw with his goddamn pipe. That's how come I almost choked him to death."

"Yeah," said Dixie, "I know, I know, but I wanna see what kind of story it made."

By the time Durwood could focus back in on what was being reported, the "story" was winding to a neat close. The powdery, coiffed newsreader was occupying front screen center.

"So, even though Woody Knight himself could not be reached for immediate comment, it certainly appears that his daughter, the victim of this bizarre abduction, mysteriously tied to the narcotics underworld, has been safely returned to her family. Let's hope that little Celia is sleeping safe and sound tonight as this unpleasant story, like a Beanstalks basketball game, comes to a winning end. Tricia Washington, our stunning new recruit here on the News Posse, will be coming up next with a heart-warming story about a welfare family in the East Bay that lucked out on sixty-five thousand dollars in the New York State Lottery. . . . That and more coming up when we continue with Channel 6 News. . . ."

Celia didn't go back to school the following day, nor the day after that. In fact, it was a week before either Durwood or Dixie thought she was ready to tackle the old routine again. The atmosphere that permeated the house those first couple of days—part guilt, part paranoia and repentance—was like the lingering smell of fried fish.

There was talk that went on into the night—consultations, as

Dixie called them—between Celia and her folks, Celia and her close friend Patsy, Celia and Leon, Celia and Moby, Celia and Lieutenant Sparrow, Celia and Gail Díaz, the family attorney. The phone jangled relentlessly, so that Durwood, when he did go out of the house on business, had given up calling home, knowing that the line would be busy.

When she wasn't talking or moping or crying, Celia played her guitar and listened to records. Actually, it was the music that turned out to be more therapeutic than anything else. Durwood came home at the close of one particularly grinding day—half of it spent at the record store and the rest at Gail Díaz's office—to find Celia, Leon, and Moby camped in the living room jamming together and having fun to boot. Celia was laughing and beginning to resemble her old self again. Durwood stood quietly in the doorway and listened while the three struggled through an old, slow Gershwin ballad—"Someone to Watch Over Me"—that Leon had charted out on composition paper. Celia and Moby weren't having an easy time getting through the chordal changes. This seemed to be amusing Leon, who, at one point, looked across the room at his dad and gave him a grinning wink. The scene had been so disarming to Durwood, given the blistering week he was having, that he caught himself envying them their ability to relax and forget themselves that way. He wanted to go dig out his old, unoiled trumpet from wherever he'd buried it and join in the fun, even though he wasn't sure if he could still remember how to finger in basic B flat, the very first scale he'd ever learned.

One icy afternoon when the sun was shining Durwood took Celia to lunch at the towering Hyatt Regency with its theatrical, glassed-in elevators, and then to a full dress rehearsal of the *Nutcracker* at the Opera House, making use of two free passes that a classical-record salesman had laid on him at the shop. They had so much fun—and was Celia ever floored!—that he wondered why it hadn't occurred to him before now to do something crazy like this with just the two of them. He knew, of course, that it never would have happened if all hell hadn't broke loose. Was he being extravagant, overly solicitous? He didn't know and he didn't care. Hadn't he always heard his grandmother say, "You can catch more flies with honey than you can with vinegar"?

Toward the close of that week, Celia came down with something the citizens of the western United States were calling the Cambodian flu—a nasty, fast-moving little bug that apparently spent its entire thirty-six-hour life cycle rendering the people who hosted it prostrate and feverish. She spent the weekend in bed, wiped out, and Durwood, in a guilty sort of way, was relieved that she would have to stay put for a while. He had grown so weary of feeling guilty *about* feeling guilty that he almost shouted "Hallelujah!" in front of Dixie when the elusive Corky Ski called to invite him to a get-together that the Beanstalks were having that Saturday night.

"Aren't I invited?" Dixie asked sullenly.

"Afraid not," he explained. "It's stag."

"Stag? I haven't heard anybody use that term in years. As a matter of fact, come to think of it, I don't believe the word's even crossed your lips since you retired."

"Retired," said Durwood. "Retired from what? I never worked so hard in my whole life as I have since I got outta pro ball."

"Well, do you know how long it's been since we've been out by ourselves together, even to a movie?"

"A movie!" Durwood thundered. "Shit, that's what we need to get the hell away from—a movie! I'm so sick of this movie we're stuck in, I'm ready to throw up."

"Then I'm afraid you're gonna have to stand in line," she said with a puckish smirk.

"Aw, c'mon, Miss Madeleine, I know you're as tired of this stuff as I am, but—"

"That isn't what I meant," said Dixie, who was sitting in the dining room trying to balance their bank book. "I went up just now to check on Nissa, and I hate to hit you with this, but it looks like she's coming down with the same thing Celia's got. I'm not feeling all that hot myself. So if you have to throw up, you'll have to line up at the bathroom door with the rest of us."

"Oh, crap! That means it's just a matter of time before I get it too."

Leon, who had a date on her way to pick him up, paused at the table and said, "I couldn't help overhearing that, and, like the man said . . ."

"Like what man said?" asked Durwood.

Leon whistled a bar of "It Ain't Necessarily So" and added, "You don't have to get sick if you don't want to. It's all in the mind." He tapped at his noodle. "It's all up here. I hardly ever get sick. Of course, a lot of that has to do with nutrition, but it's the sickness consciousness you have to be on the lookout for. That's what'll getcha."

"I appreciate your philosophy," said Durwood, "but how am I supposed to dodge all these Cambodian flu germs when they're right here cooped up in the house with me?"

"Just tell yourself you aren't gonna succumb. You aren't gonna get sick, no matter what. I know it's been rougher than rough around here these past few days, but it's getting better, don't you think? You owe it to yourself, both you and Dixie, to hang loose and keep in shape."

"And I suppose you can tell us how?" asked Dixie.

"It's easy. Just plant the seed of the idea that you're going to remain healthy and nourish that mental seed—just like you would a seed that you plant in the ground—and I guarantee you it'll take care of itself."

"You can lecture us and talk that talk if you want to," Dixie went on, much too gruffly, Durwood thought, "but you forget that we old-time meat-eaters have more experience behind us than you can get from reading those esoteric books of yours."

"I'm sure you do," Leon bounced back, undaunted, "and I respect you for it. I only hope I'm doing half as well as you guys are when I get to be your age. That's why I'm telling you you don't have to come down with the flu or any other unnecessary disease if you don't want to."

Durwood could see it happening again; the off-handed way that Leon had of stealing Dixie's thunder. Like Celia—who was the first to confess it on their way back from the ballet that afternoon—he, too, was going to miss Leon terribly when he packed and flew back to New York after the holidays. Oh, he was going to miss the hell out of that boy! Why couldn't he just move out to San Francisco, Los Angeles, or someplace close by?

"Tell me this," said Dixie, closing the bank book and pushing back her chair. "With all that talking you've been doing with Celia, how is it she's still got the 'sickness consciousness'?"

"I think she's getting better," said Leon. "She won't be down for long. In her own quiet way, she's—"

"Quiet, my foot!" cracked Dixie.

"Hey, Miss Madeleine, give the man a chance!"

"In her way, she's starting to work a lot of things out in her mind. I know she feels ugly, real ugly, about that stunt she pulled. In fact, I know it scared the daylights out of her. But I also know you two are doing a good job of giving her some kind of support, and, let me tell you, she needs that more than you might even realize. It's so easy to forget she's still a child."

Dixie said, "Well, I haven't forgotten it. I wish I'd had somebody to soothe my wounds and take me out to dinner and shows after I'd messed up and showed my folks my behind."

"Dixie," said Leon, advancing and kissing her smack between the eyes, "I don't know what I'd do without you. With you around, I really have to keep on my toes, don't I?" He eased both arms around her and, on tiptoes, gave Durwood another one of those looks that Dixie never saw.

It cracked the ice, as it always did, and Dixie hugged him back and said, "Now, you see me standing here acting all calm and understanding, but you know what I'm wondering, don't you?"

"Would you believe," he said, backing away now with hands on her shoulders, "that I'm still studying up on mind reading?"

"What I'm wondering," she said, "is if you talk that way to me and your father here, then what manner of jive do you be talking to these young ladies such as the one you're about to take out?"

"Actually, she's taking *me* out. But since you're being sweet and inquisitive, I'll tell you a secret."

Durwood was chuckling, the same as Dixie, but he did stretch his neck to hear what Leon would say. Strange, he had never really heard him talk about women or dating.

"I'm usually so scared to death of them that I do a lot of listening the first time out. I mean, I really actively listen. I'm the most passionate, affectionate listener you ever saw. I let them tell their story, and I respond, not passively but actively, like I say. And you know what? They love it, and I do too."

"You're putting me on," said Dixie. "That never would've worked in my day. Men were always doing all the talking. Your father nearly talked me deaf when we first met, telling me about how he was gonna do this and gonna do that, how smart and beautiful I was." She turned and flashed Durwood her hang-dog look, an apology that said, I-know-I-have-no-business-saying-all-this.

Durwood said, "Yeah, and I've been doing the listening ever since."

Dixie pushed him playfully. The doorbell sounded.

"All I can add to that," said Leon, "is it must have been back in your day—in another time and another place—because these young women they've got out there today can chew a man's ear off . . . even the ones that're inarticulate."

"Where'd you meet her?" asked Dixie, whom Durwood sometimes called Her Nosiness. She seemed dead set on beating Leon to the door.

"Oh, she works at this music store where I've been buying my reeds."

Durwood stood back and watched Dixie click on the porch light while Leon gave his glad rags last-minute adjustments.

"I see you had sense enough to sneak on some of your daddy's aftershave," Dixie told him as she pushed down on the door latch.

A tan woman, taller than Dixie, green-eyed and thin with indigo hair, blinked and removed her hands from the pockets of her chic vinyl raincoat. "Hi," she said with a courteous smile, "I'm Trieste. Is Leon ready?"

"He's right here," said Dixie, dabbing at her own hair. "I'm Madeleine Knight, his mother."

"Charmed, I'm sure," said Trieste, beaming down at Dixie and putting out her hand. Leon waved her inside. "And this is my father, Durwood."

Feeling awkward and unpresentable in his raggedy, around-the-house clothes, Durwood stepped forward and shook the woman's warm hand. He'd never met any of Leon's dates before, but this one, with her hair in braids, looked beautiful. And since he was very much under surveillance, he knew he had to be careful about how he reacted.

"Pleased to meet you," Durwood said in his coolest voice. "I hope you two have a nice night on the town."

"Oh, Mr. Knight," Trieste said excitedly, "I've heard so much about you. This truly is an honor. I can't believe that I'm actually touching the hand of the man who carried the ball and made all of those dramatic touchdowns for the Forty-Niners."

Leon, as smooth as maple syrup, squeezed Durwood on the arm, pecked Dixie on the jaw, and took Trieste by the hand, saying, "I'm sure Dad still can't believe it either. But we've gotta run now, Tristie, if we're gonna be on time for that set at the Great American Music Hall. Good night, everybody."

"Don't keep my boy out too late," Dixie shouted as they raced off down the steps toward Trieste's purring Datsun sports car with lights still ablaze.

Afterward, once she'd shut the front door and they were back in the dining room, free to be themselves again, Dixie broke into one of her killer laughs, which Durwood was helpless to interrupt. All he could do was wait for it to run its course.

"Touchdowns!" Dixie managed to get out between chortles. "The Forty-Niners! I love it, I love it! Aren't you glad to be slowing down and don't have to worry anymore about being with it?"

THE BEANSTALKS' PARTY WAS at Gene Jones's Telegraph Hill condominium. Gene was the team's flashy forward who had dubbed himself Gene "Genetic Action" Jones for the press, a tag that Durwood had always mildly resented. Sometimes, though, when he thought about it, he had to hand it to Gene for being clever enough to come up with a nickname that the fans and journalists were crazy about. Maybe he, too, should have given more attention from the very beginning to developing a dazzling public image. He brought it up while Brewster was busy trying to squeeze his Audi into a tight curbside space between two larger cars.

"What's done is done," Brewster told him curtly with a sigh of relief. "All I care about is right now. Hey, why don't you hop out and see if my wheels are angled enough so we won't go sliding off down this hill."

Durwood got out and took a look, then waved an okay.

Brewster rolled up the windows, then stepped out and locked his door. "Tell you, if one of these traffic machines I'm jammed in between doesn't move, we're just stuck here, you know."

"Don't worry," said Durwood, "it's still San Francisco. People don't stay in any one place too long."

They walked up the hill toward Gene's, straight into the wind. Darkness was beginning to settle in, and Christmas trees twinkled and winked from the windows of affluent apartments and smug Victorians.

"Woody, when're you gonna face up to the fact that your playing days are behind you? You can go on dreaming and rearranging your scrapbooks and sit up cursing old video tapes. But, hey, none of that's gonna change what's already gone down. Look, man, we're gonna do all right in this business of ours. We can't miss. If we play the game and be careful about the kinda P.R. we put behind it, before you know—zap!"

"Zap, what?"

"Zap, we'll be opening up Knight and Day number two, Knight and Day number three, and then—"

"Slow down, Brew! We haven't even got number one going yet. And anyway, do you know what a headache it'd be trying to keep on top of all those stores?"

"Now, *that* is your problem. You gotta have vision. You gotta get up offa this little pootbutt fantasizing and dream big. I'm surprised at you—a big old slewfoot Texan—always holding back like you do. You're supposed to dream big, act big, talk big, and do big! Now, you take Mitzi. Oh, I love that woman!

Smart as a whip! That pretty little thing just now got here off the boat from Japan, and—"

Two juice-heads—who, for some reason, had wandered far afield of their turf and were clearly out of their minds—stumbled down toward them as they were reaching the top of the hill. Durwood knew right away that he and Brewster were going to be pestered.

"Say, Jasper, I know him," one of them pointed at Durwood and gibbered. "That's O.J. Simpson. That's old O.J.!"

"Naw, it ain't either," slurred Jasper. "Winnie, you crazy!"

"Look here," said Winnie, blocking the sidewalk and breathing his Annie Greensprings wino breath in Durwood's face. "Listen, O.J. Seein as how I been a big fan of yours goin way back, do you . . . do you think you might could get us a coupla cases of orange juice and one of them Hertz rent-a-cars? See, we got this party we on our way to."

"You gotta excuse him, mister," Jasper mumbled. "He don't see too good when he under the influence, but *me*, I do know who you are."

"Well, who is he then?" asked Brewster, stuffing his hands into the pockets of his dark velvet topcoat.

"You're Dr. J., right? Am I right?"

All Durwood did was shake his head and try to walk around them.

"Well, whoever you are," said the first wino, doffing his fuzzy Russian headpiece and holding it out, "we sure could do with a little chari . . . chairut-a-bubble, uh . . ."

"Charitable," said Jasper, embarrassed.

". . . A little charitable contribution. Anything you can spare."

"You happen to be standing in our way!" barked Durwood.

"Take it easy, Woody," said Brewster as he came up out of one pocket with a crumpled, balled-up bill, which he dropped politely into the outheld hat.

The derelict retrieved the offering and, after smoothing it out, held it up for his buddy to see. "God-*damn*!" he snarled. "Jasper, you see this? A stingy, tight-ass one-fucking-dollar bill!" Then he turned to Durwood and Brewster. "I think it must be some kinda mis-apprehension goin on. See, this here is Telegraph Hill. We didn't climb up here for no bullshit chump change. It's Christmas, man, it's Christmas! . . . Joy to the world, and like that. Y'all sposed to give till it hurt, then give some more—god-*damn*!"

"C'mon, Winnie," Jasper was urging, "let's get outta here. Thank you kindly, sir, and Merry Christmas to you." He tugged at his outraged partner's arm. "This the best we done all day."

"Fuck that!" boomed Winnie. "This is Telegraph Hill, man! It was my idea in the first place, remember? Shit, a one-dollar bill ain't sayin nothin to me . . . Hell, by the time we get to the bottom of this hill, inflation'll be done et this little parkin change *up*! Say, O.J., ain't you got no tens or nothin? Shit, a five'll do! Cheeseburger with french fries and a Coke cost you five dollars now. We goin to this party and need to get us some Chivas Regal."

Durwood was gearing up to shove the drunk aside when Brewster pulled him back. Jasper took firm hold of Winnie's elbow and, practically dragging him, moved on. "Thank you, gen'mens," he hollered, "and God bless you, Dr. J."

"I'm not Dr. J.!" Durwood called down to them, but Brewster put a finger to his lips and, looking around, said, "Shhh, save your breath. This just happens to be the place."

"How come you put up with all that ratshit?" asked Durwood. They were clicking up the walkway. "You didn't have to go giving them a whole dollar. Tight as you are with money, I don't get it."

"No harm done," said Brewster as they arrived at the condo's brightly lit lobby entrance. "I don't tell many people this." He stopped at the glass door and looked up at Durwood, who, seeing that Brewster's eyes were watery, figured that this hard-blowing breeze had gotten to him. "But, you see," he continued, glancing down at the roster of unit buzzers, "my dad back in Philly—he used to be one of those people."

It was Corky Ski who answered the door to Gene Jones's apartment on the seventh floor. "Well, it's about time," he gushed. "Woody Knight and Brewster Day! I don't believe it, but if it's an apparition, please let it linger just a little bit longer.

Come on in, guys, and sample the virtues of male companionship!"

Corky, Durwood thought, hadn't changed one bit. If anything, he looked and talked and acted more like himself than ever. His hair never looked blonder, his tan never tanner, his smile never warmer. Only his style of dress was different. In what were quickly becoming the old days, Corky used to go in for white suits, dark shirts, and sizzling ties with big, hip-looking caps and shades, or fat-checkered pants with mammoth belt buckles, turtlenecks with gaudy pendants, expensive leather jackets, clear gold-rimmed glasses, and stately black Apache hats with rainbow-beaded bands set off by a pair of sharp, keen-toed boots or shoes. Now he got by in a white knit sweater, narrow shirt collar peeking over the top, Calvin Klein stovepipe jeans, Gucci loafers, and short hair. He looked like he should, and so did everybody else.

He ushered them inside while apologizing for the loud music. "Don't worry, I'll slip over there to the stereo in a minute and ease that sucker down, take that disco shit off and put on some Crusaders. All we're into here is eating, drinking, and hearsay."

Looking around the room—crammed with paintings, posters, textile hangings, and a few pieces of sculpture—Durwood was thinking how you had to be single to be able to pour that kind of bread into keeping up a show. Then again, now that he thought about it, young "Genetic Action" Jones, right from the start, had commanded considerably more income than he had. It was a new day, and a whole new breed of talented scorers were flooding the scene. The ABA and NBA, having conquered the almighty tube, were getting to the point where they could choke all the extras they wanted out of owners and promoters. It hadn't been that way when Durwood started out.

He remembered, rather sadly, how his lawyer had to wait outside the room where negotiations were being conducted. Players didn't mean beans then. Owners kicked back at the bargaining table and crossed their expensive-slacked legs with a battery of attorneys at their fingertips, coldly aware of him as being only some magical basic resource fresh off the streets. When they asked him how he'd like to travel 100,000 miles a year—and in those days that meant flying in cramped coach quarters, not first-class like now—with so many dollars a day for meals and unlimited freedom to become famous, well, hell, what else could he do but leap at the chance, and gladly? What choice did he have? He was nineteen, pulling straight C's in college, and untrained to do anything else. What did he know? It sounded to him like the greatest thing on earth.

"I wish they'd ask me now," Durwood mumbled out loud just as Corky was escorting him and Brewster toward that part of the room where all the guys and guests were clustered around a very long table, looked over by a jovial hired assistant who almost looked like one of the boys as he dispensed food and drinks. Besides crock-pot chili, the table was laid with cuts of chicken, spareribs, ham, roast beef, vegetable dishes, salads, breads, lip-smacking hors d'oeuvres of every description, crushed ice, dishes, glasses, silver, and real linen napkins, as well as bottles and carafes of liquor and wine.

"What was it you said?" Corky wanted to know. "I'm afraid I missed it."

"Oh, nothing," said Durwood. "Just talking to myself. I'm glad you guys thought to invite us."

"Everyday," said Corky. "Gene's crazy about you, in case you didn't know. Woody, I felt crummy hearing about what you and that oldest girl of yours have been through. We were out in Salt Lake when I read about it in the papers there. You know, it came across real shaky. I couldn't tell what was going on. Can you fill me in?"

"That chili's moving fast," said Brewster. "Better get up there quick if you want some."

"Hold on," Durwood told Corky, "and I'll run it down to you—what I've figured out anyway."

Gene Jones himself, sipping foam off a glass of beer, jumped right up into Durwood's and Brewster's faces, unbuttoning his sweater vest.

"Hey, Woody," he bellowed, "it's a treat to see you here, man! And, Brewster, are you ever gonna pay me back that twenty dollars you borrowed?"

"Twenty dollars?" asked Brewster while they were shaking hands all around. "When was that?"

Jones flashed his familiar, photogenic, gap-toothed smile and said, "Cleveland, my man . . . Right there in the locker room of Cleveland Arena, just before the Cavaliers moved into that new stadium of theirs." He winked at Durwood. "I know you ain't forgot Cleveland, have you?"

Durwood laughed. "That's one joint I'll never forget." He shook his head and made a face. "Ooo, you talk about raggedy! . . ."

Lincoln Rucker—the handsome Stalk center with the shiny, high forehead—moved into the circle with grease and sauce dripping from his fat mustache. In his hands was a plate of ribs, partially broken down, piled on sopping slices of Wonder bread. "Hey, Woody, Brew . . . What's goin on?"

"You got it, Link," said Durwood, sticking out his hand.

"You don't wanna shake this hand," said Rucker. "It's pretty well lubricated by now. Y'all talkin about Cleveland Arena?"

"I hated that place," Durwood went on. "Remember how you used to stand in the shower and somebody'd flush the toilet and you'd almost get scalded to death?"

"Shoot," said Jones, "it happened the other way 'round too. You never knew. I liked to froze when somebody got 'em a drink from the water fountain upstairs."

"Just a second," said Brewster, still looking ponderous. "Now, Gene, I do seem to kinda halfway remember you lending me some money someplace, but it was so long ago—"

"You better believe it was a long time ago. I been waiting on you to bring it up for, let's see, how many years has it been now?" He began counting on his fingers.

"But I can't remember no twenty dollars," said Brewster. "Where'd you come up with that? I thought it was a ten."

Everybody started laughing, and Durwood, who was laughing the hardest, realized that he was back with the gang again and that anything could happen.

"It was a ten," Jones admitted, "but the way I figure it, the least you can do now is tack on a cost-of-living increase. I mean, face it, what ten dollars'd buy then, thirty can't hardly buy now. So I thought I'd go easy on you and split the difference down the middle."

"That doesn't make a bit of sense to me," Brewster said in all seriousness. "But, here, I'm no deadbeat. I'll pay you your money."

Gene Jones immediately held out his gigantic hand. "Thank you, sir—and, please, don't come handing me none of that old toe-jam-smelling money you keep in your shoe. I want me some fresh, deodorized bills."

There was laughter again as Corky Ski got into the act with, "Uh-uh! You better watch out, Gene. If it comes up smelling like Arrid Extra Dry, you'll know where he's been stashing it."

Even Brewster had to chuckle over this one as he peeled off two crisp tens from a modest-sized pocket roll. Gene handed him back one of the bills and said, "Here you go, Brew. A ten's enough. I was just having some fun with you. We're square now, okay? Hey, let's get you two honored guests some greaze and booze. And you better not try to get away from here without trying some of my chockful-o'-chili."

"What in the world kinda chili is that?" yelled Skeeter Moss, the guard who'd replaced Durwood, from the end of the serving table.

"It's damn good chili—chili *I* made myself and named myself, that's what. Took three days to get it to act right."

They carried on this way into the evening, munching and drinking and kidding one another, swapping lies, catching up, comparing notes, and getting loose. Durwood remembered how important this kind of low-keyed, jivey interaction had always been to him when he was playing. Most people had no idea how hard it was to be a pro in this fast-moving game with pressure on you every day to keep running like hell to advance a few inches, even to stay in one place. Momentarily, he had put the family out of his mind, along with Gail Díaz, Lieutenant Sparrow, Trip and Choo Choo, Knight and Day, Christmas, and all the other headaches that had been hounding him. He hadn't fully realized how much his strength had been zapped until now. He was working on his third cognac and soda, sunk down into Jones's fabulous, endless sofa, feeling more relaxed and unwound than he had in weeks, maybe in months.

Durwood was noticing how dwarfed trainer Freddy Chu and owner Frank D'Annunzio looked as they stood joshing and arguing with some of the storky players who were gathered off to one side in front of the life-sized Advent video screen, where the evening's Raiders–Cowboy death struggle was being projected. He sat with Corky, Jones, Link, Brewster, and a promising new forward fresh out of Kansas named O'Dell Shank.

"So tell me," Corky sipped from his wine and asked, "what's it like to be liberated from the likes of this unrelenting rat race?"

Corky could say things like that and get away with it. Durwood rather liked his self-mocking properness. "Liberated?" he began, mulling the word over in his mind. "I don't know if you could say I was liberated."

"Then let's put it another way," said Jones. "How's it feel to be off the plantation for good? Face it, Wood, you gotta admit this is some hard shit to be in, and you were in it close to twenty years."

"And what makes you think I'm not still in it?"

"Hell," said Link, "just look at you. Sittin up there, done ate all you wanna eat and drinkin all you wanna drink. We can't do that." With a playful smirk intended purely for effect, he cut his eyes at light-skinned O'Dell Shank. "At least, most of us can't. I mean, maybe O'Dell here can put away a whole ham and a head of cabbage and a six-pack of Bud for lunch, wash up, then turn around and show up for practice and score seventeen points—plus, he don't even gain weight. But me, I gotta watch my diet and stick with Dr. Pepper."

"If what I saw you put away tonight is what you call watching your diet," said Brewster, "I'd sure hate to be around when you go off-regimen."

This tickled the quiet O'Dell, who suddenly slapped his knee and said, "Don't pay this gangster no mind. Why, right up there in Portland last week, the plane was late and the two of us were getting hungry. So we went up to the cafeteria and had two dinners apiece. Then you know what Lincoln Rucker did? Got on the plane—I was sitting right across the aisle looking dead at him, ask Bolo and Floyd—and not only did he eat up every bit of that make-believe food they threw at us, but, get this . . . When he saw Skeeter'd done dozed off and hadn't touched his meal, that signifying Negro over there took over Skeeter's tray and gobbled all that up too!" He clapped his hands. "Floyd Himmel and Bolo Harris be my witness!"

"Well," Rucker grinned sheepishly, "what you expect? I was famished."

"And you *stay* famished!" said O'Dell.

"Seems to me," said Corky, "that the only difference between you and Link is Link's a little more devious about how much he ingests."

"Devious, nothing," Jones slipped in. "I'd say he was downright sneaky."

While they were roasting Link, Durwood, laughing from way down inside his mellowing belly, could feel himself about to get silly. It was high time he cut the fool again. "Well," he said, patting his stomach, "I must confess I still do try to stay in shape and keep this here in proportion."

"But, see," Lincoln offered, "that's by choice. Pointer's still dockin us fifty bucks for every pound we come in overweight. I mean, I come in there sometime after a coupla days' lay-off and it's like I'm a trucker tryna dodge them interstate scales or somethin."

"I knew somebody was missing," said Durwood. "Where is Pointer tonight?"

Gene Jones looked at his jeweled watch. "Aw, Lester shoulda been here by now. He told me he was gonna be late, though."

"That is one cold-blooded coach," said Durwood. "Remember that time in Boston when my little cousin was waiting for me after we got finished dusting the Celtics, and Pointer saw us leaving the Garden with her hanging on my arm?"

"Oh, yeah," Corky grinned. "And he took you off to one side the next day and hit you with this sermon about how a married man should strive to be more discreet."

"Tell me something, Woody," said Jones. "Was that really your cousin?"

"Swear to God."

"But that girl was too good-looking to be related to you in any way, shape, or fashion."

"I believe she was his cousin," Brewster said calmly. "You know why? Because they both had that same country Texas walk." He hopped up to demonstrate by taking broad steps across the shaggy, white flokati rug. "They all kinda walk like this, you know . . . Keep the toes of them big feet aimed out, ready to kick at a rattlesnake . . . and be taking great big strides like they're tryna keep from stepping in something."

"Oh yeah?" said Durwood, laughing along with everyone else as he, too, got to his feet. "Well, at least we take our time. You Philadelphia and New York people don't even know how to walk."

Brewster spun around. "Don't know how to walk! Then what do we do?"

Durwood put them all in stitches when he took off scuttling around the chairs and hassocks and sofa like somebody in a hurry to catch a subway train on time. "That's how you guys walk, the same as you talk, like everything's gotta be right this minute." He slowed down and moved back to his seat at his own normal pace. "See, out there in Big Foot Country, we believe in taking our time. Brewster grew up where there was always something—buildings, skyscrapers, big poster signs—blocking his vision. He was always busy trying to get around corners and places to find out what was going on. But you take where I grew up, we didn't have that. You could stand at one end of town and pretty damn near see clean across to the next one. So, since we already knew what was going on, we weren't in any big hurry to get anywhere, not unless it was some kind of emergency. We took our time, one step at a time."

Attracted by Brewster's and Durwood's antics, members of the football-watching television bunch began drifting to their part of the room. Frank D'Annunzio, a corpulent gentleman, fiftyish-looking in a richly knitted, gray woolen turtleneck, wandered over and, lifting his steamy cup of coffee, said, "Woody, Brewster, I didn't get to tell you yet how great you're looking. I can't discern a spare tire between you, which is more than I can boast for yours truly."

"You're talking to the wrong person about spare tires, Frank," said Durwood.

"Which," said Corky, "is what I've been attempting to get back to all evening. Woody, would you mind breaking down some of this unbelievably tragic crap you've been caught up in lately? Now, I know that sounds awful, but I don't really know how else to put it just now. Tragic crap—sounds like a headline in *Rolling Stone,* or a punk rock group, doesn't it? We were talking about it just before you got here. What's happening with that? I've been trying to follow it in the local papers, but it's muddled. Personally—and this is pure snobbism, I know—but personally I sort of wish it'd happened on the Eastern seaboard someplace so I could have the pleasure of reading about it in the *New York Times*. At least it might've been clear. Now isn't that silly?"

"Nowhere near as silly as it was," said Durwood, downing the last of his drink and looking around for more.

Gene Jones, ever perceptive host, shouted right away to the hired help. "Hey, Sun Watt! Drag that bottle of Courvoisier V.S.O.P. Champagne Cognac out here!"

"First, I'd like to thank everybody for all the cables and phone calls and the concern you've shown. Celia's doing okay at the moment. At least she seems better."

"Well, my offer still holds," said D'Annunzio. "If there's anything I can do to help, just tell me."

Bunchy Holmes stepped forward and said, "That goes for me too, Woody. I got a son pulled a knife on me once. It's tough raising a family when you can't be there with 'em all the time."

"Listen, Bunchy, it's no bowl of cherries even when you are right there, like I am now."

"Don't underestimate Frank," said Corky. "He and Gina were a real help when Jill was generating all that anxiety. For a while there, I was thinking seriously about throwing in the towel, just hanging it up and getting an office job so I wouldn't have to go back out on the road."

"This might sound like an awful thing to say," Floyd Himmel ventured in nasal Chicago tones. He was a rugged-faced guard who had done some minor-league pitching prior to taking up a basketball career. "But I think I'd go bananas in no time flat if I had to be around my family year in, year out. Sure, I love the hell out of 'em, but that pressure can wear you out. It's the shits."

"Floyd," said Link, "six kids'd wear anybody out. And think about how Lorraine must feel."

"But you're a wonderful father," said Skeeter. "All those family projects you've got going. When I read that Christmas newsletter you guys send out every year, I wonder how you keep track of all that stuff."

"All I know," Floyd continued with a shrug, "is I can't afford to even think about throwing in the towel. Where else could I kick down the kinda money we need to hold that show together?"

"Money isn't everything," Gene Jones added.

"Look who's talking," said Billy Bohannon. "Go have you some crumb-crushers, then report back to me."

"So where do you stand, Woody, with the legal hassle and all?" One thing about Corky, he was persistent.

"It's the biggest mess you've ever seen. To make a long story very short, I'm pressing charges against the two dudes you read about, but it's gonna be tricky since Celia was in on the kidnapping. Complicity, it's called. But she's a minor. The cops think they can nail them on a couple of charges, chickenshit stuff—auto theft, possession of marijuana, malicious assault. They still haven't turned up that car that got away with the tire where the evidence was stashed. A quarter of a million in uncut coke! I can't get over that. We might get a break, though. They're working on the one called Trip to turn state's evidence and testify that his buddy was in cahoots with the couple that shot him and split. Isn't that a bitch?"

"I saw the bitch that shot him," Brewster said excitedly. "I'm the only one had sense enough to get the license plate down."

Corky whistled through his teeth and said, "Whew! And I thought I had problems when Jill ran away and got picked up on MacArthur Boulevard for prostitution. This makes that sound like 'I Love Lucy.'"

"I'd heard about Choo Choo Bell," said Bunchy, the only native San Franciscan in the room besides D'Annunzio. "He was one hell of a high school athlete at one time, a great high jumper. Too bad he had to drift into crime."

"Yeah," O'Dell quipped, "just like the rest of us."

While they were chuckling over O'Dell's crack, the doorbell buzzed, and Jones got up to see who it was. He hurried back after talking on the intercom and, grinning mischievously, announced, "It's Lester. He's on his way up. Why don't we play a little trick on him? I left the door cracked so he can get in. Let's hide in the bedroom and give him a surprise."

Durwood followed the rest of the gang into Jones's fashion-magazine bedroom. The custom-built waterbed, complete with canopy, and the spooky, mirror-paneled walls were not to be believed. As he caught a tipsy glimpse of himself in the mirror, crammed in there with all the rest of these crazy, partying storks, he had to laugh out loud. Oh, he *was* getting loose! *That can't be me*, he thought. *I don't look anything like that.*

"Quiet," said Link. "What the hell's so funny?"

"Just look at us," he whispered. "Check yourself out in the mirror."

There they all hovered, fourth dimensionally—the strangest assemblage of grown men you ever wanted to see. Their images were bouncing from one mirrored wall to the other and back again, creating a visual echo effect that used to make him dizzy at amusement-park funhouses when he was a kid.

"Someone ought to shoot a *cinéma vérité* documentary of us doing this," said Corky, who also must have registered what Durwood was beaming and quaking over—the absolute child-ishness of the situation, to say nothing of the setting.

Freddy Chu broke his silence and said, "They could call it *The Night the Stalks Stalked Off.*"

Finally it got quiet enough for Durwood to hear the front door squeak and carpeted footsteps. There was a knock and Pointer's gravelly voice calling, "Jones? Gene? Where *is* everybody?" Durwood heard applause. It was coming from the quadraphonic speakers and filled the room. The "live" jazz recording that Corky had put on the turntable was just concluding.

"Now!" Jones whispered.

And on that signal, the whole silly crew of them began filing out of the bedroom.

Durwood stopped in his tracks and laughed uproariously at the sight of Coach Lester Pointer and the surprise guest he'd brought along. Then he rushed over with the others to join in the frenzy of greetings and hand-pumping.

"Well, look what the cat dragged in!" Gene Jones said to D'Annunzio, who stood open-mouthed, staring up at Pointer's friend, his round face flushed with respect.

"Wilt!" said Durwood. "You big, rusty rascal! What's a nice Philadelphia boy like you doing hanging out with the likes of this old scalawag?"

"How you doing, Woody!" Chamberlain embraced him and unfastened that famous sports page smile—a combination of glowing optimism and wily reserve—that said: *It's wonderful to be alive, but don't you tread on me!* "Well, you know how it is," he said, looking at Durwood but speaking to everyone, really. "I have to get out and do some slumming every now and then just so I can all the more appreciate the finer things in life."

"You won't believe this," said Pointer. A bull of a man with an angular face and thinning red hair, Pointer couldn't help looking pleased with himself. "He was crossing the street way down by the Mark Hopkins when I spotted him. I pulled over and told him about this little get-together of ours . . ."

"And I told Les I wouldn't mind stopping by for a quickie, and I do mean just for a hot minute. I've got a late date, but I did want to look in and say hi to everybody."

Lincoln Rucker arched his brow and said, "Betcha that date won't be no quickie. Who you goin with these days—Miss America?"

"Close," Chamberlain shot back, "but you know me. Nothing but the best. This young lady's got a little more class than your average beauty queen." He winked at Link. "And she's prettier too." He turned and clapped Brewster on the shoulder. "Say, Home!"

Brewster, all grins and eyes, said, "What's happening, Wilt? You oughtta been here a few minutes ago and seen how your boy was raking us Philly people over the coals."

"Who, you mean Woody? What's he know about it?"

"Oh, I was just having some fun," said Durwood.

"You learned to shoot yet, man?" Chamberlain looked around to make sure everyone could hear. "Betcha this refugee from the Lone Star State didn't tell you about the times I demolished his butt at target shooting, did he?"

"Listen," said Durwood, "anytime you wanna take me on again, I'm game. I am game! How'd you like to drive down to the arcade right now and squeeze off a few rounds?"

"Ready and willing," said Chamberlain, "but, unfortunately,

265

not able to take you up on your challenge at the moment. But if I wasn't saddled down with this engagement, I'd—"

"Excuses, excuses!" Durwood yelled tauntingly. "Now, everybody heard him, didn't you? I'm asking for a return match and this joker is ducking and dodging me. How long you gonna be in town?"

Wilt sighed and said, "Aw, I have to be back in L.A. by tomorrow afternoon at the latest. Sorry, man, but it's gonna have to be the next time around."

"Then what're you doing in the morning? We can hook up before you have to be at the airport."

"Don't worry," said Chamberlain, "you'll get your chance to get shot away again, but not this trip. No way in the world I'm gonna drag myself away from a warm, lovely, feminine companion to go shoot bull's eyes on a Sunday morning with some vengeful hardleg! No way, Woody!"

After a spirited silence, Woody said, "All right, I don't blame you. Tell me what you've been up to since you quit playing. You might inspire me. I could use some ideas."

"Yeah, Wilt," asked Corky, "is there really such a thing as the light at the end of the proverbial tunnel?"

"Let me get you a drink," said Jones, who was beaming, "so you can pull up a chair and tell us about it. We've heard Woody's version, now you tell us yours."

"What's there to tell?" Chamberlain shook his head. "How would I know? I'm still out there making my way through the tunnel."

And on that comforting note, Durwood reached out and slapped cheerful hands with his legendary idol. "Hel-lo!" he laughed. "I definitely heard *that*!"

CHRISTMAS WAS THE ENEMY NOW. Public Enemy Number One. Or, as usual, was he being too subjective? Come next Christmas—as Dixie and Brewster never tired of reminding him—he would look on the season as the savior of their business; that is, if they could get the shop opened in January and hold out until next December.

The days blew by, and, as debts piled up and his energy level sank, the image of that oxygen tent he was going to need grew increasingly vivid in Durwood's frazzled brain. Already he was anticipating what the doctors and nurses would look like and how his family would act, even what they'd say when they showed up during visiting hours to sit by his hospital bed. Of course, he probably would fall for one of the nurses—someone beautiful, attentive, and understanding, whom he pictured as a composite of Leon's friend Trieste and the mysterious Audrey Spain, with a little bit of Dixie thrown into the bargain.

Audrey Spain. Her name alone had been haunting him. Now and again, when he was off by himself, he would take out the napkin on which she'd written her address and phone number and wonder if he shouldn't let her interview him. Brewster thought it a wonderful idea.

"Just make sure when you do," he told Durwood, "you be sure and get in a lotta stuff about the shop—all you can."

"I don't know, Brew. The woman struck me funny that night we met at the disco."

"Funny, how?"

"You know—strange. She's even called out to the house a couple times and left messages. Dixie doesn't know who she is, but she gets plenty upset."

"Well, quite naturally, Dixie's jaws're gonna get tight behind something like that. But *strange?*" Brewster had gone on, giving him the fisheye. "I don't understand what *strange* has got to do with it. Everybody's strange, especially nowadays. Hell, look at you. You're one of the strangest people I ever met, except for maybe Mitzi, but she's coming from a whole different background."

"And what about you?"

"Oh, yeah, of course. That's taken for granted. I know I'm out there just like everybody else, but I got my strangeness under control."

"You do, huh?"

"Sure do, and you can't let anything like that stop us from getting a good write-up for Knight and Day if this woman, like you say, is some kinda reporter or magazine writer."

Durwood said that he would have to think about it, and, indeed, he did. He kept the urge on ice at the edge of his mind, which was overtaxed with worries and anxiety over big things, little things, everything. The big things, it seemed, mattered less and less: Knight and Day, legal headaches, and getting squared away with the auto insurance people now that his tangle of a station wagon had been officially declared "totaled." Now it was the little things that were taking over and threatening to turn what little remained of the year into a fretful trickle of ant-sized nightmares. Evidently, the strain was beginning to show.

"You need to get away," Gail Díaz told him over sandwiches and coffee one afternoon. "You're a mess." They were winding up what had come to be known as a working lunch.

"You know that," said Durwood, "and I know that, but try telling it to the human-flesh-for-lunch bunch."

"Really, Durwood, is it that bad?"

He stared into his almost empty cup and reached for the percolator. What was this, his fourth cup since morning? He'd better start watching it. If Dixie could quit cigarettes again, cold turkey, then certainly he ought to be able to kick his caffeine jones, this unnecessary addiction that hadn't even existed a month ago. For one thing, he didn't like the way it affected his bladder. He seemed to be spending fully a third of his time now on the lookout for restrooms.

"All this rinkydink stuff," he told her. "It's getting to me. Look at me, Gail. You've known me a long time. Would you say I was starting to age overnight, or what?"

Gail bit into her fat egg-salad sandwich with bean sprouts on Russian pumpernickel and studied him from her side of the table while she chewed. "You aren't aging any faster than anyone else, given the time of year we're trapped in." She dabbed at her lovely mouth with a paper napkin. "I've got them too, you know."

"You've got them too? What do you mean?"

"The Decembers," Gail said. "You've got the Decembers, that's what I call them. Everything speeds up, yet everything grinds to a halt. I know how you feel. I need to get away myself. I suppose that's why I'm saying that to you."

"It's pretty bad," said Durwood, picking up his tuna fish on onion roll and sipping from his refilled cup. "I mean, it's getting terrible. Like, how do you explain my being able to cope with the hassle we're having with these partnership papers, but not being able to stand shopping, buying gifts that nobody'll like anyway. I'm drowning in dipshit rigamarole—running errands, getting the house ready for my folks to come visit, sending out cards, picking up prints at the camera store, clearing things with the Shriners so little Midge McHenry can have Christmas dinner at our place, juggling our charge cards, hand-holding my family. Plus, as if that wasn't enough, Dixie wants us to drive all the way up to Marin to one of those goddamn cut-it-yourself Christmas tree farms! I hate it! She and the kids can never agree on what tree they want. The good ones are always already sawed down, and—"

"Please, Durwood, you're making me nervous, and nervous I don't need! The Decembers are enough, thank you. I don't need any more blues on top of that."

"The middle of January!" Durwood almost choked on his sandwich. "That's when we were planning to have our grand opening."

Gail spread her arms and hunched her shoulders. "What do you want me to do? You'll have to do some juggling."

"But that's all I've been doing—juggling this, juggling that . . . Here . . . There . . . I don't even know who I am anymore!"

"Good," Gail said with a smile. Durwood loved it when she smiled and the sun came out in her warm, womanly face with its playful dark eyes, sweet cheeks, and kissable pug nose, the Latin brown hair that curled around her ear lobes set off with pendants of turquoise and silver. It was her smarts that turned him on, although she wasn't exactly colorless either. "Now you're catching up with the rest of us," she added.

"Do you think there's a future in law for women?" Durwood asked suddenly, not even knowing that he was going to say it.

Gail was unruffled. "What a curious shift. Why do you ask?"

"Dixie's been talking about applying to law school."

"Well, it's about time. It's never come up before, but I've always thought she'd make a gifted attorney."

"And why do you say that?"

"Dixie is tough—tougher, I think, than you'll ever know. And, from what I've seen of her, she's also sharp, gutsy, and persistent."

"Oh, she's persistent all right." Durwood sat for what felt like a full minute with his hands curled around the thick, warm mug. "So," he said finally, "are you saying I should encourage her?"

"No," said Gail, leaning back in her cushioned chair, "I'm not saying that at all. You asked if I thought there was a future in law for women, and I'm telling you the answer is yes." She smiled and munched on a carrot stick. "Everything's changing, Dur."

"Yes, things have a way of doing that, don't they?"

"No, I mean it on a broader scale than you might have in mind." On the wall in back of Gail hung a framed oil portrait of Chief Seattle delivering his famous "You will never be alone" oration to the white settlers. "I'm not the type to go around wearing a T-shirt that says 'The Future Is Female,' but I can tell you that from here on out you males are going to have your work cut out for you if you intend to keep holding on to the throne. I'll just leave it at that."

"It seems to me there're too many lawyers already, yet every other woman I run into wants to get into law school."

Gail laughed and said, "Well, take it from a woman who worked her tail off getting through—there still aren't enough of us. The more legislation gets passed, the more legal minds we need, and, I don't care what anybody says, most of those minds are still men's, here in the U.S.A. anyway. Check the statistics."

Seeing that Gail was slowly revving up for a speech he wasn't in the mood for, Durwood bluntly changed the subject. "You wouldn't happen to know," he asked, "what salaries are running like around the league these days, would you?"

"You're awfully clever," she told him. "Whose salary are you interested in, for instance?"

"Gene 'Genetic Action' Jones, say."

"Really, Dur, that's a taboo subject. You know that." She pinched up some bean sprouts and nibbled. "I can tell you this, though. If Gene continues at the rate he's moving at now, the only team that'll be able to afford him when his current Beanstalk contract runs out will have to be either New York or someplace in Texas. You know where the money is."

"That's what I thought."

Durwood felt cheated but, at the same time, glad to be out of the running.

A concerned look came over Gail's face as she leaned forward and said, "You aren't thinking about getting back into the business, are you?"

"Not a chance."

"Do you think you and Celia are going to hold up through all this over the holidays?"

"I think so."

"Good," said Gail, "because if you can, I can." She rose and walked around the long table desk, then planted a friendly kiss, tinged with egg salad, on Durwood's forehead. "Cheer up. We're all in this together. I'm glad I can be of help. You know I've always been fond of Celia. She reminds me of my niece Concha, my sister's oldest daughter. They're exactly the same age and going through the same miserable growing pains. It must be hell on you and Dixie."

Ah, sweet sympathy. Durwood wanted to return the kiss somehow, but thought better of it. He simply stroked the back of Gail's hand and enjoyed this unexpected moment of affection for what it was.

"How is it a sharp, attractive woman like you never got married and had kids?" he asked.

"I wonder that myself sometimes." Gail sighed and leaned against the table. "My folks are still piling on the pressure, especially my mom. Maybe it's because I never did meet the right Mr. Nice, as Lily Tomlin calls him." She gazed down at Durwood with her big, tender eyes in a way that was more intimate than physical touch. When he peered back, a warm current flowed through him. It was as though he were staring straight through all of her masks and directly into her soul. "I suppose," she added, smiling strangely, "there's such a thing as being too smart for your own damn good, don't you think?"

"You're asking the wrong person. The older I grow, the dumber I get. As a matter of fact, I wonder if I was ever that bright to begin with."

Gail smiled and wrinkled her pug nose. "There's an expression in Spanish my dad's always using."

"How's it go?"

He watched her facial muscles shift slightly as she drew her lower lip taut against her bottom teeth and rattled it off to him, "¿Pero a ver cuando hemos comido en el mismo plato?"

"Sounds pretty, but run it by me in English."

"Well, literally it translates, 'So why not let's see when we've eaten off the same dish?'"

"Which means?"

"Don't be presumptuous."

It was pitch-black, moonless, when the four of them finally got back from Mill Valley with the Christmas tree they'd selected and cut down themselves. Roping it to the top of the Vega had been anything but easy. Durwood sorely missed the station wagon but was determined not to complain, knowing how it would only give Dixie and the girls another chance to get on his case.

At Dixie's insistence, Durwood patiently sawed off two of the lower branches, then drilled holes in the trunk and stuck them elsewhere to make the damn tree stand more symmetrically. By the time he got the bushy Douglas fir snugly set up in its loathsome stand, he had run out of cuss words to mutter under his breath. He also was too tired to even think about food, but Celia, who had done the cooking for a change—cheese and onion omelets with frozen cut corn and a tossed green salad—made him sit down with the rest of the family for a very late supper.

Long after the kids were in bed, Durwood and Dixie made love. As they brushed and mashed and heaved against each other, sharing breath, bites, nibbles, scratches, juices, and musky fragrances, to say nothing of squeezes and kisses, he wondered, as he always did, how it was possible to be still in love with somebody after all these years—someone he spent fully half his time hardly being able to stand.

They were stretched out, sweating and catching their breath, when Durwood noticed that Dixie's thighs and legs were twitching.

"Hey, you wanna let's rest up and do it again?"

"I don't think so," said Dixie. "I've had it."

"What do you mean, you've had it?"

"Can't you tell? I'm all bleeped out. That was wonderful. You haven't been that passionate since our trip to Jamaica. What's up?"

"Nothing's *up* . . . I just felt like it, that's all."

Dixie wriggled around and flicked her tongue across each of his eyelids and around his nostrils before kissing his damp upper lip. "There isn't some other woman that's got you all steamed up?"

"Like who?"

She laughed. "Trieste, maybe?"

"Are you serious?"

"No. Well, who knows?"

Who knows? Who knew anything? "Why would you even say something like that?"

"She does kinda remind me of what I used to look like, back when we first met."

"C'mon, Dixie, since when have you ever had green eyes?"

"I'm only joking."

I'm only joking. It was such a natural, unincriminating human cop-out. He said it lots of times himself. He hadn't even thought about Leon's friend, not consciously anyway—and certainly not lately. What was Dixie really saying, if anything?

Pictures of Gail floated into Durwood's head, and, for the

longest time all day, he relived the peck she had placed between his brows. He took it for granted that Dixie, being a woman, had been born with a special kind of radar that enabled her to sniff out whatever she damn well pleased, and whenever she was good and ready.

"You didn't get Nissa up," said Dixie.

"I know. I'll do it in a minute. Let me rest some."

"So you admit you're as bleeped out as I am."

"What's all this 'bleeped out' junk?"

"You know, if you don't get her up now, she's liable to pee a stream through the mattress. I get sick of washing her sheets and blankets."

"Listen, I'll get her up! Take it easy."

"I finally picked up the Reno passes."

"Uh huh . . ."

"Did you know that they're due on December fifteenth?"

"Due? . . ." Durwood was wearily drifting away.

"That's when they expire. Do you know what that means? Means if I don't get up there in the next coupla days, it's all over."

"I can't go to no Reno, baby. What're you talking about?"

"I'm talking about me and Jenny using the tickets. Oscar's already volunteered to look after little Julian."

Durwood sat up. It hurt to have to return to waking time. "You mean, you and Jenny are going to Nevada on that trip you won?"

"Straight to Harrah's, honey, and I've already drawn two hundred dollars out of my mad money account to do some gambling."

"Hell, that's half your stash!"

"Riiiight . . . And we're leaving tomorrow afternoon."

"What! What am I supposed to do about Celia and Nissa?"

"I wish you'd get up and take Nissa to the bathroom."

"No, I'm asking if I'm expected to stay here and cook and pick up after those girls, and take care of my business too?"

While pretending to hug him, Dixie was softly pushing Durwood out of bed. "I've done all that for years," she said. "Now, would you please go get Nissa up?"

"We can't go on forever covering for her," he said. "She's gotta start getting herself up."

"Don't worry, she will."

"Why didn't you tell me all this before?"

"I didn't think it mattered. We're both worn out and need a little time away from each another. You'll get two days off and I will too. You can stay here and spend money, and I'll be up there winning some."

"Awfully sure of yourself, aren't you?"

"Cocksure," Dixie said, simpering mischievously as her face disappeared under the covers and came to rest at his navel.

Durwood heard someone knock timidly at the bedroom door just before the knob turned and it creaked open.

"Daddy? . . ."

Dixie's head emerged in a flash. Their hearts were beating hard. Quickly she sat up on her pillow beside Durwood and took hold of his goose-bumped arm.

"It's Nissa!" she whispered. "You think she saw anything?"

Nissa, still half-asleep, tottered toward Durwood's side of the bed and buried her head in his blanketed lap. "Daddy? . . . Daddy, how come you didn't get me up?"

"You didn't already wet the bed, did you?" Durwood's hand practically covered the whole of her back as he caressed it.

"Nope. I went wee-wee all by myself."

Dixie gathered the covers around her indignantly and said, "I told your father it was time to get you up."

Nissa scooted up the side of the bed and collapsed on top of Durwood. He could hear her tiny snore. He slipped out from beneath her as skillfully as he could, found his robe in the night-lit room, and carried her back to bed, suddenly agonizing over what he was going to get her for Christmas.

36

WELL, THIS WAS A LITTLE BIT of all right. Almost. Two full days to himself and no one to monitor his every move and thought. So what did Durwood end up doing? He worked harder than ever setting up the alphabetized racks at the shop and filling them with precious album stock. He argued with Brewster, learned some Japanese from Mitzi, and hung out in department stores and toy shops.

Attracted by its smiling yet not smiling hypnotic cover portrait, he picked up a hardcover edition of Paramahansa Yogananda's *Autobiography of a Yogi* for Leon at B. Dalton and had it gift-wrapped with a card that he filled out in his finest hand to read: "The son is always father to the man." He still wasn't sure what it meant, but, way down on the underside of his mind, he knew that he meant it.

Convinced that what Dixie really wanted was something exquisite and personal, he charged a coat made in Italy as well as a set of enameled Cruset cookware from France.

Against his better wishes, he bought Nissa a pair of roller skates and a shiny pantsuit outfit to wear with them. He halfway expected that the suit would be brought back, so he made sure he had a proper receipt.

For Celia? It took Durwood a long time to make up his mind about that purchase. He put it off and put it off until there he was, back on Dolores Street, heating up some of Dixie's beef stew from the freezer.

"Can I spend tonight at Patsy's?" asked Celia.

"Then who'll be here to babysit Nissa?"

Celia put down her spoon and glared at him. "So where are you going?"

"Out."

"Mom isn't gone one day and you're on your way out."

"Celia, I've been on my way out for years. Why don't you have Patsy come here?"

"Really?"

"Sure, then both of you could guard the place."

"Where're *you* gonna be?" Nissa wanted to know.

"Just out—relaxing, hanging out with buddies."

"That's all you've been doing lately," said Celia.

"You are your mother's daughter, aren't you?"

Nissa said, "What's that mean, Dad?"

"Would you like it better, Celia, if I paid you and Patsy?"

"Paid 'em to do what?" Nissa groaned. "Look after me? I don't need nobody to be looking after me. I can take care of myself . . . Why can't Leon stay here with me?"

Durwood chopped up the beef chunks on Nissa's plate and took a bite. "Mmmm," he said, "that's yummy. Eat up, hon. Leon's tied up at a recording session in the People's Republic of Berkeley tonight."

"You mean, somebody's tied him up—like, with ropes and stuff?" Nissa seemed delighted and repelled by such a possibility, but Durwood could tell that she was putting them on in her sly, little-girl way.

"I can see me and Patsy are gonna have us some fun evening," Celia said sarcastically, hissing through clenched teeth and picking up her spoon.

Durwood reached across the table and laid a finger to her mouth. "I know you don't like my doing this, but it's Patsy and I."

"What's the difference?" asked Nissa.

"You'll find out in due time," he said. "Language is every bit as important as dress when you're trying to make an impression on people."

"So who's trying to make an impression?" said Celia. "I was merely stating a fact."

Nissa said, "Daddy, you're kinda dressed up tonight. You gonna give another speech someplace?"

"No, I just felt like looking nice for a change."

"Talk about a change," said Celia, "I've got some good news."

"Well, we sure could use that. What is it, dear?"

Nissa giggled and said, "Deer! How come people call each other 'deer,' Dad? Is it because deers are supposed to be cute or something?"

Dropping her spoon with a clang, Celia huffed up and let her pesky little sister have it. "Nissa, would you please butt out! It just so happens to be *I* who was talking!"

"Ouch!" said Durwood. "I knew that was coming. Nissa, pipe down! I'd like to hear the good news."

"Well, it's good news for me anyway, because I've been wanting this to happen."

"What?"

"I got voted in as features editor of the school paper."

"Why, Celia, that's wonderful! I always thought you were a pretty good writer."

"Dad, how can you say that when you haven't even read anything I've done in at least a year?"

"Yes, I have too."

"Like what?"

"Oh, I don't know . . . Your mother's shown me things—poems and stuff."

"You mean, from the paper?"

"Uh, that's right."

"Aw, none of that really counts. Those are like exercises I can dash off on assignment. I've got some really literary things I haven't shown anyone yet. I'm even starting to develop a style, sort of."

"What's a fee-churz editor?" Nissa inquired with exaggerated politeness.

"You wouldn't understand," said Celia.

"Betcha I would too! Make her tell me, Daddy."

Durwood gave Celia a go-ahead nod and said, "You mustn't always talk down to your sister. The only way she's ever going to learn new things is for people to explain to her what she doesn't understand."

"Okay," Celia began. "You already know what a sportswriter is, don't you?"

"Sure, they write about sports."

"Right."

"Pretty good, huh, Dad?"

"Nissa, quit being a smart aleck and listen to Celia."

Glaring at Nissa as if she were fed up, Celia continued. "Well, on a newspaper you have different people writing about different things. Then after they finish writing something, it goes to an editor, who makes suggestions and corrections before it gets printed in the paper. So a features editor is—"

"Somebody who works on features," Nissa put in with a straight face. "But what's a feature?"

"Stuff about little unusual things that people do, such as famous celebrities, and things about movies, shows, books, and music—and interviews. Things like that."

Nissa sat there perplexed and worked her gravy-smeared mouth into a genuine pout. "But I thought you called that news."

"It is news," Durwood said consolingly, "but it's also a certain kind of news."

"I told you she wouldn't understand."

"Well, Daddy's famous," Nissa said, turning to Durwood. "You still are, aren't you? And all the pictures and words they tell about him are always in the part of the paper with the basketball and baseball and football people."

Celia shrugged and picked up her spoon. "My food's getting cold. Excuse me, please."

"Anyway," Durwood said, "I think that's just great, Celia. Congratulations. It sounds like a big job, but I know you can handle it."

"Thanks. I wonder how much all that publicity I generated had to do with it."

"What do you mean?"

"Everybody at school's been so good to me since I went back, like I'm some big hero or something. Do you think that's healthy? I mean, even kids in the twelfth grade come up to me in the hall and want to talk to me about the kidnapping and things."

"You're getting famous like Daddy?"

"But I want them to like me for just being me, not because they heard about me on television or saw me in the papers."

Durwood shook his head. "People are funny that way," he said. "Don't let it go to your head. The nice thing about publicity is that it all dies down and people move on to something else."

"Daddy?"

"Yes, Nissa."

"How come all the things I do every day don't get on the news?"

"Oh, good grief!" Celia groaned, studying the ceiling.

"Who is it decides what the news is anyway? I don't get it."

"You're about to get it from me," said Celia, "if you don't stop chattering like a ninny! And *please* don't ask what a ninny is!"

"I'll have to give your question some thought, Nissy," said Durwood, "but right now I'd like to see you finish your dinner. You've barely touched it."

Nissa frowned down at her bowl of beef stew, grimaced, and made a snoring sound. "Borrrr-ring! . . ." She yawned. "You guys're putting me to sleep."

"Good," said Celia with a smirk, affecting a stilted British accent. "Now, perchance Patsy and I shall know pree-cisely how to cope with someone of your character and disposition when bedtime arrives."

Nissa, not being up to such taunting, suddenly began to cry. "Stop her," she said between sniffs, "from making fun of me. She's . . . she's being mean."

"That's enough, both of you! Celia, you and Patsy aren't gonna pull anything peculiar on me while I'm out tonight, are you?"

"Dad, did you have to ask that? What do you think I am—hopelessly stupid?"

Durwood looked and saw how beautiful Celia was getting to be and quietly said, "I'm sorry."

It was a brisk Tuesday night. Durwood couldn't remember the last time he had spent a weekday evening out by himself with no particular place to go. At first it made him uncomfortable. Here he was, wasting his time, when he really should have been holed up someplace doing something important, like worrying. He drove around for half an hour and almost gave in to the urge to turn around and go home.

Part of the problem, he knew, was that he still had a hard time being anonymous. There were moments when he wished he were Leon, even Brewster, and could bop around town unnoticed. Most public places were intimidating. Almost inevitably somebody would approach him and ask for an autograph, or, worse yet, exhaust him with dumb-ass conversation. Basketball players, for reasons that remained inexplicable to him, seemed to bring out the shallowest sides of people. If he heard "How's the weather up there?" one more time, he was afraid he'd lose control and do something psychotic. If he were five-feet-five and weighed four hundred pounds, then things might be different.

Still, some part of him felt like being sociable, for a little while perhaps. He remembered a little neighborhood bar out in the Fillmore that used to feature informal jazz dished up by local musicians—old-timers, mostly, who had never made the big time. He headed up Divisadero in the Vega to see if he could still find the place.

Yes, it was still there, although it was no longer called the Zanzibar. The curlicue neon script now read "Tooty's Bar & Grill." But outside on the sidewalk, before walking in, he could hear the thick, bluesy sound of a tenor saxophone trying to make itself heard above a Hammond organ and drums. It was as if nothing had changed since he'd last dropped by with Dixie seasons ago. Chitlin-and-gravy music, they called it. He could already picture the patrons inside and what the atmosphere would be like.

Durwood sat at the bar and treated himself to a brandy with a Perrier chaser. It was nothing he'd ever tried before, but what the hell! Relax a little! The little trio down front in the smoke-lit bandstand area was working very hard. The saxophonist, who looked to be Durwood's age, held his horn up and slightly off to one side the way Lester Young used to do. Like a good many aging jazzmen and other entertainers, he was dressed in a way that caught the eye, but in a style that was decidedly behind the times. His blown-out bush of an Afro, flecked with gray, reminded Durwood of the way he himself had gone around looking about the time Nixon came in, and the arty pendant, the size of an ashtray, that graced the top of the musician's dashiki'd paunch was—like the bell-bottoms and high-heeled boots—just a little too quaint for comfort. Happily, the music he was blowing would always be in fashion.

Durwood had never been crazy about Hammond organs, but

the peppy little sepia lady in owlish glasses and chestnut wig who was booting the hell out of this one was making him feel pretty good. As for the drummer—a beefy, middle-aged man in a Levi's suit who looked a lot like a balding Howard Cosell—well, he, too, was taking care of business, even if the bombs he was dropping and the accents and licks he was laying down were strictly from the hard-bop fifties.

For the length of a tune, Durwood sat hunched, patting his foot on the bar rail and losing himself in the music. The customers at tables, most of them black and in pairs, seemed to know the musicians and one another. It was the kind of vanishing neighborhood joint that he'd always loved. And nobody was bothering him.

He was ordering his second brandy when a careful-stepping man in a suit with no tie walked through the door, snapping his fingers, and headed straight for the bar.

"Durwood!" the man said in a loud voice as he took over the next stool. Then he clapped his hands to get the bartender's attention and shouted, "Delano, you know who this is, don't you? Bring him a drink. It's on me. I'll have the regular. How you doin, Woody?"

When he slipped his hand into Durwood's, Durwood shook it politely and said, "Thank you, sir. Pleased to meet you, but I already have a drink."

"Aw, I can see that. I ain't blind, you know. The name's Clayton—Stanfield Clayton—but you can call me Homer. Everybody else does."

"Hello, Homer. I—"

"You don't know how long I been countin on this moment. The great Woody Knight. I'll just be god-*damned*! Delano! I'm sponsorin this man for the rest of the night. Anything he wants, just give it to him and put it on my tab, you hear?"

Delano nodded dutifully. It was clear that the poor bartender was acquainted with this blowhard on a far too regular basis. Durwood was racking his brains to figure out how to tell "Homer" that he didn't feel like talking. Why not use the direct approach?

"I do appreciate your hospitality, uh, Homer—but I came to catch the band, and I'm not exactly in the mood to talk."

Up went Homer's hands. He held them apart from one another as though he were indicating the size of some fish he'd almost caught. "I know exactly what you mean, Woody, and I'll leave you alone. You know why? 'Cause I respect the shit outta you, guy! I wish you were back in there wearin that green number eleven. The Stalks sure could use an old scrapper like you."

"Thanks. Now, if you'll—"

"Just a minute. Lemme ask you one question. One question, okay?"

"All right, Homer . . . One question."

The bartender brought the drinks, and Homer drained half of his gin and tonic in one gulp and smacked the glass back down. "What do you think about this new deal they got goin where they're talkin about how ticket sales are goin down unless they get more white players to playin basketball? I saw this with my own eyes on the 'Wide World of Sports.' Now, what you think about that?"

Durwood pondered the question and cleared his throat. "Well, what you have to remember is—"

"Now, hold on," said Homer. "Wait a minute before you answer, so I can say this." He lowered his voice and moved his face in close enough for Durwood to smell the booze on his Sen-Sen breath. "I happen to know that these people don't wanna see no colored get a break no kinda way. And it looks like to me that shit is goin backwards insteada forwards. You see, what you got here in this United States today is a buncha scared white people, scareda the Negroes and Mexicans and Chinamens and things—and don't get me to talkin 'bout these Veetnamese they bringin over here by the boatload to do all this work for nothin and put red-blooded Americans outta work. . . . See, I'm a workin *man*! I know what they doin to us. They're sellin us down the river, Woody, sellin us down the river! Just as sure as I'm sittin here and you sittin there. Tell you, and you can mark this down, 'cause the handwritin is on the wall. . ."

Durwood could barely sit still. He looked around the room. There was an empty table right up by the bandstand. Now, if he could just slip away and make it over there. No, then more people might come over to him. He rotated his stool enough to see that the bartender—a patient soul with heavy-lidded eyes—felt sorry for him. Delano shook his head and wearily, by tapping at his temple with an index finger, signaled what the matter was.

"Excuse me," Durwood said in vain.

". . . And this basketball hype they're tryna shove down our throats ain't no different from the gas thing. Hell, anybody that swallows that scam need to be locked up in Napa. It's plenty gas. You know how I know? I work right out here on Treasure Island, and the Navy gets all the gas and oil it needs. You checked out the profits these oil companies been knockin down? Can't nobody tell me nothin! But see, they got Little Charlie and all the resta these poor peckerwoods—and it's a lotta colored people believe it too—they got him thinkin it's a shortage and all that hooey—and now they determined to keep y'all from gettin in on some of that heavy coin playin basketball. And now, you see, here come the Klu Klux Klan all over again. Fuck a Klu Klux Klan! Klu Klux Klan come fuckin with me, I'll blow they ass to Kingdom Come! . . . You can build your own atomic bomb nowdays, you know . . . It's a bohunk right out there at the Navy yard where I work at got the magazine with the plans printed right in it—blueprints and everything—and he say he gon' build him one. Shit, I'll be god-*damned* if I don't build me one too! . . ."

"Excuse me!" Durwood finally woofed in a voice so loud that it caused heads to turn. "I have to make a phone call."

Homer was still running off at the mouth when Durwood made his hasty break. He hurried over to the pay phone by the door and uncradled the shiny receiver. It wasn't until he had dropped the coin in the slot that it occurred to him that he was doing all this for show. Who the hell was there for him to call?

But then, without even realizing that he was doing it, he dialed a number on impulse. It was a woman's voice that came on the line.

"Hello."

"Hello," Durwood responded automatically, still unaware of who it was.

"So you're finally returning my call," the woman said in a tone that sounded vaguely familiar and decidedly approving.

"Uh, I can't hear you so well," Durwood told her, stalling for time to pinpoint the voice. "The music's so loud."

"Where are you calling from—a disco?"

That did it! He knew exactly who it was now, but what he still couldn't figure out was how it had come to this.

"What a pleasant surprise," the woman went on. "I hope you're calling to tell me you're coming by. I'd love to see you. It's my last night off this week. Do you really feel like being interviewed? Please say yes. That's all I've been looking forward to doing since we met. You won't be sorry. There's a magazine down in L.A. I told about it, and the editor is all jazzed up on the idea."

Was it him or the brandy? The woman sounded like a breathy 33⅓ being played back at 45 rpm.

As much as he had been enjoying himself, up until Homer's dreary appearance, Durwood couldn't help asking, "How do I get there from here?"

The woman laughed. "First you'd better tell me where you're calling from."

"The Fillmore. A joint called Tooty's."

"Oh, Tooty's. It's cozy there, isn't it? Is Jolene Nolan still on organ?"

"I think that's her name."

"She's great. Who's that I hear playing horn in the background?"

"I have no idea."

"I think I know. That's Juba Johnson. I wrote him up once for the *Chronicle* pink section. Oh, I'm so excited! Now, here's what you do . . ."

Her Potrero Hill apartment on Texas Street was crammed with books and records. When she greeted him in the second-floor doorway, wearing white Wrangler jeans and an antique Chinese brocade robe, her lustrous hair piled on top of her head, the first thing she said was, "Do you mind if I hug you? I'm just so happy to see you!"

It didn't feel right, but Durwood did nothing to discourage the woman from throwing her arms around him and pressing her high-cheeked face against his chest. He even let his hands roam around her broad, strapless back.

"God, that feels good!" she murmured, pulling back and looking up at him. "Would you like a drink?"

"No, not really."

"Not even a brandy?"

"How'd you know I liked brandy?"

"Oh, I have magical powers, Mr. Knight. I can smell it on your breath."

In very little time, they were settled on her broken-down sofa draped with an Indian bedspread. The tape recorder was going and, with pencil poised, she sat turned toward him, legs tucked under her, a spiral notebook resting in her lap.

"And what would you say," the woman asked, "was the fundamental thing you learned from having devoted the better part of your life thus far to professional sports?"

"I'd say what I've learned is pretty pedestrian. Like, I know it isn't the game that knocks it out of you. It's the way the game is played."

"Could you elaborate on that?"

"Well, it's simple. On the pro scene, you've got a game going on within a game—a play within a play, I guess you might say—and it boils down to this . . . and this is what I've learned . . . Any job you accept that brings you a regular pay check, you live with that job and you think about it. You figure, well, they're paying me to play basketball, but I'm paying dues too."

"Brilliantly put," the woman muttered and ducked her head to scribble. "Go on."

"You're performing an obligation, fulfilling a contract, but you're also keeping your eye on the take at the gate, and that's where politics comes in. I used to have this poli-sci professor who told us the first day that if there's anything about politics you don't understand, just take a minute or two to look at yourself and all the stuff you want and need and how you're gonna get it. After he said that, the rest of the course was a snap."

"And, well, I gather you're making an analogy of some kind between the world and the spectator?"

"Possibly," he said, feeling important. "From what I've answered already, you might get the impression I'm against commercial athletics. Nothing could be further from the truth."

"Fine, I've got that. What are these dues?"

"That's easy. You have to know which way the wind is blowing. How the wind is blowing is another way of saying how the pay is rolling. All I'm saying is you learn everything there is to know about life no matter what line of endeavor you take up."

"And you've gathered your wisdom from the art of zen basketball meditation? . . ."

Durwood didn't even flinch. He sipped off his cheap, raw-tasting brandy and came right back at her with: "My son, Leon, whom many people know as an accomplished musician, he would respond to that by countering it with some other kinda zen coe-ann . . ."

"Koan," she offered, pronouncing it the correct way.

"Have it your way. But, to get back, what I guess I'm saying is a basketball player's got a vested interest in playing the game that's earning him a living the same as the vice squad's got a vested interest in vice, and the last thing the narcotics squad wants to see is the price of dope going down."

"Aptly put," the woman snickered and wiggled across the couch until her knees were touching Durwood's. "You know, *Rolling Stone* might even make me an offer for this."

"Something you can't refuse . . ."

Her unprofessional side came leaking through at full steam. "I have to tell you I've been thinking a lot about you since Boogie Your Boodie Off."

"Oh?"

"Don't you love that title?"

"It's cute."

"Cute? I helped name that place. Boogie's such a virile word, do you know what I mean? And when you combine it alliteratively with Boodie, there's just no getting around all those erotic overtones. Don't you think it's neat?"

"I suppose," Durwood said nervously and then shifted gears. "Would you please tell me—if I'm not getting too personal—how you came by your name?"

Audrey Spain laughed and began taking out her hair pins. "It's a real grabber, isn't it?"

"I must say . . . It's been intriguing the hell out of me for weeks."

"Have you ever heard of Nancy Spain?"

"No, can't say that I have."

"Well, she was an English author who used to be on the panel of this British program, sort of a literary quiz show from the BBC I liked listening to the year I spent in London as an exchange student. Nancy Spain. What a wonderful name for a writer! I couldn't get over it. So I borrowed my grandmother's first name, Audrey, and stole Nancy's last name. At first I only used it as a pen name; then I got to like it so much I went and had it legally changed."

"What did it used to be, if you don't mind my asking?"

"Eloise McGillicuddy."

"I see. . ."

"Doesn't do a thing for you, does it?"

"Well, I don't know. That's catchy too. Who would've ever thought [Jill] Clayburgh would go over?"

They laughed for quite a while at that one, and Audrey shook her hair loose. "I have to confess to something," she said, placing her hand on his. "As badly as I wanted to interview you, I suspect I also might've had other motives for getting you off someplace alone."

"I know."

"Not very subtle, am I? But then who is? Your wife seems to have married a traveling man like her father, right? Now that I've learned so much about you and your life, all I can see is this fascinating man with a fine family who I'd like to be on friendly terms with."

"You didn't have to tell me all that."

"I should be more like you, I suppose."

"How's that?"

"I should sit there and listen and never let on that the attraction is mutual."

Watching her blush, Durwood pulled his hand away and said, "You're okay, Eloise—Audrey. But it's getting late. We'd better get back to work."

"To the interview—yes. Look, I've got so much to work with already, maybe we ought to call it a night."

Durwood yawned and made the polite mistake of saying, "Now that you've heard all about me and my crazy life, why don't you tell me a little about yourself?"

"So you think *your* life's been crazy," Audrey said. "It's the working model of sanity stacked up next to mine. Let me fix some coffee and I'll give you the latest chapter."

And so Durwood sat and let Audrey chew his ear off, smiling to himself about just how right Leon had been concerning how much effort and talent it took to be a good listener these days. Afterward, when they hugged again at the front door, Durwood said, "Be sure and mention the shop."

"Don't worry. I'm a record-shop fiend. Record shops and bookstores—I should never go into either one. I'll probably end up being one of your best customers."

Bone tired, Durwood drove straight home and had the best night's sleep he'd had in months. He woke up knowing what people meant when they talked about being "dead to the world."

Dixie and Jenny came away from Reno with winnings of twelve hundred dollars between them from blackjack and the slots, and eight hundred of that was Dixie's. She was in such a good mood that she didn't even seem to mind when Durwood told her that Artie and Gertrude, his folks, would be arriving in two days. "After what we've been dealing with," said Dixie, "that'll be like falling off a log."

"Do you really think they're that much of an imposition?"

"No," Dixie admitted in a rare moment of candor. "Actually, I like them a lot, always have. I'll just make sure there's plenty of buttermilk for Artie and those dreadful grits you guys like. But I would appreciate it if you'd help me stop your mother from rearranging the furniture and keep her out of the kitchen! God, that's aggravating!"

"I just hope I can put up with Pop's philosophizing. You know how he likes to carry on."

"Who're you telling? For sixteen hours straight that man can talk! But I'm gonna fix him this time."

"What do you plan to do?"

Dixie smirked and slit her eyes. "I'm gonna sic Leon on him."

Christmas Day turned out to be not so bad after all. There was no complaining about inappropriate gifts. When Dixie unwrapped her coat and cookware she said, "Darling, you must've been reading my mind! I love them! But it's a good thing I won all that money." Nissa couldn't wait to hit the sidewalk so everyone could see her skating in her skating outfit. Celia was crazy about the portable typewriter that Durwood, in a last-minute burst of inspiration, had gotten her. More than that, though, she cried when Dixie told her how long she'd been wanting such a beautiful, hand-crafted necklace. Durwood was content with his shirts, ties, and cologne, but what truly got to him, what he treasured most, was the mammoth album of Knight family snapshots that his parents, in secret collaboration with Dixie, had gotten copied for him.

Midge McHenry and Leon's girlfriend Trieste were lively Christmas dinner guests. Durwood even posed for a couple of shots with little Midge when Brewster showed up after dinner with the fancy new Polaroid that Mitzi had given him. Leon was busy video-taping it all.

Durwood calculated that it was going to take him the better part of the coming year to pay for their modest celebration of Jesus's birthday. But later that night, when they all sat around the warm gift-wrap-and-ribbon-strewn living room, turning the pages of the family photo album, reminiscing over old pictures while Artie and Gertrude commented and told stories in their soft Texas tones, his money worries seemed insignificant.

"So what do you think?" Durwood asked, then stood back and gestured toward the partially filled bins of records and half-empty shelves of sports souvenirs. Framed posters of star musicians and athletes lined the shop's upper walls.

"I'm impressed," said Leon. "By the way, did you stock any of the records I'm on?"

"Everything we could find in the Schwann Catalog. Mitzi helped me track them down. As a matter of fact, I personally made a slot for them and had your name stenciled on the file divider."

"You did that?"

"Sure."

"Not that I don't believe you," said Leon, "but this is one slot I have to check for myself."

Durwood got a kick out of watching his son rush down the aisle to the "K" section to see what he'd done. Leon came back looking pleased and slapped his father on the back.

"Pops, I'm touched! . . . What can I say?"

Durwood looked at his watch. "I'll tell you what you can say. Say yes."

"Huh?"

"Hey, it's Saturday already. In thirty-six hours it'll be New Year's, and you still haven't told us your plans. Now, Christmas night you said you'd let us know when you're going back East."

Leon leaned against the counter and looked away. "Do you really have to know so soon?"

"So soon? . . . Look, you know how Dixie and the kids feel about you. And I don't have to tell you my feelings, do I?"

"Oh, boy, here we go! Trieste is after me to stick around too. Says she can't afford to be flying back to New York."

"Then why don't you stay?"

Leon made a little frown and said, "The band's got a two-month tour coming up. We open in Buffalo at the end of January, and we haven't even rehearsed for it. There's so much new material we have to go over. I have to get back." He cut his eyes at Durwood. "And Mom's expecting me to be around town on her birthday too."

"That's right, I'd forgotten Coretha's birthday was in January. That always used to get me. We'd just be getting over Christmas and then she'd hit me with that, whew!"

"So then you up and marry Dixie and her birthday's in December. You didn't do your homework, did you?"

"Don't change the subject."

"I have to get back, but we'll be winding out this way again. I've been thinking about leaving the group after that and starting a band of my own. I've met some first-rate players around here, and this record company over in Berkeley—Islander—kinda hinted the other night they'd be interested in producing something with me on it as leader."

"You're sounding better all the time."

"Oh, thanks. Glad you like my playing."

"I wasn't talking about your playing."

Leon laughed and punched Durwood on the arm jokingly. "I get the feeling we'll be seeing a little more of each other next year," he said.

"You come out with an album and I'll make a big window display, and Brewster and I'll advertise it all over the Bay Area."

"And lapse into bankruptcy," added Leon.

"Come on," said Durwood, snapping off the lights. "Let's go."

"Where to?"

"Let's go get some exercise."

"But I don't feel like jogging. I hate it. It's not all that good for you."

"I never said anything about jogging."

"Then what sort of exercise are you talking about?"

"Just trust me, all right?"

Durwood locked up the shop, and they stepped out into the sunny noon light.

"Think you'll buy this thing?" Leon asked as they motored across town.

"Not on your life."

"But it's pretty comfortable, I think, for a van. Look at all the leg space. I've always felt sorry for you in those cooped-up cars you drive."

"Oh, I'm gonna get it, all right. But buy it? *Never!*"

"So it failed the test drive, eh?"

"No, I'm liking it better every mile I make."

"Then what're you gonna do?"

"Lease."

"Huh?"

"We're gonna lease it for the shop, and I'll just use it for our second car too. Smart, huh? I can write it off as an expense and not have to worry about repairs."

"Very sensible."

"Brewster and I thought so."

"Would you tell me where we're headed?"

Durwood made a right, then an immediate left, and pulled up by a playground.

"What's this?" Leon asked.

"See for yourself."

They watched four teenage boys dribbling and shooting on the cemented court, then got out and walked to the Cyclone fence.

"Where are we?"

"This is Celia's school," said Durwood, waving. "Hey, Moby! . . . Moby!"

Moby, who was just then wheeling in for a hook shot, spun around and wiped sweat from his face with the back of one arm. He squinted to see who was calling his name.

"Over here!" Durwood cried. "It's us!"

Beaming, Moby waved back and shouted, "Mr. Knight! . . . Leon! . . . What're you doing around here?"

"You guys wanna make it a three on three?"

"Aw, Pops, do we have to?" said Leon. "I'm not even wearing sneakers like you. I can't play in these loafers."

Durwood snickered. "Sure, you can. It'll be fun. Remember, one must overcome the negative consciousness."

Leon dug one elbow into his father's side and said, "I

should've known you'd be throwing that back in my face."

"But it's true," Durwood told him, laughing. And, as they sprinted through the gate onto the playground, he meant it. It felt so good to be saying what he meant and doing it at the same time. He couldn't wait to get his hands on the ball.